WAGER FOR A Wife

a regency romance

WAGER FOR A *Wife*

KAREN TUFT

Covenant Communications, Inc.

Cover image *Historical Woman Holding Bouquet of Flowers* © Lee Avison / Trevillion Image

Cover design by Christina Marcano © 2018 by Covenant Communications, Inc.

Published by Covenant Communications, Inc.
American Fork, Utah

Printed in the United States of America
First Printing: December 2018

25 24 23 22 21 20 19 18   10 9 8 7 6 5 4 3 2 1

ISBN:978-1-52440-767-4

To Stephen.

You were and still are a sure bet. I love you with my whole heart.

Acknowledgments

WAGER FOR A WIFE WAS a unique endeavor in that it was originally written as a novella. My thanks to the team at Covenant for seeing its potential and urging me to turn my original submission into something bigger. I want to especially thank my editor, Samantha Millburn, whose patience and faith in me are of as much value as her editing acumen and encyclopedic mind for grammar. I'd also like to give a shout-out to Christina Marcano for the beautiful cover art and to Stephanie Lacy for her enthusiastic marketing. You both are stellar.

I'm grateful for my children and their spouses for their continued love and support and for giving me the most adorable grandchildren on the planet. I love you all.

And finally, thanks to Stephen, who supports my writing in the most real of ways—not merely with pep talks but with cooking and doing laundry and cleaning and encouraging me to take my laptop wherever we go. The man walks the walk. You are a true prince among men.

Chapter 1

April 1805

THE HONORABLE WILLIAM BARLOW BECAME the fourth Viscount Farleigh in the usual way—with the death of the third viscount. That the deceased third viscount was William's father was also usual in such situations.

What was less than usual was the complete apathy William felt about both the title and his father's death. Nonetheless, his life had irrevocably changed as a result. It remained to be seen if it had changed for the better or the worse. If he were a betting man, which he *emphatically* was not, he would bet on the latter.

The carriage in which he rode was taking him closer and closer to the family home he'd avoided for years. There was no avoiding it now.

He folded the missive his father's solicitor had sent and that had eventually found its way north to Edinburgh, where William had been for the past few years, and slid it into the breast pocket of his coat. He'd read it several times already since receiving it yesterday morning. He could recite it all by heart now.

Lord Farleigh, the letter began—as if that alone hadn't been enough to enlighten William as to the letter's contents—*Lord Farleigh, I regret to inform you of the untimely passing of your father, William Barlow Senior, the former Viscount Farleigh.*

William stared out the carriage window at the passing scenery. It was a particularly gray April day. Gusts of wind battered the hedgerows and whipped the trees alongside the Great North Road, bruising the young spring foliage already sodden from the slanting rain. It matched his mood entirely.

I regret to inform you of the untimely passing of you father, William Barlow Senior, the former Viscount Farleigh. His passing confers the title of viscount on you as his only son and heir. It would behoove you to return to Farleigh Manor as soon as you are able so that pressing concerns related to the viscountcy can be dealt with expeditiously. Your servant, Richard Heslop, Esquire.

It was worded in Mr. Heslop's typically overwrought manner—oh, yes, he'd had dealings with Heslop before now—but in simple language, the solicitor was telling him the viscountcy and its associated properties, that were now William's responsibility, were in a desperate state. But of course they were; that came as no surprise.

The only real surprise in all of this was that his father had managed to live for as long as he had, all things considered.

William settled back into the corner of the carriage the solicitor had sent along with the letter to bring him to Buckinghamshire, and he planted his feet firmly on the floor for balance. He slid the brim of his hat down, folded his arms across his chest, and shut his eyes, willing the motion of the swaying carriage to soothe him. He mentally recited as many verses from the plays of Sophocles as he could remember from his school days, but as they were all tragedies, they only added to his overall sense of gloom. He tried to take a nap.

Despite his efforts, his mind kept returning to the letter in his pocket—or, more precisely, to Farleigh Manor.

Farleigh Manor, the seat of the viscountcy and William's childhood home, was filled with ghosts. Haunting memories. William hadn't been there, hadn't returned home, since he'd left for Oxford. He'd rarely gone home during his time at Eton before that, having left for school at the age of ten. His mother was long dead—buried in the family graveyard there, next to the little chapel, along with other deceased viscounts and viscountesses and assorted Barlow family members.

He wondered if Matthew, the groundskeeper, was still there and if he was keeping her grave well tended. It belatedly occurred to him that his father would have a grave to be tended now as well. The father William remembered would have insisted his final resting place look distinguished, as befitting a member of English nobility.

His mother would have cared only that any flowers planted there were treated well and allowed to flourish.

And what of Mrs. Holly, the housekeeper? Or Grimshaw, the butler? Good heavens, the man had seemed ancient to William when William was a boy. Was he still alive? And then there was Samuel, who'd been stable master and had taught William to ride.

Those dear people—the servants of Farleigh Manor who had remained faithful to the viscountcy and to William—had made his boyhood more bearable. He had thought of them frequently over the years, but to what end? The last time he had confronted his father about Farleigh Manor, its tenants and servants and the general state of its finances, he had been ordered to leave and never return. William had obliged him and had moved to Scotland. It had been the ideal location—the intellectual community in Edinburgh had kept his mind occupied, and the distance between him and Farleigh Manor had kept his longing for the good people of Farleigh Manor at bay—not that he had been entirely successful.

William knew from his last encounter with his father that if things had continued on the course his father had set, Farleigh Manor would most likely be bankrupt. The man's unwillingness to change would have seen to that. William would need all his wits about him when he reached the manor and came face-to-face with the challenges he had newly inherited.

He pulled the brim of his hat farther down over his eyes. The movement of the carriage had finally done its work and had lulled him into a drowsy state. Sleep was preferable to the painful, nostalgic shards he was feeling with each servant and tenant he remembered. There was nothing he could do from the interior of a carriage anyway.

Farleigh Manor and its troubles lay ahead, so for now, William slept.

* * *

The Wilmington ball was this evening, and Lady Louisa Hargreaves had received an invitation from Lady Wilmington herself. It was the first grand ball of the year and Louisa's first ball of her first Season, so she had chosen her gown with extreme care—after consulting with her mother, the modiste, her personal maid, her mother's personal maid, and even a chambermaid who'd happened to enter the room right after she'd donned the gown just minutes ago. Presenting oneself to London Society was a greater ordeal than Louisa had imagined it would be.

Assured by them all that the gown was exquisite and would cut a fine dash, she took a deep breath and left her dressing room. It was time to join her parents and be on their way.

"Good heavens, Louisa, what is that *thing* you're wearing?" her eldest brother, Alexander, said as he watched her descend the main staircase of their London home.

Louisa came to an abrupt halt halfway down the staircase.

"It is not a *thing*, Alex," her brother Anthony said in a decidedly condescending tone, taking Louisa completely by surprise. It was so unlike Anthony, who was just older than she, to come to her defense. If there was one thing she had learned over the years, it was that *both* brothers could be terrible nuisances. "It is clearly a cloud of one sort or other," he finished.

Louisa fought the urge to growl.

"The question we must then ask is what *kind* of cloud is it? Is it a cirrus cloud?" Anthony mused, tapping his chin in thought. "But no, the dress is too"—he made circling gestures with his hand—"too . . . *puffy*. Yes, that's the word. Too puffy to be cirrus clouds, which are ethereal in nature."

"Our sister is definitely *not* what I would call ethereal," Alex said. "She planted me a facer once, and there wasn't anything ethereal about it."

"I was nine at the time, if you'll recall," Louisa said in her own defense, feeling quite proud of herself because Alex had been all of thirteen, not to mention a foot taller than she.

"You had a black eye for a week," Anthony said.

"I did at that." Alex rubbed his cheek at the memory. "Now, back to the subject at hand: cirrostratus clouds have more substance than cirrus clouds do." He came up the stairs toward her, leaning closer and raising his quizzing glass to study her appearance more thoroughly. He ran the flounce on her sleeve through his fingers. "Cirrostratus, hmm."

Louisa glared at him and swatted his hand away.

He grinned. "Look at that frowning face of hers, Tony," he said. "A storm appears to be brewing after all."

"A cumulus cloud, then," Anthony said. "She's all puffy clouds with the threat of foul weather. We are at your service, Lady Cumulus." He bowed theatrically to her as Alex offered her his hand.

She pretended to ignore them both, raising her chin as she took her last few steps down to the entry hall—and then she couldn't help herself. She giggled.

Their parents entered the hall from one of the adjoining parlors at the same moment, obviously overhearing the exchange.

"What a vision you are, Louisa," her father, the Marquess of Ashworth, said, taking both her hands in his and kissing her cheek. "Don't listen to those rapscallion brothers of yours. They wouldn't know a diamond of the first water if she were to stand two inches from their noses. One would think I had never taught them to admire beauty."

"Don't worry, Papa," she replied archly. "They were merely discussing the weather."

Alex laughed.

"You look absolutely exquisite, my darling," Mama said, giving Louisa a hug, careful not to wrinkle either of their gowns. "The gown is divine and is the perfect choice for this evening."

"Thank you, Mama." Drat her pesky, adorable brothers!

"I assume the two of you are planning to make an appearance tonight since this is your sister's first ball of the Season," Papa said.

"Certainly, Father. We would never wish to disappoint our little sister. But does that mean I must also dance with her?" Anthony asked, rubbing his leg for effect, an innocent look of inquiry on his face. "Sore knee, you know. Boxing mishap at Gentleman Jackson's the other day."

"You never mentioned a sore knee to me," Mama said, raising an eyebrow.

Alex was biting his lip to keep from laughing again.

"I didn't wish to worry you unduly, Mama," Anthony replied meekly.

"That is most unfortunate," Papa said smoothly. "Because I expect you both to dance at least once with your sister and introduce her to some of your friends. The reputable ones, that is. And as for you, Anthony, I suggest you rub liniment on that knee before you arrive at the Wilmingtons'. Hopefully the smell of it won't put off the other guests."

"If those guests include the young ladies in attendance, that makes liniment a plus in my book," Alex whispered loudly to Anthony from behind his hand. "Parson's mousetrap and all that. Wouldn't want to end up leg shackled before I'm ready, you know. Perhaps I'll discover a sore knee, too, before we make an appearance."

"Halford," their father said, calling Alex by his title, which meant the words to follow were ones he intended to be taken seriously. "I expect you to lead your sister out for her first dance. See that you are there and on time, whatever plans you do or do not have for later in the evening."

"Certainly, Father. I wouldn't dream otherwise." He waited a beat before continuing. "Nothing more fun than dancing with one's baby sister, after all." He winked at Louisa.

"You are incorrigible," Louisa said, fighting back more giggles.

Alex only laughed.

"I suppose I must dance with Louisa as well," Anthony said with a huge sigh, "despite my sore knee. I am that thoughtful of a brother, you know."

"Your chivalry knows no bounds," Papa said dryly.

"I am quite certain Louisa shall have no problem finding dance partners," Mama said. "She has caught the eye of several young men already, including the Earl of Kerridge."

"Unless she begins talking any of them into a stupor," Alex said.

"Halford," Papa scolded.

Louisa could feel her cheeks turn red, but really, Alex spoke the truth. Louisa knew that she occasionally had the tendency to rattle on in conversation.

"*Nevertheless*," Mama said in a tone that brooked no argument. "It is always good to have one's brothers there to make sure things go off smoothly at the beginning of one's first official ball, is it not?"

"Of course, Mama," Louisa's brothers said almost in tandem.

"Good. It's settled, then."

Gibbs, the head butler at Ashworth House in London, silently materialized and helped the ladies with their wraps while Papa donned his hat and took up his walking stick. "Have a good evening, your lordship, milady," he said, opening the door for them. "And the very best to you, Lady Louisa."

That was quite a speech, coming from Gibbs. "Thank you, Gibbs," Louisa said, touched.

Papa turned back to her brothers. "We shall see you two shortly, then."

"Don't worry, Father," Alex said. "Additionally, I shall introduce Louisa to every gentleman of my acquaintance this evening and then threaten them with bodily harm if they should choose not to invite her to dance, regardless of the menacing glances they get from the illustrious Earl of Kerridge."

"Alex!" Louisa exclaimed with a gasp.

"It would certainly add spice to an otherwise tedious occasion," Anthony remarked.

"Not too much violence, please," Papa said. "Very well. Let's be on our way, Lady Ashworth, Louisa. The Wilmington ball awaits, and your mother seems to think it's time you got yourself a husband."

"I didn't put it quite like that, Ashworth," Mama said. "What I actually said was more along the lines of taking your time and choosing wisely, Louisa. We want you to be happy, above all else."

Louisa had made several good friends and already had more beaux than she could have imagined, one or two of whom she found quite interesting. She really had no idea what Lord Kerridge's intentions were for her. The earl had paid her particular attention the past few weeks, and his doing so had generated a bit of a buzz amongst the *ton*, Louisa knew, but he had made no declaration to her of any sort, regardless of his attention to her. It all seemed very confusing at times.

She needn't place her hopes or expectations solely upon the Earl of Kerridge, however. There were parties and routs and musicales and, oh, lots of events to look forward to and many, many young gentlemen and ladies with whom to become acquainted. She would concentrate on enjoying herself, making friends, and practicing her flirting skills. She would stop fretting about marriage, starting now. And if the Earl of Kerridge decided to make an offer, she would consider it. Of course she would.

"Thank you, Mama," Louisa said. "But you needn't concern yourself unnecessarily. After growing up with these two for brothers, everyone else will be an improvement, by comparison."

Her father barked out a laugh while he handed her mother into the carriage. Her brothers, who stood in the open doorway in order to bid them farewell, also laughed.

"Touché, little sister," Alex said, offering her a jaunty salute.

"Adieu, Lady Cumulus," Anthony added, grinning. "We shall see you soon and vow to do our very best not to be embarrassed by the puffiness of your gown. Try not to rain this evening."

Louisa waved to them and climbed into the carriage, straightening her gown once she was seated. Her not-at-all-puffy gown, the silly wretches. Oh, but she loved her brothers, terrible teases that they were. She recalled a time when she was eight that she'd managed to retaliate against their constant teasing by sneaking frogs into their beds. That had been one of her crowning accomplishments, especially when she'd been able to hear Anthony shrieking from his bedroom. It hadn't mattered that she'd gotten a talking to from Papa or that her brothers had tossed her into the lake the following day.

She settled back into the comfortably upholstered seat of her father's carriage as the horses leapt into action. As they moved forward, she gazed out the window at the fashionable homes of Mayfair, appreciating the architecture, the flower gardens, and the lovely weather, her mind humming with excitement, a little apprehension—and hope.

* * *

The Wilmington ball was always one of the first of the Season, and Lady Wilmington, Louisa knew, went to great lengths to assure its success each year. Louisa could see rows of carriages awaiting their turns to deposit their passengers at the door, confirming that the ball was going to be a crush. The cream of Society milled about on a red carpet, of all things, waiting to enter the Wilmingtons' expansive London home and greet their host and hostess before making their way to the ballroom.

Soon it was their turn. Louisa exited the carriage, assisted by her father, who'd preceded her, and then waited, pulling her wrap a bit more tightly around her, as her mother descended the carriage steps. The sky held the last vestiges of twilight, and the dewy spring air was chilly, creating a blurry halo around the moon in an otherwise cloudless sky.

It appeared Louisa's dress was the only cloud venturing out tonight.

In contrast to the nighttime sky, the entrance hall of the Wilmingtons' residence was ablaze with light, and Louisa found herself having to blink until her eyes adjusted. A grand chandelier hung overhead, and silver sconces adorned the walls. Perfumes and beeswax mingled together, creating a heady fragrance, and the hum of conversation echoed through the marble hall. The gowns and turbans and plumes of the ladies provided a vivid counterpoint to the formal black the gentlemen wore. Louisa shivered with excitement and anticipation and a touch of nervousness as well.

After what seemed an age to Louisa, she and her parents finally made their way through the crush to Lord and Lady Wilmington.

"I daresay you are destined to break many a poor gentleman's heart this Season, Lady Louisa," Lord Wilmington said. He was a short, round man with a genial nature, and Louisa had always liked him. "What a dashing young lady you have become. But then, you were always a pretty little thing."

"You are too kind, Lord Wilmington," Louisa said, offering a demure curtsy.

"Your gown is exquisite," Lady Wilmington said. She was as short and round as her husband, but the plumes attached to the turban she wore gave her a decided advantage in height over her husband this evening. She leaned in closer to Louisa, causing the purple silk of her gown to rustle and the feathers atop her head to flutter precariously. "I rather like the gauzy fabric, my dear. Rather fluffy and cloud-like. Very becoming."

Louisa's hand darted to her bodice. Had her exasperating brothers managed to arrive ahead of her? Had her mother said something to Lady Wilmington? They couldn't have; they *wouldn't* have. *Would they?*

She looked carefully into Lady Wilmington's face but could see only the same good-hearted amiability the lady always exuded. "Thank you, Lady Wilmington," she managed to say in a rather strangled voice.

Lady Wilmington took Louisa's hand and patted it. "Are you quite well, my dear?"

"Yes." She swallowed. "I'm fine. Thank you for asking." Since Lady Wilmington didn't add anything to her earlier cloud reference, Louisa decided—hoped, rather—that it must have been a coincidence. A coincidence she had no intention of sharing—especially with her brothers, who would never let her live it down.

Couples were already taking their places on the floor by the time Louisa and her parents arrived at the ballroom, and the musicians were warming up their instruments on the dais. The first dance of the evening would soon be underway. The murmur of conversation filled the room, and as Louisa looked around the room for familiar faces, all thoughts of clouds faded from her mind.

Lord Kerridge would be here tonight, and he had asked her to reserve a dance for him. The evening would be filled with dancing, and that meant she would most likely have many dance partners, for Lord Kerridge wouldn't be able to dance with her more than two dances. She had already penciled his name on her card for one dance. Would he ask her for a second later in the evening—perhaps the supper dance? Were there other gentlemen here tonight she would find as charming as he?

What if no one else asked her to dance? The thought hadn't occurred to her before, but it was entirely possible she could end up a wallflower, sitting with Mama and her friends and fanning herself out of embarrassment and boredom. How mortifying that would be if, at her first real ball, she turned out to be an utter failure. Could a worse thing imaginable ever happen to her? She doubted it.

"Would you care to dance with me, Lady Ashworth, before you settle in with your friends and fret over which young suitors are paying court to your daughter?" Papa asked Mama, interrupting Louisa's stream of thought.

Goodness, she was so nervous she was babbling in her head now.

"You mean before you discreetly head in the direction of the card room, Ashworth?" Mama replied with a coy smile.

"Precisely, my love."

"I would enjoy such a dance, provided your daughter is not left on her own as a result."

Ashworth glanced around the ballroom. "You needn't worry. Halford will show his face at any moment if he knows what's good for him."

As if on cue, Alex and Anthony materialized at the ballroom door, both looking like lambs being led to the slaughter. Louisa hid a smile behind her gloved hand as her brothers spotted the rest of the family and made their way toward them.

"I'm off to search the ranks for willing—I mean suitable—dance partners," Anthony announced. "You shall not be left wanting, little sister." Louisa barely had time to register what he'd said before he was off like a shot and disappeared into the crowd.

"Lady Cumulus," Alex said, bowing theatrically to Louisa, a twinkle in his eye. "How soon we meet again! I would be honored to dance the first dance with you, provided you do not become thunderous during our time together."

She laid her hand on his arm and allowed him to lead her onto the dance floor. "Did you or Anthony say something about my gown to Lady Wilmington?" Drat. She'd told herself she wasn't going to say anything about that.

"Don't be silly," Alex said absentmindedly. "Wait." He stopped walking. "Are you telling me she actually called your gown a *cloud*?"

"Something like that," Louisa answered, feeling rather grumpy about the entire business.

Alex grinned.

"Stop it," Louisa said, rapping Alex on the arm with her fan, which caused both of her parents to turn and give her reproving looks. "Stop it," she repeated in a quieter tone, trying her best not to giggle. It was all so ludicrous. "I chose this gown with extreme care, you know. Does it really make me look like some sort of weather phenomenon?"

"It's a very delightful, very fluffy gown, Weezy—much better than the monstrosity you wore when you were presented at court last week."

Louisa shuddered. "That gown *was* a monstrosity—all hoops and brocade and ostrich plumes, with that horrid train I barely avoided tripping over as I backed away from Queen Charlotte after curtsying nearly all the way to the floor."

"I don't envy you at all. In fact, I applaud your ability to stay on your feet."

The music began at that moment, and Louisa turned her attention to the steps of the lively country dance.

Throughout the remainder of the evening, she found herself engaged to dance with a number of her brothers' friends: Christopher "Kit" Osbourne, the eldest son of the Earl of Cantwell; his brother Philip; Sir Richard Egan; and Hugh Wallingham, to name but a few. Obviously, her brothers had listened closely to their father's orders and done their duty in seeing Louisa had a full dance card for the evening. But they were *friends*, young gentlemen she'd met before, not suitors, really; at least, they didn't seem that way to her. She could hardly be interested in someone who felt forced to bestow his favors on her, now could she?

Dancing with her brothers' friends hadn't allowed her much of an opportunity to be introduced to other young gentlemen or to dance with some of the gentlemen with whom she'd already become acquainted. Like the Earl of Kerridge, for example.

The earl was dashing and witty and was heir to the Duke of Aylesham, making him one of the great matrimonial prizes of the Season. Louisa, as the daughter of the Marquess and Marchioness of Ashworth, was one of the highest-ranking young ladies making her come-out this year, if not the highest. While love matches were looked upon with tolerance, many noble marriages were still arranged for practical reasons, especially amongst the higher ranks. Louisa was not a fool. She knew at least *that* much about the Society into which she had been born. If Lord Kerridge offered her marriage, it would be foolish not to consider it. Marriage to him would eventually make her a duchess.

She did have a partiality toward the earl. But was this partiality love? She had no experience at all when it came to romantic love. Would she recognize the feeling when it happened? Would the attachment she felt for him grow into something more?

Oh, but she dearly wished to marry for love.

"Ahem, Lady Louisa," a male voice behind her said.

She turned, smiling, hopeful that Lord Kerridge had finally approached her to claim his dance. Her smile froze.

Baron Moseby bowed to her. The baron, a widower, had been a rather persistent suitor as of late, and Louisa was not at all interested. "Lady Louisa," he said again. "I would consider it a great honor if you were to dance—"

"Sorry, old chap." Lord Kerridge materialized next to the two of them. "I believe this dance is mine, is it not, Lady Louisa?"

She cast wide eyes at him, unsure what to say. She didn't particularly want to dance with the baron, but—

"I must apologize for being tardy to claim my dance. I was caught up in a rather involved conversation. I do hope you will forgive me." He winged his elbow out to Louisa, and she tentatively took it. "Sorry again, Moseby."

Baron Moseby bowed as Lord Kerridge led Louisa onto the ballroom floor.

"It seems, like a hero of old, I arrived in the nick of time," Lord Kerridge murmured as the lines formed for their dance. "I hope you don't consider what I did too presumptuous, but the very idea of that . . . creature . . . laying a hand on you in any way made my blood curdle."

"That comes as something of a surprise since you have been preoccupied with others this evening," Louisa said, flattered by his actions but a bit surprised by his heavy-handedness. Baron Moseby had been polite enough in his attentions to her, in spite of her lack of interest in return. Besides, she didn't want to appear too young and eager. "You haven't even said good evening to me yet."

"I must berate myself for my negligence. Good evening, Lady Louisa." He took her gloved hand in his and kissed her knuckles. "You look quite heavenly this evening—a veritable angel descending to us from on high. Since I believe this is the supper dance, I hope you will forgive my rashness just now and join me for supper."

"Very well," she replied, silently noting that his description of her was a bit cloud-like as well. "I forgive you, and I will gladly join you for supper."

"I thought you might," he replied with a knowing smile. He took her hand in his, and the music began.

* * *

The weather improved after William's first day of travel, and by the time he arrived at Farleigh Manor in Buckinghamshire, the skies were blue and the air pleasantly warm for April. Perhaps this accounted for the small degree of hope he was feeling, he thought as he exited the carriage and watched it drive off toward the stables.

The main door of the house opened, and a bent, elderly man with white hair approached. Devil take it, if it wasn't old Grimshaw after all!

He gave William a very dignified bow. "Welcome home, your lordship," he intoned in the low, gravelly voice William remembered from his boyhood.

William chose not to act on ceremony. It was *Grimshaw*, after all, who'd conspired on more than one occasion to keep William's boyish antics from getting him in trouble with his father. He grabbed the man's hand and shook it heartily. "Grimshaw, what a great pleasure it is to see you again and looking so well!"

"Thank you, my lord." The man gestured for William to precede him inside.

The entire staff was gathered in the main hall, which could only mean that the carriage had been spotted in the village and the staff at the manor had been informed of its approach. They all stood at attention now—all eight of them: Grimshaw; Mrs. Holly; Matthew; Samuel; Mrs. Brill, the cook; her daughter Mary, who was the scullery maid; and a footman and maid William didn't know. Counting the coachman who had brought William here and was still with the horses, that would make nine servants in all.

It was a small staff for an estate the size of Farleigh Manor, but as William had been anticipating the worst, it was a larger number than he'd expected. He strode over to Mrs. Holly, the housekeeper, who was first in line. She began to curtsy, but he reached for her hand and bowed over it. "Mrs. Holly, it is a delight to see you again and to find you still here at Farleigh Manor."

"Oh, you dear boy!" Mrs. Holly exclaimed, digging in her pocket and retrieving her handkerchief. "Welcome home!"

"Samuel, Matthew, well met!" They had been more like fathers to him than his own had been. He and Matthew shook hands vigorously.

"It's a fine day that you're back with us again at last, your lordship. A fine day." Matthew gave William some welcoming pats on the back.

"Boy . . ." Samuel spoke the word in a low rumble that grew into a growl and ended in a laugh as he threw his arms around William and hugged him tightly. He slapped his back and ruffled his hair—and entirely ignored the fact that William was the viscount and Samuel a mere stable master. It felt like heaven to William. He'd forgotten.

He accepted another rib-breaking hug—this time from Mrs. Brill— and one from Mary, whom William had known all his life.

"You're back, Will!" Mary cried, her arms clinging tightly to his waist. Sweet, simpleminded Mary, who had been his best friend during child-hood. "I knew you'd come back, and you did."

"Ah, my little Mary," William said. He gently extricated himself from her arms and studied her closely, holding her hands at arm's length. "You're a lovely young woman now, aren't you? I missed you the most, you know."

"Yes," she said. "Because I love you the most."

He smiled at her words while the others chuckled.

"Now, Mary, you mustn't be sayin' such things," Mrs. Brill whispered to her daughter. "Beggin' yer pardon, yer lordship."

"None needed, Mrs. Brill, I assure you." He kissed Mary's hand before letting it go.

He was then introduced to John, the footman, and Sally, the maid of all work. He was already acquainted with the coachman, a red-faced, robust man of middle years named Walter. The entire round of introductions took all of five minutes.

"May I show you to your rooms, your lordship?" Mrs. Holly asked, apparently feeling that a sense of decorum needed to be put in place for the new lord of the manor after calling him a dear boy.

"Thank you, Mrs. Holly," he said, nodding goodbye to the others and following her up the main stairs.

Once they were out of earshot of the others, however, he stopped her. He was certain the rooms Mrs. Holly was taking him to would be the viscount's rooms, but they had been his father's. William had never set foot in them before and didn't want to now. "I believe I would prefer to stay in my old room for the time being, if you don't mind."

"But—oh, of course." She nodded in understanding. "As you wish."

Mrs. Holly looked older—not as old as Grimshaw, to be sure, but there were lines on her face and about her eyes that hadn't been there before, and there were more than a few threads of silver running through the brown hair that peeked out from beneath her cap.

"Luncheon will be ready in an hour, allowing you time to refresh yourself, if you like, my lord," she said. "In the meantime, I'll have tea sent to your rooms. Ah, and Mr. Heslop asked me to inform you that he would join you here this afternoon, if that meets with your approval."

"He's not staying here, then?"

"No, my lord; he elected to stay in the village, at the George and Dragon." She curtsied and turned to leave.

"Mrs. Holly—"

She stopped and turned back. "Yes, my lord?"

"Mrs. Holly," he repeated, extending both hands out to her. "I remember many times, in the not-so-very-distant past, when you chose to call me names, such as rascal and scamp and others of a similar nature. Let's not overdo the 'my lording,' then, shall we?" He smiled and dipped his chin, waiting for her reply.

"Oh, you!" she said, clasping her hands at her bosom, and—Good heavens, William thought, she wasn't about to cry again, was she?—"You were always such a handsome little boy and a good boy, too, and just look at you! All grown up and as handsome a man as was ever born." Her tears did fall then, and she pulled her handkerchief from her pocket once again and dabbed at her eyes while William patted her on the shoulder. "It is so good to have you back home at Farleigh Manor, Master William, where you belong."

"It's good to be home." It wasn't entirely, not really, but now wasn't the time for expressing such a sentiment.

He excused himself from her and ventured on alone to his old room, which was located at the end of the same wing as the viscount and viscountess's suites of rooms. He'd had little opportunity to inhabit it since leaving for Eton. It smelled of a mustiness that came from disuse, which would explain why Mrs. Holly had initially been taken aback when he'd said he preferred to stay here. She must have had the viscount's rooms prepared for him. Knowing Mrs. Holly, however, she'd have his bedroom aired and ready for him by the time he retired to bed that evening.

The room looked exactly as he remembered it. The counterpane and curtains were the same ones from his boyhood, made of dark-blue brocade meant to assist in hiding the dirt that was inherent to young males. The same painting still hung on the wall across from the bed—a simple landscape he himself had painted while at Eton. His desk. His bookcase.

He crossed to the desk and opened the top drawer on the left, removing the object wrapped in cloth that lay inside. It was the small family portrait of him and his parents that had been commissioned when he was ten.

He carefully unwrapped the painting from its cloth and was immediately thrust back in time. There was his beautiful mother, young again, sitting in an ornate chair, with William at her side and his father standing behind her, arrogant swine that he was. William had begged his mother to have it painted so he could take it with him to Eton, and by some miracle, his mother had gotten his father to agree. William's mother had done her best to shield him from his parents' increasing hostility toward each other, but William had sensed that much was wrong within their family.

And then she had died.

He ran a single finger gently over the image of his mother before rewrapping the painting in the cloth and placing it back in the drawer. Perhaps one day he would be able to look upon it with objectivity and not with stabbing pain and anger, but not yet.

The maid, Sally, arrived then with the tea tray. He thanked her and sat near the window to drink it. From what he'd observed so far, the manor was in better condition than he'd expected, but then, he'd expected it to be entirely derelict. Perhaps he had misunderstood the tone of Mr. Heslop's letter. Perhaps the viscountcy's assets weren't in a dire state after all. Perhaps—despite his father's costly vices and decades of finessing those vices into an art form—things weren't as bad as he'd feared.

It struck him that his father's steward was not among the employees and servants he had greeted earlier. That wasn't a particularly promising sign; granted, the man may have simply tired of dealing with his father and gone on his way.

Well, he would have his answers soon enough. This afternoon, in fact. He decided to spend the rest of the remaining hour before luncheon in his room unpacking his belongings rather than asking Grimshaw or the new footman to do it. He'd always seen to such personal needs himself, and there was plenty of other work for the others to do without his adding to it.

Besides, it might be the last time he would have an hour of peace and quiet to himself for a while.

* * *

At precisely two o'clock in the afternoon, Mr. Heslop, a man of middle years, arrived from the village and suggested to William that they adjourn to his lordship's study. As a boy and even as a youth, William had never been in his father's private rooms and had been in the study only when his father was meting out punishment—not that William had required much discipline growing up. Or maybe he had, and his mother and the servants had hidden that fact from his father whenever possible. At any rate, William had eventually learned to pay special attention to the sorts of activities his father had praised and those that had merited a caning, though there had not necessarily been anything amounting to consistency.

William doubted his father had actually spent much time in the study himself. He had left most things in the care of his steward, whose small office in the back of the house near the kitchen underscored the type of priority his father had placed on the day-to-day running of the estate. Today, the study was surprisingly tidy—the desk straightened with papers neatly arranged on top. His father had been meticulous in many ways—his appearance, for example—yet erratic and impulsive in others. He would have considered anything having to do with income as beneath him, unless it had to do with spending that income. William had never been able to understand him.

Stop crying, boy. You will never win if they can read your face.

"Would you care for tea?" he asked Mr. Heslop. "Or a brandy, perhaps?"

"No, thank you," the solicitor replied. He sat and leaned his leather letter case against the leg of his chair. "I hope you will forgive me," he continued. "I'm afraid I allowed myself certain liberties of access to your father's papers upon his death. Because of the disarray I saw here when I arrived, I also brought in my clerk, who assisted me in putting things to rights."

That sounded more like the father William remembered. "You could not have waited until I arrived?" he asked.

"Perhaps, but as it took a few days for us to locate your whereabouts and then write to you and wait for your return, I judged it prudent to act. There are unusual . . . ah . . . circumstances at play here that required thorough legal examination in order to address them in the most expeditious and beneficial of manners."

The man was talking as convolutedly as he wrote. "You are speaking in riddles, Heslop. Let me be frank—I received very little instruction in estate management growing up; I believe it is because my father had little interest in it himself and felt it beneath him, so he delegated the responsibility of the estate to his steward. Additionally, I was estranged from my father for several years, as you are already aware, having had no connection to him at all after the death of my mother." William paused to let those words sink in before continuing. "In short, it would be a service to us both if you were to cease worrying about offending my sensibilities regarding my father and speak plainly."

Mr. Heslop heaved a sigh. "That is a relief to hear, your lordship. Very well, then; let us proceed."

They spent the next several hours going over the estate's books and papers, and William, who had always thought himself rather clever, soon realized just how lacking his education as a titled landowner was. He shook off the resentment he felt anew toward his father and focused on the numbers he was reading.

He and Mr. Heslop reviewed livestock quotas, earnings and losses from the home farm and the various tenant farms, repairs, and drainage costs. They went over servants' wages and pensioners' allowances. They added incomes and subtracted debits. In spite of himself, William's eyes began to swim, and his head ached from the rows and columns and pluses and minuses.

And then Mr. Heslop picked up a sheaf of papers from the corner of the desk and placed them in front of William. William thumbed through the first few pages before sitting back in his chair. He rubbed his eyes, unwilling to believe what he was seeing.

Mortgages. They were mortgages—*plural*—made against the estate.

Viscount Farleigh, William Senior, had mortgaged the estate to the hilt, and now those debts belonged to Viscount Farleigh—that would be he, William *Junior*, lucky chap that he was.

He thought of Grimshaw and Matthew and Samuel and Mrs. Holly. He thought of Mrs. Brill and Mary and the other servants, few though they may be, and the loyal tenants who still remained on Farleigh land, and what a blow these massive debts would mean to their wellbeing.

"How could my father have allowed this to happen?" he asked. And yet William knew how, remembered how his father had been.

"As best I can tell, while your father was concerned about personal debts of honor, he was markedly less so about debts owed to institutions and merchants, whom he considered beneath him, if you'll excuse my bluntness. It also appears your father's steward took his cues from your father, in that he was more concerned about seeing to his own welfare and skimming from the books than he was to the overall success of the estate. As long as your father had what he wanted—"

"He didn't care about anything else," William said.

"Quite so, unfortunately."

"The steward?"

"Long gone, I'm afraid. Our inquiries have led nowhere."

William nodded, expecting as much. "What is to be done?" He asked the question rhetorically, expecting no real answer from Mr. Heslop. He fully appreciated now why the solicitor had taken the time to thoroughly explain the gravity of the situation to him, knowing William was a young man of a mere twenty-four years with no practical experience upon which to rely.

"I have pondered that question daily since your father's passing," Mr. Heslop replied, removing his reading spectacles and pinching the bridge of his nose. "There are several critical repairs needed about the estate and the home farm. With good management, Farleigh Manor would be able to meet her own obligations within a year or two; after that, it might provide a decent income or even better than decent. Were it not for the mortgages . . ."

"Were it not for the mortgages, which put any chance of success out of reach," William said, finishing the solicitor's sentence. "We have no options, then, do we?"

"Well, there are a couple of small unentailed properties that can be sold that will help reduce the mortgage debts, *if* you're agreeable. Their sale won't clear the debts, mind you, not by half—but at this point, anything will help; however, it would reduce the overall size of the viscountcy holdings significantly."

"I'm agreeable. I don't care about the size of the viscountcy holdings; I care about the people affected by my father's behavior. I'm willing to do whatever it takes to get the debts resolved and the manor and its people thriving again."

The solicitor cleared his voice. "That is good to hear, your lordship, for that is where the unusual circumstances I spoke of earlier come into play. There is a particular detail I have been holding back that might be the key to resolving the mortgage debts and seeing Farleigh Manor ready to thrive again."

"Then tell me," William said, leaning forward in his chair. "You have spent the whole of the afternoon pointing out in great detail the dire situation the viscountcy is in. And then you tell me there is an answer? Why this drawn-out exercise? Why not simply point out the answer and let's be on with it?"

Mr. Heslop shook his head while he straightened the mortgage documents and set them aside. "If only it were that easy, your lordship. I needed to impress upon you the critical nature of your situation first. Yes, the sale of the unentailed properties will help the situation, but they will not resolve the majority of the debt or see to the repairs needed here at Farleigh Manor or to the basic funds necessary for running the estate. I said the detail I spoke about *might* be the key to resolving the debt. I did *not* say it was a simple matter. Quite the contrary, in fact. But it is, I believe, your only hope—the slimmest of hopes, if I may be frank."

"I cannot know that without being told what it is," William remarked pointedly.

"Very well. It will be up to you to decide how to proceed anyway." He picked up his letter case and removed a folder, then opened the folder and removed a document. And then, with great deliberation, he handed the document to William.

William read the words written on the document before him. He read them again and then a third time. "What the *devil?*" he exclaimed, looking up at Mr. Heslop.

"Precisely," Mr. Heslop replied.

Chapter 2

"I THINK I SHALL SET up a florist shop right here," Alex said to Louisa when he entered the main drawing room and saw the numerous flower arrangements and bouquets displayed there. "Every variety of bloom in every conceivable color is in this room. I could make a fortune, and there would still be enough flowers left over that no one would be the wiser."

What Alex was jokingly implying was very nearly true, Louisa conceded. The number of bouquets she'd received in the days following the Wilmington ball had gone beyond her wildest expectations. She understood now what people meant when they spoke of an embarrassment of riches.

"They're certainly lovely to look at, and the scent in the room is heavenly," Mama said as she sketched one of the arrangements of roses to use as a needlework pattern. "These yellow roses are particularly stunning. Who are they from, Louisa?"

"I'm not sure." She opened the card accompanying them. "Oh dear," she muttered softly. In a louder voice, she said, "They're from the Baron Moseby, Mama." She still felt a bit guilty about the way Lord Kerridge had dealt with the poor man at the ball—but really, the baron should have gotten the hint before then, especially when one considered that he was more than triple her age.

"That old goat!" Alex exclaimed.

"Who's an old goat?" Anthony, who had walked into the drawing room right at that moment, asked.

"Moseby." Alex waved his hand in the direction of the yellow roses. "Thinks he's one of Louisa's suitors."

Anthony snorted. "Didn't he try to woo you once, Mama?"

"While it is true I knew him in my debutante days," she said, "he did not try to woo me. He was married to his second wife at the time. I'm sure he is not nearly so bad as his reputation would suggest—"

"He most certainly is, Mama," Alex said, cutting her off. "There was this one time I happened to see him near Drury Lane with a certain—"

Mama silenced him with a gesture. "He has only ever been gracious to me, Halford," she said. "So have a care, if you please."

Anthony's and Alex's eyebrows rose, and Louisa threw her hand over her mouth to stifle a giggle. Mama rarely used Alex's title when the family was alone, and Louisa wasn't so naive as to misunderstand her reason for using it this time.

"Certainly, Mama," Alex said, bowing deeply to her, making her chuckle in response. Alex was such a charming scoundrel; he got away with all sorts of things all the time. His charm worked this time too. "In future, only the most sugary words shall escape my lips when referring to the Baron Moseby."

"Unless he tries to court our sister in earnest," Anthony said. "In which case, I shall very sweetly challenge him to swords or pistols."

"Precisely, brother dear. And I shall sweetly agree to be your second," Alex said.

"Good heavens! As bad as all that?" Mama asked, aghast.

"At the very least," Anthony assured her.

"Perhaps I shall sketch the orchid by the window instead," she said, flipping the page of her sketchbook. "Louisa, I give you permission to decline any offers of courtship from the Baron Moseby."

"Thank you, Mama," Louisa said, still attempting to hold back a giggle.

"Ahem." Gibbs cleared his throat discreetly to gain their attention. "Excuse the interruption, but the Earl of Kerridge is here to see you, Lady Louisa. I put him in the blue sitting room." He handed Louisa the earl's calling card.

Louisa's humor vanished, and her heart began to flutter. "Please invite the earl to join us here," she instructed Gibbs.

Alex whistled through his teeth once the butler departed the room. "What a coup. Aylesham's heir, no less. Who would have thought it of our baby sister?"

"I wouldn't have," Anthony said. "At least it isn't Moseby though, thank goodness. You certainly picked the highest plum from the aristocratic tree, Weezy. Is this overwhelming array of horticultural perfection his doing, then?"

Louisa could feel her cheeks heat up—drat her tendency to blush easily. "Don't call me Weezy. I'm not five years old anymore. And to answer your question, some of the blooms are from him but not all, or even a majority of them." There were two arrangements from the earl that she knew of: the large urn of red roses that had required two footmen to carry into the drawing room and the rare orchid her mother was now sketching near the window.

She dashed over to the gilt mirror hanging on the wall and patted a loose curl back into place. Her cheeks were too pink, but there was nothing she could do about that.

"It goes without saying that I expect the two of you to be on your best behavior for your sister's sake," Mama said. "You look fine, Louisa. Sit down." She set her sketchbook aside.

Louisa dutifully perched on the corner of the sofa.

"If it goes without saying, Mama, then you needn't have bothered saying it," Alex replied. "Ah, Kerridge, here you are. Welcome."

The Earl of Kerridge bowed over Mama's hand and then moved across the room to bow over Louisa's. He was a handsome man, Louisa thought—tall and slender, with a thick shock of hair the color of mahogany. He had taken her driving in Hyde Park twice since the night of the Wilmington ball.

"May we offer you tea, Lord Kerridge?" Mama asked.

"Yes, thank you."

She nodded to Gibbs, who then left the drawing room. "Please, be seated."

He sat in a chair directly opposite Louisa, and the five of them proceeded to chat about the usual things—the weather, the Parliamentary session, the weather . . . Louisa tried to concentrate on the conversation, all the while terrified one of her brothers would refer to her as Weezy (a terrible incarnation of her name, if there ever was one) or Lady Cumulus or any one of the myriad other embarrassing nicknames they had conferred upon her over her lifetime. Eventually, the tea arrived, and Mama poured for everyone. Louisa made a mental note that Lord Kerridge preferred his tea with cream and no sugar.

She managed to finish her tea without spilling on herself, in spite of the trembling of her hands. Afterward, her brothers eventually paid heed to the subtle gestures Mama had been giving them the entire time and excused themselves from the room.

"Lady Ashworth," Lord Kerridge said when Anthony shut the door behind them, "would you mind very much if Lady Louisa and I had a few minutes alone together?"

Louisa's heart was beating so loudly she was surprised no one else could hear it. She looked from her mother to the earl and back again to her mother, who rose gracefully to her feet and smiled. "Perhaps I shall go see if Lord Ashworth would like to take a break from meeting with his steward for a few moments. I am certain he would enjoy seeing you again."

"Thank you, Lady Ashworth. A conversation with Lord Ashworth would fit with my plans nicely." He turned his gaze on Louisa, giving her a steady, confident look that suggested he thought she was already his for the asking.

Was she? The earl was handsome and wealthy and heir to a duke—a matchmaking mama's veritable dream—and he was about to propose marriage; Louisa was sure of it.

Was he her dream?

He must be. She enjoyed his company and found him attractive, and of all her suitors thus far, he was her favorite. She had even allowed him to kiss her. It had been a brief and respectful kiss, but despite its brevity, she'd been aware of his lips on hers, the smoothness of his freshly shaven skin, the scent of his cologne.

It had been her first kiss; she had no other experience with which to compare it. And it had been enjoyable. It had made her feel . . . something. A bit daring, perhaps. More womanly—which was an odd thing, really, since she'd always been aware of her female nature, even when she'd been a hoyden of a child, climbing trees and swimming and horseback riding and chasing after her infernal brothers.

The earl's kiss had awakened a different sort of awareness in her—one she wasn't completely capable of putting into words. Perhaps he would kiss her again today so she could understand it better.

She was reasonably certain she would enjoy it if he did.

"Louisa?"

She blinked. The earl was waiting for an answer to something with a twinkle in his eye. "I'm sorry. I must have been woolgathering."

"So I surmised." He smiled. He had a handsome smile—a perfect smile, like the heir to a duke should have. "May I join you on the sofa?" he asked.

"Oh, assuredly you may." What a ninny she was being! She scooted over a bit, making more room for him on the sofa, and he sat by her, more closely than she'd expected, ratcheting up her heartbeat again. "Would you care for another biscuit?" she asked, unsure what else to say. "Or more tea? I can ring to have a fresh pot—"

"No, thank you." He paused, and Louisa held her breath. "Louisa," he said at last. "My dear, you must have noticed my particular attention to you over the past few weeks. I think I am not being presumptuous when I claim that you have received this attention favorably."

"Yes," was all she managed to say. She swallowed.

His eyebrows wrinkled. "Yes, I am being presumptuous?"

"No—I mean, yes, I have received your attentions favorably. And no, you are not being presumptuous." If she wasn't careful, she could end up being the first young lady in British history to botch a proposal.

His face smoothed with relief—and probably humor. Louisa chose not to analyze it too closely. "I'm glad to hear it," he said. "If that is truly so, then . . ." He slipped off the sofa gracefully onto one knee, and Louisa stopped breathing altogether. "I would consider it the greatest honor if you would agree to be my countess and my future duchess." He reached for her hand and turned it slowly, dropping the lightest of kisses on her wrist, of all places, completely catching her off-guard and making her tremble.

There. There it was. He'd proposed marriage. He was looking up at her, still on bended knee, his eyes dark with intensity, waiting . . .

"I will," she said.

He smiled. "You have made me the happiest of men, my dear," he answered. He rose and resumed his place next to her on the sofa. "I shall speak to your father, then. We will begin negotiations on the marriage settlement straightaway, if that pleases you."

"Shouldn't it?" she asked.

"I certainly hope it should. After I speak with your father this afternoon, I shall inform my solicitors and Aylesham's to meet with the Ashworth solicitor. I don't believe it will take too long to hammer out the arrangements. We should be able to announce the betrothal within a week or two." He studied her face; Louisa had no idea what he saw there. "You're disappointed."

"Not at all. I'm very happy."

"Good. I am too. Perhaps I may steal a kiss before we are intruded upon by your parents."

"I should like that," she said.

He leaned toward her and pressed his lips to hers, lingering, feathering his fingers along the line of her jaw before ending the kiss and moving back.

"I can hear your parents coming," he murmured.

"What?" She blinked and sat up straight, quickly placing her hands—which had strayed to his shoulders—in her lap. There was a soft knock at the door before it opened, and her father stepped inside, followed by her mother, who was biting her upper lip as though she might cry.

"I believe I was summoned," her father said, looking every inch the marquess that he was.

Lord Kerridge rose to his feet and bowed. "Yes, your lordship. I was hoping I might beg a few minutes of your time."

"Certainly. If you ladies will excuse us, it appears the Earl of Kerridge and I have business to discuss."

And just like that, Louisa found herself betrothed.

* * *

Louisa did not see Lord Kerridge at all the day following their betrothal. He sent her a note, accompanied by another large bouquet of roses, informing her that, regretfully, he would be spending the day with the Duke of Aylesham and their solicitors, hammering out the tedious details of the marriage agreement, which her father's solicitor would then need to review and approve.

Tedious, indeed.

She stayed home, feeling unsettled. How was one to go on calls or take a stroll through Hyde Park or visit with friends and acquaintances when one was betrothed and yet not officially betrothed? People had seen her in company with Lord Kerridge and would undoubtedly ask her about him. Their betrothal wasn't a secret, but it wasn't to be made public yet either. Until the Duke of Aylesham's solicitors had met with her father's solicitors and ironed out all the particulars on both sides, it would be imprudent to say anything to anyone.

It wasn't that she felt she couldn't converse with people and tactfully avoid the subjects of betrothal and Lord Kerridge and such. It was just that the entire business seemed exactly that. Business.

Which was silly because marriage *was* business. Critical business for anyone but especially for the nobility, who held lands and estates and fortunes that must be protected for posterity. Louisa understood all that. It had been ingrained in her since childhood.

And yet, today, her betrothal felt rather anticlimactic.

Never one to sit still, however, she found things to do to keep busy throughout the day. She read. She practiced the pianoforte. She sat with her mother and did needlework until she thought her eyes would cross. She read some more.

Later that afternoon, she received another note from Lord Kerridge, apologizing once again for his absence and inviting her and her parents to join him at the theater the following evening.

The negotiations are progressing, his letter said, *but not at the speed with which I had hoped. We must be patient awhile longer, dear Louisa, before we may share our joyful news with others.*

Since the marriage contracts involved three of the most highly ranked noblemen in England, she supposed this must be the usual way of things, and as such, she must be patient.

She decided to take her supper in her room and then retired to bed early.

It seemed she had barely fallen asleep when she awoke with a start the next morning as her mother opened her curtains and the midday sun struck her full in the face. "It is past time you got up," Mama said. "Regardless of the negotiations the solicitors must undertake, you and I still have a wedding to plan. Up you go, now."

Louisa moaned and rolled to her side, an arm thrown over her face to protect her eyes from the glaring sun.

"Are you ill?" Mama asked. "Is that why you excused yourself last evening?" She sat on the side of the bed. "Truly, Louisa, are you unwell?"

"No, Mama, I'm fine. I just need a moment. What time is it?"

"It's past noon."

Louisa sat up abruptly. Gracious, she'd slept for an age! "Tibbetts," she called to her maid, who immediately bustled into the room. "Quickly, draw my bath. And can you please—"

"Toast and chocolate are on their way, milady, as I took the liberty when I saw her ladyship enter your room."

"That's a relief, for I've certainly overslept breakfast. I can't believe how late it is. I must wash my hair, and we must discuss how to style it for this evening, and I need to choose a gown—something that doesn't look like it should rain at any minute, and—"

"I don't understand why you're in such a state of anxiety, darling. One would almost think you were more nervous about attending the theater with Lord Kerridge tonight than you were for the Wilmington ball. Your gown for that was exquisite, and you should not take your brothers' teasing to heart that way."

Louisa was not in the mood to tell her mother that Lady Wilmington and even Lord Kerridge had made similar cloud comments about her gown.

"At any rate, Louisa," Mama continued, "I do suggest you hurry with your morning routine. It would be a good idea to have a few wedding details in place that you can discuss with Lord Kerridge this evening. The gentlemen may argue all they wish about marriage this and marriage that, but it is the womenfolk who see to the actual event. I shall meet you in my sitting room in an hour's time."

"Yes, Mama."

One hour later, Louisa dutifully arrived at her mother's favorite sitting room, where the two of them discussed her nuptials to Lord Kerridge. "We must be assured of Lord Kerridge's approval in all of this, of course, not to mention that of the Duke and Duchess of Aylesham, who will undoubtedly wish it to be a grand affair."

Their efforts during the afternoon raised a flurry of questions in Louisa's mind. Would the marriage take place in London? At Lord Kerridge's estate in Devon? Or at one of the duke's vast holdings? What was to be eaten at the banquet to follow, and who was to attend? And then there were flowers and travel arrangements and guest accommodations and on and on and on. Louisa felt completely overwhelmed.

"Don't worry," Mama told her reassuringly. "It sounds a bit much at present, and it's true that most weddings needn't concern themselves with the preferences of a duke and duchess in addition to everything else, but it will all work out well and happily. You'll see."

Louisa hoped so.

Eventually, Mama put the list aside and sat back, satisfied that they'd at least made a decent start, which was a good thing, for it was past time they concluded in order for her to prepare for the theater.

Louisa chose a demure gown of dark-blue silk with silver embroidery on the bodice, rather than one of the lighter-colored gowns young girls usually wore during their come-out season. She sat at her dressing table and studied her reflection in the mirror, finally deciding she looked acceptable, even if the color was still high in her cheeks. She realized she was looking forward to seeing Lord Kerridge again. She wondered how the marriage contract negotiations were progressing and if he would approve of the plans she and Mama had drawn up thus far.

She wondered if he would kiss her again and how she would feel when he did.

She took up her gloves and fan and made her way downstairs to join her family for supper.

* * *

The following afternoon, Louisa was in the music room practicing the pianoforte in case she was called upon to perform sometime, which was often the case for young ladies during the Season—even betrothed young ladies. More precisely, she supposed, she was attempting to practice because, truthfully, she couldn't stop daydreaming about her time at the theater the previous night.

She hardly remembered what she'd observed onstage—what with Lord Kerridge seated beside her, sensing his nearness and the natural warmth that had emanated from his body, the scent of leather and cologne that had filled her nostrils. It had all seemed so masculine and intriguing—which was odd, considering she'd lived her entire life with a father and two older brothers. She'd certainly smelled leather and knew men were warm-blooded individuals, just as she and Mama were. Perhaps her awareness of it last evening was because she knew Lord Kerridge was to be her husband, so she had begun to notice elements of his maleness she'd not really considered before.

At the intermission, he'd asked Mama's permission to take Louisa for a stroll, and, naturally, Mama had agreed. They'd exited the box and walked down the hallway, Louisa's hand tucked in the crook of Lord Kerridge's arm, greeting others who were taking the opportunity to stretch their legs as well. They received several knowing smiles, and Louisa understood that he was making a public point of his intentions toward her, even if nothing at all official could be said yet.

He clearly had been intending to send a message to her other suitors. Louisa had noticed more than one gentleman approaching her only to change course when they saw her on Lord Kerridge's arm. The Baron Moseby, who'd been with an elegant older woman who wore too many cosmetics, had looked positively chagrined.

And then, before the intermission ended, Lord Kerridge—George, as he'd finally asked her to call him—had led her to a secluded corner and kissed her again. More than once, in fact, allowing for the brief amount of time they'd had remaining before the next act was to begin.

It had seemed delicious and rather clandestine to be pressed into a corner in such a manner and kissed by a handsome gentleman. Her betrothed. She knew he had been highly sought after by the young misses and their eager mamas. He was an earl who would be a duke one day. He'd been one of the most eligible bachelors of the *ton* for the past few years, from all Louisa had heard.

And he'd chosen her out of all the prospective young ladies.

She was puzzling out the fingering for a particularly tricky musical passage when there was a knock at the door that made her jump in surprise. Good heavens, where was her mind today?

"Sorry to disturb you, milady," the footman who opened the door said in a low voice. "But I have been sent to summon you to your father's study. As soon as is convenient."

"Thank you." She set her music aside and hurried to the study. A formal summons by her father was an unusual occurrence. It was possible that a settlement had been reached, although she doubted it, based on what Lord Kerridge—George—had told her last evening.

"Lady Louisa," her father's solicitor, Mr. Swindlehurst, said, crossing the room to greet her when she arrived. "You are as lovely as ever." He took her offered hand in his and bowed over it.

Louisa's attention, however, was diverted to her father, who was standing by the window, looking out, his hands clasped behind his back. And then she noticed her mother sitting in a chair, twisting a handkerchief in her lap, her face strained and pale. Something was terribly wrong. Had one of her brothers been injured, or worse? Her stomach clenched at the thought.

There were two other people in the room, she belatedly realized—a man who looked to be about the same age as her father and a younger man not much older than her brothers. They both rose from their chairs and turned toward her.

"Allow me to present Viscount Farleigh and Mr. Heslop, his solicitor," Mr. Swindlehurst said. "Gentlemen, Lady Louisa Hargreaves. Please, Lady Louisa, won't you be seated?" He gestured toward the vacant chair next to her mother's, and the two gentlemen resumed their seats. Her father did not move, however, but continued to stare out the window while the young gentleman's solicitor, Mr. Heslop, began ruffling through a small stack of documents in his possession.

The young gentleman, Viscount Farleigh, on the other hand, was studying Louisa closely—enough so to unsettle her. His dark eyes were scrutinizing her from head to foot, seeming to take in every detail of her appearance. It felt to Louisa as if he were assessing her rather like he would review bloodstock at Tattersall's.

Feeling self-conscious and uneasy, Louisa sat at the edge of the chair and clasped her hands to keep from fidgeting. Why did her father continue to stand woodenly at the window? Why was this young viscount watching her so closely? She was betrothed—as good as betrothed—to an earl who would be a duke one day. She was the daughter of a marquess. A mere viscount should not feel so intimidating, as though he, somehow, was the person in control of things here in her father's study. She lifted her chin ever so slightly and stared back at him.

One corner of his mouth tipped slightly upward for the briefest of moments.

"What is going on, Mama?" she asked quietly, her eyes still on the viscount.

"I am so sorry, darling," her mother whispered in a broken voice.

Mr. Swindlehurst cleared his throat. "Lady Louisa, a situation has been brought to our attention by these two gentlemen that has a direct effect on you, it would seem."

Louisa glanced at her father, who still hadn't moved, and then at the viscount and his solicitor. "I cannot imagine how. I have never met either of these gentlemen before. Have you, Papa?"

"No," he said flatly, still staring out the window.

Mr. Heslop lifted a faded document from atop the stack he'd been leafing through earlier. "Viscount Farleigh is in possession of a vowel, a guarantee of payment of debt, from the Marquess of Ashworth."

"I don't see how that concerns me. My father is a wealthy man, Mr. Heslop, and I'm sure he will fulfill the terms of the vowel. Won't you, Papa?" Louisa said.

Her father continued to stare out the window. "The terms of the vowel don't involve money, Louisa. I cannot believe the old fool did this."

She was more confused than ever. What old fool? "I don't understand—"

"Allow me to explain it to you, Lady Louisa," Mr. Heslop said. "I hope you will pardon my choice of words, but it is best to present this as frankly as possible. The terms of the vowel are this: that the daughter of the Marquess of Ashworth be united in marriage to Viscount Farleigh. You are the daughter of the Marquess of Ashworth, and as has been pointed out to you already, this gentleman is Viscount Farleigh."

Louisa's head snapped in the direction of the young man, who was still watching her intently. "This cannot be," she declared, fear curling through her like acrid smoke. "I am already betrothed to Lord Kerridge."

"Not *officially* betrothed, from what we understand," Mr. Heslop said. "And very soon, not even that. At least, *not* to the Earl of Kerridge."

Louisa struggled to breathe. Mr. Swindlehurst placed a glass in her hand. "Drink this," he said.

She obeyed him and swallowed, choking on whatever it was. Brandy, perhaps; she didn't know. She handed the glass back to him, her throat and eyes burning.

"You see, Lady Louisa," Mr. Swindlehurst said, waiting until she had caught her breath before attempting to explain Mr. Heslop's jarring words. "Based on the evidence they have presented, it appears that your grandfather, when he was the marquess, made a wager with one Viscount Farleigh—this gentleman's father." He gestured toward the young man. "Rather than a traditional bet of money or property, however, the wager was unique in that it enabled the viscount to marry the daughter of the marquess."

"My grandfather never had a daughter," Louisa said.

"Which was undoubtedly the reason he agreed to the wager in the first place. The viscount in question was a young man at the time and unmarried. The marquess had long given up on having additional children, something he'd most likely assumed the viscount wouldn't have realized when making the wager."

"What you are saying is my grandfather made and lost a wager, not caring whether he won or lost because he assumed the terms of the wager could not be fulfilled."

"Precisely, milady," Mr. Swindlehurst said.

"However," Mr. Heslop said, "the late viscount was exceptionally clever in how he wrote the vowel for the marquess to sign. He never explicitly stated *which* marquess or viscount the vowel pertained to. It is, therefore, still valid, in our opinion."

"May I see this vowel?" she asked as calmly as she could, although her heart was pounding violently.

Mr. Swindlehurst handed it to her. She read the words and then read them again. There, at the bottom, was her grandfather's signature, and there were witness signatures as well. Her grandfather had even affixed the marquess's seal to it.

"Good heavens," she whispered, handing the vile document back to Mr. Swindlehurst with shaking hands.

"As you are the first daughter of a Marquess of Ashworth to come of marriageable age since the vowel was drawn up, the current Viscount Farleigh has the right to claim the debt owed on it," Mr. Swindlehurst said in a compassionate tone that did little to soothe Louisa.

"Which he wishes to do," Mr. Heslop added briskly. "At the soonest possible convenience."

"But it *isn't* convenient!" Louisa cried, jumping to her feet. "This . . . this *obligation* has nothing to do with me. You cannot possibly mean to hold me to the terms of this vowel, which is decades old. We live in a modern age—this sort of thing doesn't happen anymore." She ran to her father and grabbed his arm. "Papa, tell them! Please!"

Her father kept his hands braced on the windowsill and took a deep breath before turning to face her.

"Papa, *tell* them," Louisa begged, clutching at his lapels. "The vowel is meaningless. I am betrothed, or as good as betrothed. You will pay him whatever he wants, won't you, Papa? There is no need for this. *Tell* them, Papa!"

"I cannot," her father said. His face was all bleak, hard lines as he looked back at her and drew her hands away from his person, then kissed each one before letting her go.

Mr. Swindlehurst rose and took her gently by the arm and led her back to her chair. "You understand, certainly, that under the law, children are considered the property of their fathers, just as wives are, although I doubt this sort of claim has ever been made before, nor do I believe they would succeed if they were to take this to court." He glared pointedly at Mr. Heslop. "I have advised your father not to honor the vowel."

"So you have, Mr. Swindlehurst," Mr. Heslop said. "Allow me to point out to Lady Louisa, however, that the debt remains; we have verified the vowel's authenticity, as has Swindlehurst here, to everyone's satisfaction."

"Not to *mine*." She blinked back the tears that threatened to spill. She would *not* cry before these men. She would not show that weakness to them, and especially not to *him*, who had said nothing so far and still watched her too closely. "You don't have to do this," she said to the viscount. "You can rip up the vowel right now."

"The viscount wishes the vowel to be honored," Mr. Heslop said. "It is a debt the Marquess of Ashworth is honor-bound to fulfill."

The viscount himself remained silent.

"Papa," she entreated again. "Mama. *Say* something."

Her mother stifled a sob.

"I cannot simply ignore the vowel, my dear," Papa said. "I don't know what my infernal father was thinking, but I cannot ignore the fact that the vowel is real. It bears his signature and seal. Honor dictates that I fulfill the obligation of the debt. That being said, however, I cannot force *you* to do so, Louisa. As I have explained to these gentlemen, you are free to decide the matter for yourself. I have taught you and your brothers to understand your worth. You are my daughter. I trust you. I must leave this in your hands." He turned back to the window.

A dull weight settled heavily in Louisa's stomach. *Honor*, her father had said. Honor was everything to a true gentleman. Duels had been fought; lives had been lost over honor. Despite her parents' efforts to hide the shameful details of her grandfather from her, Louisa knew her father had dedicated his life to reestablishing the family honor after his own father had so capriciously ruined it. Honor had been bred into her and her brothers from the cradle.

Papa could not ignore the wager or the debt of his father, however ill-conceived and negligent her grandfather's actions had been. He could not absolve his daughter of the weight of it either.

She herself would have to choose how to proceed.

"Perhaps Lady Louisa wishes to have a few moments to herself," the viscount said, speaking for the first time. He rose to his feet, clearly expecting the others to take his lead.

Surprisingly, they did.

Her mother wrapped her in a hug. "Oh, my darling girl," she whispered. "I should never have believed something like this could happen. I am in utter shock."

When the door finally shut, leaving her alone, Louisa crossed to the window where her father had been standing. The view overlooked a terraced lawn bordered with a hedge of boxwoods. A line of yews in the distance marked the property boundary and offered privacy. How could it look so peaceful and orderly when she felt like she was being torn asunder?

What was she to do?

The debt a gentleman owed another gentleman was a matter of extreme honor. Louisa knew, from listening to her brothers' conversations, that a gentleman paid his debts to another gentleman, and he did so promptly. To do otherwise was not acceptable. Dishonorable. It was beyond the pale.

Today, her father, the Marquess of Ashworth, known for his hard-won integrity and honor, had been made aware of a debt his father owed—worse, a debt the *Marquess of Ashworth* owed, regardless of who had held the title when the debt had been incurred—and he could not resolve it and maintain the family honor without it impacting the life of his only daughter.

The existence of the vowel had created a horrible dilemma for him, and he was suffering deeply, for Louisa knew her father loved her. And rather than order her to comply, as many fathers could and would have done as head of the family, he had left the decision entirely to her. He had put his honor, his family's honor, into her hands.

She moved away from the window and wrapped her arms around her middle, trying to hold back the pain and anxiety she felt. Only last evening, she had been with George at the theater, and he had strolled with her so everyone would understand his intentions toward her and had kissed her in a secluded corner.

How much one's life could change in less than a day.

Chapter 3

WILLIAM COULD BARELY CONTAIN HIS surprise.

Regardless of the fact that he and his solicitor had walked into the home of the Marquess of Ashworth and issued what had amounted to a marital ultimatum to the man and his daughter, William was being treated with unexpected, albeit frosty, courtesy. In truth, he'd fully expected the two of them to be tossed out on their ears.

They were currently in an elegantly appointed anteroom not far from the marquess's study. Lord Ashworth had offered William a drink, but he had politely declined. The day was still young; he did not want the marquess to add excessive drink to a list of grievances he must already be forming against William.

The plan he and Heslop had devised this morning was that Heslop would do the talking and William would remain largely mute. Heslop was familiar with the details, could answer the questions, and was not emotionally invested in the outcome. They had both concluded that William's interests would be best served if he maintained his silence. The odds of success were better that way.

It was critical to weigh the odds, understand the stakes—not only one's own but also those of the other wagerer. William's father had stressed this time and time again throughout William's youth.

It was also important to keep one's expression neutral. *One does not give away one's hand, ever.* It was better to remain silent, mask one's feelings and reactions, and wait for the other person to make their move. He'd learned that convenient fact over and over again whenever he'd had dealings with his father.

He had also learned as a youth that he loathed gambling in any form.

He thoroughly detested what he was doing today. If it weren't for the responsibility—the *love*—he felt toward the good people of Farleigh Manor, a loyalty to his deceased mother he'd been forced to keep buried with her these past several years, and an intense longing for home that had emerged upon his return, he would not be attempting this—even though it was perfectly justifiable and within his rights that he should do so.

He'd never met Lady Louisa; still, he'd belatedly recalled seeing her when he'd been a student at Eton. Her brothers had attended Eton during his own time there, and Lady Louisa, along with her parents, had visited once or twice. She'd been a mere child at the time, dark-haired like her brothers, and overly chatty, if he was remembering that bit correctly. He wasn't entirely sure, as he hadn't run in the same circles as Ashworth's sons and, therefore, hadn't been particularly interested in anything to do with them, other than to take the briefest mental note of a talkative little sister.

Beyond that early reference, he hadn't spent much time thinking about her in a personal sense while he and Heslop had made their plans. She had been a theoretical figure in his mind, the means by which he could salvage his home and save the people he loved, who were dependent upon him as their new viscount.

On the rare occasion when he *had* thought of her, it was with the full understanding that he was sacrificing any future hope of marital happiness for himself in saving the estate and its people this way. As a result, he'd envisioned either an Amazon of a female, tall like her brothers and full of her aristocratic self, or a twittering bird-wit of a debutante, who would undoubtedly speak nothing of sense.

But today, the young lady herself, Lady Louisa Hargreaves, had entered the study and been a radiant bloom of youthful vitality, and William wouldn't have been able to speak even if it had been in the plans for him to do so.

He'd been caught utterly by surprise, and his disposition had shifted from one of resolute and gloomy self-sacrifice to hopeful longing in the space of an instant.

His eyes had taken in their fill. He suspected he already knew every flutter of her eyelashes, the curve of her ear, the line of her cheek. He had very nearly had to sit on his hands to keep from reaching for her, so badly had he longed to touch her and assure himself that she was not a vision.

His surprising reaction had also set off alarms clanging within him. That he found himself so strongly drawn to her was an unexpected bonus, to be sure, but William could not afford to be vulnerable or show any weakness whatsoever. He could not forget his purpose in being here. There was too much at stake.

He listened as Heslop and the other solicitor quietly discussed potential marriage settlements based on what had been in progress between Lady Louisa and Lord Kerridge in the matter-of-fact way that seemed unique to solicitors, in William's estimation. The marquess had gone to stand by the fireplace and was staring at the cold grate, one arm raised to rest against the mantel. The marchioness sat like a statue nearby.

William wanted to assure them both that he would do his best to be a good husband to their daughter, but he knew the words would ring hollow. Even so, he crossed the room to stand next to the marquess, as if his nearness would lend support to the man.

Lord Ashworth sensed his presence. "I would ask again that you consider a monetary amount in exchange for meeting the terms of the vowel," he said in a low voice. "For my daughter's sake."

"I'm sorry, your lordship, but no," William replied. Heslop had explained at length that it was the *connection* to the Ashworth family that was essential—that this was more than a matter of mere money. The mortgages on Farleigh Manor were too extensive, even after any potential sale of unentailed properties. William needed the connections he would get from marriage to the daughter of the Marquess of Ashworth, one of the most powerful men in England, if Farleigh Manor was to survive and thrive. "Nothing will satisfy but the original terms of the wager."

"Come, man. There must be a price we can agree upon. My daughter's very future is at stake."

"As is mine, sir, as well as the future of my title and tenants," William replied. "I did not make the wager, nor establish its terms; two other gentlemen did. I find it ironic that their combined recklessness now holds the means of restoring my family's honor. I intend to hold them both accountable."

The Marquess of Ashworth was silent for several moments, and William watched and waited for him to speak. "Honor and accountability," the marquess finally said. "It has been instilled in the English gentleman for centuries—that he is nothing without honor. One is prepared from birth to give one's life for one's honor."

He spoke the truth. William had been taught the same—at Eton and then at Oxford and even, to a certain extent, at home from his father— not that his father had been a shining example of it. Far from it; he had exemplified the opposite and had dragged the family name down with him as a result. William intended to rectify that now that he was viscount.

"Honor is in the very fiber of my being," the marquess continued. "I have always been prepared to sacrifice my life for my family's honor. But I never expected to be called upon to sacrifice the life of my daughter."

His words cut deeply. William understood the emotion behind them, and yet he was not without some pride, after all. "I should like to think I am offering Lady Louisa a fate that is not quite worse than death."

"With all due respect, Lord Farleigh, that remains to be seen."

"As you say. The opposite could just as well be true." William nodded and moved away. Nothing would be gained by allowing this conversation to continue, and much could be lost.

A subtle knock at the door drew everyone's attention. "Lady Louisa has requested Lord Farleigh join her in the study," a footman announced upon entering.

William glanced at Heslop, who was subtly shaking his head no. It had not been part of the plan. He sent Heslop a look he hoped conveyed confidence and crossed to the doorway.

"Lord Farleigh," the marquess said, stopping William in his tracks. "Ten minutes. That is all you get, and then I will be returning to my daughter's side."

William acknowledged the words and left the room.

These could very likely be the most important ten minutes of his life.

* * *

Louisa paced, sat, and then stood and began pacing again. The solicitors had explained the situation. Her father had made his position clear. If Louisa was to make a decision, the only way to do it was to acquaint herself with the individual to whom she would find herself married and at least assure herself of his character. She would not believe that honor took precedence over marriage to a villain. It was her very life that had been wagered away, after all. Her father would surely agree.

She forced herself to sit again and be calm. She could at least be grateful that her father had left the final decision in her hands.

There was a soft knock at the door, and Louisa turned abruptly in her chair; he was here, and she must discern his character swiftly, for she knew she would have little time alone with him.

"Lord Farleigh, milady," the footman who opened the door announced. He discreetly moved out of the way so Lord Farleigh could enter the room and then closed the door, leaving the two of them alone.

The viscount bowed formally to her. "You asked for me, Lady Louisa. How may I be of service?" he said.

For some reason, his tone made Louisa's teeth clench. She rose to her feet but did not reply immediately. She would turn the tables on *him* and study him for a few moments, as he had done her. She looked him up and down, hoping she wore the same bland expression on her face as he did.

The first thing she noticed was that he was tall—not as tall as her brothers but tall enough. He was dressed suitably, albeit not in the latest style, and his boots were well polished, she begrudgingly noted. His hair was a light brown, thick and straight, and neatly cut. His eyes, by contrast, were a deep brown with full, arched brows. His cheekbones and jawline were sculpted, as was his nose.

His lips were—well, perhaps she wouldn't study them too closely.

His expression told her absolutely nothing of what he was thinking, yet the corner of his mouth twitched briefly again, as it had done earlier.

"Does what you see please you?" he asked.

"Don't be impertinent," she responded. "I am only doing what you did to me."

"Fair enough." He spread his arms out at his sides. "Look your fill."

Now that he *knew* what she'd been doing and had given his permission for her to do so, studying him was the last thing she could possibly do, and he knew it. She turned and reseated herself in her chair, her back ramrod straight. "You may sit," she said, using as regal a voice as she could, considering the tension she felt.

"Thank you." He chose the chair closest to hers and sat, resting his arms on the arms of the chair. His hands didn't move. His feet didn't move. *He* didn't move.

She, on the other hand, began to fidget. She stilled her tapping toes and fingers, intent on having the upper hand with this man who had shown up this morning to wreak havoc on her life. He wasn't at all like Lord Kerridge, who was all elegant charm. Theirs was a match that would make sense to everyone when it was officially announced.

Would *have made sense, that is,* she reminded herself. *If* she felt she must honor the vowel.

He tipped his head slightly to one side in inquiry, waiting for her to speak.

Fine, then. There was no time to waste anyway. "Why are you doing this?" she asked bluntly.

"Because I must, and I can," he replied.

"I don't believe you," she said.

"Are you accusing me of being a liar?" he asked in a low voice, the merest edge of challenge in his tone. And yet he still didn't move. It was unsettling.

"No, my lord," she said. She paused to choose her next words carefully—which truly was a difficult task, especially under the circumstances, for her words generally tended to proliferate from her mouth without her mind always keeping apace with them. "What I am saying is that I detect a flaw in your argument, and that the flaw makes me disbelieve your words. You say you *must* do this. *Why* must you? And while I agree that, based on what the solicitors have said, it appears you *can* do this, you have free will, and, there-fore, you can choose *not* to do this." Oh dear, in spite of her best efforts, she was beginning to babble; she only hoped her words had made sense.

"There is no flaw in my argument," he replied. "I must do this. It is as much a matter of family honor for me as it is for you. And as you yourself just pointed out, I can."

"You could tear up the vowel, as I suggested before," she said. "Or burn it."

"I could," he agreed.

"But you won't."

"No."

"I am newly betrothed, Viscount Farleigh, to the Earl of Kerridge, heir to the Duke of Aylesham. The marriage settlements are nearly completed, and then the formal announcement will be made. For me to cry off at this point would seem to lack honor as well, would it not?"

"That is for you to decide," he said.

She leaned forward slightly in her chair. "It doesn't bother you that you are, in essence, stealing the bride of someone who will become one of the highest peers in England?"

"No."

She tried another approach. "Perhaps you would be better off finding a bride who hasn't given her heart to another."

That got a reaction from him. She saw a muscle in his cheek twitch ever so slightly. "Are you telling me that you have already given your heart to Lord Kerridge? So easily?" he asked. "How long have you known him?"

"Two weeks, nearly three." Her answer must surely sound foolish. After a two-weeks' acquaintance, had she given her heart to Lord Kerridge? Had she fallen in love in so short a time? Undoubtedly the man before her thought not. "Whom I choose to give my heart to is my concern, not yours, my lord, and shall remain that way."

His questions got her thinking though. She rose and walked over to the window again. Clouds were beginning to gather—gray cumulus clouds that meant it would soon rain—and for a moment, she was reminded of the teasing she'd taken from her brothers a mere week earlier.

She was attached to Lord Kerridge, certainly, and had enjoyed his kisses, and . . . well, she had assumed love—deep, abiding love—would grow over time, as it had with her parents. "Love doesn't necessarily follow a timetable. It can take years or merely a glance. Who is to say one way is better than another?"

He had followed her to the window, stopping mere inches away; she could sense him standing behind her and found his nearness disconcerting, but she refused to turn and look at him. This man, with his dark-brown eyes and his plain, neat clothes and his level voice and unsmiling mouth was impossible to understand.

"Two weeks—even nearly three—is not so very long," he said in that low, even tone of his. "Perhaps after two or three weeks, you will find yourself attached to me instead, more so than you are now to him."

"I doubt it," she whispered. For some reason, she could hardly catch her breath.

"You may be right, yet I sincerely hope not, for both our sakes." He laid his hand gently on her shoulder in a reassuring gesture that made her tremble nonetheless. "For you see, Lady Louisa, I refuse to withdraw my claim on the vowel. But I give you my word that I will do all in my power to make your life a happy one."

She turned to face him, incensed rather than reassured by his words. "How can you possibly promise me that when you are giving me no choice in the matter? I shall marry you, and you shall make me happy, you say. I do not know you at all, my lord. I know nothing of your character or your intentions, beyond forcing me to atone for my grandfather's selfish actions."

"Nobody is more aware than I that I can offer you nothing but my good intentions at present. We both seem to be in the unwelcome and uncomfortable position of making things right for the sake of our families' honor."

"Honor," she spat. "I am growing sick of the term. I do not understand the sort of honor you claim gives you the right to hold an innocent person accountable for something she did not do. It makes no sense to me, and I resent it."

Lord Farleigh said nothing in reply. He simply stood there in front of her, his hands at his sides. She remembered the feel of his hand on her shoulder just a few moments earlier. An attempt at support, she supposed—or perhaps a subtle move to win her over. She didn't know. She didn't trust him.

She wanted to grab him by the shoulders and shake him. "*Why* are you doing this?" she asked again. "You yourself just said this is as uncomfortable and unwelcome to you as it is to me. If that is true, then don't do it. You have the power to free us both."

He remained silent and unmoving, holding her eyes with his own. They gave nothing away, those eyes of his. No emotion whatsoever.

How could she marry a man like that?

Perhaps she *should* shake him, if only to see if there was a man of feeling buried somewhere beneath his wooden exterior.

"You are truly not going to change your mind in this matter, are you?" she said, an awful resignation settling about her like a cheerless gray fog.

"No."

She turned back to stare out the window, at the gathering clouds that matched her mood. It had been apparent to Louisa that Papa had been horribly distressed by his father's actions. There was no more honorable man than her father, and the vowel had created a moral dilemma for him that offered no reasonable solution.

How could she back away from duty and honor simply because the choice wasn't her preference? How could she, the noble daughter of the Marquess and Marchioness of Ashworth, look honor in the eye and then shrug it off as though it meant nothing when she knew of its importance to her family?

The answer was she couldn't. Her very being wanted to push the viscount aside and run away and pretend that nothing had happened this afternoon. But she couldn't. And with that reluctant acknowledgment, she knew what she must do.

She would be as honorable as Papa, heaven help her.

She sighed. "Very well. It would seem that honor requires I make good on the debt, my lord."

Lord Farleigh bowed in acknowledgment of what amounted to her acceptance of marriage to him. "Let us rejoin the others, then, and inform them that we are in accord and the marriage will proceed." He offered her his arm, and she laid her hand upon it, tacitly saying goodbye to her romantic dreams and expectations. There had been no suitor on bended knee asking for her hand this time, no kiss that hinted of romance and passion in her future, nothing but mutual agreement upon the resolution of a debt.

She had been invited to dine that evening with Lord Kerridge and his family. It wouldn't be happening now. She must speak with him this afternoon and end their betrothal.

Lord Farleigh had suggested Louisa might form an attachment to him. She wondered if it would ever be possible. Right now, all she felt was bitterness toward the man.

"I hate you," she whispered as he led her from the room.

* * *

"That went more smoothly than I expected," Heslop said, dabbing at his forehead with his handkerchief.

"Yes," William replied. They were on their way to Heslop's London office in William's newly inherited carriage, where they intended to review the details of the marriage settlement discussion they'd had with the Marquess of Ashworth and his solicitor after Lady Louisa's agreement to the betrothal.

"I rather thought we'd be escorted out by our ears as soon as we presented his lordship with the vowel," Heslop continued. "Instead, you now find yourself betrothed to one of the highest-born ladies of the *ton*, accompanied by one of the most generous dowries I've ever heard described in my entire career. I'm quite astounded, truth be told."

William said nothing. He, too, had been shocked at the amount of money Ashworth's solicitor had quoted. Only years of training had kept his jaw from hitting the floor, yet it was Louisa's final whispered words to him that still rang in his ears.

"I suspect you have the Duke of Aylesham to thank for that," Heslop said. "I rather doubt he'd have allowed the wife of his heir to appear in anything but the most recent fashions and the most expensive jewels, and would have been adamant that the lady's dowry reflect and support his lofty expectations."

"Louisa," William said, breaking his silence.

"Eh? Beg pardon?"

"Lady Louisa. You called her 'the lady.'"

"Ah, my apologies; I was speaking in theoretical terms. No insult intended."

If William had been shocked at the size of Lady Louisa's dowry, he'd been equally as shocked when the Marquess of Ashworth had simply stated the amount that had been agreed upon with the Duke of Aylesham and had done nothing to suggest lowering it. The marquess had had a variety of motives at his disposal he could have employed to do so—punishment to William for insisting the vowel be honored or an adjustment in the amount relative to William's status as a mere viscount, to name but two. Instead, the marquess had sat silently by, much as William had, and had allowed the discussion of "pursuants" and "wherefores" to be undertaken by the two solicitors, only speaking when he was called upon to clarify a point.

The meeting had not been a particularly warm one, however, in spite of Heslop's observation that it had proceeded smoothly. Even the fireplace in the marquess's library had seemed unwilling to offer more heat than was absolutely necessary to keep the room less than frigid. Or perhaps only William had felt cold.

"Ah, here we are," Heslop said as the carriage arrived at the building that housed his law offices.

"If you don't mind," William said, "I've changed my mind. I believe I'll return home rather than join you inside." He suddenly couldn't face nitpicking over the details like a hawk over its latest kill.

"I understand," Heslop said. "One can't help but be rather dumbfounded by it all. What a stroke of good fortune for a young gentleman such as yourself. Quite a coup. Naturally, you need time to ponder it all. I shall endeavor to draft a document we can present to the marquess and his man within the next day or two. In the meantime, I suggest you think about how to proceed with haste in courting the young lady—er, Lady Louisa. I know you to be a sober sort of fellow, not inclined toward haste, but circumstances call for precisely that."

"I shall call on you tomorrow," William said.

"*Haste*," Heslop repeated, giving William a stern look to underscore his point—as if William didn't understand the stakes already. "Very well, then. Adieu." The solicitor tipped his hat in farewell and went inside.

William gave directions to Walter the coachman to take him to the London house, which was part of the Farleigh holdings, where he'd taken up temporary residence. The carriage bumped along the cobblestones, and William sat back and listened to the clopping of the horses and usual noises of people going about their business. But try as he might, they didn't drown out the discord of his own thoughts.

He'd found himself intensely drawn to Lady Louisa this morning—a turn of events he hadn't expected. He should have anticipated it, but the forced nature of the betrothal had made it seem more of a necessary evil than an opportunity for courtship.

But today, a beautiful young woman had entered her father's study, full of a brightness and joy William hadn't felt in years. And she'd behaved in the most remarkable manner. She hadn't fainted or wept when the situation had been explained to her, even though it had been apparent to William that the news had greatly distressed her.

The range of emotions William had witnessed flitting across her lovely face haunted him. When she'd entered the room, she'd worn an expression lit with curiosity yet shaded by concern. He had then watched shock, disbelief, anger, fear, resignation, and, finally, resolve take their respective places as the reality of the wager her grandfather had made had sunk in. She had not clung to either parent. She had taken the time, rather, to absorb the news and the effect it would have on her—and then she had confronted William in a passionate yet dignified manner. She'd even told him she hated him in a dignified way.

He thought he could marry such a woman.

He *must*, if he was to have any reasonable hope of saving the people who meant the most to him.

He climbed the steps of the house, opened the door, and then shut it as quietly as he could. No need to alert the housekeeper, Mrs. Gideon, of his presence—not when he needed time to himself. But it seemed that luck was on his side once again this afternoon, William thought wryly when Mrs. Gideon didn't arrive to welcome him and share the latest Town gossip.

Luck was on his side. And wouldn't that delight his father, may the cursed man forever roll in his grave. William had thrown the dice, had played the ace, had held all the trumps. He had been the victor. His father had won the wager, but William had taken the prize.

He dropped into the leather chair in front of the fireplace, unwilling to stir the coals and ease the coldness he still felt.

He would claim his prize; oh yes, he would. It went without saying that he needed Lady Louisa's dowry and family influence for his people to survive. But Lady Louisa herself had set a long-frozen corner of William's heart burning with the promise of something he had no name for and that he could not bring himself to refuse. He'd thought himself condemned to live a joyless existence in a loveless marriage, as his parents had done before him. If he were a better man, a stronger man . . .

He wanted to marry Lady Louisa.

He buried his face in his hands.

* * *

"I'm not quite sure I understand what you are telling me," Lord Kerridge said to Louisa later that afternoon. "Let me see if I have got this straight—your grandfather lost a wager, and as a result, our betrothal is at an end before it could even be announced."

She had told her parents after her meeting with Lord Farleigh this morning that as she had been the one to accept Lord Kerridge's proposal, she would be the one to end it.

"But only think, my dear," her father had said. "I have been the person negotiating with him and the Duke of Aylesham and their respective solicitors. Allow me to be the one to inform him and the others and take this burden from you."

"No, Papa," she'd replied. "I gave the earl my consent. I will be the one to withdraw it."

And so she had sent a note to Lord Kerridge, asking him to call on her as soon as was possible, and now here she was in the same drawing room in which she herself had been given the unfortunate news of the vowel, having just told Lord Kerridge their betrothal was off. He looked austere and coldly furious and every inch the duke he would become someday. She studied his face, desperate to find a hint of the charming gentleman who had wooed her with flowers and stolen kisses, but that gentleman was not to be found.

"I agree that it's confusing," she said in an effort to placate him, shaken by his angry reaction. "I admit I, too, was terribly confused at first and didn't believe it and was even shocked when it was all explained to me. Grandpapa never spoke of it to anyone. Even Papa knew nothing of its existence. Had we known, I should never have accepted your proposal and gotten you and the duke and, oh, *everyone* tangled up in all this. You must believe me."

"I find myself struggling, nonetheless, to comprehend what you are telling me. You would have me accept the notion that your *grandfather* lost a *bet*—one that occurred nearly *thirty years* ago, mind you—in which he wagered *you*, whom he didn't even know would ever *exist*, and yet *now* you and your father both agree that it is *binding*?" The words he hurled at her hit their mark and stung.

"Yes," she said—simply, for once.

"And so you are marrying this *viscount*, who has *nothing* to offer you but crushing debt and little, if any, social standing, while I, who *can* and *have* offered you wealth and prestige *and more*, have now been *cast off*. *Jilted*, as it were."

"I am so terribly sorry." It wasn't as if she'd *wanted* any of this to happen, for heaven's sake.

He shook his head in disbelief. "But it's *ludicrous*, Lady Louisa! Completely illogical and utterly archaic—like something out of the Middle Ages or an old folktale or worse. I cannot fathom that either of you actually think you are obligated in any way to the terms of this . . . this . . . *ridiculous* vowel and these lawyers' nonsensical drivel. And what does it say of the viscount's character?" he added, rising to his feet and beginning to pace the room. There'd been a lot of pacing today. "I do not know the man, nor do I wish to. That he would hold you to this—why, it's *barbaric*. Rather than the normal, refined discussions between families to determine marital property agreements meant to reassure everyone involved, he arrives with his solicitor and makes demands."

"He didn't actually demand. It was more a statement of fact," Louisa carefully pointed out.

"That's beside the point!" Lord Kerridge exclaimed, slashing his hand through the air angrily. Louisa recoiled; she had never seen Lord Kerridge angry before. It was a revelation. "Not only that," he continued. "The timing of this is highly suspicious. If this vowel has existed for thirty years, why is it only now that this pathetic *viscount*, whoever he is, comes forward—*immediately* after you accepted my proposal, hmm?" He dropped back into his chair and drummed his fingers on his thigh as though pondering the merits of this last thought.

The timing *was* rather coincidental, but Louisa suspected it had more to do with her coming of age or the previous viscount's death than the earl's attention to her. It also seemed rather self-important of Lord Kerridge to think Lord Farleigh's proposal had been made to cause *him* particular injury, Louisa thought, feeling bruised by his callous assumption.

"Well," Lord Kerridge said, his countenance shifting from burning rage to a distant, icy hauteur. "He is a fortunate man, I must say. He has obtained one of the fairest and highest-ranking ladies of the *ton* with little effort on his part."

"Thank you for the compliment," Louisa said softly.

"Not to mention the most wealthy," he added.

Louisa dropped her gaze to her lap. His remark was ungentlemanly and wholly unexpected.

He rose to his feet once more, this time in a manner meant to indicate the conversation was at an end, so she rose as well. "I believe there is nothing more to say, then, other than to wish you well," he said, albeit his tone suggested just the opposite. He bowed formally. "I bid you adieu and will think fondly on what might have been. Good afternoon, Lady Louisa."

Louisa remained in the drawing room until she was sure he was no longer in the house. The whole of the day had left Louisa exhausted and numb—a blessing of sorts, she supposed, as it would give her the appearance of composure when she eventually left to go to her bedroom. How abruptly her life had changed. This morning she had been anticipating dining this evening with her betrothed and his family. Now she would be staying home, contemplating marriage to a total stranger—her *new* betrothed. How was one to react in such a situation?

But it was more than that, for during the past few hours, Louisa had also come to understand that one man had proposed to her because of her suitable social rank, while the other was only interested in the resources a connection to her would provide his estate.

Neither had wanted Louisa for herself.

She rose from the chair and walked to her bedroom with what she hoped was a serene expression on her face, where she collapsed on her bed, unable to hold back the hot flood of tears any longer.

Chapter 4

THE FOLLOWING MORNING, WILLIAM HAD met briefly with Heslop and then had made his way to Doctors' Commons in pursuit of a special license, which was now tucked safely in his breast pocket. The vowel had been in existence for thirty-odd years, but now that it had been brought to light and acknowledged and the special license obtained, William was anxious. He would rest more easily after the marriage had been performed and duly written into the parish register, he thought as he scraped soap and stubble from his chin for the second time today, paying special attention to an unruly spot under his jaw, careful not to nick himself.

He had washed and shaved this morning, but an invitation to dine at Ashworth House this evening had arrived during his absence from home, and as he intended to look his best when he presented himself at Ashworth House again, he was repeating the process.

This was one of the few times in his life he wished he had a valet. He hadn't bothered with one in university and hadn't seen the need since, which was probably just as well, considering just how empty the family coffers he'd inherited were. He'd done well enough over the years to make himself presentable, occasionally relying on the help of a maid or laundress wherever he'd been staying at any given time.

He attempted a slightly more elegant knot than usual in his neckcloth without success, then tossed it aside and tried again with a fresh one. He must do his best to look the impeccable gentleman when he arrived to dine with Lady Louisa and her parents. He wouldn't be surprised if her brothers would be there as well, scrutinizing him closely.

William didn't usually concern himself with others' perceptions of him, but tonight was crucial. Family honor aside, if William presented himself in any way that implied their daughter and sister was headed toward disaster by marrying him, the brothers would not hesitate to intervene, he was sure.

He located his stickpin and carefully inserted it into the folds of his neckcloth, praying it would keep the knot he'd achieved in some semblance of order throughout the evening, and evaluated his appearance in the mirror.

He'd managed well enough, he supposed.

He hoped he'd managed well enough.

He sighed. If he were to be honest with himself, he would admit that, first and foremost, what he wanted was to improve Lady Louisa's opinion of him.

Heslop's words ran incessantly through his mind: "The legal aspects of the wager are thin and would not be enforceable if challenged. You must win the lady over just to be sure."

William had his work cut out, especially since she had declared her hatred for him.

* * *

Louisa sat, her back ramrod straight, on the edge of the settee in the drawing room while she and her parents and her brothers awaited the arrival of Lord Farleigh to join them for dinner. They had all dressed much finer than they normally would when dining *en famille*. The addition of Lord Farleigh called for more formality.

Alex and Anthony had been apprised of the abrupt change in her betrothal. The discussion had included a great deal of disbelief and resistance on their part, including a few unseemly remarks Papa had put a stop to before they'd gotten out of hand. However, Louisa knew her brothers well enough to know they were not about to ignore the topic as they dined with Lord Farleigh this evening, regardless of Mama's added appeal to them for discretion. Her brothers were not the type to mince words.

Louisa was not looking forward to any of this, and long before she felt ready, Gibbs announced the arrival of their guest.

"Farleigh, I presume," Alex said, crossing the room to shake the viscount's hand. "I had a casual acquaintance with the previous Lord Farleigh. I believe I won several hundred quid off him once."

"You likely did," Lord Farleigh answered smoothly but not before Louisa's father shot Alex a quelling look. "My father rarely turned away from an opportunity to wager."

"Welcome, Lord Farleigh," Louisa's mother said, rising from her chair and offering her hand to him. "We are pleased you are joining us."

Louisa assumed her mother was only pleased that he was joining them for dinner—and *not* that he was going to be joining the family. And she might not have even meant the word *pleased* at all.

"Thank you, my lady," he replied with a bow.

"Wait a moment; I remember you," Anthony said, coming forward. "Will Barlow, from Eton. You're Farleigh now, eh? Alex, you remember Barlow. He was house captain when I was a first-year boy. Gave me a rather hard time too, every once in a while."

"Only when you deserved it," Lord Farleigh said. "Which wasn't frequent, by my recollection."

"Why, so it is," Alex said, recognition dawning on his face. "It's been years. Care for a drink, Farleigh?"

"No, but thank you for the offer."

Alex poured one for himself and downed it in one swallow, earning a reproving look—this time from Mama.

How they had managed to tell her brothers about the betrothal to Lord Farleigh without mentioning his *name*, Louisa didn't know. At least now he didn't seem a total stranger to her brothers.

"Condolences on the loss of your father," Anthony said. He had always been the more solicitous of Louisa's two brothers. Perhaps it was a trait he'd developed as spare to the heir.

"Thank you, Lord Anthony. These have been difficult times," Lord Farleigh said.

Alex snorted.

Lord Farleigh ignored him. He turned instead to Louisa and bowed over the hand she extended to him. "Lady Louisa, you are a vision of loveliness."

At some point during the introductions, she had risen to her feet, although she couldn't remember doing so, anxious as she'd been about how her brothers would behave.

"Much better than the other night when she had looked a portent of foul weather," Alex murmured.

Louisa watched Lord Farleigh's eyebrows come together in confusion, and Anthony and Alex shared a look that said they thought they'd been fairly prophetic in their comments about her dress.

"One would think we'd reared our sons to have no decorum at all, Ashworth," Mama said in a tone intended to be taken seriously.

"Thank you for the compliment, Lord Farleigh," Louisa added quickly, shooting a warning glance at Alex, unsure exactly how to move the conversation along to a topic that her brothers wouldn't take down an undesirable path.

Gibbs entered the room—none too soon, in Louisa's estimation. "Dinner is served," he announced.

Louisa let out a breath. Perhaps chewing food would keep her brothers' mouths too busy to speak. One could always hope.

Lord Farleigh offered her his arm. "May I have the honor?"

She laid her hand on his arm as lightly as she could, and they proceeded to the dining room. Her father took his normal place at the head of the table, but because they were eating informally, Louisa's mother sat to his right, with Alex next to her. Lord Farleigh sat to her father's left, and Louisa was next, with Anthony seated on her other side. At least if Alex offered veiled insults to their guest, she could kick him under the table.

"Ah, Eton," Alex said as he draped his lap with his napkin while the soup was being served. "Jolly times they were, eh, Farleigh?"

"Yes," Lord Farleigh answered in a noncommittal tone.

"Hmm." Alex drummed his fingers on the table, which earned another look of consternation from Mama. "I'm trying to recollect who your mates were at the time. I must confess I avoided the older boys as much as possible— it was safer for my physical well-being that way."

"I'm sure your mother and sister don't wish to hear about the antics young men get into while at school, Halford," Papa said.

"I doubt anything I say will be a surprise to either of them, but I take your point, Father."

As Louisa had observed or been included in plenty of boyhood antics during her lifetime, she had to agree with Alex on this one, but she said nothing and concentrated on her soup.

"Alex and I went to Cambridge when our Eton years concluded, but I don't recall seeing you there," Anthony said, changing the subject. "Excellent soup, by the way, Mama."

Anthony, Louisa's more subtle brother, was fishing for information from Lord Farleigh about how he'd spent the past few years, without coming right out and asking. Louisa hoped Lord Farleigh would take the bait. She wanted to learn as much as she could about him before she was married to him. It would be dreadful to learn he was of low character *after* they were married, when it was too late to do anything about it.

"Thank you, Anthony," Mama said. "I shall pass that along to Cook."

"I was at Oxford," Lord Farleigh said. "The soup is indeed excellent, Lady Ashworth."

Mama smiled politely.

"I'm an Oxford man, myself," Papa said. "Couldn't convince my sons to follow suit, however."

"Too close to home, Father," Alex said with a wink. "A young man needs to learn, ah . . . independence . . . in a way that is best accomplished by distance from his parents."

"Agreed," Anthony said with a smile before taking a spoonful of soup.

Lord Farleigh said nothing.

Throughout the remainder of supper, Louisa was more silent than was her usual tendency. She was too busy observing her parents observing Lord Farleigh, and she was too busy observing Lord Farleigh as well. Louisa's brothers continued to attempt to engage the viscount in conversation about their years at Eton and mutual friends and acquaintances from that time. Her parents allowed them to take the lead, only offering the occasional comment during the ebb and flow of conversation.

Lord Farleigh was similar to her brothers in many ways, Louisa noted. He was congenial enough and was intelligent and well-spoken, albeit his responses were brief and seemed intended to give the least amount of information possible. Was he simply a quiet man, or did he have something to hide?

As the dessert dishes were cleared away, Lord Farleigh set his napkin down. "Thank you for your hospitality, Lord Ashworth, Lady Ashworth. Would you mind if I invited Lady Louisa for a walk in your gardens? Lady Louisa, would you care for a stroll?"

Since they were dining informally, Louisa had fully expected she and Mama would retire to the sitting room, allowing her father and brothers the freedom to enjoy a glass of port and interrogate Lord Farleigh to their hearts' content, as they would no longer be in mixed company. She looked at him in surprise, unsure quite how to respond.

"I suppose we did monopolize the conversation at supper, did we not, Alex?" Anthony said before she could articulate a reply. "But, Farleigh, you must be warned. On most occasions, Louisa is more verbal than we two brothers combined. Once our baby sister begins talking, there are few ways to get her to stop."

"Should that happen, you might be inclined to change your mind about the wager," Alex added. "She's been uncommonly quiet so far this evening. She might explode."

"Alexander, really," Louisa's mother said.

"Halford," Lord Ashworth warned.

"If he's going to be family, he deserves to know," Alex said, then took a sip from his goblet.

"I won't be changing my mind," Lord Farleigh said.

Louisa stood abruptly and tossed her napkin on the table. "A stroll would be just the thing," she said. "Thank you, Lord Farleigh. Please excuse us, Mama, Papa."

She left the room with her head high, ignoring her brothers and not caring if Lord Farleigh—or anyone else, for that matter—followed her. And she intended to give Alex and Anthony plenty of words later. She was supposed to marry this stranger, and they were making jokes at her expense.

She made her way to the drawing room, with its french doors that led directly to the terrace and the formal garden below. Lord Farleigh caught up with her by the time she reached the doors. "Allow me," he said and opened them for her.

Once outside, she walked along the terrace, stopping near the end and setting her hands on the balustrade. The moon was half hidden by the clouds and cast the garden in partial shadow. Lord Farleigh had followed her and now stood at her side.

She waited for him to speak, but he said nothing. He stood there *quietly*, as he *always* seemed to do. It was impossible to ignore him, however, though she tried for several frustrating minutes.

Finally, infuriated, she turned to face him. "Are you happy, Lord Farleigh?" she asked him.

"What do you mean?" he asked.

"It should be obvious what I mean," she said. "Are you *happy*—are you experiencing that joyful state of being in which one is full of contentment and blissful satisfaction? Happy."

The moon bathed his features in milky-white light. He looked serious—definitely not happy, which was fine with her, for *she* most certainly was not.

"I am happy to be here on the terrace with you, Lady Louisa."

"That is no answer," she replied. "Or, more to the point, I don't believe you. You don't smile. You give the briefest of replies to every question or statement put to you." She took a step closer to him and looked him straight in the eyes. "I will come to your assistance, by describing my own state of being. I am *not* happy. Since you showed up unannounced on our doorstep, I have done nothing but reflect upon the horrible truth that I have been summarily passed from one man to another during the course of a single day, the sacrificial lamb for someone else's misdeeds, because of *honor*.

"Where was honor when my grandfather made a wager that impacted someone else's life in such a way? *My* life." She blinked back hot tears she had thought she'd entirely shed already. "What of *me*? What of *my* hopes and dreams? What of love?" She turned away from him when her foolish tears began to fall in earnest. She brushed at them furiously with her hand.

Her infernal brothers were right though; now that she'd begun speaking, it seemed she couldn't stop. "I always aspired to a marriage of love, like that of my parents. Children need to be born into a loving family, with a mother and father who love each other and cherish them and don't send them off with the nurse or the governess—or off to school, poor dears, simply because they are an inconvenience. Children!" She gasped, throwing her hand over her mouth. "Oh, dear heavens, does that mean you expect that I . . . that we . . . ?"

It was his turn to look her directly in the eyes, wet and puffy though they assuredly were. "I had hoped to have a marriage in fact, my lady, and not one in name only, yes," he said evenly.

Well! He'd spoken one of his rare complete sentences—one that had succeeded in leaving her speechless for once, and, naturally, it would be on *that* subject. Men undoubtedly held strong opinions when it came to *that*. And yet his words and the intensity of his gaze had also left her feeling breathless and tingly, even though it was at odds with her general mood at present. She sniffed.

He retrieved his handkerchief from his pocket and handed it to her. "My intention has always been to be faithful to my wife," he said.

"How comforting," she said, adding a touch of sarcasm to her words.

"I'd say so, yes," he replied, leaning his hip against the balustrade. At least he was being polite enough not to stare at her while she dabbed at her eyes and blew her nose. Blowing one's nose was such an indelicate, embarrassing thing to do. "Many gentlemen aren't, you know. Faithful, that is."

"My father is not like 'many gentlemen,' then. He would never do that to my mother. He adores her, and she adores him."

"If that is true, you are exceedingly fortunate," he said.

"It *is* true."

"As you say."

He was silent then, and so was she. She dabbed at her eyes again. As a young girl, whenever she'd cried, Anthony had teased her that she was such a talented watering pot she should work with the gardener. Alex would counter that Anthony's suggestion was an impossibility, as her resulting splotchy face looked so much like Medusa, she would turn the gardener to stone. Then they would laugh uproariously while she dashed off to the nearest mirror to see if what they had said was true. It hadn't dawned on her until she was older that if what Alex had said was indeed true, her brothers would have turned to stone long since.

She'd also learned, however, that while she didn't look as bad as Medusa, it wasn't her most flattering look by any stretch either.

How utterly mortifying to be in this situation with a virtual stranger. *This* stranger.

"Lady Louisa," he said gently, "I promised you a stroll in the garden, and yet here we are, still on the terrace, when we could be enjoying the moonlight and the fragrance of the flowers." He offered her his arm. "May we?"

She felt so helpless, so vulnerable. But what was she to do? She'd already given her word regarding marriage to him. "Very well," she said.

* * *

They descended the stairs into the garden, Lady Louisa's hand tucked tentatively in the crook of William's arm, and walked along the path that led to a lush bed of roses. And all the while, William felt an aching constriction at the back of his throat. Her words had struck at him like knives.

"What of me? What of my hopes and dreams? What of love?" she had cried.

He recalled his mother's words—words flung at his father. William had been but a young lad at the time, standing outside the door of her room, eager to show her his latest drawing. *"What of me? And what of your son? Have you no love for us?"* Even at William's tender age, he'd recognized the desperation in her voice.

He pushed the thought away. "Your brothers are devoted to you," he said to Lady Louisa. He had to say something to break the silence.

"There have been plenty of times over the years when I would have called them pestilential rather than devoted," she replied in a slightly nasally voice as a result of her tears. "Including today."

William knew what a truly pestilential person was like, and her brothers didn't qualify. "They love you."

She heaved a sighed. "I know they do, and I feel the same about them. If anything were to happen to either of them—well, it doesn't bear thinking about. I worry about them, you see. I spent my childhood chasing after them; I know the kinds of mischief they got into back then. It actually served me well a time or two, as I was able to blackmail them into including me in some of their less dangerous escapades." She sniffled and wiped her nose again.

William had the sudden urge to kiss that nose, swollen and red though it was at present—for, truly, her nature was so opposite his own that he found her captivating. His eyes dropped from her nose to her lips . . .

"I don't know why I'm telling you all this," she muttered. "I suppose it's because they're right."

He pulled his attention back to the train of the conversation. "About?" he asked.

"About how once I begin to speak, I can't seem to stop."

"I haven't found that to be the case. Your brothers were only teasing." William didn't think he'd ever met anyone so ingenuous, so guileless and open as Lady Louisa Hargreaves. Did she know that every nuance of her emotions was apparent in her expressions and in her words? He doubted it.

He snapped a bloom from a rosebush with his free hand, briefly held it to his nose to breathe in its scent, and then handed it to her. "For you."

"Thank you," she said. "But don't try to make me like you, as I still feel inclined not to at present. Oh, but it does smell lovely, does it not?"

"Indeed."

They walked along in silence again. William thought carefully about what to say next. He wanted to discuss their wedding plans further, but he didn't want to broach the subject until he was certain she was of a frame of mind to do so. Considering how upset she'd been on the terrace, now was not the time—at least, not yet.

"I remember you from a visit you and your parents made to Eton," he said finally.

"Do you?" she said, looking up at him in surprise.

The moon broke through the clouds then and illuminated her face—and her eyes, still slightly swollen from her earlier tears, glowed with curiosity. If he were a true artist and not a plodding amateur, he'd paint her just as she looked right now, he thought to himself, drinking in the sight of her. She was Diana, goddess of the moon—pure and youthful and, oh, so lovely. Unattainable. His studies of Roman and Greek mythology, along with the classics, while at university were infinitely more gratifying to him at this particular moment than they had been before. And then the clouds shielded the moon once again.

"You were wearing a blue dress," he replied in answer to her query. "I remember because it matched your eyes quite remarkably. Of course, you were only a little girl and, therefore, of no interest to a houseful of sophisticated young gentlemen, including myself."

"I was always envious of Alex and Anthony," she said in a thoughtful tone. "Going off to Eton seemed such an adventure. I felt sorry for myself, stuck at home with my governess, Miss Leggett. She was wonderful company—we had a grand time together and became fast friends. We still correspond, and I miss her dreadfully. But Eton seemed vast and exciting and scholarly and . . . oh, I don't know. Mysterious."

"Let me assure you, there is nothing mysterious about a school full of boys."

She actually laughed for the briefest moment, a soft, musical sound that plucked at William's heartstrings. "With two brothers to my name, I must agree." She looked off into the distance, although there wasn't much to see in the nighttime darkness. "But I was referring to the exclusivity of the school, the subjects boys—not girls—were allowed to study."

"Most boys would have used the term *required* rather than *allowed*," he said.

"I wouldn't. My father let me join Alex and Anthony with their tutor for part of each day until they went off to Eton. Quite forward thinking of him. I was better at Latin and Greek than either of my brothers—at least, I was before they left. They've surpassed me by quite a bit now, sadly; however, my French is much better than theirs."

"Had you been allowed to attend Eton, then, you would have continued with your Greek and Latin studies?" he asked, surprised and pleased to find her so interested in academics—something he enjoyed as well.

"Perhaps. Or perhaps I would have studied mathematics—I'm fairly good with numbers too—or astronomy or architecture or philosophy or, oh,

I don't know. There are so *many* things one can be curious about, you know? Perhaps I would not like any of the subjects once I began, but I would know that for a fact afterward, would I not? At any rate, I have certainly learned it to be true when it comes to ladies' arts."

"I take it you are not a fan of needlework," he said, amused by her admission.

She snorted indelicately, then had to dab at her nose again, and William had to stifle the urge to laugh. Such a *faux pas* seemed out of character for her—and yet also completely in character. What a delightful creature she was.

"I can do needlework competently enough, and I'm not terrible on the pianoforte—although I'm not a great performer," she said, responding to his comment. "I can dance, stand, sit, and walk with deportment and even a touch of elegance. I made my curtsy to Her Majesty without tripping on my train."

"Well done."

"I thought so too. That entire day was a horrible ordeal and also a truly fascinating study in politics and protocol—and the queen spoke to me, which is quite a coup, you know."

"I do not doubt it," he said.

They had reached the end of the rose garden, where an arched trellis covered in climbing roses stood. Underneath it was a bench.

"Would you care to sit?" he asked her.

"I've been rattling on again, haven't I?" She removed her hand from the crook of his arm—William missed her touch the moment it was gone—and sat.

He sat next to her, as closely as he thought she would allow. She was like an open book, and he'd learned a great deal about her in the past few minutes—more than he'd expected to know in such a short amount of time. He actually liked everything he'd learned—even her tendency to "rattle on," as she'd put it. He hadn't planned on any of this when he'd first learned of the vowel.

"Lady Louisa," he said, "I brought you outside where we could have some privacy for a few minutes, but I fully expect one of your brothers to come looking for us shortly. Therefore, if you'll forgive me, I'll come right to the point."

He instantly felt her withdraw into herself.

It was a strange, empty feeling—to have been surrounded by her words and her open expressions and then to have them all suddenly closed off from him. It was like being a starving man who'd tasted a banquet and then had it snatched away before he could be filled. He cleared his throat and began again. "With your permission, I would like for us to discuss the matter of a wedding date. I have procured a special license—"

"No!" she cried, startling him into silence. "No special license. Please! Only yesterday I was expecting to marry someone else. I need time to think and adjust to everything that has happened. Just because I am trying to be polite and agreeable this evening doesn't mean I am anywhere near ready to marry you. It is too much! Can we not have banns read instead? That would give both of us time . . . to get to know each other, at the very least. The marriage would not appear hurried and give rise to gossip. Wouldn't that be a good thing? You have not even been in Town for people to get acquainted with you or to see us together before our marriage is announced. There will be talk. Three weeks is all I ask. You cannot deny me that. Please, I beg you."

Her words stung his conscience. He wondered again about her attachment to Lord Kerridge. She would have been seen on Kerridge's arm the past couple weeks, and people would have understood that they had been courting. Kerridge may have even told a few acquaintances that a betrothal was in the works. There was logic in her request, he knew it, and yet he didn't want to give her the three weeks needed for banns to be read. It was too much time, and too many things could go wrong during those three weeks.

But how could he not allow it when he'd taken so much from her? "Very well. You have your three weeks," he said reluctantly.

She squeezed her eyes shut and clasped her hands together. She was so young—unspoiled by the harshness of the world, a beloved daughter and sister, doted on and protected. He longed to put his arms around her and comfort her, assure her that he would do all in his power to keep her from regretting her decision to marry him, but he couldn't. How could the person who was causing her such pain now be her source of comfort? He remained unmoving at her side.

"Thank you," she whispered. She rose to her feet and briefly laid her hand on his shoulder before rushing back to the house, leaving him alone in the garden.

Chapter 5

FOUR DAYS HAD PASSED SINCE Louisa's entire life had turned upside down.

Lord Farleigh had not called upon her yesterday, which showed a great deal of prudence on his part, as Louisa had needed time to herself to adjust to her new future. Instead, he had sent her a gift—not flowers, thank heavens, as she was still receiving bouquets from hopeful gentlemen, including Baron Moseby. Those gentlemen's ambitions would be dashed soon enough.

No, Lord Farleigh had sent her a small oil painting of an oak tree, of all things.

He was escorting her to Lady Melton's assembly this evening, their first public appearance together, and Lord and Lady Melton had given permission to use the occasion of their assembly to announce the betrothal. The first of the banns was to be read in church on Sunday, two days hence. Marriage to Viscount Farleigh was becoming all too real.

Louisa's parents had already left for Lady Melton's, and Anthony and Alex had gone out with friends and would be joining them later in the evening.

Mama had stopped by Louisa's room before leaving. "You're sure you don't want us to wait for Lord Farleigh to arrive?" she'd asked.

"No, Mama, I'll be fine," she'd assured her. "If he'd wanted to kidnap me and drag me off to Gretna Green, he could have done it already rather than face you and Papa with the vowel."

"That is not particularly funny, Louisa," Mama had responded. "But I take your point. Very well, we shall see you there, then."

Louisa spent extra time dressing and seeing to her appearance, as it was critical to look her best. She'd chosen a gown of purple velvet with a high waist and short puffed sleeves.

There was bound to be gossip; she had been seen with Lord Kerridge often enough for marriage speculation to have arisen. Therefore, by arriving tonight at Lady Melton's assembly on the arm of Lord Farleigh, Louisa must present herself as a mature woman who knew her mind and had made her choice.

She fastened her pearls around her neck, which she'd deliberately chosen because they were not ostentatious, then pulled on her evening gloves and took up her reticule and lace shawl. She was dreading the evening ahead, but it had to be faced.

The knock at her bedroom door that heralded Lord Farleigh's arrival came at last.

He was waiting for her as she descended the stairway to the entry hall. "Lady Louisa," he said. "You look radiant."

He looked surprisingly elegant—and as unfathomable as usual. He wore black formal attire and had chosen a waistcoat of beige silk embroidered with gold thread, which complemented the black and the snowy white of his linens. His neckcloth was in a fashionable knot that wasn't overly fussy and was held in place by a simple gold stickpin. The gold in his attire managed to bring out similarly colored strands in his brown hair, while the black of his coat made his dark-brown eyes seem even darker. Right now, they were directed at her, and she realized she had not replied to his compliment. "Thank you," she said rather more breathlessly than she'd intended. How mortifying that he had this effect on her.

Lord Farleigh handed Louisa into the carriage and then climbed in and sat next to her rather than across from her. She should have anticipated it, all things considered, but she hadn't, and his proximity to her set her insides fluttering.

"Are you ready for this evening?" he asked once the carriage was on its way. "It will be public knowledge after that."

"What are we to tell people about our nonexistent courtship?" Louisa asked him. "There are bound to be questions along with the obligatory congratulations, and I refuse to tell people you won me in a wager."

"What do you suggest?"

"It might help if I knew a little more about you than your name and title, for starters," she replied, unable to hide the edge in her voice.

"Very well. I am an only child. My mother died when I was sixteen. I attended Eton, as you know, and Oxford and the University of Edinburgh thereafter, where, unlike many of my peers, I happened to prefer studying to drinking, wenching, and wagering."

"That's good to know. It's also the longest string of words you have ever shared with me."

"Hardly."

"Oh, yes," Louisa said. "I'm certain of it. I am so conscious of my own tendency to chatter that I'm highly attuned to others' speech as well." Despite her best intentions, she'd been affected by his words, especially his reference to his mother. She impulsively set her hand on his, causing his gaze to fix there. "I am sorry about the loss of your parents, you know. I would be heartbroken to lose either of my parents."

A muscle in his cheek twitched before he spoke. "My mother has been at peace for many years now, and as for my father, I do not particularly grieve his passing—a sentiment that must horrify someone like yourself." He raised her hand and kissed it before letting it go. "But let's not dwell upon death tonight. What are we to tell others when they ask about our betrothal, then?"

"I hate to lie," Louisa said. "But I cannot tell the precise truth either."

"I shall say it was love at first sight and I did everything in my power to convince you to marry me. And that in the end, you were unable to resist my offer of marriage."

"Hm. Except for the first part, it's all true enough, I suppose."

He said nothing to correct her. It was gallant of him to say he'd fallen in love with her as part of their plan for this evening, but it left her feeling deflated too, knowing it wasn't true.

"I can tell everyone about the gift you gave me," she said. "It's a very lovely painting of a tree."

"Not just any tree," he said.

She smiled. "I thought not. More precisely, I *hoped* not."

"It's my favorite oak at Farleigh Manor," he said. "It stands alone near a pond at the edge of the property, with a small wood not far from it. I spent many hours in that tree as a lad."

"You're a tree climber? I scrambled up more trees than I dare remember now, especially with Anthony—Alexander was there with us too when he was home from Eton."

The corner of his mouth twitched in that way of his that was nearly a smile but not quite. "Just to clarify: I *was* a tree climber," he said. "I can't claim to have climbed any trees recently."

His words sent a small ray of light into Louisa's heart—knowing he had climbed trees gave the two of them their first real connection—which was undoubtedly foolish since most young boys climbed trees, after all. "*Was* and *is* are only a matter of attitude," she said.

"I expect it shall remain a *was*, however," he replied.

"One can never know for certain." The painting meant more to her, though, now that she knew the history and sentiment behind it.

"We are nearly there," he said, glancing out the carriage window. "And there is one more thing we must settle before we arrive." Without any further warning, he leaned forward and pressed his mouth to hers, placing his hand on her cheek while he did, and catching her completely unawares.

It was not like the polite, gentle kisses she'd shared with the Earl of Kerridge. Not at all.

This kiss flared with a heat Louisa hadn't experienced before. Her senses collided—the leather of his glove on her cheek, his lips pressed to hers, the scent of his shaving soap, the steady swaying of the carriage all coalesced into a sweet yearning she didn't understand.

Long before she was ready, he ended the kiss and brushed his thumb across her chin. "Now you look like a woman who is newly betrothed."

She pushed his hand away, feeling crushed and embarrassed. "Are you saying this was part of some strategy? How dare—"

His lips returned to hers, more insistent this time, his hand at the back of her head, taking his fill and yet giving too. And her senses responded once again, betraying her when she should be angry and indignant instead.

"No strategy," he murmured a hair's breadth from her lips.

"I don't believe you," she said. For why else would he have said such a thing to her after such a kiss? She closed her eyes, struggling to regain her composure and her dignity.

"It's true, nonetheless." His hand dropped to his lap.

They sat silently side by side during the all-too-brief carriage ride that remained before arriving at Lord and Lady Melton's residence. Through the window, Louisa could see footmen in pristine livery assisting other guests from their carriages; nevertheless, when they themselves made it through the queue of arriving carriages, Lord Farleigh quickly descended and handed Louisa down himself, placing her hand securely in the crook of his arm.

"Courage, my lady," he whispered to her as they entered the front doors to join other guests waiting to be received by Lord and Lady Melton.

Courage, indeed, she thought shakily.

* * *

William led Lady Louisa through the main doors, all the while wishing he could be anywhere else. His gut churned. He could almost smell the stench that clung to him from his father's misdeeds and unsavory reputation. Beyond the Meltons' gracious willingness to allow Lord Ashworth to announce the betrothal, William was uncertain what sort of welcome he would receive. He'd taken Lady Louisa's hand and placed it in the crook of his arm, as it had seemed the gentlemanly and most confident approach to take. In reality, it undoubtedly gave him more support than it did her.

Lord and Lady Melton's residence was an impressive dwelling, which only heightened William's anxiety. The front doors opened to a spacious entry hall whose high ceiling echoed with the sounds of newly arrived guests greeting one another as they removed their wraps and handed them over to the footmen on duty. To the left of the entry hall, beyond a pair of open double doors, was an equally spacious sitting room, where William could see Lord and Lady Melton receiving their guests.

William expected to know very few of the people at the assembly this evening. There might be one or two classmates from Eton in attendance and some acquaintances from his Oxford days, but William had made few close friends during those years. He was not gregarious by nature, like Lord Halford, or even as amiable as Lord Anthony, the more reserved of Lady Louisa's brothers. He'd simply gone about his schooling, happy to have something that occupied his mind and kept his days filled. And he'd continued that rather aloof behavior upon completing his studies at Oxford by heading north to Scotland and attending the University of Edinburgh, which was where Heslop had finally caught up with him and sent him word of his father's death. He doubted any old acquaintances he'd had would even remember him.

It might have been his imagination, but it seemed to him that the echoing sounds in the entry hall increased in volume as the other guests began to notice that Lady Louisa Hargreaves was with a gentleman who was not Lord Kerridge. William was relieved to see that she was smiling, at least, even if there were signs of strain around her eyes. He doubted anyone else would notice, but William had an awareness of such subtleties of expression that his father had drilled into him. He pressed forward, his eyes firmly set on the door to the sitting room, hoping to get his introduction to his host and hostess out of the way. Meeting them would give him his first real clue about how the evening would play out.

Eventually, it was their turn. Lord Melton was a slightly built but distinguished-looking gentleman with hair the color of granite and a face creased with wrinkles that William suspected he'd gotten from smiling too much. Lady Melton was slightly taller than her husband and had similar wrinkles. They looked like a matched set.

"Lady Louisa, welcome," Lord Melton said in a cheery voice. "Look who has finally arrived, Lady Melton."

Lady Louisa slid her hand from the crook of William's elbow and extended it to Lord Melton, who bowed over it. "Thank you, Lord Melton."

William wanted to snatch her hand back.

"We are so honored to play a small part in this happiest of occasions," Lady Melton said, taking both of Louisa's hands in her own and sounding for all the world as though she meant what she said. "And you must introduce us to your young gentleman here."

"Lord Melton, Lady Melton, this is William Barlow, Viscount Farleigh," Lady Louisa said, her smile still firmly in place.

"How do you do, Lord Farleigh?" Lord Melton said, offering William a less-than-enthusiastic nod of his head. Lord Melton must have been acquainted with his father, then, William surmised. "Your parents are here already, my dear, but, assuredly, you must know that," Lord Melton added. "I believe they expressed an interest in viewing some of my recent art acquisitions in the gallery."

"Lord Farleigh," Lady Melton said, tapping her chin in thought. "I remember a young lady who made her come-out with me—I believe she married a Lord Farleigh. Sweet girl, as I recall. I didn't know her well and never saw her again after her wedding. Her name was Margaret Strickland, if I'm recalling it correctly. She was an heiress; her father had made his money in coal, I believe. Any relation of yours?"

"She was my mother. She passed away several years ago," William said. He detested speaking about her with virtual strangers. He bit the inside of his cheek to keep the flood of emotions he felt at hearing his mother's name from pouring out.

Lady Louisa was watching him too closely.

"I'm so sorry to hear that," Lady Melton said kindly.

"Thank you," William replied, ready to be done with the conversation.

Fortunately, there were more guests for Lord and Lady Melton to receive, so he and Lady Louisa excused themselves and moved through the crowd into an adjoining room, where refreshments were being served. They continued on through that room, however, and finally spotted the marquess and marchioness in the music room down the hall, where a nondescript young lady was attempting—rather badly, it seemed to William—to play the pianoforte. He and Lady Louisa stood quietly inside the door and waited for the piece to end before moving farther into the room.

William used the time to study the marquess and marchioness more closely.

Lord Ashworth was a tall man, like his sons, with dark hair that had gone silver at the temples. This evening, along with his typical aristocratic bearing, there was an air of grim resoluteness about him as he sat and listened. Lady Ashworth was fanning herself, and her lovely face—so much like her daughter's—had a drawn look about it. They weren't looking forward to the announcement to come, but then, no one was; they all merely wished the deed done.

The young lady eventually finished her performance and stood to receive the weak but polite smattering of applause that followed.

"Poor Harriet does try," Lady Louisa whispered to William as they clapped. "I will credit her that. I think her mother puts her up to it."

Now that the performance had ended, they made their way across the room to where Lady Louisa's parents were sitting. Luckily, and not surprisingly, considering what they'd just listened to, there were vacant chairs nearby. "We were on our way to view Lord Melton's latest additions to his art collection when Lady Putnam invited us to hear Miss Putnam perform," Lady Ashworth said, glancing beyond William's shoulder. "How could we possibly refuse such a kind offer?"

William turned his head and quickly concluded that Lady Putnam must be the woman who looked rather like a man-o'-war under full sail and who was heading in their direction with Miss Harriet Putnam in tow.

"Lady Ashworth, Lord Ashworth, so thoughtful of you to deign to listen to our dear Harriet," Lady Putnam gushed. "She has worked diligently at perfecting her finesse at the keyboard. I am quite delighted at her progress. And here is our dear Lady Louisa too . . . with a young gentleman, no less." She smiled at William, who presumed the man-o'-war was wrangling for an introduction, if her hungry look—*and* her daughter's—meant anything.

"I must say, your performance of the Haydn was very energetic, Miss Putnam," Lady Ashworth said tactfully. Lord Ashworth stood by, looking aloof, and said nothing.

"Thank you, my lady," Miss Putnam said to Lady Ashworth, albeit her eyes never left William, which, honestly, was beginning to make his skin crawl. "It is kind of you to say so."

"And are your two sons intending to join us here this evening?" Lady Putnam asked. "Such elegant young gentlemen, they are."

Lord Ashworth rolled his eyes skyward.

"Thank you, Lady Putnam. Yes, they should be here shortly," Lady Ashworth said.

With Lady Ashworth's assurances that her sons were planning to attend, the feral glint that had been directed at William turned immediately to focus instead on the marchioness and her words, thank goodness. He needed no complications tonight other than to get the betrothal formally announced.

There was much he had been spared by haring off to Scotland: marriage-mad mamas and their daughters, for one, besides having to watch his father's dissipation and ultimate ruin.

"Lord Farleigh, allow me to present Lady Putnam and Miss Putnam," Lady Louisa said, pulling William back from his gloomy thoughts. "Lady Putnam, Harriet, this is Viscount Farleigh."

"How do you do?" Harriet said with a deep curtsy and a flirtatious smile. "So *very* nice to meet you."

"Viscount *Farleigh*," Lady Putnam said, her eyes narrowing. "Hmm."

"A pleasure, Lady Putnam, Miss Putnam." *Ah, yes*, William thought. He'd also forgotten that he'd been spared the gossips that abounded in Town and was certain he had just met one of the most accomplished, if Lady Putnam's eyes were anything to go by. No doubt his name and title would make their way through the rooms of Melton House like wildfire.

William would not have Louisa suffer the ill effects of his father's foul reputation. Notwithstanding the cordial welcome he'd received from Lord and Lady Melton, he could not guarantee the reactions of any other guests, especially with the likes of Lady Putnam and her loose tongue in attendance. It was time to prepare for the battle that loomed ahead.

He had a great deal of work to do.

* * *

"If you would excuse us," Lady Putnam said to Louisa and her parents. "Harriet, come with me quickly. I believe the Earl of Cantwell and his brother have arrived—such charming young men. And you are looking so fetching in your yellow gown this evening. Too bad they didn't arrive earlier so they could hear you at the pianoforte." She grabbed her daughter by the hand and forged her way through the crowd.

"Formidable woman," Lord Farleigh murmured.

Louisa bit her lip.

"Very," Mama agreed. "I almost wish I had encouraged Anthony to stay at Cambridge rather than join us here for the Season. It would have kept him safe from her scheming."

"What about Alex, Mama?" Louisa said. "Are you not equally concerned about his marital well-being?"

"Lady Putnam is formidable, I'll grant you," Papa said, "but she is no match for Halford. Miss Putnam and her younger sisters will have to look elsewhere for husbands. Now then, shall we make our way to the gallery and view Lord Melton's art before it is time to make the announcement?"

Speaking of looking for husbands, Louisa belatedly remembered that she and Lord Kerridge had originally planned to attend the assembly together. She frantically glanced about her, hoping he'd had the sense and decency to stay home this evening.

The gallery was a long, narrow room that ran parallel to the public rooms the Meltons used for entertaining. Louisa wandered from painting to sculpture to painting with Lord Farleigh at her side, his hands clasped behind his back. Lord Melton was an avid collector of English works of art, she discovered, but he also had an interest in antiquities, which accounted for the occasional Greek statue or broken bit of Egyptian pottery that sat in pride of place amongst the landscape paintings and portraits. Normally, Louisa would have found such artifacts interesting, but she was having great difficulty concentrating on anything but the man next to her—the quiet man who spoke very little and still wore a mask of inscrutability on his face.

"Which is your favorite, Lord Farleigh?" she asked, unable to bear his silence any further.

"Favorite?" he asked.

His one word reply only served to increase her prickling sense of anxiety and irritation. "You know—your favorite piece of art from Lord Melton's collection. We've just spent the last half hour gazing at art and antiquities, Lord Farleigh, so it ought to be obvious what I'm asking about. If I were looking at a roomful of art, which I am, I would certainly have formed an opinion about them and would undoubtedly have chosen a favorite or two." Oh, dear. Her agitation had loosened her tongue once again. Additionally, she sounded shrewish, which was not an attractive look—*not* that her intent was to appear attractive to him; they may be planning to wed in the near future, but she wasn't about to encourage the man whose presence had altered her life forever.

"Very well." Lord Farleigh's gaze turned toward a particular landscape of a stream bordered by a copse of trees, with a small stone cottage nestled beneath it. "That one," he said, gesturing discreetly.

"Why?" she asked.

"I suppose it reminds me of Scotland," he said. He lowered his head. "Perhaps it might be a good time for you to begin calling me William. May I call you Louisa?" he murmured in her ear.

Hearing her name on his lips, spoken in such quiet tones, was startlingly intimate. Her thoughts immediately flew back to their last few moments in the carriage when he had kissed her. *Now you look like a woman who is newly betrothed.*

She drew in a breath and let it out. "Certainly . . . William." It rolled off her tongue smoothly, like rich custard.

"It is time," Papa said behind her, interrupting them and, thankfully, breaking the spell Louisa had found herself in. Mama and Lord Melton were with him.

"Louisa?" William said, looking intently at her. "Are you ready?" His face was still frustratingly impassive, but his eyes searched hers with an intensity that hadn't been there before.

She nodded her consent.

* * *

They all returned to the room where Lord and Lady Melton had received their guests. The assembly was a crush, the Melton's spacious London home full to overflowing with the cream of Society, and if not for Lord Melton, who led the way, parting the crowd like Moses had the Red Sea, they should have had great difficulty making their way through the house.

Both of Louisa's brothers were there when they arrived, looking more like they'd prefer to escort William into the mews behind the house and thrash him soundly than stand here and listen to the announcement yet to come.

"You don't have to do this," Louisa's eldest brother, Lord Halford, whispered to her just loudly enough for William to overhear. "You do not owe your entire future to our grandfather's folly."

"How can you say this to me now?" Louisa whispered back to him, her eyes wide with a hurt William didn't wish to see or acknowledge.

"Because it is never too late until you say the vows," he said.

Louisa didn't immediately respond; William tensed and held his breath.

"What if your name were the one on the vowel?" she asked Halford.

"It's not the same thing, and you know it; I am a gentleman, and Tony is a gentleman," he answered her. "You, on the other hand, are not."

William began breathing again. Halford had miscalculated; he'd said the absolute worst thing possible if he were to convince Louisa not to marry him. William knew Louisa well enough by now to know that she felt the family honor as keenly as her brothers did.

"Oh, Alex, you don't understand anything at all," she said, shaking her head—and proving William correct.

"We're with you, whatever you choose to do," Lord Anthony said, squeezing her hand. "You know that, Weezy. But Alex is right—do think about it, right now, before it becomes public knowledge."

"Thank you, Anthony," she said. "But I *have* thought about it. You cannot know how much I have thought about it. If *you* were challenged to a duel, would you go, Alex? Even if you knew it meant losing your life? If you were facing battle against Napoleon, Anthony, would you desert? I know you both, and I know you would rather face death than act dishonorably. I am no different from you. I am my father's daughter." She straightened her back and nodded to Lord Melton, who was waiting for a cue to begin.

It rankled William a bit at being compared—*once again*—to imminent death. Apparently, kissing Louisa in the carriage hadn't *quite* won the lady's affection, he thought sardonically.

The guests gradually quieted when word spread through the crowd that Lord Melton wished to speak.

"Dear friends," he began, "Lady Melton and I are thrilled to welcome you to our home this evening and hope you are enjoying yourselves. It is always an honor and a delight for us to mingle with you and strengthen our connections with one another. I am happy to announce that we have an additional treat for you this evening. Lord Ashworth, I turn the floor over to you."

The Marquess of Ashworth, looking even more stiffly aristocratic and dignified than he had a mere moment before, took his time looking about the room, and it seemed to William that he was making it clear before he spoke that what he was about to say was not to be questioned.

"Lady Ashworth and I were blessed to have but one daughter, our precious Louisa," he said. "No father could love a daughter more, nor be as proud of her as I am this evening." He turned to look at her, and William watched the marquess's face soften with emotion. William had never seen such a look on his own father's face, not even toward his mother.

And then the marquess's eyes turned on him, and William watched as the man's eyes turned steely with an implicit warning from a protective parent. "And so it is that I announce her betrothal this evening to William Barlow, Junior, Viscount Farleigh," he said.

An audible gasp could be heard around the room and beyond, followed by a brief moment of dead silence, which was then followed by a groundswell of murmuring.

And then William heard Louisa gasp.

He turned to her in concern and then followed the direction of her eyes. There, at the side of the room, standing just inside the door that connected the room to the entry hall, was a distinguished young gentleman looking directly back at her. He gave her a discreet nod of acknowledgment before turning his gaze on William. And then he left.

William went cold all over. There was only one person it could be: the Earl of Kerridge, to be precise, heir to the Duke of Aylesham, Louisa's former betrothed.

"Hear, hear," Lord Halford called out, raising the glass in his hand. "To the betrothed couple."

"To the betrothed couple," echoed some of the assembled guests. Others appeared too busy expressing their shock to join in.

Louisa was trying desperately to hide her own shock at seeing Lord Kerridge, if the overbright smile on her face was any indication. Lord Kerridge should have known better than to show his face here tonight. Or . . . perhaps no one had even thought to tell him the announcement would take place.

William should have seen to the task himself. He should have sent a note to Kerridge, informing him of their plans and asking, as a gentleman, that he not attend the assembly out of respect for Louisa and her family. Kerridge's appearance had poured salt in a raw wound—one William had created, certainly, but one Kerridge hadn't needed to make worse.

The next few hours were a blur of activity, during which he was sure he and Louisa received the congratulations of every person in attendance. There were a few people, like Halford's friend Kit Osbourne, who was now the Earl of Cantwell, and his brother Phillip, both of whom William recognized from their school days at Eton, who were, surprisingly and thankfully, genial in their congratulations to the newly betrothed couple. William hoped their affability would help convince Louisa that he was generally well regarded by those who actually knew him.

There were also, thankfully, others who seemed happy for them both. Close friends of Louisa's parents and several of her brothers' friends offered their congratulations and good wishes and undoubtedly would do their best to offer support.

Many of the guests had been unable to hide their surprise, however, while others had smoothed their faces into polite masks before offering bland congratulations. William suspected some must have previously witnessed Louisa in the company of Lord Kerridge, while others may have known William's father but hadn't wished to offend the Marquess and Marchioness of Ashworth.

All in all, William thought as he called for his carriage while Louisa chatted with friends at the end of the evening, he'd at least gotten over this first hurdle with a modicum of success. But he would not rest easy until the marriage vows had been made.

Chapter 6

THE EVENING COULDN'T HAVE GONE any worse.

Louisa slept until well past noon the following day, awaking with a terrible headache from the feigned smiling she'd done—hours and hours of smiling—until her jaw had been sore and she'd feared her face would permanently remain in some ghastly grimace afterward.

That had all been more than enough to bear—but then the absolute worst thing that could have happened had happened. The Earl of Kerridge had made an appearance at the assembly, arriving fashionably late—but just in time for the announcement of her betrothal. He had locked eyes with her at the announcement—and then left.

Brief though his appearance had been, it had been enough.

She sipped the hot chocolate Tibbetts had brought to her room, hoping it would ease her throbbing head. Chocolate was the best remedy for nearly everything Louisa could think of, and Tibbetts knew this.

"Choose something drab and comfortable for me to wear," Louisa said as Tibbetts rummaged through her wardrobe. "I don't think I can manage wearing any bright colors today." What she longed to do was go riding. If she were at Ashworth Park, she would give Athena her head and let her gallop through the countryside, just the two of them, free to do as they chose and go where they wished. That would never do in London, where she must take Tibbetts or a footman or a brother with her everywhere. Besides, that would require talking.

Louisa was not in the mood to speak to anyone today if she could help it.

Tibbetts selected a simple mauve gown for her to wear, and all too soon, Louisa had no excuse but to leave her bedroom. If she didn't, her mother would show up to see if she was unwell, and for the world, Louisa wouldn't worry her mother.

"It's about time you showed your sleepy head," Anthony said when Louisa arrived at the morning room. He and Alex were still breaking their fast, which meant they hadn't beaten her here by much. "Mama told the staff to serve breakfast later than usual."

Alex was shoveling food onto a plate over at the sideboard. "It's a good thing you finally showed up, Weezy," he said. "I may not have saved any food for you otherwise. I'm famished."

"Where is Mama?" Louisa asked, picking up a plate and nudging Alex out of the way so she could help herself to a few sausages before he could take them all. She already knew Papa would be seeing to his duty at the House of Lords, as he did every day while they were in Town.

"She promised the Duchess of Atherton she would call on her today," Anthony said. "They're probably compiling a list of suitable young ladies for Alex so he will do his duty and marry one of them." He shot a lazy grin at Alex, who was seating himself next to Anthony, his plate piled with food. "Now that you're betrothed, Weezy, I think Mama has matrimony on the mind."

The Duchess of Atherton was one of Mama's closest friends. She was short and plump, with twinkling hazel eyes that missed nothing. The duke frequently referred to her as The General, so clever she was at everything, whether it came to running her household or offering astute opinions on politics. Louisa adored her.

"Luckily for me and sadly for them, I am making plans to leave for Rome shortly, which will allow me a little more time before my heels are held to the fire," Alex said, spearing a piece of fried kidney with his fork.

"Besides, you're forgetting that Alex is as good as promised to Lady Elizabeth Spaulding, Anthony," Louisa said. "Papa and the Duke of Marwood have been planning their nuptials practically since she was born. If Mama and the Duchess of Atherton are making lists, they are most likely intended for you."

"Good point, Weezy. Perhaps I'll join you on that trip, Alex, even if Bonaparte is rattling his saber wherever he goes," Anthony said.

"He's too busy rattling his saber at Austria presently, so I'm not all that worried, and you're welcome to join me if you'd like—although I suspect Papa will insist you return to Cambridge."

"Likely true, blast it. Of course, as his heir, he may not let you go haring off to parts unknown, you know, with the turmoil from France spreading everywhere."

"You're probably right. But Lady Elizabeth is still a child, and I'm not ready to settle down and marry yet." He took a bite of eggs and chewed thoughtfully. "Perhaps I'll consider the West Indies."

"I wish I could travel to Rome," Louisa said wistfully. "I imagine Rome to be an entirely enchanting place, from what I've read. It is quite unfair that young gentlemen are allowed to travel on their own, while a young lady may only travel well escorted. It is to protect her from 'dissolute men,' Papa said." She paused, pondering the topic for a moment, in spite of her aching head. "What would qualify as being dissolute?"

"Do you really wish to know?" Anthony asked, looking shocked, while Alex choked on his tea before bursting out laughing.

"Not really," Louisa said, taking a bite of toast as Alex regained his composure. "Except—well, Grandfather must have been somewhat dissolute." She wouldn't be stuck in this mess and marrying Viscount Farleigh if he hadn't been. "And Lord Farleigh's father was apparently even worse than Grandfather."

"If you truly wish to know," Alex said with a diabolical twinkle in his eye, "some fellows like to pursue reckless indulgence, leading to excessive wagering and drunkenness . . . and then there are the actresses and—"

"A true gentleman knows his limits, Louisa," Anthony said firmly, interrupting Alex. "That is all you need to know. Stop teasing her, Alex. We don't need to scandalize our baby sister."

Alex shrugged, chuckling. "She asked."

Since Alex hadn't actually said anything Louisa didn't already know, she didn't precisely feel scandalized, and she supposed she didn't really want to know the sordid details anyway. "Tomorrow at church, the first of the banns are to be read," she said.

Alex set down his knife and fork, and Anthony reached for her hand, both her brothers' faces instantly sobering.

"How are you holding up through all of this, Weezy?" Anthony asked her.

"As well as can be expected, I suppose." She loved her brothers, truly, and knew they were there for her—but she wasn't sure she wanted to share her feelings with them. Besides, she wasn't even sure she could put what she was feeling into words.

"Truly, Weezy, we are concerned about you," Anthony said, giving her hand a squeeze. "You don't have to do this. Father would understand completely. In fact, I wonder if he wouldn't actually prefer it."

"We've talked about all this before, and the argument is always the same," Louisa replied. "If *honor* constrained you to do something you were otherwise loathe to do, serve your country in the military, for example"—she looked directly at Anthony, as he intended to buy his commission as soon as he completed his studies at Cambridge—"or were compelled to make a dynastic match, as the heir to a marquess is like to do"—she directed this remark to Alex—"you would do it, wouldn't you? Your honor would demand it."

"Yes, unquestionably, we would," Alex said in a tone that sounded suspiciously as if he were explaining the obvious to an imbecile. "But that is because we are *gentlemen*, as we've pointed out before, and *you* are *not*."

"You think I am less of a Hargreaves, less a child of the Marquess and Marchioness of Ashworth than either of you?" she challenged, trying to keep her voice low and reasonable but without success. "That because I am a female, I cannot have honor?"

"Of course not, Weezy," Anthony said soothingly.

"*Precisely*," Alex countered. "It is *not* the same thing at all. Women are weak and vulnerable, prone to hysterics, subject to fainting spells and vapors—"

"*When* have you ever known me to faint? Or Mama either, for that matter," Louisa exclaimed hotly. "I have followed the two of you all over the countryside my entire life—exploring attics and sheds, climbing trees, swimming in ponds, riding. You yourself said I was as good a horsewoman as you'd ever seen, Alex—"

"That's true, Weezy, but—"

"But *nothing*," she said, cutting off Alex, unable to control her growing irritation. "I will do what I *must*. I *refuse* to be the member of the Hargreaves family, the lone child of the Marquess of Ashworth to act with dishonor after all our father has done to restore the family name."

Anthony heaved a sigh. "Very well, Louisa; your willingness to make this sacrifice for honor's sake is one I highly respect. There is no point in arguing with her, Alex; she has made up her mind. What can we do to help, then?"

"I don't know," Louisa replied, suddenly feeling drained. She wanted to lie down and put a cold compress on her forehead. "Lord Kerridge was at the Meltons' last night."

"He was?" Alex said, his countenance darkening. "Devil take him to Hades and back! Now, *that's* what I call dishonorable—"

"None of us thought to warn him that we were announcing the betrothal at the Meltons' assembly. He wasn't there long—only enough to hear the actual announcement." She could still see his handsome, aristocratic face looking calmly at her. He'd been able to say so much with that one look: pity and irony mixed with a dash of contempt. It had pierced her deeply—she'd felt all the shame and guilt he'd intended for her to feel in that moment. He'd wounded her, and then he'd left. "I cannot blame him for his being there and can only respect his swift management of what could have been an awkward situation."

"If you say so," Alex said, looking unconvinced.

"We will be at church with you tomorrow, little sister," Anthony said resolutely. "We will smile and greet all the churchgoers, and we will not leave your side. We will be your support."

"And we shall be ready to provide Viscount Farleigh with a black eye if the situation requires," Alex added.

Louisa wouldn't put it past Alex to look for such an opportunity. "I doubt it will come to that," she said. Truth be told, she would rather have her brothers help her pry information about Viscount Farleigh from him rather than resort to violence against him. It would be much more useful, for, despite her attempts to get him to open up to her, she was still betrothed to an enigma.

* * *

William heard nothing during the lengthy church service on Sunday morning, his mind preoccupied with Heslop's words of urgency to him: *You must proceed with haste in courting Lady Louisa. You must win the lady over. You must proceed with haste . . .*

He'd arrived at Ashworth House this morning—he had arranged to drive Louisa to St. George's today, her parents and brothers following behind them in a separate carriage—trying to convince himself that while he hadn't been willing to withdraw the vowel, she'd had the right to choose whether she married him or not. He had not coerced her. Not precisely.

She'd chosen a pink muslin dress and matching pelisse to wear that brought out the color in her cheeks, and a straw bonnet arrayed with flowers the exact hue of her lips. He sorely wanted to kiss her again. Their kisses had been a revelation, an experience he'd thought about ever since and longed to repeat. Instead, he'd silently handed her up into the gig he'd discovered in the mews behind his father's house.

He didn't deserve to kiss her.

She was now seated next to him in one of the front pews of the chapel, her parents and brothers sitting on the other side of her on the same pew, poised to protect her, William presumed, if anyone in St. George's were to stand and publicly proclaim a reason why they should not wed.

And if no one stood? They would still have to go through this same ordeal two more times since he'd promised Louisa she could have the banns read and the extra days that doing so would give her. His father, may his soul rot in his grave, would have said William's promise to Louisa had been nothing more than a bluff and that Louisa had called him on it, weakening his chance to win the game.

Except it wasn't a game. There was too much at stake for too many people.

Out of the corner of his eye, William noticed Louisa's gloved hands suddenly clench in her lap, which brought his thoughts back to the services going on around them.

The rector had begun reading the banns.

"If any of you know cause or just impediment why these two people should not be joined together in holy matrimony," the man boomed from the pulpit, "ye are to declare it. This is the first time of asking."

Louisa sat as still as a statue, staring straight ahead. William, too, did not move. He held his breath, waiting—no, *dreading*—the inevitable moment someone stood and claimed knowledge of a just impediment. William himself could recite more than a few without blinking an eye.

Time stood still.

But no one stood. No one claimed knowing any impediments. There was only silence. Blessed silence.

And then, miraculously, the rector continued with the service, and William breathed again. When all was over, William stood by while Louisa and her family greeted their friends and acquaintances afterward, nodded politely, and shook hands with the rector.

The first reading of the banns had been successful. Two more weeks, two more readings, and he'd have kept his promise to Louisa and they could marry. *You must proceed with haste in courting Lady Louisa. You must win the lady over.*

Perhaps, if he were fortunate enough to win her over, he wouldn't feel such pressing guilt.

Two weeks seemed an eternity.

* * *

"You're very quiet this afternoon," Louisa said.

"What?" *Blast*, William thought. He should be conversing with her when he was with her, not analyzing the ethics of what he was doing. Or thinking about kissing—

"I *said*, you're very quiet this afternoon," she repeated. "Even more so than usual, I daresay."

"Forgive me," was his pathetic reply.

After surviving the first reading of the banns, William had invited Louisa for a drive in Hyde Park before returning her to Ashworth House. Amazingly, she'd agreed. William suspected it'd had more to do with maintaining appearances than any desire she might have had to spend time with him. He, however, hadn't been ready to return her to the protective arms of her parents—or her brothers, who'd both looked quite menacing during the church services. He longed—

"You are the most aggravating person," she muttered, interrupting his wandering thoughts once again. "I am trying desperately to understand you, but how I'm to accomplish it when you tell me virtually nothing, I'll never know."

They were nearing the park. Once inside the gates, she would be busy once again, greeting her many friends and chatting with all and sundry who went to see and be seen in Hyde Park in the afternoons—Louisa was not only exquisitely lovely, but she was also well-liked, he'd quickly learned, which would allow William to sit back quietly and watch. He would be free of her demands for conversation and her questions about his past. *To be successful, one does not give away what is in his hand all at once, nor does he allow his face to reflect what he holds at any time.*

William despised wagering. His father's vices had killed his mother day by torturous day. And yet his father's words had become ingrained nonetheless. He could still feel the burning welts on his back that he'd received as a boy whenever he'd succumbed—as his father had been wont to say—to "emotional outbursts."

They had barely passed through the park entrance when Louisa's hand moved to his thigh briefly before returning to her own lap. His eye traveled from her hand to her face, void of its color, to the source of her distress.

William had seen the distinguished-looking gentleman before. Today, he was elegantly dressed and seated in a dashingly turned-out barouche, a beautiful and lively female companion by his side.

The Earl of Kerridge.

William went cold all over.

The earl was obviously exceedingly wealthy, his carriage and horses of the finest quality. As the barouche drew up alongside William's gig, William felt a fierce stab of resentment and jealousy.

"Lady Louisa, what a pleasant surprise to cross paths with you this afternoon. Lovely day, is it not?" Lord Kerridge said. "But surely you know Miss Hughes."

William shifted the reins into his far hand and placed his other over Louisa's fist. He'd heard of Miss Belinda Hughes. She was an heiress and a wealthy young lady, in her own right.

"I am indeed acquainted with Miss Hughes," Louisa said. "How do you do?"

"Very well, thank you." Miss Hughes shot Lord Kerridge a distinctive look that William knew was intended to point out her own good fortune at Louisa's expense.

"Perhaps you would do us the honor of an introduction?" Lord Kerridge asked, gesturing subtly toward William.

"Oh. Of course," Louisa said. "Lord Kerridge, Miss Hughes, allow me to present Viscount Farleigh. Lord Farleigh, the Earl of Kerridge and Miss Belinda Hughes."

"Your *betrothed* Viscount Farleigh, I understand," Lord Kerridge said in what could only be considered a dig at Louisa. "My felicitations."

"Thank you," Louisa said in a muted voice.

"I am the most fortunate of men," William interjected, wishing he were more adept at polite conversation so he could smooth over the awkwardness of the situation for her.

"Indeed," the earl replied with a cool glance at Louisa, who dropped her eyes. "Well. I have promised this young lady an ice at Gunter's, so we must be on our way. Good afternoon Lady Louisa, Farleigh." He turned the barouche with accomplished ease. The man was a dab hand with the reins as well; blast him for all his perfections.

It was apparent to William that despite the earl's hauteur, the man's pride had been wounded by what had happened. Louisa had accepted Lord Kerridge's proposal, and William's actions had made an end of it, so Lord Kerridge had made a point of showing her he had moved on quickly from his attachment to her.

William's actions, on the other hand, were taking her from a loving family and marriage to a man she loved, who had promised her wealth and rank and security, to a dwindling estate wracked with debt and no guarantee it would be anything more than that. William's envy of their former attachment matched the guilt he felt.

He watched Louisa watch the earl's barouche as it wove its way through the other carriages holding other lofty members of the *ton*. Miss Hughes turned around briefly and waved at Louisa, the little cat.

"I must go," Louisa whispered when the barouche faded from sight at last. "Please take me home."

"Of course," William said.

They rode through Mayfair in silence.

Chapter 7

"WAKE UP, LOUISA. UP, UP!" Mama's voice roused Louisa from a blessed sleep devoid of dreams—and betrothals.

Louisa pulled the blankets over her head.

"The Duchess of Atherton is calling today, and I expect you to join me in entertaining her. You've hidden yourself away since Sunday."

"It's only Tuesday."

"That's not the point. Tibbetts, keep her awake and get her dressed for the day, and send for tea and toast."

"Yes, milady."

"One half hour, Louisa, and you had better be downstairs with me."

Louisa peeked her head out from beneath the blankets to see Mama marching toward the door. "I'd really prefer not to, if you don't mind, Mama. I don't feel well at all."

Mama stopped and turned. "Tibbetts, please leave us."

"Yes, milady." Once Tibbetts was gone, Mama sat on the edge of the bed and drew the blankets completely away from Louisa's face.

"Are you ill?" She laid a hand across Louisa's forehead. "No fever, at least," she said. "Shall I call for the doctor? Oh, I wish Mrs. Shaw were here instead of at Ashworth Park. I'm sure she could produce an herbal remedy to help you feel better."

"I'm not ill, really, but . . . Mama, did you always love Papa?" Louisa asked.

Mama closed her eyes and heaved a sigh. "Ah, I see. I should have known, shouldn't I? You seemed so sure of your decision and have handled yourself so admirably, I didn't allow myself to think that perhaps you were merely putting on a brave face. Perhaps I didn't want to see anything else." She stroked Louisa's hair away from her forehead, and Louisa wished she were a young girl again when Mama did such things frequently, as if brushing away all the childhood cares of the day. She turned her cheek to rest against Mama's palm and closed her eyes. "*Did* you love Papa back then?" she asked again in a low voice.

"I had a certain regard for him," she replied, "and that grew into an affection and then into love."

"Did he love you?"

"Oh, Louisa, such questions! It was years ago."

"I know nothing about him, Mama." She meant Viscount Farleigh, not Papa, but Mama would know that.

Mama said nothing, just continued to stroke Louisa's forehead. "Marriage is a fickle thing, Louisa, especially amongst the noble ranks. A couple can think themselves in love and then grow to despise each other—but the opposite is equally as true. But this is a conversation that needs to occur when we have more time. Visiting with the duchess will do you a world of good. She's excellent company, as you well know."

She patted Louisa's shoulder. "Besides, the duke doesn't refer to her as The General for nothing. She's more skilled than Lady Putnam at sifting through gossip, and she's infinitely more discreet. I wouldn't be at all surprised if she has discerned a thing or two about your Lord Farleigh."

"He's not *my* Lord Farleigh," Louisa grumbled.

"Nevertheless, we shall welcome the Duchess of Atherton, and we shall see if we come away with any knowledge about your betrothed. For—"

"For it is what the daughter of the Marquess and Marchioness of Ashworth would do."

"Precisely. Ah, here is Tibbetts back again, and if my nose does not deceive me, she brought you chocolate rather than the tea I ordered."

"Begging your pardon, milady—" Tibbetts began, blushing.

"She knows I prefer chocolate to tea, Mama."

"Enjoy your chocolate, then." She rose. "I shall be waiting for you downstairs in a half hour's time. Make sure she eats, Tibbetts. I want her at her very best when we entertain the duchess."

And so it was that a half hour later, Louisa was dutifully sitting with Mama and the Duchess of Atherton in the dayroom, Mama's favorite room. It was a cheerful room, decorated in pale pinks and greens, with cozy upholstered sofas and chairs, the sort of chairs one would wish to curl up in with a book on a rainy day—or any day, for that matter.

"I'm so pleased that dear Louisa is with us today, Eleanor," the duchess said as Mama rang for tea to be served. "Such news! I can hardly wait for you to share the details." The Duchess of Atherton had come out with Mama, and they had remained close friends over the years.

"Indeed. Ah, John, there you are. Tea, please."

The footman bowed and left.

"What a surprise for us all to hear the announcement of your betrothal at the Meltons' assembly last week, Louisa," the duchess said, not being one to beat around the bush.

Louisa glanced at Mama, unsure how to proceed.

Mama simply returned Louisa's look with a raised eyebrow and a nod, which, translated, meant, "This is for you to explain, not me."

Louisa opened her mouth to speak, although what she intended to say, she wasn't entirely sure—

"Here you are, my dear!" Papa poked his head through the door. "I've been looking for you—what ho! We have a guest, I see! Always a pleasure to see you, Your Grace." He strode across the room and bowed over the duchess's hand and then gave Mama a kiss on the cheek.

Louisa blinked at the sight. A kiss, even on the cheek, was a highly intimate thing for him to do in front of company, even an old friend such as the duchess. And yet it also warmed Louisa's heart to see them share their love for each other so openly.

"The combined beauty in this room quite eclipses the sun," Papa said.

"You're laying it on thick, Ashworth," Mama said with twinkling eyes.

He laughed. "Not in the least, my dear, I assure you."

"I am here to learn all about Louisa's betrothal to Viscount Farleigh." Once again, the duchess cut through the small talk to get to the point.

"Ah, yes," Papa murmured, becoming a bit more serious.

"We had expected an announcement of some sort to be forthcoming, you know, but I daresay we were all caught by surprise."

"Life does tend to offer its share of surprises, does it not?" Papa glanced over his shoulder as the footman brought in the tea service. "Here is your tea, ladies. I shall, therefore, excuse myself, as this conversation cannot be enhanced by the presence of a lowly male." He bowed and left.

It appeared to Louisa as if he couldn't escape quickly enough when he realized what the topic of conversation was to be.

"Milk or lemon, Martha?" Mama asked.

"Milk, please."

While Mama set about pouring tea, Louisa reflected on what she'd observed about the Duke and Duchess of Atherton over the years.

The duke and duchess's affection for each other was no pretense, just as her parents' love for each other was also obvious to her. It should make her feel better to know there were married couples within the highest levels of Society who actually loved each other. Such emotions were often frowned upon and were rarely even considered when brokering marriages—and yet Louisa had always yearned for such a match.

It was utterly discouraging, she thought as she sipped her tea, to think of spending her entire life with an indifferent partner.

"Viscount Farleigh has been on everyone's tongues the past several days," the duchess said. She took a small bite of biscuit and chewed thoughtfully. "I vaguely remember his father, the former viscount. I saw him on a few occasions over the years, but we were never introduced." Her tone implied that the former Viscount Farleigh's reputation would have prevented him from having any personal connection to the duke and duchess. "Handsome man, when he was younger—" Meaning, he hadn't aged well. Louisa had spent enough time with Mama in the duchess's company to infer the real meaning behind what she was saying.

"I was rather hoping, Martha, if I may be so bold . . ." Mama's words trailed off.

"Yes?" the duchess said before taking a sip of tea.

"Well, Louisa is my only daughter, as you know, and . . ."

The duchess took another bite of biscuit, obviously waiting for Mama to dig herself out of the hole she was making for herself.

"I am not nearly as adept at . . . um . . ." Mama threw her hands in the air and gave up speaking altogether.

"Leave off, Eleanor. I take your meaning and am not insulted in the least. It takes a certain skill and a bit of luck to be privy to idle chatter without actually being called a gossip. It also helps that I'm a duchess, and people seem to think providing me with juicy information is a coup of some sort."

She dabbed at her chin with her napkin before continuing. "The Earl of Kerridge, whom we all expected Louisa to marry, is the catch of the Season," the duchess continued. "As rich as Croesus, incredibly handsome, and Aylesham's heir, to boot. A future duke who isn't round about the middle and still has all his hair is a rare commodity—and he was Louisa's for the plucking, from what I saw and heard." She looked directly at Louisa with gimlet eyes.

How was she to respond? She couldn't simply blurt out that she'd been won in a wager. No one could know of those circumstances beyond the few who already did, and heaven forbid those few share their knowledge with anyone else. Louisa bit her lip, holding back the words and looking at Mama in panic, passing the responsibility back to her.

Mama cleared her throat. "Sadly, Martha, they ultimately did not suit," she said rather unconvincingly. Her eyes flickered back toward Louisa as though she knew she'd failed; it would never be enough to satisfy The General.

"'Did not suit,' you say? I'm sorry, Eleanor, but you must do better than that." The duchess set her cup and saucer down with a clatter. "There is no conceivable reason why the two of them wouldn't suit; in fact, I heard the marriage contracts were very nearly complete. Try again." She folded her hands in her lap and waited.

Mama actually began wringing her hands. "I don't know quite what to say. There was a prior . . ." Mama stopped speaking and stood to pace about the room.

Louisa, by contrast, sat frozen in place, a terrifying bubble forming in her chest.

"There was a prior . . . what? A prior understanding with Farleigh? I was given to believe the viscount was nearly a complete stranger before he arrived in Town so recently. But if there *was* an understanding, why would marriage contracts have been drawn up, and why would you be here hoping I know anything—" Her brows furrowed with confusion. "I'm at a total loss."

The bubble inside Louisa was pressing against her heart and lungs now until she could barely breathe. And it grew bigger and bigger still until it continued up her throat to her lips—and then it burst. "Lord Farleigh won me in a wager," Louisa blurted out, then threw her hands over her mouth as if to force the words back inside.

"What?" The duchess's eyes doubled in size, and she whirled to look at Mama.

Mama collapsed into the nearest sofa as if Louisa's words had taken her breath away too. She nodded weakly, laying a hand over her eyes.

"Good heavens!" the duchess exclaimed.

"Yes," Mama replied.

There was nothing for it now that Louisa had spoken the words aloud. "Lord Farleigh won the daughter of the Marquess of Ashworth in a wager.

That is to say, the former Lord Farleigh made a wager with my grandfather in which he bet a future daughter of the marquess. The wording was all rather . . . conveniently vague and . . . surprisingly legitimate . . . and suddenly, there I was, not betrothed and then betrothed again, and, and . . ." And Louisa could tell that, once again, she was beginning to babble.

"Oh, my poor girl!" The duchess rose and moved to the chair closest to Louisa, wrapping her in a hug and patting her back over and over again. "It goes without saying, Eleanor, that Louisa's words won't leave this room. Oh dear, oh dear."

"So you see, Martha, why any knowledge you can provide would be a great help. My only daughter is to marry a total stranger, a stranger who descends from an entirely despicable character. And yet, Louisa feels honor bound to do it."

"Well, I am quite without words for the moment."

"You would have done the same, I daresay," Louisa replied. "There is a reason you are called The General. I daresay women are no less honorable than men."

"Louisa!" Mama exclaimed, aghast.

The duchess waved off Louisa's comment. "I know very well what I am called, Eleanor, and I'm quite proud of it, actually, considering what other options there may have been. I hope you are right, Louisa, that if I were in a position to make such a difficult choice, I would choose honor over my personal feelings. We'll never know though, will we?" she said. "Hypotheticals provide little of value, in my opinion. Very well. I daresay I've heard nothing as of yet about the son, but the *father*, well, that's a different matter altogether . . . I shall tell you what I know about the man and what little I have heard—"

There was a discreet knock on the door, interrupting the duchess, and then John entered once again, this time bearing a salver with a calling card on it. "Lady Putnam and Miss Harriet Putnam to see you, Lady Ashworth," he said.

The duchess shook her head. "It needed only this. Well, I daresay you'll hear everything and then some about Lord Farleigh now," she said.

"Send them in, John," Mama said with a sigh. "Send them in."

* * *

Now that the first of the banns had been read, William needed to travel to Farleigh Manor so preparations could be made for the arrival of its future mistress, albeit he'd been reluctant to leave London as of yet.

It was not an exaggeration to say Louisa had been deeply upset by their chance and unfortunate encounter with Lord Kerridge on Sunday. William doubted the Earl of Kerridge would consider Belinda Hughes, a mere "miss," an appropriate wife for the heir of the Duke of Aylesham; it had been obvious that Louisa had been too upset to come to the same conclusion during their encounter.

He'd left her alone and in peace on Monday as a result, but he couldn't afford to be away from her side for too long. He needed to call on her this morning before he left Town.

He purchased a single red rose from a flower girl on his way to Ashworth House, approached the front door, and straightened his neckcloth before knocking.

"Good afternoon, Lord Farleigh," the butler said as he opened the door and allowed William to enter. "I shall inform Lady Louisa of your presence." He gestured for William to wait in a small parlor off the front door.

He felt restless. During all of William's time at Oxford, and even the past few years in Edinburgh, he'd not found himself foolishly wondering how to act around a lady, of all things. It was embarrassing.

He stood by the fireplace and stared out the window, tapping his foot. "Ahem."

William whirled around, then silently berated himself for letting his reaction show.

The butler stood in the doorway, a bland expression on his face, as though he hadn't noticed William's actions, just as any good butler would. "The ladies will receive you in the dayroom," he intoned. "Follow me, please."

If William had heard the man correctly, it meant Lady Ashworth was most likely there to receive him, as well as Louisa. That wasn't the best of scenarios; he would get a better read on Louisa's state of mind if he was able to meet with her alone.

The butler led him past the formal drawing room and down the hall. "Viscount Farleigh," the butler announced when they reached their destination.

William entered the dayroom—and five sets of female eyes turned to look at him, stopping him in his tracks. Blast it all. The situation was even more complicated than William had anticipated.

"Lord Farleigh, what an unexpected surprise," Lady Ashworth said, rising to her feet. "Welcome."

"Thank you," he answered, feeling uncomfortably conspicuous. He cleared his throat. "Forgive me for intruding," he said.

"Not at all," Lady Ashworth replied. "You have met the duchess, I believe?"

"A pleasure to see you again, Your Grace."

"The pleasure is entirely mine," the duchess said with a suspicious twinkle in her eye.

"And we have Lady Putnam and Miss Putnam with us as well," Lady Ashworth said.

He nodded graciously toward the two Putnam ladies, both of whom were eyeing him like hawks who'd spotted prey, notwithstanding their knowing about the betrothal. "An honor to see you again, ladies," he said, hoping he sounded like he meant it.

Louisa had stayed silent throughout the exchange. Considering how their last encounter had ended, he couldn't really blame her.

"Would you care to join us?" Lady Ashworth asked as she resumed her seat. "I shall send for a fresh pot of tea."

"Er, no, but thank you." He took a breath. "If you'll excuse me, Lady Ashworth, I had hoped to steal Lady Louisa away—"

Lady Putnam gasped, and the duchess bit her lip, trying unsuccessfully not to laugh—

"That is, I—" Of all the words he could have chosen, *steal* was the absolute worst he could have used around Lady Putnam, whom he'd already concluded was a gossip of the first order. William was flustered, unsure what to say next, which was intensely annoying. He glanced about the room, not knowing precisely where to look, and then turned to Louisa. "May I have a few moments of your time?"

She rose abruptly to her feet. "You may. Perhaps a walk in the garden?"

He nodded, concealing his relief as best he could.

"So good to visit with you all," she said to the other ladies before placing her hand on William's arm. "Now, if you'll excuse us, I intend to spend some time with my betrothed."

"Not *too* much time, I hope," Lady Putnam muttered under her breath.

"Of course not, Alice," Lady Ashworth said. "Lord Farleigh is the epitome of a true gentleman, I assure you." Lady Ashworth probably thought she was lying between her teeth at her statement regarding his character, but William appreciated her public display of support.

Louisa's hand dropped from his arm once he'd shut the door behind them, leaving a warmth behind that gradually faded.

William held the single rose out to her as soon as they left the house. "For you," he said as they began their stroll.

She took it from him and held the red bud to her nose. "Thank you."
Silence.

"Please forgive me for arriving unannounced," he said, hoping a conciliatory gesture would get them past this awkwardness.

"Not at all," she replied. "Your arrival was a godsend."

It was? His heart sped up.

"Lady Putnam was beginning to wear on me with all her talk. Terrible of me to acknowledge it out loud, I know, but, really, the woman would try the patience of a saint."

Not quite the reason William had hoped for—not that he should be hoping for anything anyway.

They walked through Lady Ashworth's rose garden and down a path that led toward a small folly set amongst a few young maple trees, Louisa occasionally breathing in the rose's fragrance, William clasping his hands behind his back. The property around Ashworth House was ample, despite being merely their Town residence. He could only imagine what Ashworth Manor must be like in size and opulence by comparison.

"I'm sorry the lady's company was distressing to you," he said.

She stared at him, her large blue eyes speaking volumes.

"Ah," he said. "I was the topic of conversation."

"The topic, yes, although there wasn't much to say. Apparently you are an enigma to everyone. Your *father*, however, is not."

"You knew that already."

"I did. The duchess, at least, was discreet when speaking of your father. Lady Putnam, on the other hand . . ." She stooped to brush away a twig that had caught on her skirts.

"Anything you wish to share with me?" he asked, hoping she wouldn't take him up on the offer. He loathed talking about his father—or thinking about him at all, for that matter.

"No," she said.

William breathed an inward sigh of relief—

"Just the usual sorts of things, you know," she said, apparently unwilling to talk about it but unable to let it go either.

"Like?" he begrudgingly asked.

She shrugged but averted her eye, her face turning bright pink.

"Ah," he said. "I can't say I'm overly surprised, can you?" William hoped his casual reply masked his true thoughts on the matter. "Does this mean you would like to discuss these things after all? I saw my father but once after my mother's death, so I'm afraid I haven't all the particulars of his wrongdoings. I take that back; I *do* know the particulars of his financial wrongdoings." He needed to step back from this conversation and get his thoughts in order, as he was precariously close to speaking with more excitability than was good for the situation.

"I know you do; it's why we are betrothed, after all," Louisa said.

There was clearly nothing he could add to that. The best thing for now was a change of topic. "Come," he said. "Let us set this distressing conversation aside for a while, shall we?" He offered her his arm, and thankfully, she slid her hand into the crook of his arm this time, and they strolled onward.

* * *

Louisa walked with William across the garden to the maple trees—hardly more than saplings, they were, as the groundskeeper had only added the folly and the trees the previous year. The folly itself was a small marble pavilion with a marble bench within, offering a view back toward the house. It was a pleasant place to sit and usually made Louisa feel as if she were at their country seat of Ashworth Park.

Usually—but not today.

They sat on the bench, and Louisa dropped her arm, choosing instead to clasp both hands on her lap after laying the rose on the bench next to her. The feel of him, the male strength she sensed in his arm, was beguiling, and Louisa didn't want her nascent attraction to him to interfere with her determination to learn about him. She needed a clear head in order to do that.

William adjusted his position on the bench in order to face her, causing their legs to brush together, and Louisa drew in a breath. "I'm traveling to Buckinghamshire this afternoon," he said, "and wished to take my leave of you before doing so. It will be a short trip, as I intend to be back tomorrow evening, if all goes to plan."

"That seems to be a great deal of travel for such a brief visit," she said.

"Perhaps, but it is for a good reason. I wish to personally review the preparations being made at Farleigh Manor in order to receive a new viscountess." He paused, the corners of his mouth flickering for the briefest moment in what was almost an actual smile before disappearing. "And then I'll return to London in time to escort you to Vauxhall Gardens tomorrow evening, if you would be willing to do me the honor." There was that flicker again.

She ignored it and what it did to her insides and firmed up her resolve. "Naturally, I am willing to go to Vauxhall with you; I am your betrothed, after all, and such things are to be expected. I have heard that Vauxhall Gardens are not to be missed, and I shall look forward to it with anticipation. *But—*"

"But what?" he asked.

"I have conditions that I wish to have met in return."

His eyes shuttered. He reached out and took her hand in his. With his free hand, he began lightly stroking each finger, from knuckle to fingertip.

Louisa swallowed. "Conditions," she repeated.

"Conditions," he said. "Undoubtedly, you do. You have beautiful hands, Louisa, soft hands with long, delicate fingers. And yet they feel capable and strong too. Such a paradox. If I were an artist, I would paint your hands."

"You're speaking foolishness," she said, her voice a bit shaky, which annoyed her. What did her hands have to do with the current conversation anyway? "You're not an artist, I daresay, and even if you were, I'm not sure I find it flattering that my *hands* are the subject you would choose to paint."

He threaded his fingers through hers, interlocking them, moving his head this way and that as though looking for the best angle to view them before returning his gaze to hers. "Oh, I would wish to paint your face too, rest assured. And your throat—from right here behind your ear down to your collarbone." With his forefinger, he traced the spot he'd just described without touching her; still, she could swear she felt it all the same. "The line here is exquisite. If only I'd been given a true artist's talent," he said in a low voice.

Louisa could feel herself melting, much as she had before the Melton assembly when William had kissed her the first time—

The scoundrel was making it happen again!

"Stop it," she exclaimed, pulling her hand free. "You kissed me before only to make me look betrothed in front everyone present. You flatter me with your words only to distract me from my intent. You must think me a weak female to use such tactics on me."

"Not at all, Louisa, I promise you." He turned his head away and stared outward toward the house.

"My conditions are simple ones, William. Talk to me. Be forthcoming with me. Be honest. That is all I ask."

He turned back toward her, his dark eyes burning in a way she'd not seen before. "You think your conditions are simple, but they are not." He reached for her wrist and pulled her toward him until she was pressed closely to him, their faces mere inches apart.

Louisa's heart pounded with excitement and fear and just a touch of triumph; she'd poked the caged tiger with a stick and had finally gotten a reaction.

"There is not much to tell," he said, the look in his eyes scorching her. "Anything of any import you know already. My mother died far too soon. My father died far too late to benefit anyone. The only thing of any worth he ever did was wager against your grandfather." He cupped her chin with his hand and moved so his lips were but a breath away. "And when I kiss you," he whispered, "it is because I cannot help myself."

His lips met hers then, firm and persuasive, and the entire world melted around Louisa, her senses once again colliding. Gradually, oh, so gradually, his kisses gentled and began softly exploring, and she floated into a place without time, eyes closed, receiving, taking, giving. Wanting more. Not knowing what she wanted.

Eventually, much too soon, William drew back . . . and time gradually returned. She didn't want to open her eyes. "That is all I can tell you for now," he whispered, running his forefinger over her eyebrow. "But I give you my solemn promise that I will do better. Will that suffice?"

"Yes," Louisa breathed. Her eyes fluttered open.

His dark eyes, intensely serious now, locked with hers and held her gaze—with passion, yes, she recognized that now, but also with pain. "I must go, although it gives me no joy. I will console myself with the thought that I will see you again tomorrow evening," he said. He pressed a lingering kiss at the corner of her mouth. "Adieu, Louisa."

Chapter 8

THAT KISS.

The ride to Buckinghamshire had flown by, for the private lane leading to Farleigh Manor was—surprisingly enough—just ahead. William's mind had been greatly preoccupied the entire way, so it only made sense, in retrospect. Kissing Louisa for a second time had only made him want to take her in his arms and kiss her again and again.

He'd lost whatever restraint he'd had when she'd prodded him to open up and expose his inner self to her. He should not have kissed her. Not like that. But, by thunder, she had kissed him back. Oh yes, she had. It had been a passionate kiss, a memorable kiss. It had been a victory.

But William was no fool either. It would take more than passion to win the heart of Lady Louisa Hargreaves.

He reined in his horse and came to an abrupt halt. When had this become more than simply getting his betrothed and her dowry to the altar? When had it become about winning her heart?

That she was willing to marry him at all should be enough. It *was* enough, he sternly told himself. He was *not* doing this for himself. If it had only been about him, he would have remained in Scotland, free to pursue his academic interests, and let Farleigh Manor rot.

That wasn't entirely true though, he conceded. He couldn't do that to the tenants who depended on the estate for their livings, the people who depended on him, or to the servants of the manor who'd taken care of him in his boyhood and youth. The people he loved. He couldn't do it to Mrs. Holly or Grimshaw or the others. Or to Mary.

"Look here, Mary. Soldiers march like this." Young William, *a willow stick braced against his shoulder as if it were a gun, straightened his spine and paraded about the herb garden, knees high, while little Mary tagged along behind.* "Soldiers don't skip, and they don't sing either."

"Well, they should," she replied. *"Maybe they wouldn't fight each other so much if they did."*

Farleigh Manor had always been Mary's home. How would she ever be made to understand and cope if, suddenly, she and her mother were left to their own resources? Mary was like a sister to him—the closest thing to a sibling William had ever had.

No, he couldn't do such a thing to Mary. Or to the others.

Perhaps he couldn't do it to the memory of his mother either, who had spent all her married life at Farleigh Manor, much of the time alone and abandoned by her husband, and who was buried in the family plot there.

He nudged his horse forward at a walk.

The house gradually came into view. Farleigh Manor was an estate with a reasonable amount of property and a modestly sized manor house, and Matthew had done a good job keeping the front grounds in decent order, especially when one considered that he was undoubtedly doing all the work himself. The lawns had been recently scythed; however, the bordering shrubbery needed more pruning than they'd apparently received the past few years and were a tad overgrown. Except for the scythed grass, the place looked just as it had when William had been summoned home by Mr. Heslop.

William studied the estate now with new eyes. What would Louisa's impression of her future home be?

Weeds William hadn't noticed before suddenly appeared amongst the cobblestones leading to the front entry. The shutters needed a fresh coat of paint, and the roof was missing tiles in several places. It was certainly not as well maintained as the homes a daughter of a marquess would be accustomed to experiencing.

Rather than dismount when he reached the front entry, he continued on horseback around the side of the house until he reached the stables. He spotted Samuel there, tending to the horses.

"Master William! Welcome back!" the man called, leaving his chore and striding toward William, wiping his hands on a rag.

William dismounted. "Samuel, good to see you again so soon," he said, shaking Samuel's hand.

"That's true enough, me boy—er, I mean, melord." He grinned cheekily.

"Let's take it easy on the 'milording,' shall we?" William said. "You're family."

"I'm family, eh . . ." Samuel scratched his grizzly chin as if pondering William's words carefully, the old bounder. "That puts things into a whole new light, I reckon." He rubbed his hands together with an avaricious grin.

Samuel was joking, and the stable master's casual words took William back in time. "You were more of a father to me—you and Matthew and even Grimshaw—than my own father ever was. I won't be having the lot of you bowing and scraping and tugging your forelocks at me every hour of the day. Understood?"

"Aye, boy, I do. Matthew and me—and all the others what's here—done a right good job of raising ye too. And yer mother done her best by ye, God rest 'er soul." He sobered. "She were a fine woman and gone too soon."

"Thank you, Samuel." William banished the ghost of his mother and the melancholy it invariably brought along with it. "I'm here to announce my betrothal and to see what can be done in a very short amount of time to prepare Farleigh Manor for the arrival of its future viscountess."

The look of utter shock that appeared on Samuel's face quickly became one of utter joy and excitement. "Well, ye don't say!" He grabbed William's hand again and shook it vigorously. "Well done, lad! And quickly too! Those lovely London ladies took one look at ye and fell at yer feet, did they?"

"Not precisely," William said. William and Louisa's betrothal could not be construed in those terms at all—yet there had been that kiss . . . "We must try our best to make Farleigh Manor as fit a home as possible for my bride-to-be," William said, bringing the subject back into focus. "She is a lady of high rank."

Samuel winked at him.

"Enough, man." William couldn't help but crack a small smile. "This is serious business I'm about. Lady Louisa is the daughter of a marquess. I want her to feel comfortable, and that means I'm relying on you and the others to work miracles between now and the wedding."

"I've never been very saintly, as ye well know, me boy, but I'll do me best. Me an' Walter will get things shined up here. Your father cared enough about his horseflesh and carriages that we're in better shape than most. It's what yer going to do over there"—he gestured with his head toward the manor house—"that ye need to worry about, if yer looking to make your highbred lady feel at home."

"You're right," William said. "Which is why I'm headed there now. Even so, I want an honest accounting from you of what can reasonably be done. Carriages, bloodstock, tools, paddocks. A full accounting, Samuel. We want everything at its reasonable best."

"Right ye are. And everything in the meantime will get shined up proper, don't ye worry about that. We all done our best to keep the place up for ye; we're that fond of ye, boy."

"Thank you, Samuel."

He hoped the rest of the staff received his news with the same degree of enthusiasm and optimism.

* * *

"Will!" a high-pitched voice shrieked, and William had barely enough time to brace himself before Mary vaulted herself into his arms. "You're back! You're staying for good this time too, aren't you? Oh, Will!" She hugged him with such force that he thought he might suffocate.

"Mary, my best girl and truest friend." He gently pried her strangling arms from around his neck and took a deep breath. "I am back for today and part of tomorrow, but then I must leave again—but before you frown, I will tell you that soon I will be here to stay."

"For always?" she asked.

"For most of the time. I may have to journey to other places on occasion, like London."

"That's okay," she said with a nod. "Important gentlemen go to London."

"Will you let me escort you to the house?" he asked her formally, winging his elbow out for her. It was a game they had always played growing up.

"Why, thank you, sir," she replied with a grin, placing her hand on his proffered arm.

They walked toward the herb garden together. "Mary, I have some important news to share with you," he said. "So I'm exceedingly glad you saw that I had returned and came out to greet me. I hope the news pleases you."

"It will please me, because you will be telling me that you are going to stay here now, when you don't have to go to London."

"Indeed, love. But when I return to stay—listen to me carefully, now—I will be bringing someone special. Her name will be Lady Farleigh—"

Mary's eyebrows came together in a look of confusion. "But your mama is Lady Farleigh, and she died. I cried when that happened, Will. I cried and cried."

"I know, love. I grieved for her as well, and I still do. But the Lady Farleigh I am talking about . . . will be my wife. Do you understand?"

Her eyes widened, and she stopped in her tracks. "You are getting married!" She threw her arms around his neck again. "Oh, Will! You are getting married, and you will be a husband, and you will have a wife. And that means there will be babies too. I can't wait!"

He chuckled while he again pried her arms away from his neck. "Perhaps in time there will be babies. But not right away. I am counting on you to help make the new Lady Farleigh welcome when she arrives."

Mary's sunny face suddenly darkened. "Will she like me?" she asked. "Will she make me go away? I don't want to go away, Will."

He tucked her hand into the crook of his arm this time and patted it reassuringly. "She will definitely like you, Mary. She will discover all your wonderful qualities, and she will even love you, just like I love you." And he was sure of that too. Louisa would not hold Mary's infirmities against her. He knew her well enough to be assured that it was not in her nature.

"And she will be Lady Farleigh, and not your mama anymore," Mary said as if making sure she had remembered all her facts correctly.

"That's right. Just like I became Lord Farleigh when my father—"

She shuddered. And no wonder, as the man had barely tolerated Mary over the years, putting up with her presence only because William's mother had promised to keep her out of sight.

"When my father died," he pressed on.

"I'm glad he's gone," she said in a hushed voice. "I hate him. I stayed away from him. But now he is gone, and you are here. I have missed you, Will."

"And I have missed you, my dear Mary. Shall we go find your mother and Mrs. Holly and Grimshaw now?"

"Yes," she said. "And now that you're going to be here, everything will be happy again. Oh, I am so glad you are home! And you are bringing a wife, and she will like me!"

They walked together through the herb garden until they reached the back entrance of the house, and then Mary skipped off, presumably to wash her pots and pans and do the other sundry tasks she'd been assigned by her mother and Mrs. Holly over the years. And William went in search of Mrs. Holly and Grimshaw to inform them of his news.

* * *

The staff gathered in the kitchen, the coziest room of the house, in William's estimation. They sat around the old oak table that had always been there: Mrs. Holly, Grimshaw, Matthew, Samuel, and Mrs. Brill, with William seated at the head. Mary was in the kitchen, too, but was busy scrubbing pots, and John and Sally were elsewhere in the house doing their chores.

Mrs. Brill had made a fresh pot of tea and had set it in the center of the table, along with a plate of scones that had been significantly depleted by the men present before William had even had a chance to speak.

He cleared his throat to get everyone's attention. After they quieted, he began. "I have come here today with important news and to ask for your help," he said. "I am happy to announce—"

"Will is getting married!" Mary cried out, turning abruptly from the sink, pots clattering.

There was an audible gasp around the table, and Mrs. Brill clutched her hands at her chest. Samuel, who already knew, sat back in his chair and grinned.

"That didn't take long," Matthew said.

"Well, don't just sit there," Mrs. Holly added. "Tell us who she is."

"Her name is Lady Louisa Hargreaves, and it goes without saying that she is making a huge sacrifice in marrying me," William said without explaining just *how* huge of a sacrifice it was—or the fact that it hadn't been her preferred course of action. "Lady Louisa is the daughter of the Marquess of Ashworth. I am quite lowly by comparison."

There were more gasps, of a different nature this time.

"You can't bring the daughter of a marquess *here* with the house all bare bones and such!" Mrs. Holly exclaimed. "The upper classes are demanding. There were plenty of house parties here before your time, where we were dealing with impossible demands at all hours of the day and night from your father's lofty guests. How is it to be done?"

"Lady Louisa isn't like that," William replied, hoping to reassure her.

"Food won't be a problem, milord," Mrs. Brill said. "That's something, at least. We been that careful the past years gone by to make preserves and the like. Chickens and plenty of game about too. I still got most of my cookin' tools; yer father didn't put too much stock in my kitchen."

"That's because he was too busy eating while he looked around for things to pawn," Grimshaw said. "Begging your pardon for saying so, milord."

"No pardon needed," William replied wryly. "I know as well as all of you what my father was like. I can only hope you were spared his presence as much as possible after—"

After his mother passed away.

"He had little enough to do with us the past eight years," Mrs. Holly said in a kind voice. "And as you can see, we've survived well enough. What is the lady like, if you don't mind me asking?"

Leave it to Mrs. Holly to take the conversation down a more pleasant path. "I believe you will find Lady Louisa to be kind and unpretentious, despite being of such exalted lineage."

"And?" she asked, looking at him expectantly.

And *what?* He racked his brain. "*And* she's pretty." It had no bearing on the conversation, but it was an answer, albeit Mrs. Holly looked less than satisfied.

The men began to fidget, which cleared things up considerably in William's mind: Mrs. Holly was apparently trying to discern if theirs was a love match. Unfortunately, any answer he gave her in reply would be a disappointment. "And," he continued, "when Lady Louisa arrives here, I want her to feel comfortable in her surroundings, and I don't want Farleigh Manor to put any of us to shame." He shrugged his shoulders. "At least, as much as that is possible. Thank you all, and I beg you will forgive me for asking such an impossible task of you today.

"I am expected back in London tomorrow evening, so we must roll up our sleeves and organize our plan quickly. My father didn't leave us with many options in that regard." Grimshaw muttered something under his breath that William decided to ignore. "And so we will have to be clever and resourceful about it. But if there are any people in England I trust to be clever and resourceful, it is all of you."

"Don't ye worry, Master Will," Mrs. Brill said with confidence. "Now that ye're back at Farleigh Manor, all will be well."

"We'll not let you down, sir," Grimshaw said, standing and straightening up as tall as his old bones would let him. "You can count on us."

William had asked for a miracle from them. He doubted he'd get it, but he was confident he would get everything they had to give, and what man could ask for more? But even knowing he could rely on them to do their best, he wanted to examine the manor in as fine a detail as possible himself. He'd barely glanced at the place when Mr. Heslop had summoned him home after his father's death. If there was anything now that he could see, anything he could suggest to the staff to help make Louisa's initial reaction to Farleigh Manor a positive one—or more importantly, her willingness to stay a reality—he would do all he could in the short amount of time he had to accomplish it.

He decided to begin with the house, so his first stop was the sitting room on the main floor.

As a boy, this room had been filled with elegant furniture. Now there was little of it left. The couch he remembered was still there, its upholstery now faded and frayed. Two chairs sat at right angles to it, creating as much of a conversation spot as possible. There were no tables.

The paper hangings on the walls were faded as well, except for a few scattered rectangles that clearly indicated where paintings had originally hung. There had once been a landscape Gainsborough himself had painted hanging above the fireplace mantel, one his father had won in a game of whist.

The drawing room was in much the same state as the sitting room. The dining room, which had once held an elegant mahogany table with matching chairs, was now completely empty. William suspected that his father, on the rare occasions when he'd deigned to visit, had opted to eat in his study after he'd sold off the lot. The staff undoubtedly ate in the kitchen, as they had done today.

The west wing of the first floor held the portrait gallery and music room. Those two rooms had been designed with large double doors between them so both rooms could be utilized if the family were to hold a concert or a ball. William had never seen a concert or recital of any sort performed at Farleigh Manor, nor had there been a ball here that he could remember. He did recall there being a small pianoforte in the music room at one time. A quick peek showed that it, too, was gone.

The portrait gallery, on the other hand, still displayed William's ancestors, with the exception of his father and mother. A portrait of his mother as a young bride had originally hung in the sitting room opposite the Gainsborough when William was young, a matching portrait of his father next to it. He remembered it, remembered how beautiful his mother had looked in it. When he had returned home from Eton on his first school holiday, he had noticed her portrait had been moved to the gallery. When he'd arrived for his mother's funeral, it had been missing entirely.

His father's portrait had disappeared too. He assumed Grimshaw had removed it and put it in storage; William hadn't bothered to ask. He'd simply been glad it was gone.

The east wing included the viscount and viscountess's bedrooms. William had never been in his father's room. He vaguely remembered a few occasions as a little boy when he'd been allowed into his mother's room. A review of those rooms showed that the furniture was still there, and the bedclothes were still in relatively good condition. His father would have insisted that his room be kept up suitably for his occasional visits. William surmised that his mother's room had been maintained by the staff out of respect. He already knew that his own room had been kept as it was when he'd left for school.

He hadn't really observed anything in his assessment that could be used to improve the appearances of the main rooms of the house, however, and he had but one final place to look, and that was the attic. Perhaps it held secrets that could be put to good use.

The stairs that led to the attic were located at the back of the house. As William trudged up them, he thought he heard a slight scratching sound—faint, almost inaudible, and then it stopped. He paused on the stairs and listened.

"Hello?" he said.

Nothing.

Why he'd said hello, he wasn't sure. He was behaving as if he'd heard a ghost, which was ludicrous. It was likely a mouse the stable-yard cats hadn't bested yet scurrying between the walls. He shook his head at himself and continued up to the attic. He would mention it to Matthew when he saw him. Mrs. Holly hated mice with a passion, and she would want the problem dealt with posthaste.

There was a narrow landing at the top of the stairs with just enough room for an attic door. The door creaked loudly when William opened it. He stepped inside, ducking his head to fit through it, and then found himself having to crouch. The ceiling was low and angled due to the pitch of the room, with a single gable window to his left that allowed in a stream of dusty light. Cobwebs hung from every corner like lacy shrouds, and a layer of dust covered everything—including William now.

He could make out several large items draped in cloth near the back of the attic, along with a box of old toys. A single large trunk stood just inside the door. Next to it were a few paintings stacked vertically together against the wall.

Since the paintings might be put to immediate use and were near the door, he decided to start with them. He squatted and inspected them. The attic wasn't very well lit, but even so, William could understand why these particular paintings had ended up in the attic. None of them stood out as being exceptional, and some were damaged. That being said, if they managed to fill in the empty spots on the walls of the main floor, it might be a marginal improvement.

He then turned his inspection to the trunk. It wasn't locked, so William undid the latches and lifted the lid—and then shut it quickly, placing his forehead on his hands atop the trunk. Tears stung his eyes.

His mother's dress had greeted him.

He'd been struck first by the scent that had filled his nostrils even before he'd realized what he was seeing. Bergamot and jasmine, his mother's signature fragrance. Memories of times seated at her side while she read to him or when she'd hugged him good night came flooding back.

He recognized the dress in the trunk. It was a dark-green silk she'd worn the last Christmas holiday he'd been home, the winter before she'd died. She'd looked pale and thin; her skin had seemed almost translucent. If William had only known it would be the last time he'd see her alive . . .

He eventually got his emotions under control, and only then did he raise his head and reopen the trunk. He doubted he'd find anything that would be useful in it, but he would allow himself this brief moment to indulge.

Under the green silk was a matching cloak made of velvet, lined with satin, and trimmed with fur. William stroked the various fabrics of the cloak, recalling the last time she'd worn it. They'd gone to church, and then his father had mumbled something about "business in Town," and he'd left—not that William had minded his absence. William suspected that even his mother had been relieved.

He and his mother had spent a few quiet days together conversing and taking walks when weather had permitted. He'd pulled out his oils and easel and painted while she'd sat nearby and done needlework. When William had returned to school, she'd appeared stronger. She'd smiled more.

A few months later, she was gone.

He carefully moved the gown and cloak to the side. Underneath them were a few more of her finest dresses, one or two he didn't recognize. He was about to shut the trunk when he spied a bundle at the very bottom wrapped in linen and tied with string. He lifted it out, carefully untying the string and folding back the layers of cloth. "Ah, Mama," he murmured. Within the rather large bundle were his mother's needlework projects. Until this moment in the attic, he'd not even thought about what had happened to them or to the others that had graced Farleigh Manor.

The top piece was a pastoral scene worthy of pride of place on a duke or prince's wall. He traced the details of it with his finger before setting it aside. Underneath it was a pair of woman's kid gloves with delicate flowers embroidered on the cuffs.

There were other items of equal quality: monogrammed handkerchiefs, pillow covers, samplers. He took out a handkerchief that bore an elegant W, held it to his nose briefly, and put it in his pocket.

Eventually, he closed the trunk and left the attic with the bundle, then went in search of Mrs. Holly. He found her taking inventory of the linen closet.

"Mrs. Holly, look what I found in the attic," he said. "Perhaps they can be put to use."

"Good heavens, milord; here, let me help you." She swiftly removed the bundle from his hands, setting it on a nearby chair, and then grabbed a cloth from a shelf in the linen closet. "I'm sorry to say it, but you're a sight," she said and proceeded to brush at his shoulders and arms. "So much dust!"

He nudged her hands away. "Never mind the dust; we can see to my clothing well enough later. But I have found something of value—my mother's needlework. There are some old paintings in the attic as well. If the art itself isn't up to snuff, at least the frames might be put to good use.

"Your mother always did such fine work with a needle," Mrs. Holly said, already taking stock of what William had brought her. "So talented, she was. I remember her sewing this one, in particular." She held up an exquisite rendering of the Madonna and Child. "She began it shortly after you left for Eton. I think it gave her comfort; she was the mother of a beautiful son too." She set the piece aside, brushing her hand over it, and then inspected the next.

"There are gowns of hers in the attic," he said.

"Yes," Mrs. Holly said. "Your father insisted all of her remaining personal effects be put in storage. It didn't stop him from selling off what he could get a price for though, did it?"

"I believe my mother would be pleased if we were to bring her things out of storage now and put them to good use making Farleigh Manor respectable again. If you can find a way to remake her gowns into something useful, you have my permission to do so."

"You're absolutely right—especially if it is her son's home now. I shall see what can be done," she said.

He was placing a huge burden on everyone to take limited resources and restore his home so quickly after so many years of avoidance and neglect on his part. "I'm sorry I wasn't here more often over the years. I should have confronted my father again and made sure Farleigh Manor had the resources it needed to remain prosperous. I should have taken better care of you all."

"You were but a boy then; there wasn't anything you could have done," she said. "We understood this. Your father wasn't the most agreeable of men, if you don't mind my speaking out of turn."

"Not at all." He smiled grimly. "Nonetheless, when I left Oxford, I should have come here, even though Mama was gone and my father spent the majority of his time in London." And even though his father had told him never to return. "I've been remiss, and I'm sorry."

"But you're here now, and things are going to get better," she said resolutely. She carefully stacked each of the pieces of needlework, reminding William of a question he'd meant to ask her. "When did my father begin taking the valuables from Farleigh Manor?"

"Not while your mother was still alive, thank goodness, except for the piano. He said she was too ill to play it and it wasn't doing anyone any good sitting in the music room. Even so, it nearly broke her heart—if he hadn't broken it already, that is." Her mouth set in a stubborn line as if she were tired of apologizing for speaking her mind about William's father. "After she passed away, God rest her soul, one or two items seemed to disappear whenever he visited. He always had a reason—Lord So-and-So had admired the dining table, Lady Such-and-Such had asked about the chairs. It often seemed like the only time he visited was to remove an item or two he could sell. And that knave of a steward slipped an item out here and there too; I'm sure of it."

Ah, yes, the steward who had vanished. He must do something about replacing the man sooner rather than later.

"Tomorrow morning, I will be inspecting the lands," he said. "And then I must return to London. I have a commitment I must keep." He must resume his courtship of Lady Louisa, for that was his top priority. He needed her money, but he also longed for her, heaven help him. He deserved neither.

He couldn't wait to see her again.

* * *

Louisa decided—somewhat late in the day—that she was not going to stay home simply because her betrothed had left London, even if it was only for one evening. She'd sat at home too much already in the past two weeks. Soon enough, she would be married to William and making her home somewhere in Buckinghamshire. Besides, a lady had only one come-out year, and this was hers. She should enjoy it while she could.

Unfortunately, her parents had accepted an invitation to dine with the Duke and Duchess of Atherton this evening and had already left in the carriage, so there could be no assistance from that quarter.

Alex was no help either.

"Sorry, Weezy, but I'm off at any moment to join some friends. In fact, Kit and Phillip should be here at any minute."

Botheration. "Is Anthony going too?" she asked, feeling her hopes drop.

"No, actually. He was invited but wasn't in the mood for an evening out with the rest of us. He thinks he'd rather stay home and read, poor dull chap that he is." Alex shook his head in mock sorrow. "It would do him some good to let loose a bit, but that's Anthony for you. You'd think he intended to become a vicar. Ah, the lads are here."

And Alex was gone.

Anthony was in the library, she was not surprised to discover, seated by the fire, one leg thrown over the arm of the chair, swinging lazily, while he himself was engrossed in whatever he was reading.

"Anthony?" she asked in a low voice so as not to startle him.

"No," he said and turned a page.

"Anthony." Her voice was louder this time since he knew she was there.

"No," he repeated.

She closed the door behind her and crossed the room to sit in the chair opposite his. "Seriously, Anthony, talk to me. Please?"

He closed his book, leaving a finger in it to keep his place, and looked at her with raised eyebrows.

"Mama and Papa and Alex are all out for the evening."

"Yes," he said in a tone that suggested she was stating the obvious, which, clearly, she was. "And?"

"And Lord Farleigh has gone to the country for a day or two."

"What is it you wish, Louisa?" he asked with a sigh.

"I *don't* wish to stay home, Anthony. I wish to put on my loveliest gown and have Tibbetts style my hair. I wish to go to parties and balls and routs and chat with my friends and dance with young gentlemen. I wish to feel the night air as I step out of the carriage, tingling from the excitement the evening holds in store. I wish—"

"You want to do all that *tonight*?" Anthony asked, sounding alarmed.

She wished she were free.

"Of *course* I don't want to do it all tonight," she said, exasperated. "But tonight, I at least have a chance to enjoy the Season, and I don't want to pass on this opportunity to go out and mingle and feel the romance of it all—oh, men simply do not understand!"

He set the book on the small table beside the chair. "Come on," Anthony said, rising to his feet. "We men are not so bacon-brained as all that—especially when a young lady points it out to us. I am at your service for the evening, little sister. Let's go through that exhausting pile of invitations on Mama's desk and see if there is one among them that will suit your fancy."

"Oh, Anthony!" she exclaimed, throwing her arms around him. "Thank you. This means so much to me."

"Apparently." He chuckled. "Which means you will owe me a favor at some future point in time."

"Anything! I promise."

"A huge one."

"Anything, truly!"

"I mean it, Weezy. You are forcing me to go out into the wilderness that is the *ton* and face its predatory creatures—dewy-eyed misses and their eager mamas."

Louisa laughed. It felt good to laugh. It seemed like ages since she had. "Thank you, Anthony. I shall do my best to run interference between you and anyone who attempts to get their claws into you tonight."

"I will hold you to it," he said.

* * *

The only real invitation Louisa could choose for this evening was the one to join Lord and Lady Melton in their box at the theater. It wasn't precisely what Louisa had had in mind; she'd wanted to mingle and dance with her peers, but since William would not be accompanying her, she realized it was in both their interests to keep the gossips at bay. Lord and Lady Melton were dears though, and when Louisa sent off a note asking if the invitation was still available to her and Anthony, the answer that had returned with the footman was a resounding yes.

"I'm so pleased you decided to join us," the countess whispered only a few hours later, when Louisa and Anthony, who arrived after the performance had begun, seated themselves next to the Meltons in their private box. "Always so delightful to have young people about, don't you agree, Melton?"

The earl, who was sitting on the other side of his countess, grunted softly, his attention remaining on the stage, where a line of dancers was pirouetting very prettily.

Louisa and Anthony turned their attention to the stage as well.

"I had thought," Lady Melton whispered behind her fan, "that you might be escorted by young Lord Farleigh, but it is always a treat to have Lord Anthony with us."

"My brother is good company," Louisa said, not wishing to explain William's absence. "Lord Farleigh and I intend to visit Vauxhall Gardens tomorrow evening. I have longed to visit the pleasure garden and am looking forward to it."

Anthony elbowed her and gave her a look that said she was speaking more loudly than she should and was beginning to babble. She shut her mouth and smiled at Lady Melton, then focused on the dancing.

A tenor, whose voice was exceptional, followed the line of dancers. Since he was singing in Italian and Louisa didn't speak Italian, her mind—and her eyes—began to wander.

She looked around the theater, spotting Alex and Kit and Phillip, along with a few other young gentlemen, down in the gallery—undoubtedly only their first stop in a night of revelry that would continue until dawn. Alex and Kit were a lively pair, with Phillip usually dogging along after them. Louisa half suspected Phillip remained with them solely to keep the other two out of mischief—much like Anthony tended to do.

Her eyes moved upward to scan the private boxes, taking in the elegance of all those in attendance. Gentlemen in black evening wear added contrast to the rich colors of the ladies' silk and velvet gowns. She spied Lord and Lady Wilmington, with some of their friends, in their private box. Others of Louisa's acquaintance, including Sir Frederick and Lady Putnam and their eldest two daughters, Harriet and Charlotte, were also here for the performance. Even Baron Moseby . . . She blinked rapidly.

"Goodness, Anthony," she whispered, leaning toward him. "Who is that lady with Baron Moseby in his box?" She was a rather striking woman of middle years, with coal-black hair piled high on her head, wearing a burgundy gown scandalously cut to enhance a rather ample bosom.

Anthony's eyes moved from the gallery, where he'd apparently spotted Alex and the others, and searched the private boxes until he spotted Baron Moseby and his guest. "Never you mind, Weezy," he whispered back.

"Oh . . . I see," she replied.

Lady Melton glanced at them to see if everything was all right, so Louisa smiled at her and returned her attention to the stage. The tenor finished his aria, bowed at the enthusiastic applause he received, and exited. It was intermission.

"I believe I would like to stroll for a bit and stretch my legs," Lady Melton said as she and Lord Melton rose from their seats. "Would either of you care to join Melton and me? Or perhaps you'd rather remain here and take in the sights before you? It is nearly as entertaining to watch the people at the theater as it is the performance itself."

"I believe I shall remain here, but thank you for the offer," Louisa said, still reeling somewhat from the sight of what she assumed was Baron Moseby's mistress. The baron had been attempting to court Louisa not so many days ago. She shuddered at the thought.

After the Meltons left the box, Anthony stood. "I think I shall find Alex and the others," he said. "Since you pried me from my comfortable fireside and book, I may as well see what plans they have for the remainder of the night."

"What about me?" she asked indignantly. "Are you intending to leave me to the Meltons and ask them to take me home afterward? It was kind of them to allow us to attend the theater and join them in their box on such short notice. If you dash off and I must beg their assistance in returning home as well, I shall be utterly mortified."

"Don't worry, Weezy," Anthony replied. "I will see you home safely first, regardless of what follows. I'll be back in a trice."

Louisa was alone in the box.

Alone. It was the complete opposite of how she'd intended to spend the evening.

Feeling more than a bit disgruntled, she leaned forward so her elbow rested on the railing in front of her—*not* a ladylike thing to do, and her mother would be horrified if she were to see her right now—but Louisa didn't particularly care at the moment.

She watched Anthony enter the gallery and join Alex and the others. He gestured up toward the Meltons' box, and Alex and Kit and Phillip and the other young gentlemen all turned as one to look in her direction. Kit and Phillip waved, and Alex, the silly wretch, blew her a kiss.

She rolled her eyes and sat back.

Anthony hadn't intended to go with them, but now he probably would, and Louisa should have expected it. The Osbourne estate bordered Ashworth Park, and they'd all grown up together. Alex and Kit had always been the two who seemed to find trouble wherever they went—and still did, for that matter.

Was William like those two? Was he the type of person trouble seemed to follow? Did he have a mistress like Baron Moseby did? She marveled that the baron had brought the woman to a public place like the theater. Perhaps if Louisa were to look around the theater again, she would be able to discern other gentlemen in attendance with their mistresses. And surely, still other gentleman of the *ton* kept their mistresses a secret.

Such things had never been discussed in Louisa's presence.

But now she was to marry a total stranger, and she realized there were things she didn't know and couldn't understand about men, about marriage, about what to expect. She knew she would not enjoy being married to someone, even of the finest quality, if he were inclined toward such selfish indulgences. William had been right, she realized, when he'd told her she was extremely fortunate her parents' marriage was a loving and faithful one, a fact about which she had no doubt and, until recently, had taken for granted.

There was a soft knock on the door of the box, plucking Louisa from her thoughts. The door opened, and Lord Kerridge entered, closing the door behind him. "Lady Louisa, I hope I'm not intruding," he said.

The night needed only this.

"Lord Kerridge, this is not a good idea," she said, even as she felt all the blood in her body congeal in her stomach.

"I will take only a moment of your time, and then I will leave. You have my assurance of this."

"Very well," she said. She glanced about the theater, at the gallery and the other boxes. Everyone seemed occupied with their own conversations, including her brothers and their friends. Plague Anthony for leaving her alone!

"Lady Louisa," he said once she'd given permission for him to remain. "I have no wish to cause you any more scandal than your current betrothal already has, but I must speak to you."

"Lord Kerridge—"

He held up his hand. "My apologies. That was an ungentlemanly thing for me to say. Allow me to start over: I observed that you are here tonight without your betrothed, and I realized it gave me an opportunity, perhaps a final one, to speak to you and assure myself that you have clearly thought the matter through." The earl slid smoothly into the chair Anthony had been using. He was fitted out in his elegant evening wear, a burgundy waistcoat embroidered with gold thread contrasting with the black of his coat. The light from the theater sent shots of deep red through his chestnut hair. He was a handsome man, and right now, he was looking at her with grave concern, his brows low over his eyes, his mouth—a mouth she had *kissed*—curved downward.

"Lord Kerridge," she repeated—she could no longer call him George—"I am grateful for your concern, truly. But—"

He laid gloved fingers over her lips, stopping her from speaking. "You must hear me out, and then I will go." When he sensed that she would not speak, he removed his fingers and continued. "Your Viscount Farleigh has been absent from London and its society for several years. I can find few people who know him, *really* know him. In my estimation, it seems he has few acquaintances and even fewer friends. He is an utter unknown—except for the reputation of his pater, who was a walking scandal, as you well know. How do you know his son is not like him? I cannot imagine you in a match with such a man."

"Lord Kerridge, you must cease speaking to me in such a way," she said, trembling.

"Please, allow me to finish," he said, drawing closer. "I have never, nor will I ever, offer marriage lightly to anyone. I have current and future responsibilities to consider and will marry only a lady I feel worthy to be a duchess—to be *my* duchess when the time arrives. You are the daughter of a marquess, your upbringing has been impeccable, and that makes you worthy. And so I ask you to end this sham of a betrothal, which is based solely upon other men's follies. Marry me. I offer it to you once again."

She gasped and fought to regain her composure. "You honor me, sir, but I *cannot*," she said.

"Hush," he said. He took her hand in his. "There is no need to answer me tonight. I only ask that you consider what I am saying and understand that there is another path you may take, another offer of marriage that is open to you. I admit I was angry when you broke our betrothal—"

"Oh—"

"But," he interjected, "I have had the past week or so to think about what happened, and I am no longer angry—and even commend you for your courage and your willingness to do what you believe to be honorable. I forgive you. Tonight, the opportunity arose for me to have this private moment with you and to urge you toward caution and let you know that you have another choice. Cease this foolishness, Lady Louisa. The *ton* will soon forget you had this lapse in judgment."

"What of Miss Hughes?" Louisa managed to ask.

He smiled. "Were you jealous, then? Miss Hughes is a delightful young lady, and I have enjoyed getting to know her. But regardless of her fine qualities, she is hardly suitable to be the wife of a future duke." He turned serious again. "Very few young ladies are, you know. You are the rare exception."

There was a noise outside the door, and he quickly arose, just before Lord and Lady Melton entered the box. "Good evening, Lady Melton, Lord Melton," Lord Kerridge greeted them. He looked once again at Louisa. "Think on what I said." He bowed to them and left.

Oh, Lord Kerridge should not have come into the box to speak to her. He should *not*. But she had given him permission. She had felt an obligation to listen to him and hear him out. He'd had time to think about things, he'd said. Louisa knew what it was like to be confronted with unexpected news—news that changed the course of one's life. She knew it took time to sort through thoughts and feelings and come to some sort of conclusion. She had owed it to him.

She had not expected to hear what he'd said, however. And he had not allowed her to reply; he had left the offer open, unresolved. And he had forgiven her, he'd said, for her "lapse in judgment."

She drew in a few breaths to steady herself. The normal Louisa would be pacing the corridors of the theater and wringing her hands and undoubtedly chattering unceasingly and nonsensically to whoever was nearby. But tonight, she was a guest of the Meltons, and she wouldn't, for the world, do or say anything to distress them—or to divulge what Lord Kerridge had said.

She heard and saw nothing during the second half of the performance, so focused she was at keeping her emotions hidden from the others. Much like William always did.

What an illuminating thought.

Chapter 9

WILLIAM SPENT THE MORNING VISITING the tenant farms, accompanied by Matthew, whom he subsequently saw in a different light—with the eyes of a nobleman who had responsibilities and not as a boy looking for a father figure.

Matthew must have been but a young man when he began working at Farleigh Manor, for he appeared to be only of middle years now, not at all like Grimshaw, who looked as old as Methuselah and always had. Matthew was strong and capable, and William had always known him to be trustworthy. Today, he discovered that Matthew had been essentially acting as steward, as there had been no one else to take on the task once the prior steward had absconded. Unbeknownst to William, Matthew had received a fairly decent education as a youth—he could read and write and add columns of numbers with impressive competence, and he also had a keen eye and creative mind when it came to the estate and what was needed to make it prosperous once again. He also knew all the tenants well—those who had remained—and had a good working relationship with them.

William had no difficulty offering the job to him. "Sadly, Matthew, I cannot dismiss you from your responsibilities as groundskeeper just yet," he said when they completed their tour. "I am asking you to do both for the time being, and for the same pay you currently receive, which I presume has been next to nothing for the past while. But I believe that between the two of us—with help from Samuel and the others—we can, over time, return Farleigh Manor to a state of respectability, at the very least."

Matthew shook William's hand and agreed with enthusiasm to the pathetic offer he'd been given. It was a great relief. Then William said goodbye to everyone and left Farleigh Manor for London, knowing there was someone in charge of the estate while he was gone, someone he trusted to see to its best interests and those of the people there.

It had been a busy and instructive morning, and William had arisen early to make sure he had time to assess everything. He should be tired, especially as he had a long ride back to London, but the glimpses of hope he'd had at Farleigh Manor had given him a sense of optimism and a renewed sense of energy.

Were it not for the mortgages on the property, Farleigh Manor could be thriving, albeit modestly, within four or five years.

Were it not for the mortgages, he could—and would—release Louisa from the vowel. He was not mercenary by nature. He had no driving need to be vastly wealthy, well connected, or highly esteemed by his peers beyond being recognized as a decent and honorable man—the opposite of what his father had been. He'd been happy enough in Edinburgh, where he had been able to sit at the feet of some of the greatest minds in both Scotland and England and hear and even discuss their ideas on engineering, economy, medicine, law, and the like. But life could not be as it had been. There was no going back.

William liked to think that even as a penniless, unknown viscount, he could have endured the Season and the London marriage mart and found a bride, perhaps even in short order. It would have been possible, even probable. Under normal circumstances, he would never have considered forcing a young lady into marriage against her will.

But any other young lady would not have been Louisa.

He had told her he would escort her to Vauxhall this evening, and he intended to keep his word. He was finding himself drawn to her more and more, to her openness of speech and expression. It beguiled him, and yet he was also uneasy about it. Sharing so much of one's self was a prelude to disappointment and betrayal and hurt, in his experience. And yet it seemed he couldn't resist the pull of it, or her either. He reminded himself again that he had not forced Louisa into this betrothal. He had given her a choice.

If only he could believe what he was telling himself.

He arrived back in London with the barest amount of time to wash and dress before taking a hackney to Ashworth House. The Marquess of Ashworth had offered his carriage since he and the marchioness were to accompany them as chaperones. William took a deep breath as he approached the front door and then stopped on the threshold to straighten his clothing and smooth his demeanor before rapping the knocker on the door. The butler greeted him formally and showed him to the sitting room, where the others were already awaiting his arrival.

"Ah, you're here," the marquess said, rising to his feet and shaking William's hand. "When Louisa told us of your quick trip to Buckinghamshire, I wasn't sure you'd arrive back in time."

"I wouldn't have missed it," William replied. He turned to the ladies. "A pleasure to see you again, Lady Ashworth, Louisa."

Both ladies returned his greeting, but he immediately sensed that something was off in Louisa's demeanor, that she seemed subdued despite smiling when she'd greeted him. What could have caused it? He'd been gone only a day, and they had parted on excellent terms, if her response to his kiss had been any indication. Her request that he be more forthcoming with her had been agreeably made, and he had promised he would be—as much as he dared, he'd silently added to himself. Had she regretted the kiss, then? He hoped not; he wanted to kiss her again.

Within a few minutes, they were all in the carriage and on their way to Vauxhall. Conversation was polite and dealt mostly with the weather, which had been unusually fine and was this evening as well. Lord Ashworth asked him about Buckinghamshire in general terms. They eventually arrived at their destination, yet it seemed to William that the carriage ride must have surely taken longer than his ride into London this afternoon, so impatient was he to spend time alone with Louisa.

She had said nothing during the entire journey.

"Have you been to Vauxhall Gardens before?" he asked her while he assisted her from the carriage.

"No, and I am excited to be here. I've heard such fascinating stories," she said distractedly. She seemed anything but excited, from William's point of view—at least not in the way he typically expected her to be.

It was full dark by the time they arrived, and the hundreds of lamps that hung in the trees and elsewhere—and that Vauxhall was famous for—spilled their light, creating a fantasy world of illumination and shadow. William took in the surroundings. The faintest of orchestral melodies occasionally broke through the murmur of the guests. The trees and flowers gave up their earthy scents and mingled with the perfumes of London's elite.

"Oh my," Louisa exclaimed as she looked about her. "It is even better than I could have imagined."

Perhaps the atmosphere of the gardens would restore her to her usual self, William thought hopefully. Perhaps he'd only been imagining things. One did not have to be effusive every minute of the day and night, after all, and certainly Louisa was no exception.

They walked onward, down the tree-lined avenue toward the orchestra building. The marquess and marchioness had gone on ahead of them, greeting friends and peers, and were soon lost in the crowds of people who had come to take in the amusements the garden had to offer. They had arranged to meet in an hour's time at the supper box the marquess had reserved.

William recognized very few people, only those he'd met since returning after his father's death. Louisa walked beside him, her hand tucked into the crook of his arm, and introduced him to her acquaintances as they passed. He doubted he would remember any of their names, but then, he doubted Louisa would be able to call any of them to mind if he asked her, so detached she seemed from the conversations taking place around her.

She was most certainly not herself. There was no use pretending. He needed to discover what had upset her.

They continued on down the grand avenue and into the heart of Vauxhall Gardens.

* * *

Louisa relied upon years of training to smile and converse and introduce William to her acquaintances as they strolled toward the orchestra building. She could barely put names to faces or even recall what anyone—including herself—had said.

She'd hardly slept a wink last night after Lord Kerridge had spoken to her at the theater. She had gone through the conversation so many times during the night that she knew it by heart and could recall every expression on Lord Kerridge's face. She was exhausted—and not merely from lack of sleep. Her entire being felt at war with itself, a myriad questions demanding answers until her head throbbed.

"He is an utter unknown—except for the reputation of his pater, who was a walking scandal, as you well know. End this sham of a betrothal, which is based solely upon other men's follies. Marry me."

He'd told her Society would forget her "lapse in judgment" and that he'd forgiven her. *Forgiven* her. Forgiven *her.*

Why was it that men could bring their mistresses to the theater and duel and feel obligated to fulfill their debts of honor, and yet, when *she* had chosen the honorable thing, she'd apparently had a "lapse in judgment"? When *she'd* felt compelled by honor to fulfill the terms of the vowel, *she* was the one who needed forgiveness?

Her entire body fairly vibrated from the pressure building inside her. "Louisa!"

She and William both turned in unison to see who had called her name. It was Alex, which was a total surprise, as he'd not indicated he would be at Vauxhall this evening—and he was not alone. Lady Elizabeth Spaulding, the daughter of the Duke and Duchess of Marwood, was on his arm.

"Look who has been released from the schoolroom to enjoy an evening in company for a change, Weezy," Alex drawled.

"Elizabeth!" Louisa exclaimed as they embraced. Elizabeth was but fifteen years of age, but Louisa had met her on several occasions.

"I could not believe it," Elizabeth said excitedly, "when Papa *himself* said I was invited to join Lord Halford and your parents this evening! He knew you were all to be here and said it would be a good opportunity for me to further my acquaintance with Lord Halford. Under strict chaperonage, of course." She turned her head, and Louisa's gaze followed hers to the girl's parents not far away, watching them closely.

"The strictest of chaperones, I daresay," Alex said with a complaisant shrug of his shoulders, obviously not worried at all. "Lizzie, allow me to present Louisa's betrothed, Viscount Farleigh. Farleigh, this is Lady Elizabeth Spaulding, daughter of the Duke and Duchess of Marwood—who has not yet made her come-out." Elizabeth looked up at him with sparkling eyes.

"An honor, Lady Elizabeth," William said, extending a gracious bow to her.

Alex's eyes flickered in the direction of his parents. "And it seems we are being summoned, Lizzie; duty calls. A supper of thinly sliced ham awaits." He sighed dramatically. "It is a good thing I ate a hearty supper before coming here. I hope you all did the same." They strolled off to join the duke and duchess.

"I take it theirs is an arranged marriage," William murmured.

"Yes," Louisa said. "The Duke of Marwood has been promoting the match since they were born." Seeing Lady Elizabeth reminded Louisa of their similar and yet very different circumstances. At least she and Alex had been given time to accustom themselves to the idea, and an affection of sorts had grown between them, unlike her own present situation.

"*Thinly* sliced ham?" William asked her, looking comically as if he'd just received a death sentence.

"Apparently so. I suspect Alex will be returning Lady Elizabeth home early, which would be why they're eating now. May we walk and take in more of the sights?" she asked.

"Certainly," he replied. "I must build up my appetite for the thinly sliced ham."

She puffed out a breath at his little joke. She really wasn't in the mood for light humor.

William led her away to stroll down a less crowded path near a wooded area of Vauxhall. Louisa had heard these wooded areas were designed for couples seeking privacy—and from what she could now see, they could do it quite successfully. She suspected many gentlemen had traipsed these wooded areas with ladies over the years.

She wouldn't think about it.

She didn't want to think about any of it.

"What's troubling you, Louisa?" William asked her. "All seemed well enough between us when I left you yesterday. I thought we had reached an understanding."

Louisa looked about. They were out of earshot of anyone, but probably for the first time in her life, she was unwilling to open her mouth. She was afraid that if she spoke, a Pandora's box of hurt and resentment and angry questions would be released and would never be contained again. "Nothing is troubling me," she lied. "I don't know where you got such an absurd notion."

* * *

Something had definitely upset Louisa since he'd left her yesterday. She was behaving wholly out of character.

On impulse, he grabbed her hand and pulled her none too gently toward a path that led into one of the denser wooded areas.

"People are watching," she said, trying to pull her hand from his grasp.

"Then don't struggle. You'll only draw more attention to us."

"I'm not struggling!"

"Yes, you are."

She stopped trying to yank her hand free, and he led her into the trees with as much decorum as he could. The narrow path twisted and turned, and soon they were well away from anyone—and possibly lost. William did not care.

He turned her to face him. "Talk," he said.

"There's nothing to say," she replied.

"With you, there is always something to say."

That was all the prompting she needed. "How dare you!" she hissed, slapping him hard across the face. "This is nothing to you, is it? You have your bride and her dowry. You have everything you bargained for, with no consideration for my feelings at all. And then you have the temerity to insult me as well, at the worst possible moment. I hate you! I hate you both! I hate you all!"

This was better, he thought as he rubbed his stinging cheek. Punishment for his crime. He clasped her upper arms and held her firmly, thwarting her attempts to wriggle free. "Keep talking," he said, though her words would be painful to hear.

She glared at him with those magnificent blue eyes of hers. He needn't have urged her to speak, because now that she'd begun, the words tumbled from her unbidden. "You want me to keep talking? Very well. You have your wish, *my lord*, and I despise you for it. You came into my life waving an old piece of paper claiming a debt is owed because two loathsome *gentlemen*"—she spat the word—"had the stupidity or the conceit not to realize that whatever they placed in writing might possibly have a bearing on someone other than their wretched selves. If my grandfather were alive, I would spit in his face.

"But let us leave the dead out of this for the moment. They have gone to their Maker, and He will hold them accountable for their actions since I cannot. And now there are two other *gentlemen* whose sole purpose in pursuing me is for their own selfish interests. Not for love. Not because they have any consideration for me as a person. There is not much difference between them and the first two, is there?"

William felt her accusations like deep cuts from a blade, his throat tight with emotion. Never had the word *gentlemen* held so much condemnation. He ran his hands up and down her arms, trying to soothe her.

She shook herself free of his touch. "I am also trying to understand who you are in an attempt to understand my future, but you tell me nothing!" she cried. "You wear a mask so fixed I cannot tell if you are happy or angry or bored or amused. I could list what I know about you on the fingers of one hand."

"Louisa—"

"No!" she cried. She held up one of her hands, her fingers clenched. "Watch and see. One"—she held up her first finger—"both of your parents are deceased, and your father's death made you viscount. That is two things"—she held up her second finger—"so I will count them as two, just to be generous. Three"—a third finger joined the other two—"your father left you in poverty, and I would wager—ha, wager, indeed." She chuckled humorlessly at her irony. "I would *wager* that you are also *deeply* in debt through his actions. Four, as a result, you have but one item of any value, and it is of *great* value, at least to me, for what is more valuable than a human life? For that item is the vowel that holds me—my very *person*—wholly accountable for my grandfather's sins. Lastly—"

"Enough, Louisa, please," William said, feeling as if his soul was being torn asunder. He'd wanted her to speak, had urged her to, but he could no longer bear to hear the pain he had caused her. "You have made your point."

"Lastly," she continued, ignoring him. "You are counting on my father's love for his only daughter to see you clear of your debts and obligations through the financial benefits marriage to her—to *me*—will bring you."

"Louisa, stop," William said, again taking her by both shoulders, more firmly this time. Her eyes were large, and her cheeks were streaked with tears, but she looked back at him with fire and defiance. His entire body ached from the strain of hearing her words, words he'd repeated to himself over and over again since that fateful day when Heslop had shown him the vowel. He longed to assure her that she could trust him, that he would do anything for her.

He opened his mouth to speak, but he couldn't do it. His father's words were a never-ending drumbeat in his mind: *Stop crying. You're supposed to be a man. Act like one . . .*

"I am a fool," she said in a dull voice. "There was never the hope of love for me, was there? Not with you, certainly. And the Earl of Kerridge has once again asked me to marry him. I am one of very few ladies who meet the high standards of the future Duke of Aylesham, you see, and have been *forgiven* for my flawed judgment in thinking that I—a mere *female*—should act with honor. I have only ever been a means to an end when it comes to men and marriage—merely a source of income or the breeder of heirs. What a glorious future I have."

The bleakness of her words left William cold and hollow, the lump in his stomach a great dead weight. He had brought this terrible injustice upon her. And the knowledge that Kerridge had proposed to Louisa once again—after having the temerity to forgive her for acting honorably—made him want to do violence to the man. He drew her close and wrapped his arms about her, giving her what comfort she would take from him. Thankfully, she came without resistance.

"There," he whispered in her ear. "You will feel better now that you've shared this, Louisa. You are a verbal creature. Words are your friends, as they are not mine. Be at peace."

He kept his arms around her, simply holding her, until at last he felt the tension begin to ease from her body. He kissed her on the cheek and then handed her his handkerchief while keeping his other arm around her.

She dried her eyes and blew her nose. "I must look a sight."

"You look as beautiful as ever; trust me," he assured her. "No one will be the wiser."

She looked up at him with skepticism and then heaved a sigh. "Well, at least it's dark. I shall simply avoid getting too close to any of the lanterns for the remainder of the evening."

"No one will suspect a thing."

She tried to hand him his handkerchief.

"No, you may keep it."

They remained silent for several minutes while he held her close, reluctant to let her go, desirous to ask her more about Kerridge without upsetting her further. "Louisa," he eventually said with the gentlest of tones. "Will you tell me about your encounter with Lord Kerridge? The conversation was clearly upsetting to you."

"There is not much to tell. Anthony and I joined the Meltons at the theater last evening, and Lord Kerridge came to their box during intermission when I was alone. He said no one knows anything about you beyond the reputation of your father and that I should act with caution, that everyone would eventually forget my 'lapse in judgment,' as he called it, and that his offer of marriage still stands."

The dead weight in William's stomach turned into a mass of strangled knots, and he could hear his father's voice taunting him now. *He's raised the ante, boy. He's called your bluff.*

William drew in a slow breath before speaking. "I promised you before I left for Buckinghamshire that I would answer your questions. And I shall. But it is time to return to your parents now, or they will become concerned— if, that is, you are ready to join them."

Her gaze dropped to the ground at her feet. "I'm fine."

"Are you?" He would not, for the world, make her face the crowds of Vauxhall until she was ready.

She took several even breaths before lifting her face to his, looking to him as if she'd successfully mastered her emotions. "Truly, I'm fine now, thank you. Besides, they might send my brother out looking for us, and I would hate that above all things."

William nodded. Perhaps the worst of it was over. Perhaps he had mitigated the damage Kerridge had caused, blast the arrogant man, although he doubted it. He took her hand in his—no struggling this time, thank goodness—and led her out of the dark wood and back to the lights of Vauxhall and genteel society.

Oh, and to a plate of thinly sliced ham. Considering the state of his stomach, it would surely be more than enough.

Chapter 10

WILLIAM AWOKE THE FOLLOWING MORNING feeling a bit unsure. Today, he was going to have to speak openly about his past with Louisa.

On their way to the supper box, where Louisa's parents, brother, the duke and dutchess, and Lady Elizabeth had, indeed, been awaiting their return—some more anxiously than others, he'd noted when he'd glanced at Louisa's parents—he had promised her again that he would call upon her the following afternoon. They had agreed that they would spend the time in the garden of Ashworth House, weather permitting, and she could ask him any question she wished about him.

William would answer her questions as candidly as possible. He wasn't sure, however, that their individual definitions of *candid* were in total accord, and he wouldn't know until the matter was put to the test.

He had nearly completed his morning toilet when there was a knock at the door. He wiped the lather from his face and went to investigate.

"Lord Farleigh," the rusty voice of Mrs. Gideon called after knocking again. "There's a man here to see you. Says his name is Wilcox and he was sent here by a Mr. Heslop. He's got a letter for you and refuses to leave until he's delivered it personally to you."

What could Heslop possibly want that would require personal delivery of this sort? "Thank you, Mrs. Gideon," William said after unlocking and opening the door to thank her face-to-face. "Tell him I'll join him presently."

He pulled a shirt on over his head and tucked it into his pantaloons and then tugged on his boots, buttoning his waistcoat on his way down the stairs to the sitting room just off the main entrance. He doubted Wilcox, who was one of Heslop's clerks, would care whether he was properly dressed or not.

Wilcox jumped to his feet the moment William entered the room. "Good morning, your lordship," the man said, bowing deferentially to William before producing a sealed letter and handing it to him. "Apologies for the early hour, but it couldn't be helped, I'm afraid. The matter is urgent, and Mr. Heslop was most insistent that you receive this and respond to it as soon as possible."

William broke the seal on the missive and read it. He read it again, his head beginning to throb. He rubbed his forehead and pinched the bridge of his nose between his thumb and forefinger. "I should have suspected something like this," he muttered to himself. "I assume you arrived in a hackney, Mr. Wilcox?"

"Yes, your lordship. It's waiting outside."

"I need but a few minutes to make myself more presentable, and then I shall be accompanying you back to Mr. Heslop's office."

"Mr. Heslop said to expect that would be the case."

William returned to his room, taking the stairs two at a time. He tied his neckcloth into the quickest, most basic knot he could and grabbed his coat and hat. Thank goodness he'd finished shaving before Wilcox arrived.

Wilcox gave the driver directions and urged him to make haste. When they arrived at the solicitor's office, Wilcox paid the driver while William rushed inside. He felt a wreck.

"I'll let Mr. Heslop know you've arrived, your lordship," his other clerk, Jamison, said, rising to his feet from behind his desk. The clerk stepped into the next office, and William could hear murmuring beyond the door, albeit he was unable to tell how many people besides Heslop were in the other room or what they were saying. He removed his hat and ran his hand over his hair. *Always keep a cool head, boy. Keep your thoughts to yourself.* Ironic that his father's words were the ones that once again came to mind in a crisis since the infernal man had created all the crises William had been dealing with.

Fathers left their mark on their children, for good or for ill.

Heslop left his office and came forward to shake William's hand. "Is it true?" William asked him, unable to even greet the man properly first.

"It appears so, yes," Heslop replied. "This all comes as quite a shock, to be honest. There was nothing I could find in your father's papers to indicate he'd . . . done this. But it's a bit more complicated than even that, I'm afraid."

"What do you mean?" William asked, not really wanting to hear the answer.

"It's best you see for yourself."

Heslop opened the door to his office and stood back so William could precede him inside.

William closed his eyes briefly, braced himself for what he would see, and then opened his eyes and entered the office.

There, seated facing Heslop's desk, was a slender, brown-haired woman who appeared to be not many years older than William. She turned at the sound of the door.

And William instantly understood what the additional complications Heslop had mentioned were—for a little girl sat on her lap, and a young boy a few years older than the girl sat stiffly in the chair next to her.

"Lord Farleigh," Heslop said. "Allow me to introduce the dowager Lady Farleigh and her two children, Peter and Daisy Barlow."

"Except I never was Lady Farleigh, was I?" the woman said in an evenly modulated tone. "I was only ever Mrs. Barlow, and now I'm not even that."

Heslop shot a somber look at William. "Miss Jane Purnell, then," he said softly. "Miss Purnell, this is William Barlow, Junior, Viscount Farleigh. Your husband's son by his first wife."

William's vile, accursed, selfish father—oh, there were not enough unsavory words in all the English language to describe the man—had married another woman, but the woman's words added a dreadful layer of foreboding to Heslop's letter.

William watched the boy and girl closely. The boy, Peter, sitting as stiffly as ever, glowered at William. He was brown-haired like his mother and looked to be nearly the age William had been when he'd been sent off to Eton. The little girl had large, dark eyes and curls the same yellow color as William's own when he'd been a lad. On the little girl, it looked like spun gold. She was chewing her lower lip and watching William closely. He doubted she knew what was going on around her beyond sensing that it was serious.

The letter Heslop had sent had informed him that his father had taken a second wife and that it had created unforeseen complications that needed immediate attention. William had been an only child, however, so it hadn't dawned on him in the slightest that those "complications" would be a half brother and half sister. For that was what they were: his siblings.

Good heavens.

"Perhaps this is a conversation better had without the children present," William suggested in a low voice, his lips barely moving.

"No!" the boy, Peter, exclaimed. "I'm not leaving Mama. And Daisy isn't either, are you, Daisy?"

"Mama," the little girl said, burrowing deeper into her mother's lap.

"We can speak in front of the children, Lord Farleigh," Miss Purnell said. "They are generally aware of the situation in which we find ourselves. I doubt the details will be any more stressing than the generalities already are. And I would prefer to keep them by my side."

"It might be possible to find a suitable person to tend your children while we discuss matters best suited to adults, however," William said in what he hoped was a gentle tone. He was still trying to gather what remained of his wits and maintain a smooth facade. "I doubt the conversation will be of interest to them."

"I am keeping my children with me nonetheless," she said firmly. She was an attractive woman, which shouldn't have surprised him, considering the singular taste for fine things his father had always had. It certainly applied to his choice of women.

Heslop looked at William and gave a subtle shrug. "Very well," the solicitor said. He scooped up the folder of documents on his desk and handed it to William. "These are the papers she brought to me yesterday, including a few I have added since then."

William rested his hip against the corner of the desk and perused the documents one by one before looking up. "It says here that your marriage to my . . . to the former Viscount Farleigh, was on—"

"Christmas Eve 1796. That is correct, milord."

"But that's—"

"Before the first Mrs. Barlow, Lady Farleigh, was deceased. Yes, I know that now. I did not know it at the time and only discovered the truth of it yesterday when we came to talk to Mr. Heslop; he has been very kind in explaining the particulars to me. My marriage is null and void, I have come to understand, and my children, therefore, are illegitimate."

Confound his father! He'd betrayed William's mother in the most heinous of ways, but he'd used this woman just as badly. The guilt and shame William felt over the actions of his father fell on him like a heavy mantle that threatened to suffocate him.

Peter—William's *half brother*, for heaven's sake!—obviously knew what the word *illegitimate* meant, if the scowl on his face was any indication. "I hate him," the boy muttered.

"Allow me to summarize, your lordship," Heslop said. "Your father married Miss Purnell under false pretenses—"

"He told me he was a widower," Miss Purnell added. "That he was Mister William Barlow. I never even knew he was a viscount."

Heslop nodded in acknowledgment and then continued. "As he was at Farleigh House in London rather than with Miss Purnell when he died, the servants there had his remains escorted to Buckinghamshire for burial in the family cemetery at Farleigh Manor, leaving Miss Purnell none the wiser."

"He was often away, sometimes for several weeks at a time," Miss Purnell added. "He had responsibilities, he said, though he never talked about them, and I stopped asking. I didn't know anything was wrong until a man showed up asking me for the mortgage money; he said back money was owed as well." She blinked back tears, and William couldn't help but feel compassion for her. He'd watched his own mother struggle with his father over similar things when William was no more than Peter's age now, and things had only gotten worse over time. "William always told me the house was mine," she added. "That he'd bought it for me and Peter and Daisy. I thought it was all paid for." She fumbled in her reticule for a handkerchief and dabbed at her eyes and nose, then she straightened her back and lifted her chin. "I'm sorry, Mr. Heslop. Please continue with your explanation."

"Miss Purnell discovered my name and direction amongst the viscount's belongings. She arrived here yesterday with questions."

"Ah," was all William could think to say.

"I didn't become worried about him—he'd been gone only a few weeks, you see—when your betrothal announcement was printed in the papers," Miss Purnell said. "It listed your name, William Barlow. Just like his name. It was such a coincidence, and I couldn't ignore it. It got me wondering . . . He would never speak about his past, you see. I should have persisted in asking, I see that now, but I never did. He was older than me, so very imperious . . ." She looked down at her children. "Well, it doesn't matter, because eventually, he spent little time with us. And then when the man, the landlord, I suppose he was, showed up, demanding money . . ."

Heslop took up the rest of the story when she faltered. "Sadly, I provided her with the answers she needed but did not expect," he said. "I thought you had better be a participant in our conversations."

"What of your own family, Miss Purnell?" William asked.

"I have no family. I met William when I was a governess, but those days are long behind me. He was an acquaintance of my employer; at least he attended a house party my employer hosted. That was when we met." She dabbed at her eyes again. "I didn't know he was dead," she whispered. She patted her daughter's curls and held her close; still, William suspected she was mostly comforting herself. The little girl had lost interest in the adult conversation around her and had fallen asleep on her mother's lap.

"Will you excuse Lord Farleigh and me, Miss Purnell?" Heslop asked her. "Perhaps you could use a few minutes alone."

"Yes, thank you."

He and William left the office and moved slightly away from the closed door. Wilcox and Jamison were busy at work, dutifully minding their own business. Heslop had trained his employees well.

"I have informed Miss Purnell that even if the legitimacy of the marriage had been proven sound, there wouldn't be any inheritance—that you are the rightful heir. I also mentioned the debts. She's a bright woman, milord; she understands that she has been left with no home, no source of income, and two children to support in addition to herself—all while discovering that her marriage was a sham and that her illegitimate husband died without her knowledge. It'd be quite a blow for anyone, poor woman."

"She's well-educated, which accounts for her former position as a governess. She's fought out of dire straits before this, I imagine," William said. "The lady has a great deal of poise. I must think. Blast it all; her children are my blood relatives. I cannot in good conscience abandon them."

He already knew what he must do, may his cursed father rot in Hades for all eternity. "Do you have a paper and ink I may use?" he asked Heslop. "I'm afraid I have a letter to write to my betrothed, informing her I will not be seeing her this afternoon after all. And then I will be escorting Miss Purnell and her children to Farleigh Manor. God help me."

How he was to explain any of this to Louisa, he had no idea. He'd promised her an afternoon dedicated to candid answers to all her questions. Now he would not only be canceling their afternoon plans, but he would also be dashing off to Buckinghamshire once again—this time with a secret he felt unable to share regardless of his promise of honesty to her. For it was Miss Purnell's secret to tell, not William's, and the poor woman needed time to sort out her life and settle her children into a safe home before concerning herself with the scandal and humiliation brought upon her by her bigamous fraud of a husband.

William's father.

He loathed even acknowledging the familial connection to the man.

He would find a way to be back for the second reading of the banns. He would find the words to reassure Louisa that his travel to Buckinghamshire—for the *second* time in less than a week—was reasonable and necessary and not suspicious in the least. Without telling her the reason for it, no less.

He doubted she would believe him. *Of course* she wouldn't believe him—it was ludicrous to think otherwise. Oh, but he should take her in his arms and explain what a bad choice of a husband he was. He came with a family and a past that would be unfair to any young lady but particularly to Lady Louisa Hargreaves, who could have any suitor she chose and, in fact, still had an offer from one of the most eligible and high-ranking gentlemen in England. She was open and artless and loving. One only had to witness her interactions with her brothers or see her face light up when chatting with friends to know this. William was drawn to that light like a moth to flame. He longed for her warmth and brightness.

He dashed off a note, explaining that once again he'd been summoned to Buckinghamshire. He apologized, assuring her he would be at the church for the banns on Sunday, and vowed that he would dedicate his time upon his return to answering all her questions. They would get better acquainted, he promised. He would allay her worries. He wanted to know her better just as she claimed she wanted to know him.

It sounded like drivel, but it was the best he could do on short notice, especially with his mind scrambling to come up with a solution for these people—including *children*, for heaven's sake. With Wilcox's assurances that he would deliver the note directly into Lady Louisa's hands, William rejoined Heslop and Miss Purnell.

* * *

Louisa had been struggling ever since Lord Kerridge had approached her at the theater night before last. At the time, she'd been taken aback by his remarks about her decision, and then she had been embarrassed by them. That embarrassment had turned to bitterness that had manifested itself in angry words flung at William, who had caused all of this to occur. Her words to him had not been ladylike at all, and her mother would have taken her to task over her lack of propriety if she'd been present, despite the unique circumstances involved.

Oh, but it had felt *good* to say those words.

She woke up the following morning and decided to stay in bed for a few minutes, propping herself up with pillows. She wanted time alone to think before her day began. It had dawned on her at some point that despite her lashing out at William at Vauxhall, he had been solicitous and understanding. He'd urged her to speak her mind. No one had ever really done that for her before. Her brothers tended to tease her about her excessive wordiness—never out of meanness, certainly, even if it had occasionally stung. But William had understood her innate need to express herself, and he had comforted her and held her in his arms until she'd regained her composure, even though most of her vitriol had been directed at him.

Unlike herself, however, William was not an open book. He always replied to her questions with the fewest words possible. He rarely even smiled—in point of fact, he gave away little by way of expression. But yesterday, Louisa had learned that he was kind. Considering his unwillingness to free her from the vowel, the discovery had surprised her.

The man was a paradox.

"Oh, good, milady, you're awake now," Tibbetts said, peeking through the doorway. "Here's your chocolate and toast." She set the tray on the table next to Louisa's bed and poured her a steaming cup. Louisa took it gratefully from her and breathed in its aroma before taking a careful sip. "Mm, thank you, Tibbetts."

"We've finally got us some English weather for once." She went back into Louisa's dressing room and brought out one of Louisa's favorites, a pale-blue muslin dress and a matching shawl. "It's cloudy and threatening rain."

"Rain? Are my brothers still at home?" Louisa asked, taking a bite of toast. If they were here, they'd be calling her Lady Cumulus again, regardless of the different dress, and accusing her of causing the rainy weather. "So far, we've had a London spring filled with very un-English blue skies." She took another nibble of toast.

"That's to be sure, milady. Oh, I nearly forgot. You need to dress quickly, as there's a gentleman downstairs says he won't leave until he's delivered a letter into your very hands. He wouldn't give it to Gibbs, and he wouldn't give it to me either, even after I told him I was your personal maid. I told him you were asleep and I had no intention of waking you, and he said he'd wait until you did."

"Who is it, Tibbetts? Did the man give his name?" She was sure the staff would recognize William and Lord Kerridge both. It was odd that the man insisted on staying to deliver the letter only to her. She set her cup aside and got out of bed, allowing Tibbetts to assist her in removing her nightgown and stepping into the dress.

"It's a Mr. Wilcox," Tibbetts said as she buttoned up the back of Louisa's bodice. "That's all he said: Mr. Wilcox, and that he'd come to personally deliver a letter to you and wasn't leaving until he put it directly into your hands. Gibbs put him in the small parlor, he was that annoyed."

"Hmm," Louisa remarked. "I've never heard of a Mr. Wilcox." She sat in front of her dressing table and began unbraiding her hair. "Do something simple, Tibbetts. I'm curious to find out who this letter is from and what it contains."

There were really only two people who could have sent Mr. Wilcox here. He was either one of Lord Kerridge's servants, Lord Kerridge perhaps feeling it beneath himself to request an answer to his marriage offer this time around. Or it might be someone acting on behalf of William; however, she couldn't imagine why since she was seeing him this afternoon. He'd promised her last night that they would finally spend time together and that he would answer her questions openly.

Tibbetts fashioned Louisa's hair into a simple knot at the back of her head, and after a quick check of herself in the mirror, Louisa left her bedroom and descended the stairs, her heart beating a bit faster than usual in anticipation.

She found Mr. Wilcox in the small parlor, where he was pacing back and forth.

"Mr. Wilcox," she said.

The man immediately stopped pacing and turned to face her.

"I am Lady Louisa Hargreaves. I understand you are here to see me."

"Lady Louisa," the man said, bowing politely.

"I was only just informed that you were here," she said, crossing the room to sit in one of the upholstered chairs in front of the fireplace. "I'm sorry if it caused you any inconvenience. Would you care for tea?"

"No, thank you kindly, milady. No inconvenience at all. I don't mean to take up your time, only to give you the letter I was asked to place into your hands." He reached inside his coat and removed the letter in question.

"A letter. But from whom?" she asked, yet she was confident she already knew the answer. Mr. Wilcox was not dressed in the Kerridge livery. He wore the plain, modest clothes of a London businessman, which meant William had sent him. Her spirits began to diminish, and that surprised her. If it was important enough for this Wilcox person to give her the letter personally, it wasn't good news.

He handed her the letter. She examined it briefly and then broke the seal and unfolded it.

My dear Louisa,

Unforeseen circumstances have arisen that require I leave immediately for Buckinghamshire once again. I am profoundly sorry that I cannot spend time with you this afternoon, but I assure you in the strongest possible language that I will be at the church on Sunday for the reading of the banns, and I promise I will dedicate all of my time upon my return to you and to our getting more fully acquainted with each other. I sincerely hope you will forgive me.

With the greatest regard, William.

Mr. Wilcox had moved a few steps away from her, allowing her to read privately.

"Thank you, Mr. Wilcox," she said with a surprisingly steady voice. "Was there anything else?"

"No, milady," he said, but then he made a noise that sounded to Louisa as if there might be something else.

"Yes?" she asked. "Speak up, Mr. Wilcox, if you indeed have something to add. This letter gave me information, but no real knowledge. And I suspect you know more than you are telling me about the situation."

"It is not for me to say," Mr. Wilcox replied. "Nor do I wish to speak out of turn. I was instructed to deliver the letter into your hands by Lord Farleigh and Mr. Heslop, my employer, and that I have done. Anything more than that is for them to explain. But I can assure you that the reason was urgent and not to be taken lightly."

"But you will not tell me what this reason would be," Louisa said.

"It is not my place, milady."

She wasn't going to learn anything more from Mr. Wilcox, then. She wasn't about to press the man for more details; she actually admired—albeit begrudgingly—his loyalty to his employer and William.

"Thank you, then, Mr. Wilcox," she said. "Gibbs will show you out."

The man made his bow and left.

* * *

On Saturday afternoon, Louisa found herself seated once again at the pianoforte in the music room, wreaking havoc on a Scottish air she usually played rather decently. Huffing out a breath, she began again, paying the strictest attention to the notes written on the page, and yet her fingers still stumbled over them.

She set the music aside and selected another, but it went no better.

"What was that terrible racket?" Alex strolled into the room and planted a kiss on Louisa's cheek. "Thank goodness it has ceased; my ears were nearly bleeding from the pain. Now they will have a decent amount of time to recover before I must show my face at the Marwoods' musicale this evening."

"Another opportunity to spend time with Lady Elizabeth under her parents' noses, eh?" Louisa said with a smile.

"More like an edict," he replied with a dramatic sigh. "I might find I could tolerate the chit if her father weren't so emphatic that our connection begin *now*. She's not even made her come-out yet, and it seems everyone is already slavering over the dynastic union to come."

"I suspect they're afraid you'll get snatched away by a scheming young lady before you realized what has happened," Louisa said.

"Heaven forbid. I shall have to go into seclusion somewhere—the antipodes, most likely. I am beginning to think Rome not far enough."

"Come now, Alex, I know very well you like Lady Elizabeth."

Alex ignored her and fiddled with the lace on her sleeve. "Young ladies are getting younger every year," he drawled, trying to sound comically philosophical—if that was a thing.

"Ah, it's you, Alex," Anthony said, poking his head into the music room. "I thought I could hear a dog baying at the moon, and yet it is still daylight."

Louisa bit her lip.

"What you undoubtedly heard, *little* brother, were the melancholic tones of our poor, dear sister's attempt to make music on the pianoforte, for which the instrument will assuredly never forgive her."

"It was hardly me who was baying at the moon," Louisa countered. "What have you come to complain about today?" she asked Anthony. "Alex is bemoaning the efforts of certain parents to thrust him and Lady Elizabeth together, although neither of them is ready. And I—well, never mind."

"I suspect yours has to do with the mystery of the missing husband-to-be," Alex said.

"We expected you to make some sort of appearance last night with him, and yet you were not to be found," Anthony said.

"I told Mama I had a headache, which was true enough, and that I wished to stay home. *Must* a person go out into Society every night of the week?" She could feel herself getting defensive.

"Assuredly not; don't be silly, Weezy," Alex said. "But as a newly betrothed couple, especially when the gentleman is a virtual unknown—I shall be polite and refrain from mentioning the *known* facts of his predecessor—then appearing in public is essential; even I know that. We are not total fools, you know. We can tell when something is amiss."

"What is going on, Louisa?" Anthony asked, seating himself next to her on the bench, while Alex leaned against the side of the piano. "You clearly have not been yourself the past day or two."

She retrieved the letter from her pocket. She'd been carrying it around with her since Thursday, when Mr. Wilcox had delivered it, and had read it several times over the past two days. "William had to go back to Buckinghamshire again," she said, handing the letter to Anthony.

He read it and passed it to Alex.

"It's probably nothing," Alex said, shrugging and handing the letter back to her.

"Alex is right," Anthony agreed. "He's the new viscount, and we already know his father left the property in shambles. Undoubtedly, there are matters he must see to that have been left languishing for too long. I shouldn't worry, if I were you."

"Will Barlow wasn't a bad sort at Eton, if it's any consolation," Alex said. "Quiet, but a generally decent chap. Older than either Tony or me, so I didn't know him well. I think if there'd been anything untoward about his behavior, though, it would have spread through the school like wildfire. That's what usually happened. In fact, a good share of the boys enjoyed having a rather devilish reputation."

"And if there had been anything untoward about his behavior, Alex would have probably been involved," Anthony added.

"Sadly true," Alex said, winking at her, trying to lift her spirits.

"I keep trying to think back," Anthony continued. "But I am so much younger than he and would have been a new boy trying to hold my own with the older boys. My attention was riveted on survival back then. You know how boys' schools can be."

"No, actually, I don't, as you two dolts tend to forget," Louisa replied with impertinence, their words beginning to make her feel a bit better.

"Oh, that's *right*," Alex said, slapping a hand to his forehead as if he'd had an epiphany. "She is our little *sister*. How could we have forgotten, Tony?"

"If it helps, I've asked about Farleigh in the gentlemen's clubs," Anthony said. Louisa looked at him in alarm. "Discreetly," he added. "Good heavens,

Weezy, I do have some sense, you know. I found few who knew him personally. I learned a bit more about his father though—not that I feel inclined to share the details with my sister."

"I didn't know Lord Kerridge well enough, I am discovering," she said. "But I know almost nothing about William, and yet I am to marry him in little more than two weeks' time. I have tried to get him to tell me about himself but haven't made much progress, even though it was a condition I insisted upon when I agreed to the betrothal—that he allow the banns to be read so I had time to get to know him before . . ."

"Before you were bound to him for life," Anthony said softly.

"Yes."

They were silent.

"*Such* a heavy mood," Alex said theatrically after a few moments, strumming annoyingly at the strings inside the pianoforte and making a terrible sound. "I hope you appreciate that few brothers would do as we are presently doing, Weezy. Our very manhood would be brought into question if it got out that we were fretting and wringing our hands and consoling our little sister about her love life. It is the role of mamas and sisters and spinster aunts and giggling young ladies." He shuddered. "Certainly not something gentlemen are expected to concern themselves with. Even the *most devoted* of brothers."

Louisa smiled, and Anthony laughed.

Anthony rubbed his hand over his mouth in thought. "What if there were an honorable way to get out of the marriage, Weezy?" he asked, finally. "Would you want that? What if it were proven, for example, that Viscount Farleigh was a scoundrel? No one has seen him since he left Oxford, and a man can change significantly in a few short years."

Louisa thought about how he'd let her rage at him at Vauxhall and had held her afterward and accepted her need to speak from her soul. She reflected on his promise to be more forthcoming, despite its being thwarted in each attempt so far. She thought he'd been sincere, but she'd yet to see any evidence of it. She remembered his kisses, passionate kisses that hinted at his otherwise unspoken feelings for her, and that she had little experience with men with which to compare them. She had enjoyed Lord Kerridge's kisses; she would be lying if she denied it. But William's kisses had been a revelation, a sharing of emotions that ran deeper than a mere reaction to the physical sensations. And in the letter in her pocket, he'd written, "My dear Louisa." *Was* she dear to him? Had he meant it? On such short acquaintance, even though they were betrothed, he could have simply written "Louisa," and it would have been entirely appropriate. Had he meant it, then? He was such a paradox.

"I don't know how to answer your question," she said to Anthony at last. Both brothers were watching her closely. "If he were proven to be a scoundrel, I would end the betrothal. I do not believe I am required to sacrifice myself if such turned out to be the case.

"The problem is I simply do not *know*. He claims he will be here for the banns at church tomorrow, and I must believe him until he proves the contrary. He says we will spend next week getting better acquainted. *How* one can get acquainted with the person one is to marry in a week's time, I do not know, but marriages have been made on less."

"Sadly true," Alex acknowledged.

"Which is precisely why you are being sent to play escort to little Lady Lizzie this evening, dear brother," Anthony said.

"Sadly true again," Alex said.

"You *like* her; I know you do," Louisa remarked.

"And *that* is sadly true too," Alex said with a grin. "And I had best be off to get ready. I must look the part if I am to be glared at all evening by the Duke of Marwood."

"And I am off to White's," Anthony said. "But, Louisa, rest assured that I shall continue to do all in my power to find out anything I can about Lord Farleigh. Don't worry"—he held up his hand in reassurance when Louisa tried to caution him—"I shall continue to be discreet. But you are running out of days to change your mind, so there is no time to be lost."

"I too shall do my best to seek out information on him," Alex said. "Granted, I doubt I'll be able to ferret out anything much, considering the company. You had better make the rounds tonight, Tony, and not spend all your time at White's." He leaned across the pianoforte and kissed Louisa on the cheek. "Never fear, Weezy dear, you have two gallant heroes at your beck and call should anything be required of us. Now, I must bid you both adieu."

"He's right," Anthony said. "We will not stand by and have you sacrifice yourself in marriage to someone who is unworthy of you."

"Thank you, Anthony, and you too, Alex. I don't know what I'd do without you both."

"Never fear, Lady Cumulus. We are ever in your corner," Alex said.

She watched her brothers leave the music room and then stared at the pianoforte, mindlessly poking at the keys and creating a sort of somber melody.

Tomorrow, the second banns were to be read, and William said in his letter that he would keep his promise to her and be there. If he did not, she would end the betrothal, vowel or no vowel.

She wished she understood why it hurt her heart to reach that conclusion.

Chapter 11

WILLIAM ASKED WALTER TO HAVE the carriage to London ready to leave at dawn Sunday morning. He intended to be at the church well ahead of the scheduled service when the second banns were to be read. Besides, he was ready to take a break from the estate.

The past few days had been a trial for everyone at Farleigh Manor.

After a lengthy conversation between Miss Purnell, Heslop, and himself, William had finally convinced Miss Purnell that there was a place for them at Farleigh Manor and that as head of the family, he could not and would not allow her and her children to fend for themselves, with no income and no other persons to whom they could turn for help. For, regardless of the illegitimacy of her marriage to his father, they were family; Peter and Daisy were William's blood relatives. There was a modest dower house on a corner of the property, he had explained to her. A very modest dower house that was not much bigger than a cottage, but with room enough to hold her and her children comfortably.

He and Matthew had actually discussed leasing the dower house as a means of bringing in income, something the former steward should have arranged to be done years ago—but that was no longer an option now. Since Miss Purnell would have been the dowager viscountess had his father not played false with her by marrying her while William's mother was still alive, it seemed only right that Miss Purnell and Peter and Daisy make it their home.

She had reluctantly agreed, on the condition that William help her find employment in the village. She was an educated woman and had worked as a governess before marrying his father, she'd reminded him, and would do whatever she must to see to the welfare of her children and not simply rely on the charity of others.

William had felt a begrudging admiration for her. His own mother had been a lovely and genteel woman of means who had also fallen for his father's guile. He would allow Miss Purnell the same benefit of the doubt.

Due to the threat of eviction by her landlord, Miss Purnell had already packed most of their personal belongings before making her first visit to Mr. Heslop on Thursday morning. Her efforts had ended up saving them all a great deal of time and had allowed them to begin their travel early that afternoon.

William hadn't pushed her for further details, considering the poor woman had only just learned that the man she'd thought was her husband had died, that she was penniless, and that her children were illegitimate, and William had no desire to add to her grief. Heslop had laid all the legal facts out clearly enough, and as far as William was concerned, it had been sufficient for the time being.

He had opted to take his horse to Buckinghamshire so she and her children could ride in the carriage alone and would not feel encroached upon by a stranger. The ride had taken longer than usual, with multiple stops for the children to have comfort breaks. During those stops, William had conversed with Miss Purnell while they watched the children stretch their legs and play, and she had confessed to him that while her marriage to his father had started out happily and well, it had deteriorated over time and that, eventually, she hadn't minded his long periods of absence. In fact, she had preferred them. It had been enough that she'd had her home and her children and had only needed to tolerate him on occasion. Glowing words, indeed.

They'd arrived at Farleigh Manor late Friday afternoon, where the staff had formally greeted them in the courtyard the minute the carriage had come to a halt at the front doors. William had quickly jumped from his horse and quietly explained to Mrs. Holly and Grimshaw who the occupants of the carriage were before assisting Miss Purnell from the carriage. Peter had scrambled from the carriage on his own.

William had helped little Daisy down, picking her up and keeping her in his arms. Whatever the reason, Daisy had come to accept William on friendly terms at some point on the journey, and as she was his half sister, he wasn't inclined to object. Peter would take time to win over, and William understood better than most the reason why.

Mary had burst from the ranks almost immediately, eyes huge, her arms waving wildly. She'd run straight to William, crying, "You brought a wife! And you brought babies!"

Miss Purnell had frozen in place, and Peter had looked ready to throw fists at being referred to as a baby, so William—with great care and patience—had explained to Mary that Miss Purnell was not, in fact, his wife but that the three of them were special guests who were to live in the dower house and be welcomed by everyone, and he had left it at that. More explanation would have to occur over the course of several days or even weeks before Mary would comprehend it completely.

At the mention of the dower house, Mrs. Holly and Matthew had come to full attention. Until William's comment, the dower house had dropped in priority, the preparation of the manor house for the impending arrival of a Lady Farleigh being the most important consideration. With the arrival of Miss Purnell, work on the manor house had been diverted to the dower house early the following morning.

In the meantime, Mrs. Holly and Sally had set about cleaning the nursery and airing out a guest room so Miss Purnell and the children would have somewhere to sleep. William had left the trio in the capable hands of Mrs. Brill, who would see that they were well fed, and then he had gone out with Matthew to review the improvements that had been set into action on the estate. Since it had been mere days since William had been at Farleigh Manor, there hadn't been much to see, but he'd listened and looked and made suggestions.

He had also spent time with Miss Purnell—Jane, as she'd asked him to call her—after supper, wanting to assure himself that she felt comfortable at Farleigh Manor. She'd told him that she did and even opened up a bit again, although she'd shared few particulars—but what little she'd said had been enough. It had sent him careening back to a dark time in his childhood, so familiar were her words to ones his mother had spoken so many years earlier. Birchings, sarcasm, punishments for small childhood infractions, like dirty clothes and crying, all reared their ugly heads. *Toughen up, boy. You're an embarrassment. You got your mother's weak character, you sniveling little pest.* But then there were the other times. *That's right, my boy, you've got it. You're like granite; they'll never win now. Never let them win.*

Jane had been careful in her choice of words, but William knew what his father had been like with his mother. He had ears, after all, and his father hadn't been particularly discreet during his rants. *You're dull and tedious; it's no wonder I can barely stand to come home anymore. Stop crying. You're so weak it's pathetic. I need a drink.*

William felt a kinship with Jane. He understood her, and he was starting to recognize the wounds that had been inflicted on all of them by his father. It explained his own stoicism, albeit his reticence to show himself to others, really share himself, and not hide behind a facade, had begun to show a few cracks in the past couple weeks.

Thanks to Louisa.

And now he was on his way back to London with the hope that Louisa would accept his explanations and answers—lacking though they surely would be—with the generosity of heart he knew was inherent in her character. He could not tell her about Jane and the children, however. It was too scandalous, and their betrothal was too precarious. But he could try to tell her more about himself, as he'd promised. And eventually, when he was more secure in their connection, he would explain the appearance of Jane Purnell to her.

He settled into the seat of the carriage, placing his feet on the seat opposite and crossing his ankles, then slid his hat down so the brim covered his eyes. It had been an exhausting three days. It had been exhausting trying to read between the lines and discern truths from carefully chosen words and vague expressions. He'd begun to understand why Louisa had reacted as she had at Vauxhall. He owed her a huge apology. And he owed it to her to open himself up to her.

He tapped his hat firmly in place over his eyes and tried his best to sleep while the carriage bumped along on the road back to London. He needed a fresh head and his wits about him when he was reunited with Louisa this afternoon. He may understand that he needed to share himself more fully with her, but he hadn't the vaguest idea how to actually go about doing it.

* * *

Louisa peered out the window of the carriage as she and her parents and Anthony arrived at the church, right before the noon service was to begin. She saw William standing outside the doors, looking as he always did: tall, handsome, modestly but neatly attired, and completely unreadable.

Her heart leaped at the sight of him. He was here. Whatever business had taken him from London the past few days, he'd told her he'd be here today for the banns, and he was. She had at least a hundred questions to ask him, but the two most pressing ones were simple and straightforward: *Are you going to be forthcoming with me today, and will I be able to tell if you aren't?*

His current expression didn't give her a great deal of hope.

They made it through the church service, however, along with the second reading of the banns. They sat side by side, her parents on one side of her in the pew and Anthony seated next to William on his other side. Louisa clasped her gloved hands in her lap, and William did the same with his. It was all very appropriate, as it should be—especially during church—but it did nothing to allay Louisa's concerns about the conversation they were to have afterward.

"Lord Farleigh," her father said after they had all exited the church and shaken hands with the rector and greeted several acquaintances. "I would ask you to join us at Ashworth House for dinner, if you are agreeable." Knowing her father as well as she did, Louisa recognized it as a command rather than an invitation.

"Thank you; I shall," William replied. "Perhaps Lady Louisa would care to join me in my carriage for the journey there." He looked at her with his usual impassive face, but his eyes gleamed with awareness. He had not forgotten his promise to her after all.

Mama glanced from Louisa to William and back to Louisa. "I'm not sure—"

"I shall be fine, Mama," Louisa said. "The drive is a short one, and we are betrothed. We won't scandalize anyone." She looked at William and raised her eyebrows in defiance. "Will we?"

The corners of William's eyes crinkled just the slightest bit at her declaration. "We will maintain the highest level of decorum," he said. "I have missed my bride-to-be, and we must take every opportunity presented to us to get better acquainted. It is my fault, I know, and I hope to remedy it in the remaining time we have before our marriage."

Their marriage! Good heavens, Louisa thought, she'd been so focused on getting him to open up to her and getting through the reading of the banns that she hadn't even considered an actual wedding date, though she and Mama had made a few essential dowry purchases while William had been absent. William had wanted to marry quickly; they'd be married already, in fact, had she not asked for the three weeks with the banns. He would not want much time to pass before their marriage took place once the final banns were read.

She could be a married woman within two weeks.

"Very well, then," Mama said, shooting William a severely arched eyebrow meant to put fear and trembling into him. "Come, Ashworth, Anthony. I suppose I must eventually learn to trust Lord Farleigh if he is to become my son-in-law."

"I will be spending time in my study this afternoon, Farleigh," Papa said. "I expect you to join me there at some point."

"Understood, your lordship," William said.

Anthony said nothing at all, which was unusual for him. He'd been that way all morning, come to think of it. Alex had still been in bed when they'd left for church; no one had said anything about it, and Louisa suspected that even if he had spent the early part of the evening with the Marwoods and Lady Elizabeth, he had probably spent the rest of his night visiting gentlemen's clubs. Anthony had been planning to go to White's, but Alex had suggested he—how had he phrased it?—"make the rounds." Had he learned something Louisa needed to know while he'd been out making these so-called rounds?

William extended his hand to Louisa and assisted her into his carriage. He looked tired. That came as no surprise, considering he'd ridden to Buckinghamshire and back twice in the past week, in addition to whatever he'd done there. She wondered again what his urgent business had been about.

He gave directions to the driver, then climbed in and seated himself next to her. "For the record, I do not intend to take the quickest route back to Ashworth House," he said. "I hope that doesn't distress you. I wished to spend some time alone with you, without your parents or brothers about, so we—I—can communicate more freely, for that is what I promised you earlier this week."

"I am not distressed," Louisa said.

His eyes did that crinkly thing again for just a moment, and Louisa realized it was the faintest beginnings of a smile. It didn't extend to the rest of his face or reach his mouth, but—

She really had to stop looking at his mouth so much, she thought as she felt her face heat up.

The corners of his mouth twitched.

"Maybe I am a bit distressed," she remarked rather lamely.

His mouth twitched again, but he didn't say anything to her in return, which was a surprise, considering he'd caught her in the act of staring. Her brothers had teased her so incessantly over the years about absolutely everything that she'd come to expect it as a matter of course. William, however, had not subjected her to any teasing.

It was a nice change.

By this time, they'd reached the outskirts of Mayfair, and the carriage took them down a street lined with respectable houses before coming to a stop in front of one of them. "Welcome to Farleigh House," William said. He jumped out of the carriage and set the steps for her, then gave her his hand. "You wished to learn more about me. I thought I'd begin by showing you this."

He led her to the front door and unlocked and opened it and then allowed her to precede him inside.

Louisa's immediate reaction was that it was a man's domain. The wallpaper in the entry was bold, the woods dark in color. The sitting room, which was just to the left of the front entry, was similar in tone. A sofa upholstered in brown-striped silk faced the fireplace, while two leather armchairs sat on either side of it, facing each other. The painting over the marble fireplace was of a hunting scene, with men on horses and dogs in pursuit of a fox. A sideboard held an array of decanters, full of a variety of spirits, with a selection of drinking glasses nearby.

"This was my father's domicile; his place of refuge," William said matter-of-factly. "I didn't even know the place existed until I went through the estate holdings with Heslop after my father's death. It was a well-kept secret. I don't recall my mother ever accompanying my father on a trip to London, though he traveled here frequently. My own first time in London was with school friends when I was at Oxford. We came to Town only a handful of times, usually for academic symposiums and the like—not very exciting, I know. After that, I moved to Edinburgh and remained there. Until now." He ran his hand along the back of the chair nearest him. "Would you care to see the rest of the floor?"

Louisa nodded, trying to figure out what his demeanor and tone meant. He was still unreadable, but there was an edge to his voice now that he was unable to completely hide from her.

He showed her the dining room, which held a fine oak table and chairs with an elaborate chandelier hanging above them. Next was a man's study with a connecting door into a decently stocked library.

Louisa wandered through each room, surprised at the level of prosperity she saw. But there was nothing personal, no pictures of family, nothing that helped her understand what William's father had been like. Even the books in the library seemed to be more for show than anything—shelves of tomes in similar bindings that appeared never to have had their covers opened or their pages read.

They returned to the hallway. "Down those steps at the back of the house is the kitchen. There is a small apartment beyond it where the housekeeper, Mrs. Gideon, lives. According to her, when my father was here, her nephew acted as his valet. I have not employed his services—something she wasn't particularly happy about when I first arrived."

"Was she your father's housekeeper here for many years? May I meet her?"

"Ten years, give or take. Assuredly, you may meet her, but it will have to happen at another time; Sunday is her day off, and she's not here. She also gets half days on Wednesday." He led her back to the front entry. "These stairs, as you might surmise, lead up to the bedrooms and guest rooms, but they can wait for another time, as they are essentially much the same as you see down here. Bachelor lodgings for a man who was not a bachelor. Besides, it's past time that I take you home."

They returned to the carriage, and Louisa pondered what she'd seen. He'd given her a piece of the puzzle, a bit of clarity, to be sure, but she couldn't see the entire picture yet.

When they were back on their way to Ashworth House, William turned slightly, angling himself toward her on the carriage seat. "Did you learn anything on our little tour?" he asked blandly.

Louisa gazed at his face. There were no crinkles at the corners of his eyes, no smile lurking behind his lips. His face was as impassive as it had been the first time they'd met, save the dark circles under his eyes were more pronounced. "Yes," she said at last. "I have learned that if your father left the estate in tatters, it was due to selfishness. The house here in London is in excellent condition, which means that he lived well, and I must, therefore, presume that he did so beyond his means.

"There was no portrait of your mother, no mementos of any kind, nothing of sentimental value anywhere that I could see. I doubt it is because you cleared away anything of his, although I suppose you may have instructed Mrs. Gideon to remove them. I am sorry, William."

William stared out the window beyond her, but she suspected he saw nothing but shadows from his past. He was far away. "When one is reared by such a person and it is all one knows, it is difficult to change."

Louisa wanted to reach for him, to take his hand in hers and comfort him, but she did not. He had shown her a glimpse into his life but only a glimpse, and it was not enough. Not yet. Not when he still wore a mask he kept so firmly in place. Not when he still had so many secrets. He was making the attempt to keep his promise to her, but she wasn't sure it would be enough, that he could open himself enough to address her concerns and give her the reassurances she desired.

A week from today, the last of the banns would be read, and then there would be no excuse to delay the marriage further. She had asked him for three weeks, and he would have given them to her.

She must have her answers before she was out of time.

* * *

When William and Louisa returned to Ashworth House, they found her family in the drawing room, with a sleepy Halford also in attendance. Conversation was polite and amiable. Halford and Lord Anthony were rather serious in their questions toward him and prodded him further about his time at Oxford and his years in Scotland.

"But why *Scotland*, Farleigh?" Halford asked him. "No offense, but it seems to me there is plenty to see and do *here*, by comparison, and with somewhat better weather . . . although, arguably, not by much."

"There is an extraordinary group of academics and innovators in Edinburgh," William replied. "And I discovered not long after I arrived that I enjoyed their association and, therefore, decided to stay. I confess that I had little to contribute to the group but found it humbling—and enlightening— to be a part of that society." The fact that it was several hundred miles from Buckinghamshire had only added to its appeal.

His answer seemed to carry some weight with Louisa's parents, who doubtless suspected he was a reprobate like his father had been. Lord Ashworth gave the slightest of nods at his words, and Lady Ashworth looked up from her needlework.

Even with William seated on an elegant sofa with Louisa next to him, he was unsettled by the experience, which, today, felt more like he was standing before a magistrate than contributing to a casual conversation.

After luncheon, Alex and Anthony invited him to join them in a game of billiards, which William agreed to after a quick glance at Louisa since he'd promised her they would get better acquainted this afternoon. Her smile seemed to indicate that she would be fine with him spending an hour or so with her brothers.

Playing billiards was usually intended to be an enjoyable pastime, but William quickly discovered he was facing more interrogation. He was a decent player—one had to be to survive Eton and Oxford—but wasn't nearly in the league of either Halford or his brother, he immediately discerned as they took shots to warm up. They had obviously spent many hours bent over this very table, hitting balls into pockets.

"Scotland. And academia," Halford drawled, leaning against the wall, while Lord Anthony prepared to take his first shot. They had decided amongst themselves that Lord Anthony would challenge William to the first game. "I confess, I was only too glad to put Cambridge behind me when I completed university. But you *chose* to go to Edinburgh to study further. Are you a glutton for punishment, Farleigh?"

"He must be; he wants to marry Weezy, after all," Lord Anthony said. He took his shot, sending his ball across the table, short of its mark. "Blast it, Alex. Stop speaking when I'm trying to concentrate."

"Edinburgh is an amiable city, full of history and interesting people," William said. Definitely more interrogation disguised as small talk.

"I knew you weren't going to put that ball in the pocket; your angle was completely wrong," Halford remarked to Lord Anthony. "Amiable, eh?" he asked while William studied the table for his next shot. "Amiable as in long-winded lectures on mechanics and philosophy, or amiable as in assemblies and balls and flirtations, by any chance?"

William hadn't been entirely virtuous since arriving at his majority, but the few liaisons he'd had as a very young man had left him feeling empty inside. His father had hurt his mother with his own infidelities. Even as a boy, William had understood that something had been amiss between the two of them, and it hadn't taken much time after arriving at Eton for him to put two and two together. Boys will be boys, after all, and boys will talk about such things with crassness and bravado.

"Edinburgh is amiable in all those ways," William replied as obliquely as possible to Halford's question before shooting his ball into the corner pocket.

Lord Anthony eventually won the first game, and Halford had just challenged William to the next when a footman arrived to tell them Lord Ashworth requested a few minutes of Lord Farleigh's time.

"That's too bad," Halford said, "as I'm quite certain I could have won a bit of money from Tony over who would beat you by the most points. Well, we shall have to give it a go another time."

"Another time," William replied. He had no plan to return to the billiards room after his meeting with Lord Ashworth, especially not if there was to be wagering involved. Besides, it would be past time to be with Louisa.

The footman knocked on the door to Lord Ashworth's study.

"Enter," the marquess replied.

"Lord Farleigh," John said.

"Thank you, John. Come in, Farleigh; have a seat. We have unfinished business to attend to." He gestured to the seat across from his own, next to the fireplace. William had expected the marquess to be seated at his desk in a position of power, with William on the opposite side. Instead, they were seated informally. William's mind began to scramble: did the marquess intend their meeting to be informal and open, then? Or was it a strategy to catch William off guard? *Read the clues; look for the tells.*

"For a man intent on wooing my daughter, you have been remarkably absent this week," the marquess said, getting right to the point. "Or have you decided you need not bother since she has chosen to act with honor and marry you regardless?"

"I am here today to woo your daughter," William replied as coolly as possible. "But it would seem the men in her family think time with me and asking pointed questions, which I am willing to answer, by the way, are part of that wooing."

"She is our diamond and our delight. You will forgive us if we are protective of her and entirely suspicious of you until proven otherwise."

"I understand completely, Lord Ashworth, and would expect nothing less."

The marquess did not appear convinced. "I shan't keep you long, so you may go about this so-called wooing. I wanted to inform you, however, that the marriage contracts are drawn up. If you haven't heard this from Heslop yet, you may presume it is because you have been off in the countryside doing who knows what. Don't be surprised to hear from him tomorrow."

"Thank you, your lordship. For the record, I was seeing to matters at Farleigh Manor that needed my personal attention."

"As you say. Well, that is something, at least." The marquess gestured with his head toward a stack of documents atop his desk. "The marriage contracts are there, awaiting our signatures. We could sign them today and have it done . . ." He paused, drumming his fingers lightly on the arm of his chair. "*However*, I am not pleased at your absences this past week, even if you claim to have had good reason. I have watched my daughter closely, you see, and she has been unhappy. She would never say so, but as her father, I can tell that this is the case. I will not elaborate on it further, for that is for you as her *future husband*"—he nearly spat the words—"to discover for yourself. And I expect you to do so to my satisfaction." He leaned forward and said in a low, threatening tone, "For, you see, Viscount Farleigh, I will not put my signature to these marriage contracts until I am thoroughly convinced Louisa is willing to subject herself to this vowel you hold over her. Do we understand each other?"

Don't let him get a read on you. "Clearly, your lordship."

"Excellent." The marquess stood, indicating that he had said what he'd intended to say to William and now wished for the conversation to be done.

William rose to his feet, bowed formally, and took his leave.

* * *

Louisa had excused herself from sitting with Mama in the drawing room and had wandered into the music room, something she seemed to have done a lot over the past week or two. Not because she was what anyone would call a musical proficient but because reading the notes gave her something to concentrate on beyond her present concerns, and the melodies soothed her in spite of the occasional wrong note or two or several.

She had asked her brothers to learn what they could about William, so she should hardly have been surprised when they'd dragged him off to play billiards, but she had been nonetheless. She'd expected them to be a bit more covert about the whole business. She should have known better.

Her fingers stumbled over a passage in the Mozart sonata she was attempting to play. She stopped and worked out an agreeable fingering and then played the passage several times until her fingers began to go where she willed them. Herr Mozart's music was a bit more challenging than the pieces she usually attempted to master, but today, she needed something that required her complete concentration.

Except she wasn't concentrating on the sonata at all. She was reminding herself of all the reasons she needed to concentrate on something else—which meant she was really concentrating on all the reasons why she needed to concentrate on something else.

Goodness, she was babbling inside her own head now. She might well go mad if she wasn't careful.

The sound of the door shutting behind her made her jump. She twisted around on the piano bench to see who it was, hoping it was William come to spend time with her at last.

It was. He stood silently by the door, his hands behind him. "May I come in?" he asked.

"It looks to me as if you already have," she said.

"Touché," he replied. He didn't move any farther into the room, however. "Will you play for me?" he asked.

"Play for you?" she asked stupidly. She'd performed piano pieces at parties before—what young lady of quality wasn't required to do such a thing, or something similar?—but William asking for a private performance flustered her.

It was silly, she told herself.

"I would appreciate it above all things," he said.

She took a deep breath and ordered her fingers not to tremble. "Very well, but not the Mozart." She wouldn't be able to hit a single correct note in the passage she'd just practiced with William standing by listening to her. She set it aside and thumbed through the small stack of music on the music stand, choosing a more tranquil—in other words, *slow*—movement from a Bach suite.

He crossed the room quietly after she began to play. She could hear his steps and see him out of the corner of her eye as he seated himself in a chair not far away. And then she turned her attention to the music. He, she noticed after she finished the piece, sat without moving, his eyes closed, so she chose another piece and played it and then another.

After the fourth piece of music, she stopped, folded her hands in her lap, and watched him. He gradually opened his eyes. They were dark and soulful and, Louisa realized with a start, utterly bleak. And then he blinked, and the window into his soul closed once again.

But Louisa had seen what she'd seen.

"Thank you," he said.

"May I ask you a question?" she asked.

"You may."

"Will you tell me more about the tree? The tree in the painting you gave me?"

"It's a tree at Farleigh Manor that I painted from memory while at Oxford."

"*You* painted it?" she asked, surprised by this new revelation. She'd not been able to decipher the signature on the canvas. "You're a painter?"

"No, not at all, but what young boy or girl hasn't had some tutoring in it as part of his or her education? I enjoy painting on occasion, and on one such occasion, I chose to paint the tree."

"Why did you give it to me?" she asked.

He shrugged. "Perhaps I wanted to show you some of the beauty of the place since it is to become your future home."

He'd painted the tree, and even if he claimed to be an amateur, he'd managed to create an image Louisa found appealing, one that offered sunshine and shade . . . and peace. He'd given it to her in a less-than-peaceful time, and yet she'd sensed what was within the painting.

"Tell me about your mother," Louisa said.

* * *

"Tell me about your mother," Louisa had said. She was waiting for him to reply.

William was no musician, but Louisa's performance had moved him. He'd had to fight back the desire to weep. He hadn't wept in years—not that he'd succumbed this time either, fortunately. He attributed this unusual swell of emotion to the music and to the vision of Louisa at the piano, her face, even in profile, a work of beauty. His mother had been such a beauty when he was a boy; back before his father's choices had exacted their toll on her.

"I'll race you to the oak tree, Mama," five-year-old Will shrieked and then took off running. When he stopped briefly to catch his breath, he saw Mama, her skirts clutched in her hands, running to catch him, smiling and full of sunshine. He waited for her to catch up to him, and then they ran and collapsed at the foot of the tree, laughing and hugging and enjoying the shade in a glorious, free afternoon.

Louisa's request caused a tumult within his soul. What words could possibly explain everything his mother had been to him? She had been gentle and kind and beautiful, at least to the young boy who'd adored her. She had been his world, his safe place. And then he had been sent to Eton and had been allowed home only on school holidays. And she'd changed during those years while he was at school, withdrawing into herself, intent on her needlework and interested in little else. And then she'd died.

Words were wholly inadequate.

And what words would the specter of his father even allow him to say?

Louisa was watching him closely, waiting for him to speak.

"She was . . ." His mind flailed about. "She was everything to a small boy."

Pathetic.

Louisa looked at him as if she thought so too.

He heaved a sigh. "What specifically do you wish to know?"

"What did she look like?" Louisa asked. "Who were her people? Where was she from? Do you look like her or your father? Did she play with you when you were a boy? Did she read you stories? What are your favorite memories with her? I want to *know* her, William. In knowing *her*—and even your father—I can get to know *you* better too."

William had promised her he would be forthcoming, so he tried again. "My coloring is more like my father's. In fact, I'm afraid I look more like him than I do her. She was fair and blue-eyed." There. He'd said something about both of his parents.

He loathed dredging up anything that had to do with the past, but he forged onward. "She was Margaret Strickland before marrying my father and becoming Viscountess Farleigh. She was an only child, brought up near the Lake District to genteel but poor people, from what I know. She moved to London when she was offered a governess position, and it was in that capacity that she became acquainted with my father, who was—at the time—a friend of the family with whom she was employed.

"My father, as you already know, hailed from Buckinghamshire. He met and married my mother; I was born into that union a few months later. I was sent off to school at the age of ten, my mother died when I was sixteen, and I never went home again. Rather Gothic, wouldn't you say?"

He ceased speaking, his stomach in knots, the scars on his back aflame with memories.

Louisa left the piano bench and came to sit by him.

"Thank you, William," she said, placing her hand on his arm. "That wasn't so difficult, now was it?"

She had *no idea* how difficult and utterly dreadful it had been for him to speak those words. But then, she'd been protected her whole life and, therefore, had the luxury of innocence.

What an enviable life for a child to have experienced. If he were so fortunate as to have children of his own, he would want them to be brought up with that type of innocence and tranquility. Louisa would be the kind of mother who would insist on her children learning and growing with the assurance that their parents loved them.

He wanted Louisa to be the mother of his children. He wanted it fiercely.

He sprang to his feet and crossed the room, gripping the windowsill and staring out at the garden beyond. He needed to be as far away from her as possible, unsure if he would pull her into a desperate hug or shake her for the pain she was making him feel.

"William?" she asked softly.

"I have done what I can for today, Louisa. I can do no more," he choked out.

She was silent. He waited to hear her footsteps, terrified that she might come near him. Thankfully, she stayed where she was.

He breathed deeply a few times, willing himself into some semblance of control, as he had on more occasions than he could count. When he thought he'd contained his emotions, he turned. "I must leave you now," he said. "But I shall call again tomorrow, and we shall resume our conversation."

"William," she said softly. He could barely stand to hear her say his name. It caressed him and offered solace—solace he didn't deserve, didn't want. Not now.

He gritted his teeth until he thought they would crack. Dash it all, he had a vowel. He *would* have its terms fulfilled. His people deserved it, and he would do it for them. It didn't matter that he didn't deserve it. He would woo Louisa, he would convince her father of her willingness, and he *would* marry her. He *would* make sure that the people of Farleigh Manor had nothing to worry about, that their lives and livelihoods were taken care of.

He could see Peter's worried, defiant face, so much like his own had looked at that age. He could see little Daisy, aware that something was not right in her world but too young to understand it yet. He could see their mother's face too—the betrayal and resignation so clearly like his own mother's. He would *not* let his father ruin their chances of survival and happiness too. He would *not* allow history to repeat itself. He would not allow his half brother to live as he had done; he wanted Daisy to grow up as Louisa had—feeling loved and secure.

He would do everything in his power to make it happen. He would dedicate his life to Louisa's happiness over the years to come, even if it was a futile endeavor. Even if she ultimately hated him. But he would do it. He saw no other choice.

Louisa sat in the chair as if frozen, her eyes stricken. He couldn't bear to see her that way. He had to choose between the people he loved, and heaven help him, he loved Louisa. She was everything he desired in a wife and in life, everything he longed for.

She had a family who would be there for her always, without question. Parents and brothers who would do anything to protect her and who would always love her, who could bear her up should William ever fall short in his devotion to her.

The people of Farleigh Manor had only him.

He forced himself to walk toward her, take her shaking hand in his, and kiss it. *Never show what you're feeling.* "I can say nothing else tonight, Louisa; I'm sorry. I will call on you tomorrow afternoon, if I may," he said, grateful his voice sounded normal to his ears. "And we will talk some more. Now, if you'll excuse me, I'll show myself out."

He turned and left and didn't look back.

Chapter 12

AFTER A SHOCKINGLY BRIEF CONVERSATION, William departed so abruptly that Louisa was utterly dumbstruck. He had attempted to tell her about himself and his family, and she'd watched him contort over nearly every word he'd uttered. Oh, he assuredly thought he'd been keeping his emotions intact, but this time—*this time*—he hadn't succeeded. Louisa had witnessed a whole host of emotions being pitched about within him. His entire being had vibrated with it, his face rigid from the effort to contain it all.

She remained in the music room for several minutes, unsure what to do next.

In less than a week, the third and final banns would be read, and the marriage would proceed in the days following. Tonight, he had tried to keep his promise to her, had struggled to overcome whatever stranglehold there was inside him about speaking of his family and his past. Louisa's heart had gone out to him. But she still resented the constraint the vowel put her under, and she was running out of time. It could take weeks, months, even *years* for him to ever open up to her—if ever. She didn't have the luxury of time.

She eventually went back to the drawing room, not knowing where else to go. Mama was still there, reading, having set her needlework aside.

The sight of her in such a tranquil setting was eerily reminiscent of what William had told her of his own mother, a genteel young woman with no money and few prospects who'd happened to catch the eye of a viscount. She'd borne a son and seen him sent away when he was only ten. William had alluded to the fact that there had been troubles in his parents' marriage, even early on.

How lonely Lady Farleigh must have been to have her only child sent away so young and to have been married to a man who left her in the country while he himself spent the majority of his time in London. It had been difficult for Louisa to see her brothers go off to Eton, but they'd come home for school holidays, and the family had visited them at school on regular occasions.

Mama closed her book and set it aside. "Lord Farleigh has left, I take it," she said.

"Yes."

"Perhaps this is a bit indelicate of me to say, Louisa, but it must be said nonetheless: I chatted briefly with Martha, er, the Duchess of Atherton, and she hasn't been able to learn much of anything about Lord Farleigh—and if anyone should be able, it's Martha, you know. Perhaps there is nothing to learn, but I find the lack of information about him disconcerting. Are you absolutely *certain* you want to marry this man?"

"No, Mama, of course I'm not certain. Is anyone certain when they're facing a sacrifice born of honor?"

"Well, something must be done. Your father will be at the House of Lords tomorrow, and I think I shall suggest that he discreetly ask about Lord Farleigh—the son, that is, *not* the father—while he's there. I, on the other hand, have promised to deliver food baskets to some of the more needy within the parish, which will take up a good share of my day, so I doubt I shall learn anything helpful, but I will certainly try. You must set aside time in the evening after dinner for us to discuss things. Time is of the essence. Perhaps I shall ask Halford and Anthony to assist as well."

Louisa went over and kissed Mama on the cheek. She didn't mention that Alex and Anthony were already seeing what they could find out. "I believe I'll retire now," she said. "I'm tired."

Mama drew her in for a hug, and, oh, how Louisa needed it, how it made her feel like a little girl again, safe and loved within her mother's arms. "Good night, my darling girl. Rest well."

"Good night, Mama."

Louisa wasn't sure how well she would rest. The image of William agonizing while trying to express what should have been the simplest things about himself kept running through her mind over and over again. She had a lot to think about.

She had barely entered her bedroom when there was a soft knock at the door, and then Alex opened it a few inches and poked his head inside. "I've been waiting for you," he whispered. "May I come in?" He shut the door silently behind himself without waiting for her to answer and then stood where he was, looking at her, his brows wrinkled, his mouth in a deep frown.

She'd noticed earlier that, besides Anthony, Alex, who was usually so lighthearted, had been in an atypically sober mood throughout the day. She'd assumed it was because she'd asked Anthony and him to help her and he'd decided to actually take his role seriously while William was here today. Apparently, she'd been wrong, for something was truly troubling Alex—and few things troubled him. She wrapped her arms around her middle. "You know something," she said.

"Yes," he said.

"Is it very bad, then?" she asked, regardless of the fact that the look on Alex's face had already answered that particular question.

"Come; let's sit," he replied. He led her to the small sofa in front of the fireplace and sat next to her, draping his arm around her shoulders.

There was another soft tap at the door, and then Anthony poked his head into the room.

"What a surprise," Alex muttered.

"I've been waiting for you to come upstairs ever since I heard Farleigh leave," Anthony said. He glared at his older brother. "What are you doing here?"

"I asked you first," Alex drawled.

"No, you didn't," Anthony countered. "But I'll tell you anyway. I came to check on my little sister to see how she's doing. Farleigh left rather early for someone intent on wooing Louisa—and who has been gone the better part of a week. What's *your* reason, Alex?"

Alex looked at Louisa for direction.

"You may as well say whatever it is you have to say in front of Tony too," she answered.

He glared at Anthony. "I suppose he'll find out sooner or later anyway. Very well. Kerridge was at the Marwoods' last night—at least for part of the evening," he said. "You didn't mention that he'd offered for you again, Weezy."

"*What?*" Anthony asked, except, really, it was more of an exclamation than a question.

"I didn't say anything because I didn't know what to think!" Louisa said. "He showed up in the Meltons' box Wednesday night, told me he *forgave* me, of all things, and then proposed again. It seems I am of sufficient status that London Society will quickly forget what happened and move on. Kerridge suggested that I am simply to end the betrothal to William and marry him—just like that." She snapped her finger to make her point. "But it also became patently obvious that he doesn't care about *me*, not really, no matter what he said. I'm *supremely suitable*, you see, so it's worth his time to give me another chance. That's what he was really saying, and the more I've thought about it since, the angrier I've gotten." She didn't tell them about her fiery conversation at Vauxhall with William; what she'd said was sufficient.

Imagine that, she thought with irony. She'd been *judicious* in her use of words and hadn't *babbled*, despite how turbulent her emotions and her stomach were at the moment.

"The devil you say," Anthony said. "I wish I'd known about it before now."

"At any rate," Alex interrupted, "Kerridge asked to speak with me privately, which is when I learned of his second proposal, by the way. Perhaps you aren't giving him enough credit, Weezy. Perhaps he cares about you more than you think. He told me he was worried about you, so I agreed to go with him briefly and hear what he had to say." He took a deep breath and then cleared his throat. "Weezy . . ." He trailed off and then slid closer to her and pulled her to him in a gentle hug.

"Is it really that bad?" she asked.

He didn't immediately respond; he simply held her close and stared somberly at Tony, who pulled up a chair to sit across from them, their knees nearly touching. Finally, Alex heaved a big sigh. "Louisa, Kerridge said he saw Farleigh assist a woman into a carriage, follow her inside, and drive off together. A fairly young, unusually attractive woman, she was, according to Kerridge."

"The *devil* you say!" Tony hissed.

Louisa's stomach convulsed, nearly doubling her over. Of all the things Alex could have said, she would never once have suspected anything like that.

Alex began rubbing her back. "Are you all right?" he asked.

"No, of course I'm not," she managed to grind out. The world swirled around her in a haze of black and red. She fought for breath and squeezed her eyes shut. A young, attractive woman surely meant only one thing . . .

"Does she have any smelling salts?" she heard Tony ask frantically.

"I don't know! Maybe at her dressing table?"

Louisa heard rather than saw Anthony jump up and begin rummaging through her things. "I'm fine," she said. "I don't need smelling salts."

"No, you're not." Alex's ministrations to her back became even more vigorous. "I'm not fine, so you can't be fine."

"I promise you I'm not going to faint." She opened her eyes and immediately closed them again, surprised by how dizzy she was. She could still hear Anthony opening drawers and cabinet doors and muttering some fairly harsh language he would never say in mixed company in other circumstances. She concentrated on getting her breathing under control. "Tony, sit down. You're only making things worse."

He walked over and dropped heavily into his chair.

Louisa tried opening her eyes again. The world around her had ceased to spin, so she sat up, which forced Alex to stop rubbing her back—frankly, it had been getting on her nerves too. "What more do you know that you haven't said yet, Alex?" she asked, bracing herself. For there had to be more, else he wouldn't have been so grave all day long or as upset as he was now.

"There was luggage on the carriage, Weezy. *Her* luggage, according to Kerridge, and quite a bit of it. Kerridge owns a house nearby and was in the process of leaving that morning when he saw Farleigh with the woman, although they didn't see him."

"And this happened . . . ?" It was a pointless question; she knew when it had happened. But she still had to hear Alex say the words aloud.

"Thursday morning, when you received his note informing you that he was again leaving town," he answered quietly.

"I see." She doubled over again, clutching her middle to hold the pain at bay. Alex pulled her even closer to him, and she turned and buried her face in the folds of his shirt. She could feel Tony patting her knees.

She felt cold and hot and empty and small.

A mistress. The woman was surely William's mistress. Kerridge and Alex both thought she was. Undoubtedly, Anthony did too. They knew more about such matters than she did, and from what Kerridge had seen and told Alex, it seemed likely. Was William so desperate for her money and connections that he would hide something like this from her? Would he manipulate her in this way? He'd seemed truly sincere in his care for her at Vauxhall, and this evening, his emotions had been raw as he'd tried to open up to her. And he *had* tried; she *knew* he had.

And yet, he held things so deeply inside that she didn't know him well enough to be confident either.

Gradually, the black and red began to clear from her vision, and she released herself from her brother's arms and stood. She walked over to the window. She needed space. She needed to think.

"Whatever you want me to do, Weezy, I'll do," Alex said. "I'll go to Farleigh's place and pummel him into the ground, if you like. Tony will too; won't you, Tony?"

"It would be my pleasure," Anthony replied.

"I know I've brought you bad news, and I'm truly sorry about that," Alex said. "But in the long run, it's better to learn about it now, while you still have time to change your mind about marrying the chap."

She continued looking out the window, out at the garden lit by a large, bright moon, and mulled over what she'd learned so far. "This is what I have concluded about Lord Kerridge," she said. "He has been arrogant and condescending and, quite honestly, Alex, I doubt he can look at anything William does with the least amount of objectivity."

"Are you saying you don't believe him?" Anthony asked. "Do you think he made it up to cause trouble?"

"No," Louisa replied. "I don't think he would outright lie to create an advantage for himself. Kerridge saw what he saw and felt he needed to share it." She turned to face her brothers. "Do you have a mistress, Alex? Do you, Anthony?" she asked.

Both brothers went as red as a beetroot. "I cannot believe you just asked us that," Anthony exclaimed, a look of utter horror on his face. "Nor is it a question I will answer. Good *heavens*, Louisa, whatever has gotten into you?"

"You know very well what has gotten into me," she answered indignantly.

Alex remained silent, his face gradually returning to its usual color. "In answer to your question, Weezy, I do *not* have a mistress, no," he said. "Nor have I ever. That is not to say I am a saint, however. That being said, our father taught both Anthony and me that fidelity in marriage is honorable and preferable to the selfishness of taking a mistress. One has made vows before God when one marries, you see, and therefore, marriage is not to be taken lightly. But this is not a discussion about Tony and me or our personal behavior; this is about you and Farleigh and what Kerridge claims he saw."

"You're right. And since I have questions about William I intend to have answered before the final banns are read, I have decided I will find those answers for myself," Louisa said. She stalked over to the door of her dressing room. "Tibbetts," she called softly.

The door opened, and Tibbetts, yawning, her hair tucked in a night-cap, appeared. "Yes, milady?"

"I wish to pack for a two day's journey. Nothing too elaborate; clothing suitable for the countryside."

Tibbetts curtsied and left.

"Our little sister is hatching something devious, it would seem," Alex whispered loudly behind his hand to Anthony.

"There is a definite glint in her eye," Anthony replied. "It has me quaking in my boots."

"Enough, both of you," she said. "If I am to consign my fate to him, I will do so with both eyes open. I am determined in this."

"If that is so, Weezy," Anthony said, "then, assuredly, Alex and I will help you."

"Thank you. For I wish to go to Buckinghamshire, to Farleigh Manor. Tomorrow morning, at first light. I want to speak to the people there, the people who actually *know* William and know him best."

"You have our undivided attention," Alex said.

* * *

Louisa awoke early the next morning, clear-headed and with a sense of resolve.

Buckinghamshire was a mere half day's journey from London, and since she intended to be there for only a day or two, packing was easily completed and the carriage readied by ten o'clock. It was fortuitous that she had known Mama and Papa had both planned to leave the house early, Papa to the House of Lords and Mama to deliver charity boxes.

It had been agreed amongst the siblings that Anthony would remain in London to explain Louisa and Alex's sudden absence and deal with any unforeseen trouble that might arise. Trouble meaning Lord Farleigh. Anthony had assured Louisa he could ward Farleigh off for a day or two with excuses that she had been shaken by their encounter—which was true enough—and wasn't ready to see him yet as a result.

Additionally, Anthony was to tell their parents that Louisa and Alex were visiting Farleigh Manor so she could become acquainted with her future home—also essentially true, albeit not the entire truth since they had not been *invited* to do so by William, but Mama and Papa would assume so. If either parent raised questions regarding the suddenness of the trip, Anthony was to weave a colorful fabric of explanations that would reassure them, especially when they knew Alex would be at Louisa's side the entire time, along with Louisa's personal maid, Tibbetts.

Louisa and Alex made good time and arrived in the village of Farsham, the seat of Viscount Farleigh, by midafternoon. Louisa wasn't sure what she'd expected to find and was pleasantly surprised by what she discovered. The village was small but boasted, among other things, a bakery and a grocer, a millinery shop, a lovely ancient church, and a pub called the George and Dragon, which seemed to be doing a thriving business at the moment.

They learned from a friendly and curious villager that if they followed the high street, they would come to a road on the right that wound around a nearby hill, and on the other side of the hill, they would find Farleigh Manor.

They found the road described, and Louisa stared out the carriage window as they rounded the hill, taking in every rock and tree and flower and trying to imagine William here as a boy. They eventually spotted a tree-lined lane that marked the entrance to the manor and turned onto it. And then the house came into view.

Farleigh Manor did not compare by half to the grandeur of Ashworth Park, the country estate of her father, but had a modest, rustic charm. It was constructed of red brick, covered in ivy, and had two stories and an attic. It was laid out symmetrically with a generous use of windows.

As the carriage rolled up to the front entrance, the doors of the manor house opened, and an elderly, white-haired man with stooped shoulders stepped outside.

Alex exited the carriage first and then assisted Louisa from the carriage. He handed his calling card to the man. "The Earl of Halford," he said, using his most bored, aristocratic tone. "And my sister, Lady Louisa Hargreaves, daughter of the Marquess of Ashworth."

"Welcome to Farleigh Manor, your lordship, your ladyship," the man said with a deep, formal bow. "Grimshaw, the butler, at your service. We've been expecting you." He looked about. "But where is Lord Farleigh? Has he been detained?"

"Still in London, I'm afraid," Alex drawled. "But we chose to come anyway. Hope that isn't a problem."

"Not at all, not at all," Grimshaw said. He gestured for them to enter. "As I say, we've been expecting you."

A woman wearing a neat gray dress stepped outside to join them. "Indeed, we have," she said, her eyes sparkling. "Welcome to Farleigh Manor."

"May I present Mrs. Holly, the housekeeper," Grimshaw said. "Mrs. Holly, this is the Earl of Halford and his sister, Lady Louisa Hargreaves."

"Oh, and just look at you!" Mrs. Holly exclaimed. "You're as pretty as I hoped you'd be. Prettier! But where have my manners gone? Gracious me!" She quickly curtsied to them both before clutching her hands to her breast. "Goodness, but you are a dream come true after all these years! When our dear boy—"

Grimshaw cleared his throat.

"There I go again," she said. "What I mean to say is, when Lord Farleigh sent word for us to prepare for the arrival of a new viscountess, we were beside ourselves with joy. But now that you're here, seeing you . . ." Her voice trailed off, and she searched in her apron pocket, retrieving a handkerchief that she used to dab at her eyes.

"Please forgive Mrs. Holly," Grimshaw said. "She was that fond of his lordship as a lad. We all were, come to that." He gestured for them to enter Farleigh Manor ahead of himself and the housekeeper.

The Ashworth butlers, Gibbs and Buxton, would never have spoken in such an informal manner, especially to utter strangers, nor would the house-keepers. It simply wasn't done. But Louisa thought their candid comments surprisingly sweet, and she had to bite the inside of her cheek to keep a serene look on her face.

Alex couldn't hide his amusement, however, and chuckled as they preceded the others into the house. "What a place," he whispered in Louisa's ear.

Indeed, she thought but not quite for the same reasons as Alex.

* * *

Notwithstanding the best of intentions, William had a difficult time leaving his house Monday morning. He'd planned on seeing Louisa first thing—well, as soon as it was socially appropriate to call upon her. Ladies had par-ticular hours for such things, he knew, not that he knew precisely what hours were considered appropriate.

He'd decided, therefore, to call at one o'clock. It was early enough to be considered a morning call, and late enough not to be seen as gauche. He thought.

He really had no idea.

It hadn't helped that he'd barely slept a wink. He must have repeated the utterly mortifying conversation he'd had with Louisa in his head hundreds of times during the night. He'd viewed his words from every conceivable angle, and his conclusion had always been the same: they had been gut-wrenching, ludicrous, and wholly inadequate.

He'd hunted down Mrs. Gideon and asked her with extreme politeness if she would put his best suit of clothes into the best order possible. Normally, she had a girl who saw to William's shirts and linens, considering it beneath her role as housekeeper to do laundry. But after a bit of cajoling and pressing a few quid into her palm, she'd agreed.

It took her an hour or so to brush his clothes and iron a few neckcloths while he polished his boots, and she did it without too much grumbling, for which William's aching head was truly grateful. He was definitely going to consider the pluses and minuses of hiring a valet in the future—it might be worth the expense after all.

He bathed, took his time shaving so he didn't miss any stubble lurking in the corners of his jaw or by his ears, dressed, and tied his neckcloth.

He pulled off the neckcloth and tossed it aside, taking another.

He pulled that one off as well.

After the fourth neckcloth, which resulted in an irate Mrs. Gideon stating unequivocally that if he removed *this* neckcloth, she would *not* iron another for him for the rest of her days, no matter *what*, he decided—reluctantly—that it would have to do.

He checked himself one last time in the mirror by the front door and left home . . . only to return when he realized he'd forgotten his hat and gloves and pocket watch.

Blasted fool.

Finally, at two minutes after two o'clock—he checked his pocket watch to be sure of the time—he arrived at Ashworth House, silently hoping no one had seen his approach yet so that he still had the option of changing his mind. Then he mentally kicked himself for wanting to change his mind. He was a coward as well as a fool.

He straightened, walked to the door, and knocked.

The door immediately opened, but it wasn't the Ashworth butler standing before him. It was Lord Anthony.

"Ah, Farleigh, I thought that was you I saw through the window," he said in an overly gregarious tone. "Never mind, Gibbs, I got the door," he called over his shoulder. But instead of inviting William inside, he came outside and pulled the door shut behind him.

"I'm here to call on your sister," William said, although, really, it needed no explanation. Lord Anthony would deduce the fact by William's simply being here. If his head didn't throb like a beast, he would be able to think more clearly.

"She's not receiving visitors today," Lord Anthony replied.

"Is she unwell? Is everything all right?" The idea that their conversation last night may have distressed her made William's head throb even harder.

"She *was* rather upset last evening . . . after you left." Lord Anthony let his words linger on the air for the few moments, but even so, William couldn't come up with a reasonable response before Lord Anthony continued. "Say, Farleigh, I was just on my way to take in a few rounds at Gentleman Jackson's. Are you a boxer, by any chance?"

One didn't survive boy's school without quickly figuring out how to use one's fists, yet William couldn't precisely recall the last time he'd actually done any boxing. "Well, I—"

"Excellent! You must join me, then. What finer way for future brothers-in-law to become better acquainted than a few gentlemanly rounds of boxing." He threw his arm around William's shoulders and led him rather aggressively back toward the street.

William skidded to a halt. "Wait. What about Louisa? She and I have a conversation to finish. I have a promise to keep with her."

"And keep it you must. But it shan't be happening today, old chap; I can tell you that with a high degree of certainty. Where is your carriage?"

"I, uh, hackney," William said. He hadn't wanted Walter to be present, in case he'd ultimately chosen the cowardly route.

"Follow me, then." Lord Anthony took off in the direction of the private lane that led to the mews behind Ashworth House, and William mutely followed.

Lord Anthony located one of the grooms, a boy of about eighteen, and instructed him to get his curricle ready. In no time at all—William was quite sure he'd shut his eyes for only a moment—the groom returned with a fine curricle William couldn't help but admire and even covet just a bit.

"Thank you, Tom," Lord Anthony said. "Good man. We're going to Gentleman Jackson's. Hop on back."

Lord Anthony climbed into the curricle and took the reins from Tom, who jumped into his seat at the back of the curricle. "Come on, then, Farleigh. Let's be off," Lord Anthony called. "Time is our enemy."

That statement was true enough, William thought as he climbed into the curricle. Time was definitely his enemy, as he had once again lost an opportunity to speak with Louisa. She had been upset enough to not accept visitors today. William concluded that by "visitors," she'd meant him. It was also highly likely that at least one of her brothers was fully aware of the situation.

And William had just agreed to a few rounds of boxing with him. He hoped he and his head survived.

* * *

The first thing Louisa noticed when she stepped into the entry hall of Farleigh Manor was its overall emptiness. There were no paintings accenting the walls as there were at Ashworth Park and Ashworth House, except for a single piece of framed needlework. Dark rectangles on the walls showed where paintings had hung—the rest of the wallpaper having faded over the years, leaving the artworks' drab ghosts behind. At Ashworth Park, a great chandelier with shining crystals illuminated the entry hall, but Farleigh Manor boasted no such extravagance, beyond a telltale mark in the high ceiling where a chandelier of some sort must have hung.

Mrs. Holly excused herself and bustled out of the room, leaving Louisa and Alex with Grimshaw, but in short order, she was back, leading a small group of people into the hall single file—the service staff of Farleigh Manor. A few of them were wiping their dirty hands on aprons or shirtsleeves, and Louisa heard Alex snort.

They were introduced to Matthew, the steward, who'd "recently been promoted from groundskeeper, milady"; the cook, Mrs. Brill, and her daughter, Mary, a sweet girl who appeared to be slow-witted and rather childlike; Samuel, the stable master; as well as a young girl, Sally, and a boy, Jim, who served as maid- and man-of-all-work.

"I'm very pleased to meet you all," Louisa said, smiling, hoping she came across as kind and approachable. She needed to earn their trust quickly if she was to learn anything of import in the next day and a half.

Mary, the simple girl, broke the line and rushed toward her, her arms outstretched. "You're the *real* one, then, what's marrying our Will and giving 'im babies! Not the one—"

Mrs. Brill darted after her and quickly grabbed her arm and pulled her back into line. "Hush, Mary, dear," Mrs. Brill murmured. "Apologies, milady."

"Not to worry," Louisa said, taken aback. Mary's innocent words had provided the first real evidence that another woman was involved somehow, but they weren't at all what Louisa had hoped to hear. "Perhaps, if you would be so kind, you would show my brother and me to our rooms so we can get settled in. Afterward, I should like to tour the house and get to know each of you better."

"Very good, milady," Mrs. Holly said, nodding.

Old Grimshaw bowed. "Jim will see that your trunks are taken upstairs."

"Sally, get some fresh water and towels for Lady Louisa and Lord Halford," Mrs. Holly added. The housekeeper was beaming. "*Such* a pleasure to have you here at last, milady! And you too, milord," she hastily added.

"Hmph," Alex said, arching his eyebrow and looking down his nose at her, but Louisa knew he was actually laughing inside.

Mrs. Holly led the way up the stairs and showed each of them their guest rooms. The rooms were sparsely furnished, the quality not much better than that of a rustic inn, but Mrs. Holly was gracious and helpful and unapologetic about its appearance, which Louisa appreciated.

After a quick review of his room, Alex excused himself, telling Louisa he wished to go outside and get better acquainted with Samuel, the stable master, and Matthew, the groundskeeper-slash-steward.

"If you would meet me in the entry hall in fifteen minutes, Mrs. Holly, I would be grateful. And then you may show me the house," Louisa said.

"Very good, milady." Mrs. Holly curtsied and left.

The tour began in the sitting room. Louisa checked the condition of the few pieces of furniture, then carefully inspected the draperies for holes. Mrs. Holly hovered nearby, ready to answer questions. "We have done our best to keep the house in good repair, I assure you," she said.

Louisa nodded in acknowledgment. She ran her fingers over the mantelpiece, noting there was another framed piece of needlework hanging above the fireplace. "This is lovely. Who was it done by?" she asked.

"The current Lord Farleigh's mother," Mrs. Holly said. "Such a talented lady, she was too. An eye for color such as few people have, I daresay. She had a sketchbook she kept for her ideas, but—well, it's gone now. But her son got her talent, as I'm sure you already know."

Louisa did know. William's painting of the oak tree was ample proof.

So far, she'd found Mrs. Holly's work exceptional. So exceptional, in fact, that regardless of how threadbare the rugs were or the wear on the upholstery of the single sofa facing the fireplace or the removal of paintings from the walls, one still felt a sense of tidy respectability. The tables—there were but two small ones—were lacking ornamental pieces one would normally find on display in the homes of the upper classes but were dressed with inexpensive crockery overflowing with flowers instead. Louisa didn't ask, but owing to what she'd learned so far about the former viscount, she assumed anything of value had been sold to cover his debts at various points in time.

Louisa followed Mrs. Holly upstairs to the private family rooms, specifically the viscount's private suite, located in the wing opposite those of the guest rooms she and Alex were using. The viscount's rooms, done in dark woods and shades of burgundy, were not in the same shabby state as the rest of Farleigh Manor and had been cleaned and aired recently—no doubt in preparation for the new viscount, yet Louisa could see no evidence that William had stayed here.

The adjoining viscountess's rooms were decorated in pale greens and pinks, the bed neatly made. A lone bud vase with a single pink rose sat on a table by the window, and another framed needlework William's mother had made hung on an otherwise bare wall. There was a sad emptiness here, and Louisa ached for a boy who had been separated from his mother too soon and then had lost her.

They proceeded down the hall, and Mrs. Holly pointed out William's room. "Not that there's much to see there that you haven't already seen in the other rooms, milady," she said.

Mrs. Holly was right—the room, while smaller, wasn't much different from the master suite, with the same dark woods and deep colors giving it an overtly masculine look. The four-poster bed had a dark-blue counterpane and bed curtains, with matching drapes at the window. A landscape hung on the wall above the fireplace, which had been cleaned and laid with tinder for its next use. Louisa examined the landscape, appreciating the bold strokes the artist had used, the contrast between light and shade. It had the same artist's signature on it as the oak tree, but she'd already observed the similarities in style of both pieces. William had painted this one too.

She moved to the four-poster bed and ran her hand along the slightly faded counterpane and then wandered over to the writing desk. The inkwell was full, the quills sharpened, the blotter neat and ready for use, but there was nothing here that made the room uniquely William's beyond the painting. Disappointed, she had said as much to Mrs. Holly.

"He's been gone from us for so long, now, milady," Mrs. Holly said. "We always kept the room as it was while Lady Farleigh was alive, God rest her soul, but afterward—well, I don't wish to speak ill of the dead, but we were ordered to box Master William's personal items up and store them in the attic, along with Lady Farleigh's. Except—" She stopped abruptly.

"Yes?"

"Nothing. One small item, that's all. I was going to have one thing for Master William to come home to, should he ever feel inclined, now, wasn't I? And he did come home, and it does our hearts good to see him, handsome, worthy man that he's become, and to see what a lovely bride he's bringing to be mistress here."

"Thank you, Mrs. Holly. It's very kind of you to say so."

Louisa heard a noise outside the room, a scuffling sound, and glanced toward the door, trying to figure out what it might be, hoping it wasn't vermin. Not an appealing thought, but the house *was* in need of attention—

"Don't you worry, milady; that's just Mary. She's a sweet but slow girl, is our Mary. She works as a scullery maid so her mother can keep a close eye on her. *Not* that she gets into trouble, mind," Mrs. Holly hastily added. "But she's so trusting, she's bound to be taken advantage of by those who would be so inclined."

Which, Louisa took to understand, meant something of the sort had happened before.

"She busies herself about the place when she's not doing chores," Mrs. Holly continued. "Likes to roam about and hide in rooms and the attic and such. We're all fond of the girl, and William was always kind to her. Such a good lad." She smiled at some long-ago memory.

The scuffling stopped eventually, the afternoon turned to evening, and before Louisa knew it, it was time to dress for supper. She and Alex were to discuss everything they had learned during supper and strategize for tomorrow. Louisa had gleaned quite a bit from Mrs. Holly, but the housekeeper had stayed so close to Louisa all afternoon that she hadn't had the opportunity to speak to Mrs. Brill or the little maid, Sally. And she'd failed to learn anything about the mysterious woman, other than what Mary had blurted out when they'd first arrived. She wanted to talk further with Mary . . . but the girl had vanished, and Louisa hadn't seen her since.

She would not share William—or any husband, for that matter—with another woman. If he was the kind of gentleman who saw marriage as a duty with pleasure found elsewhere, he was not for her. But what other reason could there be for William to have been with an attractive, unknown woman? And why else would Mary have called Louisa "the real one" and begun to mention someone else, only to be stopped by the others?

Nothing she had learned so far had allayed her fears about this unknown woman. She hoped tomorrow provided the answers she needed and hoped she was sufficiently prepared for the answers, especially if they were ones she didn't want to hear.

Chapter 13

LOUISA AND ALEX DECIDED AT supper that they would tour the estate grounds together. So the following morning, bright and early, Samuel met them outside with two saddled horses, as arranged.

"Sorry the sidesaddle isn't as up to snuff as ye're used to, melady," Samuel said after greeting them both. "The former viscountess didn't use it much at the end, and then there weren't no need." He looked down at his feet.

"I'm sure it will be fine," Louisa replied. "Did she use to ride a lot before then?"

"Oh, here and there, in the early days. After our William—er, the current viscount—were born, she stopped for the most part. O' course, the viscount were away in Town a good share o' the time, and she preferred to spend time with the baby, like any good ma." He paused and scratched at his chin. "Mostly got out o' the habit, I'd say."

He wasn't telling her everything, but she didn't press him for details. He assisted her into the saddle while Alex mounted his own horse.

"Ye be visiting the village, then?" Samuel asked.

"No," Alex replied. "We've decided to tour the estate."

Samuel looked alarmed before quickly smoothing his features and saying, "T'ain't much to see on the estate these days, I'm afraid. Only a bit o' the farmland is bein' used at present. Matthew will tell ye that several good tenants up and left after Lady Farleigh passed on. Now, the village, that's a lively place, and if I were going wid ye, I'd suggest a visit to the George and Dragon, and there's a shop on the corner makes the best apple tarts—"

"Oh, *there* you are!" A harried-looking Mrs. Holly rushed toward them, her skirts and apron blowing about her. "I didn't realize you'd finished your breakfast," she said, breathing quickly from her exertion. "Mrs. Brill just told me. I had thought we'd be spending time today going through the inventory, and Mrs. Brill said she'd love to have you tour the kitchen in detail."

Matthew came loping around the corner of the building. "Lord Halford, if you have some time, I'd like to show you the records for the estate in more detail. What do you say?"

Louisa and Alex shared a glance. It was patently obvious the others were doing everything they could to keep them from exploring the grounds; they hadn't even flinched yesterday when Alex had toured the stable yard and Louisa had been shown the manor house. But now they were scrambling to keep her and Alex occupied and away from the estate grounds, which only convinced Louisa that she and Alex were on the right track.

"Thank you, Mrs. Holly," Louisa replied. "I would enjoy doing both of those things. But it's a lovely day, and the estate is beckoning me. I think Halford and I will use it to our advantage. Perhaps the two of you can set aside some time for us this afternoon after tea."

"Any objections?" Alex said, looking at each of them with a raised eyebrow that meant he had better not hear any.

"No, milord," Mrs. Holly said. She shot a look at Matthew.

Matthew took a step forward, picking up on her cue. "I'd like to go with you, then, if I may," he said. "I don't wish to speak out of turn, mind you, but as groundskeeper, I know the land better than anyone here about, shortcuts and such." He waited for a reply, looking up at Alex meekly, a look Louisa suspected he most likely developed over years of dealing with the former viscount. She'd gotten the impression earlier that Matthew was smarter than most people gave him credit for. Except for William, that is, who had recognized intelligence in him and had entrusted him to oversee his land as steward . . .

"Very well," Alex said with a bored sigh reserved for exclusive use by noblemen. "Get your horse. But be quick about it."

Samuel and Matthew both dashed to the stable to saddle up a horse.

"Are you sure you're up to something quite so vigorous after your long journey from London yesterday, milady?" Mrs. Holly asked, obviously unwilling to simply capitulate.

"Quite sure," Louisa replied.

"Thank you, Mrs. Holly," Alex added firmly.

She curtsied deeply and scurried off to the house.

"I believe we're finally onto something," he whispered when Mrs. Holly was out of earshot.

"Yes," Louisa said.

Matthew was approaching them on horseback now while Samuel stayed back by the stable doors. "I thought we'd start by meeting some of the tenants still working on the home farm," Matthew said. He pointed south. "This way."

"I believe we'll go north," Alex said.

"But—"

"North," Alex said again.

Matthew slumped in his saddle. "Very well, milord. North it is."

They headed down a small lane that led from the courtyard at the front of the house around one side of the stable and continued on in a northerly direction. It was considerably overgrown, but it appeared that a conveyance of some kind had recently used it, based on the wheel marks and freshly crushed plants that were visible.

The horses traveled at a walk, with Alex taking the lead and Matthew and Louisa following closely behind. It was unseasonably warm, and the heat of the sun filtered through the trees that grew on either side of the lane and down onto Louisa's shoulders. The farther north they went, the quieter Matthew became. He responded politely to Alex's questions along the way, but his answers became shorter and shorter.

After what seemed like forever but was probably no more than fifteen minutes, they rounded a corner that took them to the right. The foliage had blocked their view, but now, in the distance, Louisa could see a cottage. It wasn't a large place, but it was of finer construction than the typical tenant's cottage, and its appearance made Louisa's heart race and her hands tremble. They were close to getting the answers they'd come to Farleigh Manor to get; she could feel it.

Alex gave his horse a nudge forward, and Matthew shot a somber look at Louisa, confirming her suspicions. She urged her own horse forward until she was riding next to Alex. They were nearly to the cottage, and Louisa desperately wished to go right on past and continue down the lane and away from the inevitable truth of the mystery woman. It would take them to, to . . . who knew where . . . But Louisa didn't care. She wanted to leave. Now that the truth was before her, she didn't want to know—

The door opened, and a woman who appeared to be in her early thirties stepped outside onto the threshold.

An attractive woman.

Louisa gasped—and everything went black.

"Louisa!" she heard someone call from far away.

Then there were arms around her, arms that lifted her from the horse, that carried her out of the heat and into coolness. Blessed darkness . . .

She opened her eyes and blinked several times to bring the world back into focus. She was reclining on a sofa, and Alex was kneeling in front of her. Matthew stood behind him, his eyebrows drawn together in concern.

"What happened?" she asked. She felt a bit queasy, which was odd. She didn't remember feeling queasy before.

"You fainted," Alex said gently.

"I never faint," she replied indignantly.

"You did this time," Alex said.

As her vision cleared further, she saw another person—the woman—standing off a ways, watching. Watching Louisa's disgrace.

Louisa squeezed her eyes shut, blocking the woman out. "Who is she?" Louisa asked Alex in a whisper, mortified that whoever she was, she was witnessing all of this.

"There's time enough for that later," Alex murmured. "Ah, thank you." He took a glass of water from a young boy who suddenly appeared out of nowhere and then handed it to Louisa, keeping his hands on the glass until he was sure she wasn't going to spill it all over herself. "Steady now. Just a few sips to start."

She sipped the water. It was cool and tasted good. Her mouth was dry, so she took another sip and then another. She handed the glass back to Alex and attempted to sit up, but dizziness forced her to lie back. Her head felt as if it were stuffed with cotton. This wasn't like her at all.

"I don't faint; I never faint," she grumbled. "Have you ever seen me faint?"

Alex chuckled. "Clearly, you're beginning to feel more like your usual self, Weezy." He handed her the glass, and she drank more water. "You *have* been under more strain than usual the past week or two, you know. It was bound to catch up with you sooner or later."

"Well, it couldn't have picked a worse time."

"You gave us a bit of a scare there, Lady Louisa," Matthew said. "Luckily, your brother has quick reflexes and caught you before you hit the ground. It was quite remarkable, really," the man continued with a thoughtful look on his face. "Him leaping from his horse like that and catching you as you fell forward off your sidesaddle."

She covered her eyes with her hand and groaned in embarrassment. The woman was still there, watching, the young boy standing at her side—and when had a little girl joined them?

"I may as well be introduced," Louisa muttered. She lowered her hand from her eyes and sat up, slowly moving her feet from the sofa to the floor, and then straightened her skirts. The only way to get through a difficult situation was straightforward—at least, it was in this case. She couldn't exactly sneak out of the room and return to the manor house at this point.

Matthew cleared his throat, looking resigned. "Lord Halford, Lady Louisa, may I present . . ." He paused as if searching for the right words, which was odd. "Allow me to present Miss Jane Purnell and her children, Peter and Daisy."

The woman curtsied, as did the little girl. The boy bowed stiffly. "How do you, your lordship, your ladyship," the woman said.

She was Miss Purnell. She had two children, but she was a *miss*. Louisa shut her eyes again, in defeat this time. She must be William's mistress after all, but Louisa never in her wildest thoughts expected there would be children—

"Er," Matthew said. "There is more that needs to be explained."

"Then please do so, man. Don't leave us in suspense," Alex drawled. He folded his arms over his chest.

Louisa hunted with unsteady hands through the pocket of her dress for a handkerchief.

Matthew looked at the floor as if for inspiration before turning to look at the woman—*Miss* Purnell.

Alex began tapping his foot. Loudly.

Matthew heaved out a large breath.

"Never mind, Matthew," the woman said. "I can speak for myself, if they'll permit me."

Alex gestured for her to do so.

Miss Purnell crouched down by the children. "Peter, will you please take Daisy out into the garden? Perhaps you can help her pick flowers to give our guests."

"Yes, Mama." Peter took little Daisy by the hand and led her from the room.

Louisa heard a door at the back of the cottage open and close.

Miss Purnell stood straight and looked directly at Louisa. "Until recently, I was Mrs. William Barlow. Senior," she quickly added. "Or at least I thought I was. Only last week, I received word that my marriage was a fraud and that, as a result, my children are illegitimate and we are destitute. When Lord Farleigh—the current Lord Farleigh, that is—learned of our situation, he offered this house to us."

"I don't understand," Louisa said. Perhaps she was still suffering ill effects from the fainting spell, but the woman's words made no sense.

"Allow me to put some tea on," Miss Purnell replied. "It is a story that will take some time to tell."

* * *

William braced himself to call upon Louisa the afternoon following his encounter with Lord Anthony. Perhaps it had been a good thing he hadn't seen her and that she'd had time to herself—time away from *him*, to be more precise. He'd reflected at length, once again, upon their conversation Sunday night, specifically his ineptitude at sharing himself with her. How frustrating he must have been, and must be, to her.

And how presumptuous he had been with her. He'd had the temerity to suggest at their initial meeting that she could not have become attached to Lord Kerridge after a mere two weeks' time. He had been wrong on that score, because he'd known Louisa for an equally short amount of time, and at some point during the past two days, he had realized he was in love with her. Well, most assuredly, he was. He'd been struck speechless by her the moment he'd laid eyes on her and had been enchanted by her ever since. She was bright and candid and vulnerable and strong—how could William not have fallen in love with her?

He'd brought the little family portrait with him to London this time. He'd looked at it several times over the past two days and studied it again now. There he was just older than Peter, standing next to his mother, who was seated. His father stood behind them both. The artist had managed to capture the indiscernible expression his father had always worn.

William's mother sat gazing serenely on, her back straight, the beautiful viscountess she'd always been readily apparent, albeit William had only ever thought of her as his loving mama. Age and experience did much to expand one's perspective. Perhaps, when this painting was done, his mother had still had hope for her marriage. Perhaps not. William did not know.

William looked beyond the portrait to the blue sky showing through the window, then shook his head. It was time to call on Louisa again, apologize for his disappointing lack of openness, and proceed with the marriage plans. He washed and dressed sensibly once again, taking care as he shaved so as not to irritate the swelling and bruise that had formed on his jaw after its encounter with Lord Anthony's fist yesterday at Gentleman Jackson's. Louisa's brother had been able to land a few heavy blows in what was supposed to have been a friendly bout of boxing for the sake of exercise. William's jaw hurt like the very devil today, as did a couple of ribs.

He called for his horse to be readied and rode to Ashworth House, knotted up inside with guilt and shame and desperation—and a love he'd not expected to find.

Too soon, William reached his destination, lifted the knocker, and braced himself. For what? Silence? Silence was what he was used to, and he was comfortable with it. Louisa was not a silent person by nature, however. It was one of the things he loved most about her.

Words, then. He braced himself for more words, potentially with the same volatile delivery he'd received at Vauxhall. He would welcome her words and give her the freedom to share them and not keep her feelings to herself. He would not be responsible for destroying what was uniquely her, as his father had done to his mother.

Gibbs opened the door. "My lord," the butler said in greeting, giving no indication of what William could expect to face once inside.

"Good afternoon, Gibbs," William said. "I am here to call on—"

"Farleigh! Is that you again?" Lord Anthony nearly pushed Gibbs aside in his rush to greet William and welcome him into the house. William had to give the butler credit, as the man didn't even blink an eye at the rough handling; he merely closed the door and faded from sight. Butlers would make good gamblers, he thought. He suddenly hoped Gibbs had a nice wife waiting for him at the end of a long day.

Lord Anthony practically dragged William into one of the smaller drawing rooms. "Good to see you. Ah, it appears I left some damage in my wake yesterday," he said, eyeing William's swollen and purple jaw. "Sorry about that, old man. I spotted your poor nag out there—I must take you to Tattersall's one of these days; we'll get you set up with a nice piece of horseflesh. Perhaps we should go this afternoon. I was there just the other day, and—"

"He's not a nag," William managed to wedge into Lord Anthony's flood of words. Apparently, the man had more in common with Louisa than

William had originally thought. "He's not of the highest of quality, perhaps, but he's a decent chap, as horses go. I'm here once again, as you well know, to call upon your sister."

"Drink, Farleigh?" Lord Anthony asked, picking up a decanter on a side table and pouring a small amount into a glass.

"No, thank you; it's rather early for that. I'd prefer you simply inform Louisa that I am here."

"Yes, well." He took a sip. "As to that, I'm afraid she is still unavailable."

Something was wrong. A sense of uneasiness began to coil inside William. "Perhaps later this evening would be better?" he asked.

"I don't think she's going to be available then, either."

The unease congealed into a solid gray mass. "I see. Well. Perhaps tomorrow, then." He turned to leave, having no more reason to stay and not being in a mood for further conversation about horses or, heaven forbid, receiving another invitation to box, when the drawing room door opened. "Lord Farleigh? I thought I heard your voice," Lady Ashworth said as she entered, looking for all the world as if she was in shock. Lord Anthony, William noticed, downed the rest of his drink in one big gulp. "But how can it be?"

"Ah, Mother!" Lord Anthony said in an overly cheerful tone. "Look who has come to call! I must be going—"

"You stay right where you are," she ordered, pointing a finger at her son, who immediately stopped in his tracks. "Why are you here, Lord Farleigh? I was distinctly given the impression"—she shot a fiery glare at Lord Anthony that should have singed the man's eyebrows—"that you have been at Farleigh Manor the past two days playing host to my daughter and son."

The gray mass in William's stomach shot up into his throat. "I . . . what?" he choked out.

"Anthony, would you care to explain to Lord Farleigh and me what precisely is going on?" Lady Ashworth asked in a commanding voice, which meant it wasn't a question.

"I think you must have figured it out for yourself, Mama," Lord Anthony answered sheepishly.

William went cold all over and sought to steady himself. Louisa had gone to Farleigh Manor. She would know by now what a wretch she had agreed to marry. She would have seen how destitute the estate was. She would have met . . . devil take it!

In being less than forthcoming, he had deceived her horribly. How could someone as open and honest as Louisa think otherwise or ever forgive him?

There had been so much at stake that it had truly seemed the right approach, the *only* approach, with the situation intensified by the discovery of Miss Purnell and Peter and Daisy. He should have been forthright with Louisa from the beginning and trusted her honorable nature rather than hold everything tightly within himself.

"Lady Ashworth," he said, "if you will excuse me, I must be on my way."

"I think that's an excellent idea, Lord Farleigh," he heard her say as he swiftly took his leave. "And Ashworth and I will be right behind you."

Chapter 14

A DEEP SORROW HAD WELLED up inside Louisa over the past two days and deepened further while they conversed with Jane Purnell—Louisa loathed referring to her as "miss" since the poor woman hadn't known her marriage was bigamous.

It was midafternoon by the time she and Alex bade Jane Purnell farewell after their visit. They had learned about William's father's courtship of Jane and the little house in London that she had thought was where they would always live. They had spent time with the children, Peter and Daisy. Peter was a handsome little boy but had seemed overly cautious for one so young and had stayed close to his mother, assuming a protective stance. Little Daisy had presented flowers to Louisa and shown her her doll and had told her the doll's name was Charlotte, like the princess. They were sweet, well-mannered children. They were William's half brother and half sister.

When Alex and Louisa and Matthew eventually returned to the manor, Alex announced that he was going to continue on with Matthew to view more of the estate. "Lord Halford here has given me some fine suggestions about the farms already, milady," Matthew said, "and I should like to hear more of what he has to say."

Louisa looked at Alex in surprise, and he smirked. "You see, I *was* paying attention all those years when Father was droning on about such matters."

Their decision was completely fine with her; at the moment, what she wanted was time alone to reflect upon everything she'd learned upon arriving at Farleigh Manor. Besides, there was one thing at Farleigh Manor she still wished to see—but she wanted to be alone when she saw it.

Matthew helped her dismount, and the two men left to return Louisa's horse to the stable and continue on their way. Louisa went inside and sought out Mrs. Holly, eventually finding her in her little office tucked behind the dayroom, reviewing the household accounts.

The woman set her papers aside and stood.

"We met Jane Purnell," Louisa said.

The woman sagged. "It was bound to happen sooner or later, I suppose," she said, folding her hands in front of her.

"I imagine her arrival came as quite a shock."

"When Master William arrived back here so soon with her and her two little chicks in tow, it was a bit of a shock. We never heard a peep about her over the years, you see, even though the viscount was briefly here at Farleigh Manor a few times each year. It *wasn't* a shock, however, to learn that he had married the poor woman under such circumstances, I'm sorry to admit."

"She's a very nice person," Louisa said. "Her children are sweet."

"The viscount at least recognized quality in a woman when he saw it," Mrs. Holly said. "Not that he knew how to respect and honor that quality. Selfish man—if you'll pardon me for saying so."

"No apology necessary, Mrs. Holly. I think I have figured out at least that much about him myself. And yet you all stayed."

"For Master William, you see. We had to stay for Master William. His high and mighty lordship wasn't here often. He could be especially cruel to Mary, poor duck, but Mary knew how to stay away from him; don't you worry. She hated the man. We all did, and that's the truth. But we stayed for her ladyship and, afterward, for Master William."

Louisa's heart was already sore, and she thought she could bear no more. "I understand there is a particularly fine oak tree on the estate," she said. "I received a painting of it from Lord Farleigh—the current Lord Farleigh. I should dearly like to see it in person."

"We've several oak trees on the property. But if you're looking for a particular oak . . . hmm." Mrs. Holly tapped her chin in thought. "There is one that comes to mind. It stands alone beside a pond just over the small hill on the east side of the house. It's a lovely spot once you get there."

"That sounds like the tree I'm interested in." Mrs. Holly's description matched the tree in the painting perfectly.

"It's not difficult to find. Mary can give you the best directions to get there; she's been there too many times to count, especially when she and Master—Lord Farleigh—were children."

Louisa went with Mrs. Holly to the kitchen in search of Mary. It had been a thoroughly illuminating two days; her discoveries today, in particular, had been shocking and sad. She hoped time alone would help her sort through her thoughts before she and Alex returned to London tomorrow morning.

A wonderful aroma met them the closer they got to the kitchen, and Louisa's stomach growled, reminding her it was well past time for luncheon.

"I'll leave you to it, then," Mrs. Holly said. "Have a nice afternoon at the oak tree, milady."

"Thank you, Mrs. Holly."

The housekeeper nodded and went on her way.

Louisa poked her head through the kitchen door and saw both Mrs. Brill and Mary busily preparing a variety of dishes. "Something smells heavenly in here, Mrs. Brill."

"Thank you, m'lady. What with you and the earl here and all, I couldn't resist cooking up some of Master Will's favorite dishes to celebrate. Mary, slice them potatoes thinner, luv."

Louisa wandered over to Mary, who was standing next to the table, slicing potatoes with admirable skill. "Excellent work, Mary. I can hardly wait for supper so I can taste what you and your mama have created for us."

Mary grinned at her, then looked confused, unsure how to curtsy with a knife, then gave up. "Will loves potatoes," she said. "And I love Will."

"I'm sure he does, and I'm sure you do," Louisa said, shooting an understanding glance at an embarrassed Mrs. Brill. "Mrs. Holly told me Mary here could give me the best directions to an oak tree Lord Farleigh was particularly fond of," Louisa said.

"*Lord Farleigh?*" Mrs. Brill exclaimed, looking shocked. "Oh, right, our young Master Will." She dabbed at her cheeks with her apron. "Goodness, what a start you gave me! I'm still gettin' used to him bein' the viscount now after so many years of t'other one. Them potatoes look much better, Mary."

"I know the tree," Mary said, continuing to slice the potatoes while she spoke. Her mother had trained her well; Louisa was impressed. "It's Will's tree. Mine and Will's."

"Aye, the one what you and Will was always sneakin' off to when you shouldn't ha' been. Oh—now, don't you worry, milady. Master Will was always a good one to our Mary," Mrs. Brill added by way of clarification. "They went there hidin' from the viscount a time or two. And teachin' my girl her letters when his tutor were done with him." She chuckled. "At least tryin' to teach her, poor lass. Never could quite figure them out."

The cook's words conjured images of a lonely boy looking for friends, a boy who'd been willing to share what he knew with the cook's slow-witted daughter.

"I can show you, milady. Here you go, Mama." Mary set down her knife and wiped her hands on her apron, then took the bowl of potatoes over to her mother.

"There's a good lass. Now, you go point out the way to that tree for Lady Louisa here and then come right back, mind."

"Thank you so much, Mary," Louisa said with a smile. "And then I'll be on my way, so you both can get back to your work." She really was hungry, however, and the aromas in the kitchen were unrelenting. "Perhaps I can beg a roll from you to take with me?"

Mrs. Brill looked chagrined. "Oh, what have I been thinkin'? O' course you can, m'lady." She set about putting together a basket with a generous supply of rolls, cheese, butter, jam, and a jar of lemonade. Louisa could get lost on the estate for days and not starve to death, she was certain.

After an elaborate and detailed description from Mary of every rock and plant Louisa would encounter along the way to the tree, and being sent off with a basket of food, Louisa started out through the herb garden, carefully maintained by Mrs. Brill and flourishing as a result, and then on past William's mother's rose garden. This garden hadn't fared quite as well as the herbs had. The roses needed pruning, their beds choked with weeds.

Louisa also noticed that the grounds at the back of the manor weren't as well maintained as those at the front, those in public view. Matthew had more than one man could do on an estate the size of Farleigh Manor; it made sense that he would put his efforts into the areas that mattered most. A small ornamental garden, regardless of how sentimental it might be, couldn't afford to be a priority to him.

Her destination was not the garden, however, so she continued on across the lawns to the small hill at the east end of the property. She set the basket down so she could remove her bonnet and fan her face with it as she walked—it was quite a trek from the manor house, and she was hot. Hopefully her skin wouldn't burn too severely in the afternoon sun.

She recognized the oak tree the moment it came into view. It looked nearly the same as the painting William had given her but from a slightly different viewpoint. It was a magical place, a world all its own, green and shady, and would be an idyllic refuge for any child. She set the basket and bonnet down next to the tree and then placed her hands on a massive trunk that attested to its longevity. She gazed up at sturdy, leafy branches perfect for climbing and even for sitting on that would offer a wonderful, woodsy view of the pond.

Rather than climb those branches today, however, Louisa retrieved the basket and bonnet and settled comfortably in the shade on the far side of the tree, away from the manor house and facing the water. She spread butter and jam on one of the rolls and ate, soaking up the serenity of the place while she did so.

A picture formed in her mind of a quiet boy who had tried to make sense of a mercurial and bewildering father and a mother who had eventually given up and withdrawn. Of faithful servants who had remained steadfast through the years, waiting for the boy they loved to become a man and take his rightful place, and doing everything they could in the meantime to guard his inheritance for him.

Farleigh Manor may have been sorely mistreated by its former viscount, but it had a small, loyal staff that had not abandoned it or its heir. It said much about William that this was the case. He had been loved as a boy, and he was loved still.

Such love and loyalty could only exist if they were reciprocated.

And then just mere days ago, William had learned of another woman—a genteel woman—who had trusted William's father as William's own mother had trusted him. Another woman who had borne the man children and been treated shabbily by him, and William, despite the added strain it would put on his meager resources—not to mention the public scandal it would potentially cause—had invited her and her children to live at Farleigh Manor.

Louisa rested against the tree trunk. Ducks flapped their wings and skidded across the pond, scolding each other and setting the water rippling. What a blessed life Louisa had lived. She knew nothing at all of hardship, absolutely nothing. The vowel William had presented to her father had created the first ripple of adversity she'd ever experienced.

Her eyes closed as the rigors of the past two days caught up with her, and soon the rustling of the leaves and gentle sound of water became too much to resist, and she slept.

* * *

William arrived at Farleigh Manor after a blistering ride, taking only enough time along the way to rest and water his horse. The poor beast was blown, its sides heaving from the strain of exertion. William dismounted and patted the horse's neck in apology. "Sorry, my friend, but desperate times call for desperate measures, as the old saying goes. I'll make it up to you."

"*I'll* make it up to him," Samuel said as he walked over from the stable and took the reins from William. "S'pected ye'd show up sooner rather than later, son."

"Tell me what's been going on," William said.

"His high and mighty lordship has been busy askin' questions of all and sundry as if he owned the place, though he's pleasant enough about it. Knows his business too, that's for certain."

The Marquess of Ashworth would have made sure his heir was fully educated in the management of an estate, as William's own father had not. "And?" William asked.

Samuel shrugged his shoulders and spat. "And nothin', really, other than him being a lord and so the rest of us is bowin' and scrapin' and tuggin' our forelocks and answerin' all his questions about everything like a bunch o' lackeys."

"I was afraid of that once I realized he and Lady Louisa had come here. Unplanned, as it were."

"Unplanned, eh? I wondered about that, what with ye not being here with 'em, but what was we to do?"

"You did precisely what I would have wanted you to do. They are guests, and Lady Louisa, God willing, is to be my wife. Their questions were valid ones, anyway." He could only hope the answers they'd gotten so far didn't amount to William's undoing.

Samuel cleared his throat. "About the young lady . . ." he began.

"Yes?" William said.

"I wouldn't wish to be speakin' out of turn, melord—"

"Samuel, you used to call me 'that cursed boy' on occasion, including a time when you threatened to tan my backside."

Samuel chuckled. "Mebbe I did, at that. But if I did, 'twas only 'cause ye deserved it. Only then, mind. Ye was always a good lad, in truth."

And there it was again, the pang in William's heart that inevitably came with the desire to save the people dearest to him, like Samuel. The people of Farleigh Manor didn't know how dire its finances truly were and were in for a cruel shock when they learned of the debt that existed from his father's mortgages. William's mortgages now.

He realized he'd fallen silent and that Samuel was watching him with a keen eye, so he shook off the bleakness that had encroached upon him with his thoughts. "You mentioned something about Lady Louisa."

"Aye." Samuel was still studying him too closely. "She's been doin' the same as her lofty brother inside the house but with a lighter touch. And she met yer new guests . . ."

William moaned and covered his eyes with his hand.

"Just this mornin', she and his lordship had that distinct honor. Matthew did his best to steer 'em away from the cottage, but they insisted on goin' up that way." He paused. "Almost like they knew what they was searchin' for," he said.

William looked up in alarm. He'd only just met Miss Purnell himself before scuttling her and the children here to Farleigh Manor. Louisa couldn't have known about her.

"I figured it were because of Mary's blatherin'," Samuel said. "She were going on about Lady Louisa bein' the real wife and children and the like, was our Mary. But I think yer lady would have found it out sooner or later anyway. She's a clever one, her ladyship is, and there's no mistakin'."

"Yes, she is," William said.

"And," Samuel continued. "If ye're interested, I seen her out walkin' alone not long past in the direction of a certain oak tree a lad I once knew were fond of. She has yer heart, don't she, son?"

"I believe so, Samuel," William replied. "Heaven help me."

"Go find her, then," Samuel said.

* * *

The oak tree looked much the same as it had when William had last seen it on the day after his mother's funeral. Perhaps a bit taller, its trunk a tad thicker, but it was still the same tree that had been his refuge from the tension that had been a constant undercurrent in the house. Only Samuel and Matthew had been aware of how much time he'd spent there during his holiday visits home.

He spotted Louisa sitting beneath its canopy just before he reached it; she'd been hidden from his view by the trunk before then. When he came near enough, he discovered she was sound asleep, so he used the opportunity to simply gaze at her.

He wished he had his oils and brushes with him.

She had a picnic basket with her; bless Mrs. Brill's good heart for seeing to her needs. She wore a simple day dress of light-blue muslin and had removed her bonnet, which sat on the lawn next to her. A dark curl had escaped its pins and occasionally flitted about her cheek, depending on the whims of the breeze. That was what he would paint, if he could. It would make a beautiful, serene portrait. But Louisa was more than that—she was clever and kind and honorable and honest in her emotions—a specific quality he himself had not learned from his own childhood and still struggled with mightily but held in high esteem now.

William's heart ached as he gazed at her. It hadn't felt like this since his mother's death.

Oh, how he loved Louisa.

And in that moment, looking at her, he realized he could not shackle her by force to the same fate he had endured. He must destroy the vowel.

Ironic that for a man who loathed gambling as much as he did, he was about to make the biggest wager of his life. Freeing Louisa from the vowel meant he would lose the woman he loved and make the lives of everyone else he loved more difficult.

Unless she loved him and chose to marry him anyway . . .

He smiled humorlessly. He'd been nothing but a plague to her, forcing her to end a betrothal to Lord Kerridge and commit to marrying him. He'd been unable to get past the wall he'd built around himself and allow her to know him. He'd kissed her, and she'd accused him of manipulation. Except for that one time . . .

A single kiss, passionate though it may have been, could not be construed as love.

He sat next to her, drew up one knee, and rested his arm on top, still gazing at her, praying for the strength to do what he knew he had to do. He sensed more than saw her stir, and then her hand fluttered up to her eyes as she gradually awakened. He waited until he thought her fully awake before alerting her to his presence. "Hello, Louisa," he said softly.

She sat up abruptly, blinking to clear away the fog of sleep. "William? What are you doing here?"

"Watching you sleep." And grieving that the moment of truth had arrived.

She fumbled for her bonnet, which he gently took from her hands before she could put it on and cover her beautiful dark hair. "I didn't realize I was so tired, but it seemed the minute I sat down . . ."

"This place has that effect."

"It's your oak tree, isn't it? The one in the painting. I knew when I saw it."

"Yes."

"The painting is lovely; you did a wonderful job." She yawned. "It was quite a hike to get here, which must account for my sleepiness—although Alex and I have been rather busy the past few days too, not to mention the long ride in the carriage that brought us here. Mary showed me the way—to the tree, naturally, not the manor." She was being her typical, Louisa-like self upon awakening, overflowing with words as usual, but her eyes betrayed her worry about his arrival at Farleigh Manor.

The time had come.

"Louisa, there is something I must say to you," he said.

She took a deep breath. "Before you do, William, there is something I must say first. Please don't be angry with Alex for bringing me here uninvited. It was my idea—"

William placed his fingers on her lips to silence her words. "Shh," he said gently. "I am not angry. I am ashamed."

Before he could continue, she took hold of his hand and removed it from her lips, clasping it in both of her hands. "But there is no need to be ashamed," she said earnestly. "Farleigh Manor is special. Oh, it's definitely in need of repair, but that can be remedied once we hire more servants, and I don't entirely know what Alex has learned from his inquiries into the home farms—he and Matthew are working together right now on that very thing—but I'm sure—"

"Louisa," William said, interrupting her, loving her even more for her hopeful outlook. "My dear."

"I'm talking too much again, aren't I?"

"Not at all. But I'm afraid what I have to say cannot wait." He must speak before he lost the will to do so.

He rose to his feet and walked a few paces away, bracing himself before turning to face her. "My shame isn't because of the condition of Farleigh Manor. It is because in blaming my father for it, valid as it may have been to do so, I took my own actions too far by using the vowel to force you into marriage. I convinced myself it was necessary—a connection that would provide a means of rectifying the situation here as well as the debts my father accumulated. It was unforgivable of me. But my sins are worse than even that. You asked me to be honest and forthcoming with you, and I failed. And when Miss Purnell—"

"William," she said, but he held up his hand to stop her from speaking. He had to finish what he'd come to say.

"I had to do *something*, don't you see?" he asked. "My father—"

"*William*," she interrupted again. "I thought she was your *mistress*."

"My . . . what?" he sputtered.

"Lord Kerridge told Alex he saw you with Miss Purnell. He watched you get into a carriage with her. It seemed the likeliest conclusion; he and Alex both assumed—"

William groaned.

"I had to know for *myself*, William. I didn't have the luxury of time to wait for you to tell me, and I wasn't sure what you would say if I confronted you. It was time for me to get the answers I needed on my own since the last of the banns are to be read this Sunday. You see that, don't you?"

"You thought I had a mistress," he said more to himself, really, than to her. He nearly laughed at the absurdity of it, except that it wasn't funny in the least.

He looked her straight in her eye. "Louisa, my whole life, I watched my mother waste away from my father's abuses and infidelities. She died well before her time. And then less than a week ago, I learned that my father had treated another woman with the same selfish disregard—and that he had fathered children by her. Peter is almost the age I was when my father sent me off to school, and Daisy is a sweet little thing who deserves to be brought up with family who loves her and treats her with respect—as you yourself were loved and treated by your family. I want Miss Purnell to know that my brother and sister will not suffer from my father's misdeeds, that they will have the happy childhood I was never allowed. I will never, *never* do to my family what my father did to *both* of his."

"I wanted to believe this of you, William. I think I already knew, but I had to be sure," Louisa said, her deep-blue eyes dark and earnest.

"When Mr. Heslop first showed me the vowel, it seemed a rational and justifiable plan. But it became less supportable the more I got to know you." He longed to tell her that he loved her, but it would be unfair to weigh her down with that confession now. "It was utterly wrong of me to assume I could hold you to this. I cannot in good conscience burden you with marriage to me and to life at Farleigh Manor and all the struggles that will entail. They were not of your doing."

He reached into his breast pocket and retrieved the vowel.

* * *

Louisa watched, stunned, as William held the vowel he'd taken from the breast pocket of his coat, after having just listened to him string more words together at one time than all the other times he'd spoken to her combined. And with a surprising bit of theatrical bravado that was completely out of character for him, he held up the vowel and tore it in half and then in half again and again until there were only small squares of paper left. And then he knelt before her on one knee and held the squares of paper out to her in offering, looking for all the world as if he were about to propose in earnest.

How ironic that his romantic gesture was intended to end their betrothal.

"I shall leave at first light for London to inform your father and mother of the change of plans and to offer my deepest apologies. I am to blame, and I will do everything in my power to make things right for you," he said. He looked at her with heartbreaking tenderness before dropping his gaze. "I will take my leave of you now, unless you would like my escort back to the house."

Louisa scrambled to her feet in a rather frantic, unladylike way before he could extend a hand to assist her. "William, you cannot simply give a speech like that and then walk away," she exclaimed. "It is *my* turn to speak now."

"What have you to tell me that I do not already know?" he said. "I am a poor man, Louisa. Worse than poor, for I am a man saddled with huge debts and few resources. It will likely take my entire life to pay off what is owed, and perhaps not even then. I have discovered family who is dependent on me, for they have even less than I. I have nothing to offer you, my dear. Quite the contrary—I have cost you a great deal."

"You are so certain of all this, are you, without hearing what I have to say?" she asked.

"Yes," he said.

"And that's it? Suddenly you have come to your senses and torn up the vowel, and you tell me I am free to go home—after ending my betrothal to another man, making a formal, public announcement with you, and reading banns in church."

He looked out across the pond, his eyes squinting as if focused on some faraway object, and said nothing.

"William?" she said.

Silence. Stillness.

"Speak to me! You promised me you would speak to me; you said you would. You gave me your word." Her breaths were coming in tiny gasps.

"I have said all I have to say," he said stoically. "Except, perhaps, to tell you that I rejoice in your freedom and wish you well in your marriage to Lord Kerridge."

Louisa felt as though she had been slapped.

He continued staring out at the pond.

"I see," she whispered.

She stooped to retrieve her bonnet and then walked away, her back straight. She was determined that she would not look any less than the daughter of a marquess when she left him.

He would not see the tears running down her face. Not this time.

Chapter 15

BEFORE LOUISA ARRIVED AT THE house, she had successfully forced back her tears, which was a good thing, for Alex was heading in her direction.

"Ah, there you are," he said when he reached her side. "I was instructed with some emphasis to—and I quote—'Go and fetch the two of them, and do not return until you do'—unquote." He sighed dramatically. "I should be dreadfully lonely out here by myself with only the occasional sheep or goose wandering by for company, not to mention getting rather hungry, if I didn't find you both. Oh, and by the way, Weezy dear, in case it wasn't obvious *who* had given me those instructions, I should tell you that our illustrious and highly anxious parents—*both* of them—and our wholly incompetent brother have just arrived on the scene and have commandeered the place. Considering how swiftly they got here on the heels of Viscount Farleigh, I wonder if they took the time to pack so much as a comb before leaving London. Brace yourself, little sister. I have already felt their stinging wrath for accompanying you here uninvited."

"I think when it comes to expansive speech, you're more like me than you'd like to admit," Louisa said, managing for the most part to sound normal.

"Ha! I doubt that. But where is Farleigh? I was to bring him back as well."

"I think Mama and Papa will be content if I am with you," she said.

"Very well. They are not upset at *him*, anyway, but only at us. We are the ones who conspired to come here without his knowledge."

Grimshaw met them when they arrived back at the house, doing his best to look the part of the serene butler but appearing flustered nonetheless.

Louisa couldn't help but feel sorry for him. "The Marquess and Marchioness of Ashworth are here and are awaiting you in the sitting room, Lady Louisa," he said with as much dignity as he could, poor man. Louisa knew how austere and intimidating her father could be on occasion. This, without a doubt, was one of those occasions.

"Unfortunately, they are awaiting me as well," Alex muttered. "Or I'd conjure up an excuse to disappear."

Louisa wished she could disappear as well. When the old butler opened the door, Louisa firmed her resolve and went inside. It was jarring to see her elegantly dressed parents in Farleigh Manor's sitting room—the counterpoint of their finery against the faded shabbiness of the furnishings brought William's words back to her. *I am a poor man, Louisa. Worse than poor, for I am a man saddled with huge debts and few resources.*

The gulf between them widened at this revelation. William had made it perfectly clear that this was a disparity he wouldn't overlook.

In addition to Mama and Papa, Louisa belatedly noticed Anthony lurking near a window, looking as if he'd been subjected to their parents' censures over the entire length of the journey.

"Sorry, Weezy," he said glumly.

Alex followed her into the room, and Grimshaw closed the door.

"Your brothers, who I always assumed had more sense than they apparently do, have already given us the particulars," Papa said in his most imperious voice. "You all owe Lord Farleigh an apology for imposing upon his hospitality without permission and intentionally intruding on his privacy. I am appalled at your behavior. *All* of you." He glared at Alex and shook his head as though expecting him, as heir, to know better, which, unquestionably, he did. Her brothers would not be in this mess if it hadn't been for her. "Rest assured," Papa continued, "that I will deal with each of you appropriately as soon as we return to London, *which journey* we will commence *immediately*, notwithstanding the long travel your mother has already been subjected to by your foolish actions."

"Papa . . ." Louisa began, unsure what to say that would not have her weeping again. She refused to shed any more tears over William, especially in front of her parents and brothers. She should be relieved that he'd released her from the vowel. And she was, of course.

"There, you see, Father; Louisa would like to speak with you," Alex piped up. "Perhaps it would be best if Anthony and I slip discreetly away and leave the rest of you to talk . . ." He edged toward the door.

"Don't go too far," Papa growled. "I'm not done with the two of you yet."

Her brothers hurried from the room as if the devil's hounds were at their heels.

"Please don't be too angry with them, Papa," Louisa said. "I was the one who convinced them to help me. I needed to discover more about William than I knew, and I decided the only way that was going to happen was if I sought out the people who knew him best. And those people are here."

"And what have you discovered?" Mama asked, studying Louisa too carefully.

Louisa fumbled in her pocket for the small squares of paper that had been the vowel and held them out, her fingers trembling. "That I am free, Mama. This is the vowel, and William"—she choked on his Christian name; she had no right to use it anymore—"has torn it up. I am free."

"What?" Papa said, his brows furrowing. He took the papers from her and examined them more closely. "What of the marriage, then?"

"I am freed from that too, apparently. Oh, Mama!" Louisa ran to her and collapsed in her arms. "I want to go home." Why was she crying again? She was so tired of crying. "Please take me home."

Papa walked to the bell pull and yanked it. Unfortunately, the frayed cord came off in his hand. He stalked to the door and opened it.

"Yes, your lordship?" Louisa heard Grimshaw say in a wobbly voice.

"Lord Halford and Lady Louisa's belongings are to be packed and brought to my carriage immediately. We are leaving." He handed the bell pull cord to Grimshaw.

"Yes, your lordship. My apologies, your lordship."

Papa shut the door with a thud. "Louisa, you will remain here with your mother while I look for your infernal brothers. And Lord Farleigh had better not cross my path during that time. I am of a mood to call him out."

"Ashworth! No!" Mama cried. "Not a duel."

"Of *course* not, Eleanor. I said I was in a *mood* to call him out, not that I *would*. But I can assure you that time and distance from him will be necessary if I'm to discuss this with him—*which*, I assure you, I fully intend to do—and have any objectivity at all. Now, if you'll excuse me, I am going to find our sons."

Twenty minutes later, Louisa stood next to her father's carriage in the front courtyard of Farleigh Manor. She and Tibbetts were to ride with her parents, while Alex and Anthony had been consigned to Alex's carriage, the one that had brought Alex and her here. She thought she might sleep the entire way home, so exhausted she felt. The sun seemed overly bright and stung her eyes. She pulled the brim of her bonnet down a bit and waited for the coachman to assist her into the carriage.

"Stop!" a voice shrieked. "Stop, stop!"

Louisa turned at the sound, as did everyone else. Mary was running toward them, her hair loose from its mobcap, apron flying, arms waving frantically. She was out of breath by the time she reached them.

"Where are you going?" she cried, panting. "You can't go! You're Mrs. Will, and you're going to have babies! He told me!"

Oh, Mary.

Louisa glanced at her parents. Mama's eyes were wide with shock, and Papa's expression would surely shatter glass, considering he was already in a foul disposition. Mary's innocent words had apparently put him over the edge.

Louisa went to the poor girl and put her arm around Mary's shoulder.

"Have you been compromised?" her father asked in a quiet, menacing tone.

"Certainly not!" That was *all* she needed—for her father to think he must now force *William* to marry *her*. It was utterly absurd and so farcical under the circumstances that Louisa felt the urge to laugh hysterically.

Mary started wringing her hands and shaking her head. "You can't go. You can't go," she muttered over and over. "Will said everything was going to be better. Lady Farleigh is gone, and you're Lady Farleigh. There will be babies. And the bad one's never coming back. Will said so. He said so."

Louisa didn't know what to say to comfort her. She kept her arm around Mary and simply let her speak. *You will feel better now that you've shared this, Louisa. You are a verbal creature. Words are your friends, as they are not mine. Be at peace.*

Oh, William.

Mrs. Brill hurried over, followed by Mrs. Holly and Grimshaw. Out of the corner of Louisa's eye, she could see Matthew and Samuel coming around the corner of the house toward them too.

"I'm so sorry, milady," Mrs. Brill said, taking a sobbing Mary by the hand. "Come on, now, luv. It'll be all right. You'll see. We're all in a bit of a state, your lordship, your ladyship, and my poor lamb here meant no harm. Come on, Mary, luv."

"You can't go," Mary said again, turning pleading eyes on Louisa. Mrs. Brill looked like she didn't know what to do.

Louisa hugged Mary close as she dashed tears from her own eyes with her gloved hand. "I have to go," Louisa choked out in a whisper. "He changed his mind, you see." Louisa broke free and quickly climbed into the carriage. She could bear no more.

Tibbetts got into the carriage and sat silently next to her. Mama and Papa followed. Papa gave a rap on the ceiling, letting the coachman know it was time to leave.

Louisa looked out the window—she couldn't help herself—and saw the people of Farleigh Manor standing there in the front courtyard: Mrs. Holly, Mrs. Brill, and Mary, Grimshaw, and Matthew. Samuel stood to the side, his arms crossed over his chest.

William wasn't with them, not that Louisa had expected him to be. He had said all he had to say at the oak tree.

There was no reason for an additional farewell.

* * *

The sun was low on the horizon and cast the sky in shades of rose and gold when William began his trek back to the house, picnic basket in tow. A mere glance at the house told him Louisa was gone, as though Farleigh Manor itself was grieving her absence and William could sense it somehow.

He trudged inside, left the basket in the kitchen, and went directly to his study. First order of business was to write Richard Heslop and inform him that there was to be no marriage. After that, he would speak to Matthew. The two of them needed to determine where their best efforts would generate the most yield and income from the estate. But he was not ready to see Matthew yet; he wasn't in a mood to speak to anybody.

What was he to say to them that would explain this mess? They knew nothing of the original wager or the vowel. They were probably going about their evening tasks right now, wondering what had happened to make Louisa leave so abruptly. Or maybe she'd told them about the vowel before she'd left, and they were appalled by how low William had sunk.

He pulled out a sheet of paper and dipped his quill into the inkwell. "Mr. Heslop," he wrote. "I am not sure if I came to my senses or lost them, but I have torn up the vowel affecting Lady Louisa Hargreaves. Any suggestions you can offer dealing with the estate's debt would be greatly appreciated. Yours, William Barlow, Junior, Viscount Farleigh."

He folded it, sealed it, and set it aside. It was dark outside now. Good. It suited his mood perfectly.

He would speak to Matthew tomorrow.

He went to his room, ignoring the worried looks of Grimshaw and Mrs. Holly and the others.

* * *

On Sunday, braced on both sides by her parents and brothers, Louisa walked into St. George's Church, praying that all her years of training as a nobleman's daughter would not abandon her while she did so.

They proceeded up the aisle to their usual pew, and Louisa sat looking straight ahead, trying desperately not to think about the final banns that were to have been read today. But the very fact that she was trying *not* to think about them meant that that was all she could think about.

There was a part of her that wanted to look about the chapel for William, wondering if he would be here just to see if she would not object to the reading of the final banns. But it was fanciful thinking on her part. Papa had already spoken to the rector.

There would be no final banns read today.

She hardly heard a word spoken during the services, except for a few murmurs that arose in the congregation when the time for the banns came and went. She supposed it didn't help that the rector paused ever so briefly, shooting a glance at her and Papa as if waiting to be corrected, before continuing on.

Eventually, none too soon for Louisa, the service concluded. "Nearly done now, little sister," Alex whispered in her ear as they arose. "Only the escape, and then you are through the worst of it."

She nodded, acknowledging his words of encouragement.

But the escape proved a difficult one. They had barely stepped out of the pew into the aisle when Lady Putnam pushed through the crowd. "I believe I shall see that the carriage is ready," Louisa heard Papa whisper to Mama just as Lady Putnam reached them. Papa had little tolerance for the lady and her gossipy ways.

"Lady Ashworth, Lady Louisa, a fine day, is it not?" Lady Putnam said in greeting. "And here are your handsome sons as well."

Alex and Anthony both nodded to her and then quickly excused themselves, leaving Louisa and Mama to face Lady Putnam alone. Louisa should be put out at them for abandoning her, but it was *Lady Putnam*, after all, so she couldn't help but sympathize with their innate need to flee for survival's sake.

"Ah, well, there they go," Lady Putnam said, watching with an upraised eyebrow. "Young gentlemen are always in such a rush these days, it seems. And speaking of young gentlemen . . ." She waited, and the expectant pause that followed grated on Louisa till she thought she might scream, which would be the worst thing she could possibly do in a chapel.

"You are absolutely correct," Mama said. "It seems I can hardly keep track of what Halford and Anthony are doing these days. It does my heart good to see that they still make time to join their family at church services, would you not agree?"

Lady Putnam's face dropped when it became apparent to her that Mama was not going to talk about William. "Yes, very admirable, I must say. Just as well that my Harriet was unable to attend today since your sons had to leave so quickly. She awoke with a bit of a sore throat, and I encouraged her to remain home and rest."

"Excellent advice," Mama replied. "I hope she returns to full health soon."

"Thank you. Ah, there is Charlotte with her papa. Well, a happy Sabbath to you all. Best of wishes, Lady Louisa, *and* your betrothed, of course." She nodded politely, but her knowing smile meant she knew something was amiss.

"That's enough for today," Mama said. "Even without being told anything, you can bet Lady Putnam will spread the word that the final banns weren't read today—she will most likely share her opinion as fact that the betrothal has ended."

"She won't be wrong, Mama." Louisa winced inwardly at Mama's use of the word *bet*, for it reminded her of William. "The betrothal has ended."

"Ahem," a male voice said behind them.

She and Mama both turned at once to see who'd tried to get their attention, but Louisa had already guessed. Because with Louisa's run of misfortune lately, who else would it be?

"Lord Kerridge, what a surprise," Mama said, her face a bit paler than it had been moments ago.

"You are looking well, Lady Ashworth." He turned to Louisa. "Lady Louisa, always a pleasure to see you."

"Thank you," she managed.

"May I escort the two of you to your carriage? I noticed that you seem to be without any of your gentlemen at the moment."

Was he referring to Papa, Alex, and Anthony? Or was he dropping a none-too-subtle hint that he, too, had noticed that the final banns had not been read?

"That's very kind of you, Lord Kerridge," Mama said. "Isn't it, Louisa?"

"Yes," Louisa replied. "Thank you."

He winged out an arm for each of them, and Louisa dutifully slipped her hand into the crook of his elbow, as she had done on other occasions. So she was utterly caught off guard when something—not a voice, exactly but *something*—within her heart and mind whispered, "This feels wrong."

She pulled her hand away.

"Is everything all right?" Lord Kerridge asked her, a concerned look on his face.

She was being foolish. She had simply become more accustomed to William in the past few weeks, that was all, so being with Lord Kerridge felt less familiar now. His offer of marriage still stood. She should be appreciating his thoughtfulness—and she did. "Yes," she said simply. She placed her hand back in the crook of his elbow.

They greeted a few acquaintances on the way out of the church and then complimented the rector on his sermon, eventually joining Papa at the carriage, Alex and Anthony having already left in their own conveyances.

"Thank you, Lord Kerridge, for seeing to the needs of my womenfolk," Papa said.

"It was an honor and a pleasure, I assure you," Lord Kerridge said. "Please allow me to assist you into the carriage, Lady Louisa."

He held out his hand to her, and she took it. "Dear Louisa," he murmured as she prepared to enter the carriage. "Allow me to offer my condolences at what appears to be the dissolution of your betrothal."

She paused and turned her head slightly toward him, waiting to hear what he would say next, hoping he would leave it at that. She was not ready to discuss William, especially not with Lord Kerridge.

"You have not given me an answer to my question yet," he continued. "Nor will I push you for an answer. But I would like to call on you this week, if I may."

"I think it is too soon," Louisa said.

"Nonsense," he replied. "The sooner your life resumes as it was, the sooner Society will forget this little *contretemps* ever occurred." He smiled reassuringly. "We shall see that your reputation is fully restored and *his* is utterly returned to the gutter, where it belongs. You can count on it. Good day, Lady Louisa."

He kissed her gloved hand and assisted her into the carriage, bowed to her parents, and left.

"Well, I daresay it was quite gallant of Lord Kerridge to escort us to your father, considering what we've put him through," Mama said when they were finally on their way back home.

Mama didn't know that Lord Kerridge had been the one to inform Alex of Jane Purnell's existence and to imply the woman was William's mistress.

"Indeed," Louisa replied. She herself thought Lord Kerridge's motives had been anything but gallant, that they had been utterly self-serving. *The little contretemps,* he had called her experience with William. And she was alarmed at his assurance to her that he intended to destroy William's reputation.

"I got the impression that he'd like to pick up where the two of you left off," Papa said. "How would you feel, Louisa, if that were the case?"

"I don't know, Papa. He mentioned that he would like to call on me later in the week." The last thing she wanted to do right now was talk about Lord Kerridge. She couldn't even remember if she'd told her parents that he had offered marriage to her a second time—her mind was a jumble at the moment. It was better not to mention it, then, just in case.

She was choosing *not* to mention something. She wondered how William would react to knowing that. Perhaps in the past few weeks she'd learned to choose her words more carefully. By the same token, she hoped William had learned to trust enough to share his words more openly. It would be nice to think that something of value had come from all this.

"We shall wait, then," Mama said. "This is only your first Season, and there is nothing to say that you must marry immediately, regardless of the circumstances of the past month. In the meantime, what do you say you and I sit down together this afternoon and go through the invitations we've received? I'm sure we'll find two or three that will be diverting." She patted Louisa's hand reassuringly.

"Your friends will be glad to see you again, and soon your beaux will be lining up to dance with you, and flowers will be arriving in vast numbers at the house again, and all will be as it was before," Papa said.

"I couldn't agree more, Ashworth. There. It's settled, then." Mama smiled at Louisa and nodded.

Louisa turned her face to stare out the window.

* * *

"It's been nigh on a week since that lady o' yers up 'n left," Samuel said when William went to the stable to saddle a horse.

William had made it very clear that, firstly, he was to blame for Louisa's departure, and secondly, it was not up for discussion. He was fairly sure everyone would concede the first part, but he was absolutely confident he and Louisa had been on everyone's minds and tongues since she'd left Farleigh Manor—and him.

"What is your point?" William said while he hoisted the saddle into place on the back of his horse.

"I'll do that," Samuel said, nudging William aside. "Me point is, *yer lordship*, that we all know ye love the girl, but ye've done nary a thing to bring 'er back." He cinched the saddle and handed the reins to William.

"That is correct, Samuel," William said, boosting himself up into the saddle. "I released her from the betrothal, and that is an end to it."

Samuel spat. "Hogwash," he said. "I saw the way ye looked at 'er, and I'm not sich a fool that I couldn't see t'were the same way she looked at ye, boy."

William's heart thudded in his throat. "You're mistaken, my friend, although I confess that I wish you were not. I took her from another man, another betrothal." He waited to see how Samuel would react to that admission, but the man gave away nothing.

It was utterly annoying.

What a frustration William must have been to Louisa, asking everything of her, barely willing to give an inch himself. Even his best attempts had been withering failures.

"Do you understand?" William exclaimed. "I held a vowel, which made her and her family beholden to me. She agreed to the marriage out of honor, and honor alone." He was a bit surprised at his honesty with Samuel, feeling shameful at his confession but a bit lighter too. "In the end, I couldn't do that to her. I tore up the vowel. There. That is the truth of it." He nudged his horse, but Samuel blocked him. "Move out of the way," William said.

Samuel grabbed the horse's bridle, his face like granite. "Not until ye've heard me out." He pointed his finger at William. "I've known ye since ye were but a babe in arms. I know better'n anyone what ye've gone through all these years; I saved yer hide plenty o' times, so I *should* know. Ye were the boy I never had, though I be puttin' meself too high and mighty to be sayin' so.

"Even so, it's with the love of a father that I tell ye this: ye been dealt a bad hand all yer life, one ye never deserved. Ye've *earned* a bit of happiness after all that. Go to the girl. Look at her face. Ye'll see what I'm sayin'."

"If what you say is true," William replied, "that is all the more reason why I cannot go to her. I have *nothing* to offer her. *Nothing*, Samuel. She was betrothed to the heir to a dukedom. If we were in London, we would have read the announcement of their betrothal in the papers already. I cannot take that away from her again and offer her poverty and debt in its place. Now, let me go."

Samuel let go of the bridle. "Ye're makin' a mistake, son. I think ye're afraid, afraid of really lovin' someone an' lettin' 'em in here." He thumped on his chest. "'Tis past time for ye to love someone who isn't dead or a servant o' Farleigh Manor. Ye have plenty to offer the girl, for there's nothin' of more value she could have than yerself, Will Barlow. Deep down, the girl knows it too. An' if ye don't believe I'm tellin' ye true, ye can ask anyone else here, an' they'll tell ye. Now, off wi' ye." He slapped the rump of William's horse, sending them on their way. "Go."

William was more than happy to comply; he urged his horse to a gallop and let the wind blow hard in his face. How dare Samuel talk to him that way! He knew nothing of the situation with Louisa.

He eventually reached the home farm. It was past time William arrived; Matthew was already there and hard at work. An afternoon of heavy labor would do William a world of good. William had two good hands and a strong back, and if he was going to make Farleigh Manor survive, it meant giving his all.

It would be hard penance, good for the soul—and it would keep him from his thoughts of Louisa and Samuel's haunting words.

Chapter 16

WEDNESDAY AFTERNOON, LORD KERRIDGE CALLED upon Louisa, as he'd promised he would. Louisa was in the drawing room with Mama when he arrived, so he was invited to join them there. Wednesday wasn't one of Mama's receiving days, so they'd had no previous callers all afternoon. It had been a blessedly quiet afternoon thus far, and Louisa had been grateful for it. Mama had done needlework while Louisa had read. They'd occasionally chatted but then had fallen into comfortable times of silence.

"Lord Kerridge, how kind of you to call," Mama said. "What a welcome diversion you are! Louisa and I have been sitting around all day like a pair of lazy cats. Please have a seat and join us."

"Thank you, Lady Ashworth. I would like nothing better."

Lord Kerridge's arrival was not a welcome diversion, as far as Louisa was concerned.

"How is Aylesham?" Mama asked him, setting her needlework aside. "I haven't seen him about much this Season. Is he well?"

"Quite well, Lady Ashworth, considering his age. Great-Uncle Aylesham spends most of his time at the House of Lords during the Season, pestering everyone there to agree with him politically. When he's at home, he's pestering me—but only in the best of ways." Lord Kerridge smiled at his little jest.

Mama chuckled. "I can envision him in just such a manner. What a dear man he is, the rogue; I always enjoy his company. You will be sure to tell him hello for me and that I look forward to seeing him again soon."

"I certainly shall," he said. He cleared his throat, and Louisa held her breath. "If your ladyship doesn't mind, I wonder if I might be so bold as to invite Lady Louisa for a ride in my phaeton to Hyde Park. It would be a shame to waste such fine weather."

"I do not mind at all; I am content to do my needlework, and Ashworth will be joining me shortly," Mama said.

He stood and extended his hand to Louisa, intent on assisting her to her feet. He hadn't even asked her if she wished to ride in his phaeton or go to Hyde Park where all and sundry would be out walking and riding and seeing and being seen. She wasn't sure she wanted to be seen in Lord Kerridge's company so soon after . . .

So soon after William had torn up the vowel and told her she was free.

Louisa didn't feel particularly free at the moment.

She allowed him to assist her to her feet, all the same. "I think I should prefer to stay here, if you don't mind, Lord Kerridge," she said. "Perhaps a walk in the garden instead." She didn't ask him but intentionally phrased it as a statement.

"Very well." He strode to the door and opened it for her. "Good afternoon, then, Lady Ashworth."

Mama nodded her farewell to the earl and picked up her needlework.

When the two of them were in the corridor and alone, Lord Kerridge suggested once again that they go for a ride in his phaeton. "The ponies are quite new; handsome creatures, they are, and longing for a bit of exercise. They would relish a turn about the park. What do you say?"

"I say thank you, but I would prefer not to go to Hyde Park today."

He looked puzzled. "If that is your wish. I must confess that I do not understand. Come, then; we will walk in the garden."

They were silent until they reached the garden, and Louisa was sufficiently satisfied that no servants were nearby to eavesdrop. She had things she needed to say to Lord Kerridge, and they needed to be said in private.

Eventually, they ended up in the rose garden, near the bench where William had agreed to give her the three weeks needed to read banns rather than use the special license he'd procured.

He could have forced the issue. He could have demanded they marry using the special license. She would be a married woman by now if he had, and he would have his marriage settlements and the income they would have provided. But he had relented and given her those weeks. He'd known it was a risk to do so—she knew him well enough now to know that he understood wagering and the odds involved.

"You seem far away at the moment," Lord Kerridge said.

She sat on the bench, and Lord Kerridge sat next to her. "Jane Purnell is not William's mistress," she said. She didn't explain who Jane Purnell was; Lord Kerridge was intelligent enough to figure it out for himself.

"She's not? I'm glad to hear it."

"Are you?"

"Of course I am. It is one less thing to explain away when the dust settles. I am a fairly patient man, Lady Louisa, as I'm sure you've discovered by now. I have not pressed you for an answer to my proposal, you know. Most gentlemen of my rank and position would be more demanding."

"Thank you, Lord Kerridge," she said. "I believe I am prepared to answer you now."

He smiled, obviously fully expecting an answer in the affirmative.

"I am aware of the great honor you previously bestowed upon me and extended to me again," she said, "and I thank you most sincerely for it—but I'm afraid I must respectfully refuse."

His brows furrowed. "You refuse? I don't understand. You were willing to marry me mere *weeks* ago—the solicitors met regularly, and we were set to announce the betrothal formally—until this . . . this . . . ne'er-do-well arrived on the scene with a *vowel* in his hand."

"Lord Kerridge—" Louisa began.

"Aylesham is not as well as he pretends to be, and he is zealous in his pursuit of acquiring more heirs. I am encouraged rather vigorously to marry and marry quickly, you see, and to begin a dynasty of my own so the man may die in peace, knowing the dukedom will thrive. You are the perfect bride, and Aylesham thinks so too. He was willing to overlook what he referred to as your 'peccadillos' regarding Lord Farleigh because of my assurances to him that you would come to your senses. And you did return to London without Farleigh, and the final banns weren't read. What am I not understanding? Why can we not simply announce our betrothal now and marry?"

"Because I love someone else," she said.

"Love? When has love been a consideration?" he asked her as he stood and paced away from her. "Marriage amongst the highest nobility, as you well know, is about maintaining property, wealth, and power, not love. It is about the training one receives from birth that provides leadership and decorum in the home and for Society at large. Providing heirs is critical as well, so the noble lines will continue. Love is all fine and good—but not of paramount importance. There is too much at stake." He crossed back to her and sat, taking her hand in his. "That being said, you would make a wonderful duchess,

Lady Louisa, and give the Aylesham line strong sons and daughters. And I am genuinely fond of you, or I should not have been so patient. Tell me you've reconsidered your answer."

Louisa's heart was heavy. Lord Kerridge was not a bad man; he was a fine gentleman, and she truly was honored that he considered her a worthy mate. "Too much has happened in the past few weeks," she said softly. "We cannot go back to the way things were."

He dropped his gaze and released her hand. "I see. I am sorry to hear this and will not impose upon your time any longer." He rose to his feet. "Farewell, Lady Louisa. I hope you find happiness in the choice you have made." He made a stiff, formal bow and strode across the garden and out of sight.

Louisa waited awhile, pondering the words Lord Kerridge had spoken to her. He wasn't entirely wrong in his opinions. Louisa had simply realized at some point that their priorities didn't match. Especially when it came to love.

Lord Kerridge had offered her marriage out of duty to the Duke of Aylesham and Louisa's own suitability as daughter of the Marquess of Ashworth. His pride had been stung by Louisa's refusal, but he would recover in time, and Louisa had no doubt that he would find another suitable bride.

William had demanded marriage out of love for his home and his friends. But then he had torn up the vowel—he'd said—because the more he'd gotten to know her, the more he'd realized he couldn't force her into marriage to him.

Louisa suspected—hoped—there was another reason he'd torn up the vowel, even if he hadn't spoken the words.

By the time she returned to the house, she had made a decision. She only hoped her family wouldn't think she was utterly mad when she told them what it was.

* * *

Today, rather than do manual labor—William had developed a great deal of respect for Matthew over the past several days—the two of them spent the morning going over the ledgers. It was dull, depressing work but had to be done. William had received several letters from Richard Heslop regarding the status of the mortgages and what the solicitor had learned by speaking to the creditors. "While it may appear upon first perusal that the news regarding the debts is grim, there was some willingness on the part of a few of the creditors to negotiate, surprised as they were to learn that they might see any reparations at all."

Heslop must have spun quite a tale to them, for after the past fortnight of backbreaking work with Matthew, William had realized he'd undertaken a nearly impossible task. He needed more men to do the work if they were to make any real progress. Word had gotten out in the village what William was about, and while a few of the tenant farmers had returned, it was not nearly enough. But it was something, at least, and William would take any blessings that came his way.

After Matthew and he had gone over the ledgers, Mrs. Brill had fed them both, and then Matthew had gone into the village to check on Miss Purnell. It surprised no one that Matthew had taken a liking to the lady. William had been able to find her a job—not much of a job, but she'd been grateful nonetheless—assisting the teacher two days a week at the village school. Since Peter and Daisy both attended the school, it worked out well for everyone.

Miss Purnell wasn't ready to have a suitor after all she'd been through, William suspected, but she hadn't rejected Matthew outright either.

William was feeling restless and out of sorts. There was plenty to do, but he couldn't settle on any one task. He wandered back to the kitchen, where Mrs. Brill was washing the dishes after luncheon. "Where's Mary?" he asked. "That's her job, isn't it?"

"Oh, she's here and there," Mrs. Brill said. "She's not been feelin' quite herself the past few—well, I've just let 'er have some time to herself, is all."

William grunted in reply and stalked out into the herb garden, swatting at a few bees that buzzed about his head. He broke off a rosemary leaf and ran it through his fingers, inhaling the pungent scent. Perhaps he would ride into the village. He could go to the George and Dragon, get better acquainted with the people.

Except he'd have to go to the stable for a horse, and Samuel would lecture him again about going to see Louisa.

He wasn't in the mood for a lecture. He saw Louisa everywhere as it was.

Blast it all, she was probably at an afternoon tea with Lord Kerridge at this very moment, he thought grumpily. Wearing the light-blue muslin that brought out her eyes. She would be smiling and flowing with words, like cool water through a parched desert . . .

He didn't know what to do. Hard work hadn't driven her from his mind. The image of Lord Kerridge at her side hadn't deterred him. Perhaps he should write another letter to Heslop, telling the man to search for William's legal heir, for if he didn't get Louisa out of his head—and his heart—he would be doomed to remain a bachelor.

What a depressing thought.

He must exorcise her from his mind, so, fool that he was, he headed to the one place at Farleigh Manor that reminded him the most of her.

The oak tree.

* * *

It seemed only fitting that Louisa would find William at the oak tree. He sat, his back resting against the trunk, staring out at the pond.

He had been willing to stake his own future happiness on an unseen wife for the sake of those here at Farleigh Manor. Louisa understood this now.

A faithful old butler, a meticulous housekeeper. The aromas of favorite recipes coming from the kitchen. The devotion of a simpleminded girl.

And then there were William's kisses, different from Lord Kerridge's, enticing her, attracting her. Oh, yes, she found him attractive. He was a beautiful man.

A beautiful, honorable man.

She loved him.

"William," she said softly, not wishing to startle him.

He turned at her voice and stared at her as if he were seeing a ghost. "Louisa, is that really you?" he asked.

"Yes," she said, her heart full.

"But what of Lord Kerridge? I presumed—"

"You presumed wrong." She walked closer.

"Wrong?" he repeated as if he couldn't understand the word. "You're really here, aren't you? And your parents? They let you—"

"They are here too. And so are Alex and Anthony. We are all here, William."

He shook his head as if to clear it. "Well, you may inform them that they may exact their pound of flesh from me. I deserve no less."

"That is not why we are here, William."

He turned to stare at the pond once more and said nothing in reply.

"I told them I was returning to Farleigh Manor to see you. And when I explained my reason to them, they agreed to accompany me. We have unfinished business between us, William, whether you acknowledge it or not."

He remained silent for a while, and Louisa waited for him to speak, her heart in her throat. "I owe you an apology," he said at length. "I have already apologized to you for the worst of my deeds and tried to make amends, although I doubt that will ever be possible. But I also promised to tell you about myself and I failed, and for that I am gravely sorry."

"Hush, now," she said. She walked to where he was sitting and offered him her hand, and he took it, lending her his strength as she sat next to him. To feel his hand around hers again was heaven. "You have no need to apologize. Not to me."

He ignored her words of reassurance. Now that he'd begun to speak, it appeared he could not stop. "My earliest memories are of my mother," he said. "She was a quiet, gentle woman and beautiful, at least to a small boy who adored her. But I wasn't there for her when she needed me most."

"You were a child. You weren't responsible for her unhappiness," Louisa said. "William, I know what happened to you as a boy. And while I hope you continue to tell me more, you don't have to apologize. I want only for you to trust me. I want to not wonder why you can't talk to me."

"I couldn't risk it. Don't you see?" His eyes looked so desolate that Louisa grasped both of his hands, anything to give him support. He clutched them to his chest as if by doing so, he could contain all the emotions threatening to burst free. "I have been haunted by my father my entire life. The vowel was a sure bet, and the odds were too great if you discovered what marrying me would really mean."

"William, my love," she said gently, freeing a hand so she could lay her palm on his cheek. "I know what marrying you will mean. I have learned that you will do whatever is possible for those you love. I have seen it in Grimshaw's loyalty to you, in the proud housekeeping of Mrs. Holly, in the cooking smells coming from Mrs. Brill's kitchen, and in Matthew's neatly kept front grounds. I have seen it in Samuel and Mary.

"They all love you, William, and have stayed at Farleigh Manor because they knew your time would come, and they intended to do their part in making sure you had something of value to return to. They do not depend on you; they are offering you their support."

Her cheeks were wet, she knew, but she wanted to share everything in her heart with him. "Marriage to Lord Kerridge would have offered wealth and status but nothing more. Not love. Oh, William, you can give me a life he cannot—the one I want," she said. "I am not afraid of challenge, William. And I am not afraid to marry a man who loves others as deeply as you do and is willing to sacrifice his own happiness for them. There is no gamble for me in that."

His eyes, which had looked so anguished only moments ago, were now bright with unshed tears as they searched her face. He reached into his pocket for his handkerchief and dabbed at her cheeks. "This is what I love about you," he said softly. "That you speak your feelings so openly and that I can read your every thought and emotion on your beautiful, expressive face. It is a relief, this transparency you have, after so many years of living with the opposite."

He pulled her into his arms then, and she held him and held him, her face nestled snugly against his chest, his arms wrapped just as tightly around her. She breathed in the wonderful, warm scent that was William and listened to the solid beating of his heart. It felt natural and right for her to be there.

"You called me your love," he whispered into her ear.

"I wasn't sure you were paying attention," she whispered back. It was a wonderfully intimate thing, to be held like this, secure and exciting both.

"I could hardly miss the words I've been longing to hear you speak."

"You said you loved me too." She nestled even closer, if that were possible.

"Did I?" He nuzzled her ear.

She drew back and glared at him. "You know you did!"

He chuckled, even as a tear finally escaped and ran down his cheek. William, the man who had seldom smiled until now, actually chuckled—at *her*, at a time like *this*. And then he threw his head back and laughed. "You are such a delight, my darling Louisa. I did say it, and I will say it again. I love you. I will even declare that it was love at first sight, for you were not at all what I expected when I walked into Ashworth House."

"What did you expect?" she couldn't help asking.

"Not you. I could never have expected to find someone as wonderful as you. Oh, my dear Louisa, my love, I have lived with famine my entire life, and you are a feast for my soul." And then he lowered his mouth to hers, and they feasted together.

* * *

They were silent as they walked back to the house, but Louisa didn't mind and simply allowed herself to enjoy the peacefulness. Their conversation heralded the end of misunderstandings and the dawning of a new life together, one of love and challenge and companionship. There was more that still needed to be said between them, but she was confident now that those conversations would happen. William might never be the sort who volunteered everything on his mind or in his heart, but she understood that heart and mind now and trusted him. Honest conversations were an important part of marriage, and she would help him learn to trust having those with her.

They were nearly back at the house when they spotted Alex heading in their direction.

"Ah, there you are," Alex said when he reached their side. "And you're together. Excellent. Once again, I have been assigned to summon you to our parents, Louisa. And you too, Farleigh." He looked thoughtful. "I always liked to think that the title of earl would amount to more than being an errand boy, but alas."

William actually laughed at Alex's silly joke. For the second time in one afternoon, William laughed.

Alex shot him a look of mock disdain. "Well, what do you know. My baby sister discovered a human being behind that block of wood you call a face."

"That she did," William said, grinning, before planting a huge kiss on Louisa right in front of her eldest brother and making her face heat up. "What a magnificent woman she is."

"She ought to be after the inordinate amount of time and money my parents spent to make her more than the veriest nitwit. It was all Anthony and I could do to tolerate her most of our lives. She only became interesting quite recently, in fact."

"Who precisely is this nitwit you are speaking of, brother?" Louisa asked, arching an eyebrow at him. "The one who constantly outshone you at mathematics and spoke such excellent Latin that you begged the tutor to make me leave? The one who shot the bull's-eye during a country archery tournament? The one who—"

"Enough! I surrender," Alex said, raising both hands in defeat. "You see what Tony and I have had to put up with all these years, Farleigh. I don't envy you a bit."

William laughed again, and Louisa thought her heart might escape the confines of her body and soar heavenward with joy.

Grimshaw opened the door when they arrived back at the house. "Lord and Lady Ashworth and Lord Anthony are in the sitting room," he informed them. "They are expecting you."

"Excellent," William said.

Grimshaw shot him a puzzled look as he opened the door to the sitting room.

William strode into the room. "Lord and Lady Ashworth, Lord Anthony, welcome back to Farleigh Manor, such as it is. You are my welcome guests, and we will endeavor to make your stay as comfortable as possible—even if that means securing lodging in the village at the George and Dragon." He smiled.

Louisa watched with glee the shocked looks that came over her parents' faces.

Her father recovered his senses first. "Lord Farleigh," he said, "I apologize for my progeny, who recently imposed upon your hospitality without permission and intentionally intruded on your privacy. I beg your pardon."

"No apology is needed, your lordship," William said. "I am glad they came. I should have invited Louisa here sooner. You see, Lord Ashworth, Lady Ashworth, it is I who owe you an apology, not the other way around," William said. "I put you all through the strain of a forced betrothal for the sake of my own interests, after all."

"He makes himself sound so selfish, Papa, when the opposite is the truth. He would sacrifice his own happiness for the people of Farleigh Manor."

"It is turning sickly sweet in here," Alex drawled, wandering over to the window.

William ignored him. "I love your daughter with my whole being," he said. "I cannot imagine a life without her. Lord Ashworth, Lady Ashworth, may I have your permission—your blessing—to make Louisa my wife? I am acutely aware that I have little to offer her other than my heart and my promise to do all in my power to make her life a happy one." He reached into his breast pocket and withdrew a folded paper.

"Stop!" Louisa cried, panicking. "If that is the special license you told me you'd obtained, don't tear it up! Mama, I don't want to wait to marry William. And there is a family chapel here, a lovely little place; William's parents are buried next to it. I should like to be married there. Is that all right with you, William? I know it's not a large London wedding, and I am your only daughter, Mama, but I don't need that, truly. I would rather be married here since all of you are already here and Mrs. Holly and Grimshaw and Mrs. Brill and Mary and Matthew and Samuel and—oh, everyone—is already here."

Mama turned to Papa. "It is a good thing I instructed your valet and my maid to pack for an extended stay after all, Ashworth. It appears we are going to be here for a few days."

"I daresay you are correct, my dear. However, we have some marriage settlements to finish discussing first, Farleigh—unless you'd rather wait for your solicitor to be present."

"Not at all, your lordship. And if you have any concerns about Farleigh Manor, I expect your eldest son has gathered all the information you will need."

"You are undoubtedly right," Papa said. "And if he hasn't, then I'll be doubly ashamed of him."

William laughed. Oh, how Louisa loved seeing him freed to do something so simple as laugh! And then, in front of her entire family, he dropped to one knee and took Louisa's hand in his. "My beautiful Louisa," he began. "Here, with your parents as my witnesses, I declare my love for you. If my father did only one thing right in his life, it was to wager and win against your grandfather and require he sign a vowel; otherwise I would not have met you. Will you consent of your own will to be my wife?"

"Yes!" Tears spilled from her eyes, but she didn't care, because tears were welling up in his too. Her William was a man of intense emotion, something she never would have guessed on their first introduction.

Her William.

He rose to his feet, and right there in front of her parents, he kissed her.

Papa cleared his throat. "Enough of that, now," he said. "You're scandalizing Lady Ashworth."

"Nonsense," Mama said. She was smiling and, perhaps, shedding a tear or two herself.

"I will inform Mrs. Holly and the rest of the staff that our wedding will take place day after tomorrow," William said softly, kissing each of Louisa's hands while gazing into her eyes. "If that meets with your approval, my love."

"Yes," Louisa said. "Oh yes, my dear William, it does."

* * *

William sought out Mrs. Holly and asked her to gather the staff. She scurried off, and before he could almost blink, the entire staff had joined them in the sitting room, standing at attention. Obviously, they'd all known something was up and had already collected in the kitchen, curious to find out what was going on at the soonest possible moment.

Lord and Lady Ashworth sat together on the aged sofa, Halford leaned his shoulder against the fireplace mantel, and Lord Anthony rested his hip on one of the shabby tables in the room. William led Louisa to the better of the two chairs, and she sat, and then he took his place in front of the staff.

"There are no words to express what I am feeling right now," he began—and then he laughed. "I'm so inexperienced with words that I doubt I could find the right ones anyway, but I shall try." He paused and looked at each person in the room, and then he knew what to say. "I owe you each a debt of gratitude for safeguarding my inheritance for me. Farleigh Manor is my home, as it is your home too. It took me far too long to understand this, and I hope you will forgive me."

"No forgiveness needed," Grimshaw said.

"Indeed not," Mrs. Holly echoed.

William smiled, suspecting that Louisa's parents might be somewhat appalled by the informality of his staff. He doubted Gibbs would have spoken up in such a way. "Nonetheless, I want the words said," William said. "My fondest memories of Farleigh Manor involve all of you—even you, Sally and Jim. You remind me of how young Mrs. Holly and Matthew were when I was a boy and how loyal they have remained. You remind me that Farleigh Manor has new life and a new future in store."

"They don't remind you of me though, do they?" Grimshaw said. "I was born old."

William chuckled. "You undoubtedly were, Grimshaw, my good man. Let us say that you lend the estate *gravitas*."

Grimshaw nodded, pleased.

William took Louisa's hand and assisted her from her chair so she could stand with him. "Now, it is with great pleasure that I announce that Lord and Lady Ashworth have given their permission for Lady Louisa and me to marry, and furthermore, she and I have decided to marry posthaste. I possess a special license, which I have kept safely in my pocket, and with your help, we wish to wed here, at Farleigh Manor, in two days' time."

"It goes without saying that everyone involved will be pulling off a miracle to be ready in time," Lord Ashworth said. "I hope your staff is up to the challenge, Farleigh."

"I believe they are, your lordship," William said.

Mary suddenly made an odd sound, and everyone turned to look at her. She was flapping her hands wildly.

"Mary, hush now," Mrs. Brill said in a low voice, trying to calm her. "Isn't it lovely? There's to be a wedding, right here, at Farleigh Manor. And you and I, we're going to make the cake, and it will be a nice gift for our Will and his new viscountess from the two of us. There, now." She tried to put her arms around Mary, but Mary fought her off, her hands still flapping about.

William was dumbfounded by Mary's reaction. She knew of his intentions toward Lady Louisa, and he'd been relatively certain she'd understood what he'd been saying and had even been happy about it. He cleared his throat to regain everyone's attention. "Well, that's enough for now. I'm sure my bride and her mother will wish to consult with you on the particulars, Mrs. Holly, and you too, Mrs. Brill. Thank you all."

"Congratulations, me boy," Samuel said, pumping William's hand vigorously before shrugging and wrapping him in a bear hug. "Ye know I can't be more thrilled than I am for ye."

"Thank you, Samuel," William said.

"But I might not let ye soon forget t'was the girl who came after ye and not t'other way 'round."

William laughed. "I should have listened to you."

"I been tellin' ye that yer whole life boy." He hugged William again. "Ye were a lad set upon by troubles ye didn't deserve, but ye grew into a fine man. I'm that proud of ye, son. My felicitations to ye and yer bride."

Grimshaw came forward next and, surprisingly enough, patted William energetically on the shoulder. "Many congratulations," he said.

"Truly, sir, best wishes," Matthew echoed, taking the next opportunity to shake William's hand.

The three men offered their congratulations to Louisa, too, as did Jim and Sally.

"Oh, Master William, our dear, dear boy," Mrs. Holly said, hugging him too. William couldn't remember receiving so many hugs before. "What a happy day this is! I couldn't be more thrilled."

Beyond her shoulder, William could see Mrs. Brill take a mumbling Mary firmly by the hand and leading her out of the room. William started toward them, but Louisa put a hand on his shoulder to stop him.

"Let them be," Louisa said. "I'm sure her mother will take care of her."

"Lady Louisa is right," Mrs. Holly said. "No need to worry. This is a time for celebration."

"I've never seen Mary like that," he murmured. "And the wedding is not a surprise to her—only the fact that it will be here and sooner than expected." He really ought to check on her. He couldn't think of what he'd said in his speech that would cause such a reaction from her.

The staff eventually dispersed and went about their duties, and Louisa and her mother began discussing plans for the wedding while her father and brothers talked about the estate and what Halford had learned during his stay here. William tried to take part in the men's conversation but found himself distracted by Mary's reaction.

"And what do you think about that, Farleigh?"

"Er, what?" William said. He wasn't sure who'd asked the question. Halford rolled his eyes.

"Halford suggested turning some of the farmland into additional pastureland for grazing and bringing in more milkers," Lord Ashworth replied.

"Oh. Good. Yes, more milkers." Good heavens, he'd not even realized it was his soon-to-be father-in-law, Lord Ashworth, who had spoken to him. That was imprudent on his part, especially if he wished to stay on his lordship's good side. Had Mary been distressed by the formal announcement? Perhaps she'd been overly excited about the prospect of a wedding at Farleigh Manor. Perhaps that was it. Perhaps Mary didn't know how to express—

"Go and take care of the matter, Farleigh," Lord Ashworth said with a sigh. "You're going to be worthless in any discussion we have until you are assured that the girl is all right. Halford mentioned that the two of you grew up together and have a special bond, that she's like a sister to you. Go on, then. Be off with you."

"Thank you, Lord Ashworth." He took his leave of the men, went to Louisa's side to bid her and Lady Ashworth adieu, and made his way swiftly to the kitchen.

William found Mrs. Brill alone sweeping the kitchen floor. "Where is Mary?" he asked.

"That foolish girl," Mrs. Brill said, shaking her head as she continued to sweep. "I says, 'Mary, what's got into you, luv?' And she says, 'I got him,' over and over again—don't have a clue what she meant by that—and then she rushes out of here as if there was fire at her heels." Mrs. Brill brushed the dirt into the dustpan and emptied it into the bin. "She'll be back when she's good and ready though, like she always does. Don't you worry."

Louisa approached him after he'd concluded his search of the main floor. "You haven't found her?" she asked, a look of genuine concern on her face. "Have you checked her room?"

Blast him for a fool. "Let's go see, shall we?" He took Louisa's hand in his, comforted to have her with him, and they went upstairs to the servants' quarters, knocking on each door and calling Mary's name. Again, there was no response.

With few options left to consider, he ascended the narrow stairs that led to the attic, Louisa following closely behind, and opened the attic door, holding up the lantern so he could see the shapes and shadows. "Mary," he called. "Mary, Louisa and I are looking for you. Are you here? Please answer me!"

Nothing.

He went inside and lifted the dust covers to peer underneath them and searched behind boxes. "Mary! Where are you?" He waited, listening intently. Still nothing.

Discouraged, he closed the door, and they turned to leave.

Louisa suddenly stopped. "Shh," she whispered. "I thought I heard something."

He froze in place.

"When Mrs. Holly showed me the attic before, I thought I heard scuffling sounds," Louisa whispered. "I assumed it was a mouse hiding in the wall, and I didn't think any more about it. Do you think what I heard was Mary? Are there any other rooms up here?"

"Not that I know of . . . but perhaps . . ." He handed the lantern to Louisa and began feeling the wall of the corridor opposite the attic door, looking for anything that might indicate a hidden cubby or small room that had been forgotten over the years. It was possible, he supposed. There had been a faint sound when he'd inspected the attic upon returning too.

His fingers searched, starting at the top of the wall near the ceiling and working downward and back and forth. He could feel nothing that stood out beyond the normal irregularities in the wood and plaster. He crouched down, searching farther . . .

That was when he spied it—the tiniest thread of light escaping where the floor met the wall. It was so slight, it was difficult to see and would be easily missed.

Louisa crouched beside him and held the lantern close while William painstakingly ran his fingers over the wall once more. It took several minutes, but he eventually found what he was looking for—a small notch cleverly hidden behind the joining of two wallboards, which he'd missed the first time, that connected to a lever of some sort.

He locked eyes with Louisa, and she nodded back in acknowledgment. "Well, Louisa," he said in a carrying tone, still looking at her. "I don't think Mary is up here after all. We'd better check the rooms on the next floor."

"I think you're right, William," Louisa replied, matching his volume.

Then William put his finger to his lips . . . and they waited.

They didn't have to wait long before they heard it again—the scuffling noise Louisa had described. The sound was definitely coming from behind the wall, and seemed to be getting closer. As it did, William pushed on the notch in the wall . . . and a portion of the wall shifted out toward them. William immediately slid it to their left.

On the other side of the door was a guilty-looking Mary, her eyes huge in the dim light.

"Well, what do you know, Louisa? Here's our missing Mary," William said. "I never knew about this place. I didn't have the foggiest idea Farleigh Manor had a priest hole."

"Don't be angry, Will," Mary said. "They said everything was to be yours when *he* was gone, and we was to save it for you. I saved what I could, but it got trickier and trickier. And now he's gone and you're here finally. I hate him."

"Oh, Mary," William said. He made his way through the little door— he had to crouch down to do so, and once he was through the threshold, Louisa watched him wrap his arms around the girl. "Mary, what have you done?"

It was then that Louisa got her first real look inside the room, beyond Mary and William. She gasped, her hand flying to her throat.

The tiny room—priest hole or whatever it had originally been intended to be—was filled to the rafters with urns, paintings, small sculptures, decorative tables, and other items. Farleigh Manor had been stripped of her finest adornments, but it appeared that a good share of them had made their way into this room. Thanks to Mary.

"*He* was taking this and that, Will, and we couldn't stop him. But I *got* him. I got him in the end. And that other his lordship can't have them. I won't let him."

"What do you mean, 'that other his lordship'?" William asked her gently.

Louisa's heart was full as she watched William talk to the obviously distressed girl. He was so kind and patient. What a good father he would be.

"You know. *His lordship.*" Mary's voice went pompous sounding.

William laughed. "Do you mean Louisa's father?"

Mary nodded and then ducked her head.

"He's a very reasonable gentleman, Mary. You don't need to have any concerns about him."

"He won't take things?"

"No, he won't take things. In fact, he's going to help us make Farleigh Manor the lovely place it used to be. Isn't that grand?"

"But he won't take things? They're *your* things, Will. Not his."

"No one is going to take anything else," William reassured Mary. "We can return all these lovely items you protected for me to their places in the house. You'd like that, wouldn't you?"

She nodded.

"That's good, then. We'll leave them safely in here for tonight and go downstairs to join the others."

"Everyone was concerned about you when you got upset." Louisa said, speaking for the first time. She took Mary's hands in her own. "Mary, I am so glad William had such a good friend as you when he was a boy and that you are friends still. For, you see, I love William."

"I love Will too," Mary said. "But not in the married way, like he explained to me. You can marry him, and I will be his friend."

"I hope you and I can be friends too, Mary," Louisa said. "I should like that above all things."

"If you love Will and take care of him and don't sell his things, we can be friends," Mary said.

Louisa couldn't help herself. She laughed and pulled Mary in for a big hug. "Oh, Mary, I vow to you that I won't sell anything that belongs to him unless he has given me permission to do so. Is that sufficient?" She pulled back, smiling, and looked closely at Mary's face.

"Yes," Mary replied seriously.

"I'm glad you approve. And in two days' time, when William and I get married, I shall vow before God to love him always."

"And then there will be babies!" Mary exclaimed.

Louisa choked, but William broke out in the biggest laugh Louisa had ever heard escape his lips.

It was a glorious sound.

Epilogue

THE HONORABLE WILLIAM BARLOW, THE fourth Viscount Farleigh, became a married man in the usual way. What was also usual was that he was surrounded by the people who loved him and whom he loved. What was unexpected was the fact that he, who had thought he would be the only member of the Barlow family present for the nuptials, had discovered a stepmother and a half brother and half sister in the past week, and they were present to share in the joy as William married the love of his life.

The family chapel where the marriage took place was a small stone edifice dating back to James the Second. It had gone through several refurbishments since that time, one of which included the addition of a stained-glass window. As today was a particularly glorious morning in May, the sun streaming through the window threw rainbows of color on the walls, which matched William's mood entirely.

Miss Purnell—Jane—sat next to Louisa's mother, with Halford and Anthony joining them on the same pew. Peter acted as ring bearer while little Daisy scattered flower petals up the small aisle to the altar.

William pondered his good fortune as he stood next to the parish priest near the altar, with Samuel at his side as best man, as they awaited Louisa's arrival.

And then she walked toward him on the arm of her father, wearing a light-blue day dress that set off her radiant blue eyes. Her father and brothers shared the same distinctive family trait. William hoped one day he and Louisa would be blessed with at least one child with the Hargreaves' blue eyes. She had also chosen to wear a pair of light kid gloves with tiny blue forget-me-nots embroidered around the cuffs, and William had a monogrammed handkerchief in his pocket, both of which had been stitched by his mother.

The service proceeded more quickly than William imagined it would, and before he knew it, they had spoken their vows and signed the register and exited the chapel as man and wife—man and wife!—and were met by cheers and the requisite shower of more flower petals. Matthew and Samuel and Grimshaw joined in, as did Louisa's brothers, and even Louisa's parents chose to toss a few petals. Lord Ashworth's solicitor, Swindlehurst, and Richard Heslop were in attendance, flower petals in hand, smiles on their faces. William had dashed off letters to both of them the day Louisa had accepted his marriage proposal, informing them of the wedding and inviting them to attend.

Upon the arrival of both solicitors, William and Lord Ashworth had read over the marriage contracts together, eventually coming to full agreement and signing the documents. He and William had met in William's study the day before their arrival—just the two of them. They had spoken frankly about the status of Farleigh Manor, Halford having already reported his own findings to his father, about William's regard for Louisa, and about his plan to put Farleigh Manor to rights.

William had discovered that the contracts were much more generous than he had initially hoped and had even been further amended by the marquess, increasing the amounts significantly. Dumbfounded, William had thanked the marquess for his generosity, telling him he understood Lord Ashworth loved his only daughter and William would do everything he could to see to her comfort. Lord Ashworth had replied that he'd found William a worthy partner for his daughter after all and was only too willing to lend his resources to the success of their match.

William had been truly humbled by the marquess's words. He'd never heard anything remotely similar from his own father, and it had evoked an emotion in him as to bring him to ungentlemanly but well-received tears.

William and his bride now stood outside the chapel doors, their hands clasped together, and watched Mrs. Brill and Mrs. Holly scurry back to the house to put the finishing touches on the wedding banquet while the other guests mingled together and enjoyed the sunshine. Suddenly, Mary rushed up to William and gave him a crushing hug, tears streaming down her cheeks, a big grin on her face. "I love you, Will, and I love Mrs. Will too," she cried, quickly hugging Louisa too before dashing off to help her mother.

Were there any better words of approval than Mary's? Words shared entirely from the heart and expressed with openness.

Much like his Louisa was inclined to do.

His Louisa.

"May I escort you back to our house, Lady Farleigh?" William asked her.

"I would love nothing better," she replied, smiling up at him and glowing and looking, oh, so beautiful.

He led her to the house, which felt more like a home than it had before the discovery of Mary's hoard, each piece having been returned to its original place. They had found the portrait of his mother among them, and it now hung in pride of place over the sitting room mantel. Mary had managed to explain, eventually, that every time William's father took something—which William understood, even if Mary did not, that he'd intended to pawn to cover his debts and expenses—Mary would sneak out of her bedroom at night and hide one or two things in the priest hole. How she had discovered the priest hole, William still wasn't entirely sure. Mary's explanation had been a bit jumbled, but it came as no surprise to him that she'd chanced upon the room since she had always been inclined to go off on her own and knew the grounds and the house better than anyone else.

Soon everyone was seated in assorted mismatched chairs that surrounded a large makeshift table in the dining room. Mrs. Holly had covered the table with a white linen tablecloth that she had washed, ironed, and scrupulously mended, and she had adorned it with a bouquet of wildflowers someone had picked from the grounds of Farleigh manor. Lord and Lady Ashworth had not blinked an eye when William had informed them earlier that he wished for the wedding banquet to be informal, with the servants of Farleigh Manor joining them at table, creating a wedding party of friends that varied greatly in rank and status.

Mrs. Brill outdid herself with the menu, and they feasted on fish and pork and wild game until they were sated from good food and congenial company. Grimshaw dabbed his mouth with his napkin and then took to his feet. "Here's to my Lord and Lady Farleigh; much joy to them both. He was always a good and proper lad, and I dare anyone to say otherwise—even if I did have to send Mrs. Holly to the nursery a time or two for a clean change of clothes. Now, I won't be saying it was because he'd fallen into the pond catching frogs or had been caught mucking about in the stables—"

"It would be me sayin' he were mucking about the stables," Samuel interjected, causing the others to laugh.

"Right you are, Samuel. Right you are," Grimshaw said.

"I preferred keeping company with the horses," William couldn't resist saying. "They didn't gossip, if you take my meaning."

"It isn't gossip if one is trying to keep a young lad clean and presentable, not to mention alive," Grimshaw said, smiling and raising his goblet. The old butler had let down his facade too, William noticed, just as he himself had done. "As I was saying, to the young lord and lady of Farleigh Manor. Cheers."

They all raised their goblets in a toast, and then Halford stood. "I would be remiss if I didn't toast the bride and groom. And lest you worry about reprisals, Grimshaw, I will tell you that my little sister was just as prone to dirty clothes as a child as Farleigh was."

"True enough," Lord Anthony chimed in.

Louisa glared at them both, and William grinned.

Halford continued. "Ruffly little dresses and petticoats, lacy stockings and ribbons and such always found themselves caught on branches and twigs, and Tony and I were forever having to untangle her from all sorts of predicaments. I don't know how her nurse managed to mend them all and keep Weezy above the suspicion of our parents."

"She didn't," Lady Ashworth said, sending a wave of laughter around the room once again. "What kind of mother would I have been if I hadn't been able to spot such unladylike behavior in my daughter? I was just as unladylike as she was as a child. I recognized the signs."

"Hear, hear, Mama. Like mother, like daughter. Please, everyone, raise your glass to the newly married Viscount and Viscountess Farleigh," Halford said, his own goblet held high. "Notwithstanding, you shall always be dear little Weezy to me."

Louisa rolled her eyes as everyone joined in the toast.

And then Lord Ashworth stood, and the room went silent. "A father is concerned—rightfully so—about his children. One never knows what the future holds in store." He gazed about the table, his eyes resting briefly on Halford and then Lord Anthony and finally on Louisa. "Lord Farleigh is a good man, Louisa. With great joy and relief, I am assured of this. Take care of my daughter, Farleigh."

"I intend to, sir," William replied. "With my whole heart."

Lord Ashworth nodded. "To a lifetime of happiness together."

"To a lifetime of happiness," the guests echoed.

William took Louisa's hand in his now. "Will you walk with me, Lady Farleigh?" he asked her in a low voice. "There is a place I should like to visit today, and I would appreciate having you with me when I do."

"You have no need to ask. I would love to go with you."

He stood, and she rose to her feet as well. "Thanks to you all, dearest friends, and the warmest welcome to new family members. I am a man who is truly blessed. My heart is full."

Cheers of congratulations and well wishes met his words.

"My bride and I will leave you to enjoy yourselves. Mrs. Brill, please bring on the desserts for our guests. Eat, drink, everyone, and Louisa and I will join you again shortly."

"Little chance of that happening," Alex drawled, drawing a few chuckles and raising a blush on Louisa's cheeks.

"Alex!" she hissed.

"Halford, really!" Louisa's mama scolded.

William himself merely ignored it. He was in too good a mood to do anything else. He laced his fingers through Louisa's and led her out of the dining room and eventually outside.

He took her back to the chapel.

It was midafternoon now, and the sun was shining at a different angle and with a different sort of light than it had this morning. The stained-glass window painted the interior walls with deeper hues than it had earlier in the day. There was an air of welcoming solitude and peace about the place, especially now with just the two of them here.

They sat side by side on the first pew, not speaking. William knew he would always be a man of few words. He was not of a gregarious nature.

"You will not miss London or your friends there?" he asked Louisa after a few minutes.

"I expect we will visit on occasion. You will have your place in the House of Lords and must see to your duty."

"That isn't what I asked," he said.

She smiled. "I know. I do not need London to be happy, William; quite the contrary. What I need is to be at your side, creating a life and a family together with the wonderful people who are here."

"I love you; you know that, don't you?" William said, lowering his head to kiss her—rather chastely since they were in a house of worship.

"Yes," she replied, her eyes twinkling. "And I love you with all my heart. But there is something important I would have you know."

"What?" He couldn't resist stealing another quick kiss.

She placed her hands firmly on his shoulders and looked him squarely in the eyes, which was a total pleasure as far as William was concerned. She had a serious look on her face, however, that quickly sobered him. "I am officially informing you that I shall be calling you William in private only. You are Farleigh now, and I intend to refer to you as such whenever we are not alone. It is time the title Viscount Farleigh become known for its honor and integrity."

Spoken like the daughter—and wife—of a nobleman. It also reminded him of his reason for bringing her here. "There is somewhere I would like to take you this afternoon," he said.

"I suspect I know where that might be," she said. "And I'm glad of it."

"Wait here for a moment."

He kissed her hand and went to a small alcove, retrieving the small painting of him with his parents. He'd brought it to the chapel early this morning, wanting to have both his parents present at the ceremony. Then he led her to the family churchyard on the east side of the chapel and to his mother's grave. His father's fresh grave lay next to it.

His mother would have loved Louisa dearly had she met her and would be utterly thrilled with their match; of this William was certain. He expected his father would have at least appreciated the irony surrounding the original wager and William's subsequent use of the vowel—and the end results.

He handed the portrait to Louisa after removing its cloth covering. She ran a single finger across it, from William's mother to his father and finally to William.

"It's a handsome family, William."

"I have been intensely angry at my father since meeting Jane and Peter and Daisy. I have been angry at him for a long time before that, Louisa, for letting me down and for letting my mother down. For ruining his health and hers and all but destroying his inheritance. And yet I would never have met you if he had not done these things. And so I must forgive him." He ran his hand over the newly laid tombstone. "I must forgive him, but I'm not sure I can."

"I think forgiveness must take time, William," Louisa said. How wise she was for one so young. "I think we must choose to forgive and try to remember what goodness there may have been. And perhaps one day in the future, we will think about how things were and discover that the pain is gone. That the forgiveness is complete."

"That day is not yet," William said. "But I believe you are right. I can at least begin to forgive him when he has given me such a gift as you." He paused before continuing. "You once asked me if I was happy."

"I remember."

"Are you happy, my love? Are you experiencing that joyful state of being in which one is full of contentment and blissful satisfaction?"

"I am," she said, smiling at the words she'd tossed at him in anger only a few short weeks prior.

"I am too," he replied.

He drew Louisa into his arms and kissed her—a long, sweet kiss that filled his soul with contentment and blissful satisfaction and joy for the future. "Do you think those who rest here have had their peace disturbed by that kiss?" he asked her afterward.

"I think they would welcome any kind of true affection and love," Louisa said, clever, sweet woman that she was.

He kissed her again and then placed her hand in the crook of his arm and led her from the churchyard toward their home and their future.

Author's Note

WHEN I WROTE MY FIRST Regency novel, *The Earl's Betrothal*, I introduced a young married couple named Louisa and William. Louisa was Anthony, my hero's, younger sister, an open, sparkling young woman with a reserved, devoted husband. As I created them, they stole my heart, and I decided it would be fun to go back in time to give them their own romance. And *Wager for a Wife* was born.

My Regency novels can be read as standalones; they are complete stories by themselves. But if the reader wishes to read them in chronological order, at present, that would be: *Wager for a Wife* (Louisa and William), *The Earl's Betrothal* (Louisa's brother Anthony and Amelia), and *The Gentleman's Deception* (Anthony's friend Lucas and Lavinia).

Happy reading!

About the Author

KAREN TUFT WAS BORN WITH a healthy dose of curiosity about pretty much everything, so as a child she taught herself to read and explored the piano. She studied composition at BYU, graduated from the University of Utah in music theory, and was a member of Phi Kappa Phi and Pi Kappa Lambda honor societies. In addition to being an author, Karen is a wife, mom, grandma (hooray!), pianist, composer, and arranger. She likes to figure out what makes people tick, wander through museums, and travel, whether it's by car, plane, or paperback.

ENJOY THIS SNEAK PEEK OF HEIDI KIMBALL'S NOVEL,
COMING MARCH 2019,

A GUARDED HEART

Herefordshire, 1816

ELEANOR GRIPPED THE BANISTER AT the head of the grand staircase. The dark wood anchored her against what waited below. She could feel the blood leeching from her fingers and imagined her hand turning the same milky white as her glove. Loosening her grip, she exhaled, smoothing her dress and her nerves in one determined motion. If people were going to gossip about her, she would hold her head up high while they did it.

Her stomach clenched as she descended, reminding Eleanor of her coming-out. Everyone had seemed so welcoming back then, before she'd learned how quickly one could be cast aside. It felt strange and terrifying to be on the brink of reentering that world. The Warwicks were anxious to help ease her back into society, but Eleanor still felt quite alone.

The room hushed as she came into sight. Faint whispers snaked through the line of guests—so many more people than Eleanor had been led to expect would be there.

Miss Warwick stood at the bottom of the staircase. Her face lit up at the sight of Eleanor. "Oh, there you are! I was about to set off in search of you."

If not for her kind and open nature, Eleanor would have found her cousin intimidating. Miss Warwick was a dramatic beauty, elegant in her wine-red dress and with her dark hair fashionably swept up. She pulled Eleanor's arm into her own, as if they were lifelong friends.

Unaccustomed to this sort of camaraderie, Eleanor had no defense against it. She turned desperate eyes on Miss Warwick. "Miss Warwick, I thought—"

"Please, I *insist* you call me Caroline. We are cousins, after all."

Eleanor took a breath, keeping her voice down. "Caroline, you said tonight would be a small gathering of neighbors. This looks like a formal country ball."

Caroline waved away her concern. "Darling, these *are* our neighbors. And what better way to introduce you to everyone?"

Despite the reassurance, Eleanor's insides twisted with apprehension.

Mrs. Warwick hurried over, followed by her husband. "Oh good. There you are, Eleanor. Let us not keep our guests waiting."

"Good evening," said Mr. Warwick, greeting her with a fatherly smile. "Shall we begin?"

Caroline touched Eleanor's elbow, turning her toward the waiting guests. "Ah, here are the Bartletts. Mr. and Mrs. Barlett, may I introduce our special guest, Miss Eleanor Hayward."

Heartbeat gaining speed, Eleanor forced a smile, steeling herself for her first introduction in three years.

After thirty minutes in the receiving line Eleanor's heart had resumed its regular rhythm, but her head spun with the effort of remembering names—a skill at which she was sorely out of practice. Most of the guests were warm and inviting, though some looked at her with too much interest, as if they were trying to remember something they'd once heard and surmise whether it was true.

Eleanor craned her neck. Just beyond the entryway, the ballroom teemed with couples, candles flickering and music playing. The sound of chatter and gossip filtered through the room, foreign and familiar all at once.

"Miss Hayward, this is Mrs. Sheffield," said Caroline. She gestured toward a woman with a jeweled turban much too large for her small frame.

Despite her diminutive stature, the woman managed to look down at Eleanor, sniffing with disdain. As the woman walked away Eleanor heard her muttering, "After what her brother did . . . It's a disgrace."

Fighting against the tightness in her chest, Eleanor exhaled. *The woman is just an old coward,* she told herself. *One who didn't dare voice her condemnation aloud and risk ties to a wealthy family.* She glanced up the staircase longingly, wishing to escape.

The line began to wane, and Caroline bit her lip in concern. "Are you doing all right, dear? I know it's a lot. I told Mother you wouldn't want to be flung into a ballroom without knowing anyone, but she insisted it's the best way. Oh, here is Mr. Rowley." She leaned in, a smile playing on her lips. "He's quite handsome."

A tall man with dark hair stepped forward, and Caroline turned to face him. "Mr. Rowley, may I introduce our special guest, Miss Hayward. Miss Hayward, Mr. Nicholas Rowley, our dear neighbor."

He gave a slight bow. "A pleasure. I hear you've come a great distance to join the Warwicks."

"Yes," Eleanor admitted. "All the way from Kent. And although I've spent a day recovering, I find I still cringe at the thought of a carriage."

He laughed. "I can imagine." His gaze turned toward the ballroom, shifting through the crowds. "And what did the Warwicks do to entice you so far from home, pray tell?" he asked, still distracted.

Caroline answered for her. "Mother and the late Mrs. Hayward were second cousins and grew up together. So, you see, she's family."

After glancing toward the ballroom one more time, Mr. Rowley extended a hand. "If it's not too early, Miss Hayward, would you care to join me on the dance floor?"

Caught off guard, Eleanor shot Caroline a look of distress.

Caroline nudged her forward. "The line is all but finished," she whispered.

"I'd be delighted, sir," Eleanor said, recovering her manners. Mr. Rowley seemed like a safe option. Given his air of distraction, she could likely stick out her tongue at him without fear of observation. He'd be the last to notice if she was a little distant or her dancing out of practice. For tonight, he was the perfect partner.

He led her toward the ballroom as couples lined up for the next set. A small pit formed in Eleanor's stomach, the earlier nerves returning. Would she even remember the formations?

Paying close attention to the other couples, Eleanor let Mr. Rowley take the lead. To her surprise, she fell into her old, easy step quite naturally. The couples stepped forward and back and then weaved in and out of the group. Mr. Rowley smiled at her, and Eleanor surprised herself by answering with a smile of her own.

"Was it still raining when you arrived, sir?" she asked, moving back a step, knowing he wouldn't answer until he circled her.

"It was." He reached out and took her hand. "But the weather had the good manners to rein it in to a drizzle."

She turned to face him. "How very polite."

Just then he looked across the room and almost missed a step. "You'll have to pardon me." He gave her a sheepish smile. "When I dance it is not my feet but my mind that gets me into trouble."

"No harm done," Eleanor reassured him, trying to glimpse what had captured his attention. A tall gentleman obstructed her view, and Eleanor found herself intrigued by the mystery.

The dance ended with the requisite bows and curtsies, and Eleanor grew heady with success. Perhaps tonight wouldn't be as bad as she'd imagined. She had the sudden whim to feed her curiosity. "Mr. Rowley, if you would be so good, do you mind escorting me to the punch table? My throat is quite parched." The balcony doors remained closed, and the air had grown stifling. She had all but forgotten the press of a ballroom.

"Of course, Miss Hayward. It would be my pleasure."

There were two punch tables, but as Eleanor suspected, they worked their way over to the one near where Mr. Rowley's gaze had been steadily drawn. He took a drink for each of them, and Eleanor watched him as he sipped. The focus of his attention turned out to be a young woman in blue, and Eleanor could see why. She had dark, shiny hair and a face that seemed incapable of forming a frown.

"Have you already met the Drews?" asked Mr. Rowley. "I think I saw them come in while we were dancing. Allow me to introduce you."

Mr. Rowley approached a trio of women, where the young woman in blue stood. "Ladies, I'd like to introduce Miss Warwick's special guest, Miss Hayward. Miss Hayward, meet the Drews—Miss Drew, Miss Marianne, and the youngest sister, Miss Vivien."

Miss Vivien smiled at Mr. Rowley, dark eyes dancing. "How good of you to introduce us, Mr. Rowley, as if you knew we had been especially wishing it!" She turned to Eleanor. "As dear friends of Caroline, we have been anxious to meet you."

"Oh yes." The other two nodded.

Miss Marianne stepped forward, her dark curly hair framing intelligent green eyes. "We wanted to let you get settled but are anxious to come visiting. I love a good ball, but it does not provide the same intimate setting as having tea together." She put a hand on Eleanor's arm. "I hope we'll soon be good friends."

Eleanor nodded, taken aback at the thought of someone who wanted to be her friend. "I'd like that." She took another sip of punch, feeling her cheeks flush with the heat of the room.

"I believe the quadrille is next, Miss Vivien. Would you do me the honor?" Mr. Rowley asked.

Miss Vivien took his outstretched hand, and Mr. Rowley beamed. Eleanor tried to hide her amusement. No doubt his eyes wouldn't wander as he danced with *her*.

"And what do you think of Herefordshire so far?" asked Miss Marianne, taking a step toward Eleanor.

Eleanor exhaled, grateful to have been introduced to someone who put her at ease. "I haven't seen as much as I would like, but so far I've been quite taken by its beauty."

"We think it's lovely too, but we are a bit biased." Miss Marianne laughed, turning toward another group. "Miss Hayward, have you met our cousin? He's visiting from Derbyshire. Edmund, do come meet Miss Hayward. She's just as lovely as we expected."

Eleanor startled when she heard the name. As he turned her heart stopped.

Edmund Fletcher.

"Of course, I'd be very happy to . . ." His voice trailed off as he caught sight of her.

Eleanor blanched, and she felt all the blood drain from her face. Though she hadn't seen him in nearly three years, how often this man had occupied her thoughts. His brown hair, slightly disheveled, his arresting blue eyes. Seeing his handsome face was like a hazy dream come to life. Eleanor feared she might spill her drink, her hands began shaking so badly.

Edmund—*Mr. Fletcher,* she corrected herself—exercised better control than she did, however. He cleared his throat to cover a small noise of surprise. "Miss Hayward, is it?" he asked, bowing. He emphasized the first word, *Miss*, managing to ask two questions as one. He gave no other sign of recognition, and Eleanor felt a stab of pain. But what else should she expect, given the callousness he'd shown her when last they'd parted?

"Miss Hayward, are you well? Your face is rather pale." Miss Marianne's mouth turned down in concern.

Eleanor recovered enough to give an overdue curtsy. "It's a pleasure, sir," she said, voice catching in her throat. Her mouth had grown dry, despite the drink in her hand. "I do believe the heat is . . . I . . . I might go out for some air."

"Let me come with you," Miss Marianne pressed. "Here, Edmund, take her drink. And help us over to the balcony doors. Let's get Miss Hayward some air before dinner."

No, Eleanor almost said. But Miss Marianne had already taken her arm. Eleanor risked a glance back at Edmund. The look of disdain on his face caused a misstep that made her thankful for Miss Marianne's steady arm steering her toward the doors.

***

Hands clenched, Edmund shook his head as it began to sink in just whom he was following. A face he thought he'd put out of his head forever. He never imagined he and Eleanor Hayward might cross paths again. A strange tightness filled his lungs. Marianne's introduction had caught him so off guard he hadn't even been able to acknowledge his prior acquaintance with Eleanor. He supposed no one here would know about it, and it seemed unlikely Eleanor would mention their past association, tainted as it was. Let her make it what she would.

As they approached the balcony he stepped around the two of them, pushing the doors open. The cool evening air was a welcome change from the oppressive heat. The rain had slowed to a gentle and irregular patter.

Before he could give them proper warning, Eleanor brushed by him, stepping to the edge of the parapet. She took in large gulps of air, a hand at her throat. Turning, she sank back against the balcony railing. "I'm sorry to be an inconvenience." She spoke to Marianne, pointedly avoiding Edmund's gaze.

Taking another deep breath, she closed her eyes. Color slowly returned to her cheeks as if the night air were an elixir that breathed new life into her.

Edmund took the moment to study her. She was still pretty, her blonde hair lighter than he remembered, her features just as carefully sculpted. But there was something different about her, though it was difficult to pinpoint. The smile that had always lit up her face was noticeably absent, her expression more reserved. She seemed a little faded, like a garment that had been out in the sun for too long.

His mind raced back to the first time he'd seen her, at a small dinner party hosted by the Clarks. Her laugh had carried across the room, the sound joyous and full, yet somehow still ladylike. He had instantly wished to know her.

She was beautiful in a rather unique way, her cheekbones high, her almond-shaped eyes almost exotic. But it was her warm and unpretentious manner that had drawn him in, the happiness she exuded. For a moment he saw her as he did back then, before the warmth of the memory was broken by his recollection of their last night together.

And now she stood directly in front of him, a different creature, so altered. And so oblivious to the raindrops that were beginning to fall with more rapidity.

Her eyes opened to his scrutiny, and her cheeks bloomed with color. "Thank you, Mr. Fletcher," she said curtly, "for your assistance. I won't keep you any longer."

How easily she dismissed him. *Just like before*, he thought resentfully. Yet, however Eleanor chose to behave, he would act the part of a gentleman. "Miss Hayward, let us find you a seat inside, before you get thoroughly wet."

Marianne stepped forward, tugging at Eleanor's shoulder. "Miss Hayward, you'll be drenched. Come out of the rain."

Eleanor allowed Marianne to pull her inside. Droplets of rain trailed down her neck and cheeks, and her dress hung more limply than before, but she seemed not to notice. Edmund averted his eyes.

They moved to a small alcove behind a pillar. There Marianne promptly demanded Edmund's handkerchief and began wiping away the rain from Eleanor's face and hair. "At least your face has some color," she murmured. "You are feeling better, I hope?"

"Yes, thank you. I hate to be such a bother." Eleanor did not even glance in his direction.

"Nonsense. You're not a bother. Edmund, be a dear and escort us in to dinner."

His heart sank at the thought. Spending the next hour in Eleanor's presence felt like more than he could bear. He silently cursed the timing of this visit to his cousins.

He bowed. "Of course."

After serving themselves at the extensive sideboard, Edmund helped Marianne into her seat and then pulled out Eleanor's chair, taking the open seat between them as etiquette demanded.

"Now, my dear, tell us all about your journey," implored Marianne. "I have never been to Kent, but I believe Edmund has. Didn't you have a school friend you visited there several years ago?"

"Yes," he replied. "But my visit was relatively short, and I haven't been back since."

Eleanor brushed back an errant strand of damp hair. "It's quite far from this part of the country. And very different."

Edmund took a drink, setting his glass down with more force than he intended. "Yes, it's nothing like central England." He forced back memories of an afternoon when he'd described Derbyshire for her in detail.

Eleanor looked up. "Kent has its own beauty," she said, her voice defensive. The hand that held her fork trembled slightly.

"Ah yes, the white cliffs of Dover," said Marianne with enthusiasm. "I long to visit. Is your home near there?"

Eleanor shook her head. "No, we are a little farther inland. But my grandfather had an estate in Dover we used to visit every summer. I have fond memories of my time on the beaches there, watching the ships come in and enjoying the splendor of the cliffs." Her expression took on a distant quality.

"Perhaps we'll have to visit sometime, Edmund. I daresay with Miss Hayward as our guide you might find it more enjoyable."

"Perhaps," he answered, his manner stiff.

Marianne ignored his curtness, but the pinch between her brows served as a subtle warning. "And do you still pass your summers there, Miss Hayward?"

Eleanor set down her fork. "No, the estate was . . . sold. I haven't been back since."

Edmund's cousin began speaking with one of the guests across the table. A minute passed, an awkward silence unfurling between him and Eleanor.

"What brings you to Herefordshire, Mr. Fletcher?" Her face appeared serene, but the twisted napkin in her lap indicated she was ill at ease.

"I am here visiting my cousins." He would give what civility required but saw no reason to make this easy for her.

She exhaled, her breath almost a sigh. "I suppose neither of us realized our cousins are neighbors."

"No. It is unexpected, to say the least."

Eleanor's chin dropped. She took a sip of water, and he could almost see her give up, her efforts at polite conversation visibly exhausted. He felt a momentary stab of regret for behaving so callously. But then old memories encroached, and anger swept in. She deserved no pity.